KIM

Praise for The L...

'Like its predecessors, The Lante... place and an awareness of the r... The climactic bicycle race across the fens, foregathering all the suspects, will take your breath away' *The Times*

'As ever, creepy Norfolk folklore is skilfully blended with the ongoing saga of the personal lives of Ruth, her friends and colleagues (and now, their children). Warm, but never cloyingly cosy, this is the most lovable of current crime series' *Sunday Express*

'Elly Griffiths's great achievement in her Dr Ruth Galloway series has been to create an atmosphere as comforting as that of any traditional detective story and yet introduce to it credible crimes and lifelike characters with convincing preoccupations' *Literary Review*

'Once again, Elly Griffiths delivers witty, insightful and brilliant storytelling as the redoubtable Dr Galloway burrows away to expose the Lantern Men's dark secrets' *Daily Mirror*

'A deftly plotted thriller, and most likeable entertainment' *Irish Independent*

'The writing is excellent. It puts me in mind of the late, great Ruth Rendell ... the characterisation is perfect ... a cracker of a book' *The Bookbag*

Elly Griffiths was born in London and worked in publishing before becoming a full-time writer. Her bestselling series of Dr Ruth Galloway novels, featuring a forensic archaeologist, are set in Norfolk. The series has won the CWA Dagger in the Library and has been shortlisted three times for the Theakston's Old Peculier Crime Novel of the Year. Her Brighton-based mystery series is set in the 1950s and 1960s. She lives near Brighton with her husband, an archaeologist, and their two grown children.

Also by Elly Griffiths

ELLY Griffiths

The Lantern Men

A DR RUTH GALLOWAY MYSTERY

First published in Great Britain in 2020 by Quercus
This paperback edition published in 2020 by

Quercus Editions Ltd
Carmelite House
50 Victoria Embankment
London EC4Y 0DZ

An Hachette UK company

A CIP catalogue record for this book is available
from the British Library

PB ISBN 978 1 78747 755 1

10 9 8 7 6 5 4 3 2 1

Typeset by CC Book Production
Printed and bound in Great Britain by Clays Ltd, Elcograf S.p.A.

For Sheila de Rosa

. . . a wand'ring Fire . . .
Which oft, they say, some evil Spirit attends,
Hovering and blazing with delusive Light,
Misleads th' amaz'd Night-wanderer from his way
To Boggs and Mires, and oft through Pond or Poole
There swallow'd up and lost . . .

John Milton, *Paradise Lost*

PROLOGUE

10 July 2007

She has been walking for a long time. It's funny but she hadn't thought that there was so much *space* in England. The map, which she printed out in the library at school, seemed to show the youth hostel here, somewhere in this sea of green, but now that she's walking, in her special shoes with her backpack on, there's no sign of any buildings anywhere. Her phone is out of battery and she feels very alone. All she can do is keep walking.

Youth Hostel near Cambridge. The words evoked images of honey-coloured buildings, women in long dresses and men in bow ties, those boats that you row standing up. Images that, in the grey concrete of her home town, seemed as exotic as if they had been beamed from a distant star. But now, as the rain starts, easily finding its way through her supposedly rainproof cagoule, she wonders if it was all, in fact, imaginary. Did the England she pictured ever really exist? Is this what summer here is like? There is something oppressive about the landscape: fields, ditches, fences, the occasional blasted-looking tree. It's as if she has claustrophobia and agoraphobia at the same time; she feels as if she's crawling over the surface of the earth and at the same time hemmed in on all sides, unable to escape.

It's getting dark now. Her parents were right. She should never have come interrailing on her own. She should have travelled with friends; even now they'd be drinking warm wine in a dormitory somewhere, laughing at the day's adventures. But that's just it. She wanted adventures, not just the same photographs to stick on the wall of whichever indifferent university she ended up gracing with her presence. But walking for miles across grey fields doesn't seem especially adventurous, especially as her new walking shoes are pinching badly. She looks at her watch. Ten o'clock, just dark. Should she look for shelter somewhere? But the rain-washed landscape offers nothing, not even a hut or a generously branched tree. The rain falls as if its one aim is to make her miserable.

She sees the light first. That's the thing about this road, you can see for miles. A car – no, a van – travelling quite fast, moving in her direction. Should she hitch a lift? Her father begged her not to do this but the alternative seems to be sleeping in a ditch. Yet something stops her. There's something about the vehicle – she can see it quite clearly now, dark blue with blacked-out windows – that seems rather frightening, as if it is intent on some nefarious nighttime business. She stands back, pressing herself against the hedgerow, pulling her hood over her face.

But the van is slowing. It stops beside her and a window is lowered.

'My poor child,' says a voice that seems to come straight from her Cambridge fantasies, 'you're quite drenched. Jump in.'

CHAPTER 1

18 May 2018

The last of the light is fading as Ruth sits on the terrace looking out over the fens. Her laptop is open in front of her and she has just typed the words 'The End'. A bit silly and melodramatic, she'll delete them before she sends the manuscript to her editor, but for the moment she likes to look at the screen and feel the satisfaction of having one thing in her life that is completed, finished, accomplished. She leans back in her basket chair and feels the dying rays of the sun on her face. The weather has been wonderful all through this week-long writing retreat, amazing weather for May in England.

'How's it going?' Crissy has made one of her noiseless entrances, crossing the deck with a tray holding something that looks very like a gin and tonic.

'Finished!' Ruth turns to grin at her.

'Fantastic.' Crissy puts the tray on the table. 'You deserve this then.'

She had thought that Crissy looked a little preoccupied earlier but now she is smiling at Ruth with such warmth that Ruth feels herself smiling back, almost grinning. So many things about this week have been surprising, thinks Ruth, as she takes a delicious, juniper-scented sip, but making a friend in such a short time is definitely one of the biggest surprises. Ruth has a few, carefully selected, friends: Alison from school, Caz and Roly from university, Shona from work, Judy and Cathbad from . . . well, Cathbad would say that they are gifts from the universe. And yet she has never felt such an immediate connection as she did with Crissy. They have nothing in common really. Crissy is slightly older than Ruth, she wasn't even sure what a forensic archaeologist did until Ruth explained, and seems to have no interest in the haunted fenland landscape around her. As far as Ruth knows, Crissy has no partner and no children. But she is such a serene, kindly presence, drifting around in her flowing dresses, her greying blonde hair in a ponytail that reaches almost to her waist. It is Crissy who turns Grey Walls, the squat stone house in the middle of nowhere, into a real sanctuary, full of soft lights and delicious smells. Ruth has been able to finish her third book, about Neolithic stone circles, in record time and has been able, temporarily, to forget the other worries that dominate her life: her work at Cambridge, her relationships, her aging father. She has not forgotten Kate, her daughter, or Flint, her cat, but she hasn't worried unduly about them either. This despite not being able to get a mobile phone signal unless she stands at the bottom of the garden.

Crissy sees her looking at her phone. 'Your husband rang,' she says. 'He's on his way to collect you now.'

The word gives Ruth a jolt. Should she say something? But Crissy is already drifting away. So Ruth sits on the terrace and drinks her gin until Frank's car appears, visible for miles in the flat landscape.

DCI Harry Nelson is checking the news on his phone when DI Judy Johnson comes bursting into his office.

'Guilty,' she says. 'On both charges.'

Nelson leans back in his chair and shuts his eyes for a moment. 'Thank Christ,' he says.

It was one of the worst moments in a police officer's life: waiting for the verdict. Almost two years ago Nelson had arrested Ivor March, assembled a portfolio of evidence against him and handed the case over to the Crown Prosecution Service. Now, after several expensive weeks at the Old Bailey, justice has been served. March has been found guilty of the murder of two women and, with any luck, will spend the rest of his days behind bars.

Judy, who was Nelson's second-in-command on the case, looks almost as relieved as he is.

'I was sure it would be guilty at first,' she says. 'I mean, there was so much evidence. All those forensics. But when he just started denying everything, he sounded so plausible. I really thought they might believe him.'

'Oh, he's plausible all right,' says Nelson.

He thinks of the moment when he read the charges to March. He'd wanted to do it himself, to see the look in

March's eyes, to say the words: 'Ivor March, you are charged that you did murder two women, Jill Prendergast and Stacy Newman, contrary to common law.' That last bit always seemed self-evident; it would be a pretty black day when murder wasn't against the law. But March had just smiled and made a gesture, with palm outstretched, as if to say, 'Over to you now.' He'd been confident even then, Nelson realises, that he'd get off.

'Phil Trent made a mess of the forensic archaeology,' he says. 'Ruth would have done it better.'

'He was OK,' says Judy. 'Juries never like expert witnesses.'

'He confused them with all that stuff about soil pH,' says Nelson. 'The point was that March killed the women and buried them in his girlfriend's garden. His DNA was all over them and on the rope and on the plastic. There was hair from his cat, for God's sake.'

'I can't believe the girlfriend is standing by him,' says Judy.

'There's a certain sort of woman,' says Nelson, 'who's attracted to a man like March. They think he's an alpha male because he kills people.'

'Be careful,' says Judy. 'You're sounding like Madge.'

Nelson grins. Madge Hudson, criminal profiler, is known to King's Lynn CID as 'Queen of the Bleeding Obvious'. Superintendent Jo Archer, Nelson's boss, is a fan though and insisted that Madge be involved with the March case. Madge gave it as her perceived wisdom that March 'liked inflicting pain'.

'Have you told the super?' asks Nelson.

'No,' says Judy. 'I came straight to you.'

Nelson grunts to hide his satisfaction. 'You should tell her,' he says. 'You know how she likes to get a case ticked off her list.'

Judy looks at him. They have worked together for a long time and sometimes they don't need words.

'Is it ticked off though?' she says at last.

'No,' says Nelson. 'No, it isn't.'

Kate comes running across the deck to meet her. 'We went shopping,' she says. 'We bought steak and oven chips and really smelly cheese. You can smell it in the car.'

Ruth hugs her daughter. Kate is nine now, a restless sprite with long, dark hair. She has shot up in the last year and her head now only just fits under Ruth's chin.

'I love smelly cheese,' she says.

'That's what Frank said. He bought wine too and chocolate brownies for me.'

'Sounds like a successful shopping trip,' says Crissy.

'This is my daughter, Kate,' says Ruth, trying not to sound too proud.

'She looks like you,' says Crissy.

'I look like my dad,' says Kate, which is true. Ruth has, rather to her surprise, confided in Crissy about Kate's parentage. Crissy smiles at her now and waves at Frank, who is standing by the car. He has obviously held back to let Ruth have her moment with Kate. Ruth turns to Crissy. 'Thank you so much. I had a wonderful time.'

Crissy envelops her in a hug that smells of patchouli and lemongrass.

'I'm so glad,' she says. 'Come back soon.'

But Ruth doesn't know when she'll next be able to afford the luxury of a week on her own. The writing retreat had been Frank's idea, put forward as a solution to the ever-present stress of Ruth's looming deadline. 'Take a week and just concentrate on writing,' he said. 'No students, no worrying about Kate and Flint. Or me,' he had added as an afterthought, perhaps realising that, for Ruth, part of his charm lay in the fact that she never had to worry about him. Well, it had worked. Ruth had finished the book, tentatively entitled *The Devil's Circle*, and she feels more relaxed than she has for a long time, ever since the move from Norfolk, in fact.

John, the gardener and handyman, appears with Ruth's suitcase. He's another one who knows how to make a silent entrance, but he's a gentle soul who has told Ruth some very interesting things about local folklore. Ruth thanks him and offers her hand to say goodbye. After some hesitation, John shakes it heartily.

Frank comes forward and takes the case. Then he kisses Ruth. 'Good stay?'

'Great. I finished it.'

'That's fantastic, honey.' He hugs her. It never ceases to please Ruth when Frank calls her 'honey'. Goodness knows why because she usually hates those sort of endearments. Perhaps it's because it sounds so American.

Frank puts the bag in the boot (or trunk, as he calls it). Kate jumps into the back seat. Ruth thanks Crissy again and they are off, bowling along the road that is the highest thing for miles around. The fenlands glide past them, purple with loosestrife, secret pools gleaming in the twilight.

'How's Flint?' Ruth asks Kate.

'He's fine. He slept on my bed all week.'

Flint is the one who has taken the move to Cambridge hardest. At first Ruth was scared to let him out and he sat grumpily in the window of the townhouse, probably dreaming of his old life amongst the abundant wildlife of the Saltmarsh. Now he does go into the garden and has established himself as the alpha cat in the neighbourhood, but Ruth still imagines that he looks at her rather resentfully. And he never sleeps on Ruth's bed now, probably because Frank is in it.

It's nine o'clock by the time they get home but it's still not quite dark. Not long until June and the longest day, thinks Ruth. The summer solstice. As ever, the idea of a pagan festival makes her think of Cathbad. She must ring Cathbad and Judy soon. Frank carries Ruth's case into the house. Ruth follows with her laptop, looking out for Flint. In the first-floor sitting room, Kate switches on the television. Ruth is about to protest but then she sees the face on the screen; a strong, almost belligerent, face, with greying dark hair. 'DCI Harry Nelson, Norfolk Police Serious Crimes Unit,' runs the caption.

'Daddy!' says Kate in delight.

'There was overwhelming evidence against March and we're relieved that he was found guilty,' Nelson is saying, 'but we would still like to question him about the disappearance of two other women.'

Frank comes into the room. 'The steak won't take long,' he says. 'Shall I open the wine?' Then he stops because both Ruth and Kate are ignoring him, staring at the man on the television.

CHAPTER 2

Nelson is gathering up his things, ready to leave, when Superintendent Jo Archer appears in the doorway.

'Leaving already?' she says.

Nelson doesn't rise. It's six o'clock and Jo is always telling him not to do overtime. 'That's right,' he says. 'Half day off for good behaviour.'

Jo laughs and comes to sit in his visitor's chair. She persists in believing that they have the best of working relationships. 'We wind each other up all the time,' she said once, 'like brother and sister.' Well, Nelson has two sisters and this is something entirely different. Jo is his boss, for one thing; for another she sits on a balance ball to conduct interviews and once tried to make him attend a mindfulness seminar. Despite all this, she's not a bad copper and he doesn't altogether dislike her.

'You must be pleased about March,' she says.

Nelson sits down opposite her. 'There are still the other two women,' he says. 'Nicola Ferris and Jenny McGuire.'

Jo stops smiling. 'Their bodies were never found,' she says.

'I know,' says Nelson, 'but March killed them, I'm sure of it. He had a very specific physical type. Jill Prendergast and Stacy Newman were both tall and blonde with blue eyes. Nicola and Jenny were very similar and the same age, mid-thirties. Both women were living in north Norfolk and both attended March's evening classes. And neither of them have been seen since the summer of 2016.'

'I agree there's circumstantial evidence,' says Jo, 'but without forensics we've nothing to link them to March. Their DNA wasn't found on anything in his house.'

'He's too clever for that,' says Nelson. 'With Jill and Stacy the only DNA evidence was buried in his girlfriend's garden.'

'We've dug up that garden,' says Jo, 'and only found the two bodies.'

'They're buried somewhere else,' says Nelson. 'I'm sure of it.'

'It might have been wiser not to mention it in the TV interview all the same,' says Jo. 'It gives false hope to the families.'

Nelson knew that this was coming. Jo didn't trust him in front of the cameras. He was too intimidating, she said, not warm enough. He scowled at reporters and barked out one-word answers. Jo thought that all media interviews should be handled by Judy. Or, better still, by Super Jo herself.

'March loved being on trial,' says Nelson. 'He loved the attention. Maybe he'll confess just to get more of the limelight. He's going to have a pretty dull time of it in jail, even with all those delusional women writing to him.'

'I wouldn't bet on a confession,' says Jo. 'And, hard though it is, we can't keep on throwing money and resources into the case.'

'So that's it for Nicola and Jenny? Case closed?'

'We'll keep on looking,' says Jo. 'It just can't be a priority.'

Nelson knows that she's right but he hates unfinished business. He knows that Nicola and Jenny are going to haunt his dreams. Just like Lucy Downey did, all those years ago.

'Go home, Nelson,' says Jo. 'Baby George will cheer you up.'

'He's not a baby any more,' says Nelson, 'he's nearly two and a half.' But his face does lighten at the thought of his son.

But, on the drive home, Nelson finds himself thinking about Nicola Ferris and Jenny McGuire. Nicola was thirty-four and single. She lived near Cley, on the edge of the north Norfolk marshes, and taught at the local secondary school. She was also a keen amateur artist and had attended an evening painting course at her local community centre. It was run by Ivor March. In July 2016 Nicola went to the pub for end-of-term drinks with the other students. She left at ten p.m. to ride her bicycle home and was never seen again. Jenny was thirty-six, divorced with one child. She lived in Holt and worked in the gift shop in a nearby stately home. She too had attended one of Ivor March's evening classes at the community centre, this time in creative writing. One morning in August, Jenny had left for work, cycling through the mist. She'd never arrived.

Nelson and his team had seen the links immediately. They had questioned March along with the other students and course leaders. He had admitted to knowing both women but had an alibi – his girlfriend – for the dates of their disappearances. Then, in September, another woman had vanished. Jill Prendergast, a thirty-five-year-old teaching assistant from Cromer. Jill was last seen at a bus stop near Cley, on her way to visit a friend. She was, by all accounts, an outgoing, vivacious woman, devoted to her job and to her pet cat, Ferdy. She had a boyfriend, an electrician called Jay, and he was, of course, their first suspect. But Jay had an alibi, working a long shift at the hospital. Then, going through the list of Jill's friends and relations, Judy had come across the connection to Ivor March. Jill had been friends with March's girlfriend, Chantal Simmonds. The two women had met at an exercise class and had socialised several times with their respective partners. Jill and Jay had even attended Ivor's fiftieth birthday party. March had an alibi – Chantal, naturally – for the night of Jill's disappearance but Judy had got a warrant to dig up the garden of Chantal's cottage at Salthouse. There they had found not only the remains of Jill but also of Stacy Newman, an office worker who had disappeared five years earlier.

Stacy, who was thirty-eight and divorced, lived in London, which was why Nelson's team hadn't been involved in the case. And it was, arguably, easier to disappear in London than in rural Norfolk. But there was a link, though it had eluded everyone at the time. Stacy had known Ivor March. They had met when he was a student at St Martin's and had kept in touch over the years. Stacy had also been to one of March's parties. 'He's a wonderful host,' Chantal told Judy, eyes shining. Stacy had probably also been March's lover but Chantal would never admit this. What was unarguable was that March's DNA was on both bodies and on the rope that had bound them. There were also fibres from his house and hairs from his cat, Mother Gabley. March, of course, insisted that the police had planted this evidence.

From the start Nelson had been sure that March had killed Nicola and Jenny too. He had links with them both and it was true that all four women were of a very similar physical type, tall and blonde with blue eyes. Interestingly, Chantal Simmonds was short and dark. Nelson's team had excavated every inch of Chantal's garden, they took apart her house and March's flat in King's Lynn. But no trace of the missing women was ever found. Without forensic evidence, there was no chance of March being convicted. Nelson had to be content with charging March for the murders of Jill and Stacy and watching and waiting. The trouble is that patience isn't his strong point.

Nelson turns into his drive, enjoying, as he always does, the moment when the garage doors open as if by magic. Michelle's car is in the drive and he wonders who will win the race to greet him today, George or the family's German shepherd, Bruno.

It's George but only because Bruno hangs back, good-naturedly.

'Daddy!' George flings himself at Nelson's legs. He is very pro-Daddy at the moment which, Michelle informs Nelson, is 'only a phase'. She's probably right but Nelson is enjoying it while it lasts.

'Hi, Georgie.' Nelson swings his son up into the air. Bruno watches them both anxiously – there have been accidents involving light fittings before.

Michelle appears from the kitchen. 'Be careful, Harry.'

'He loves it,' says Nelson, throwing George up again. Bruno gives a short bark.

'Bruno knows it's dangerous.'

'He's an old woman.' But Nelson puts George down and pats the dog, whose solicitude for the family does sometimes verge on obsessive.

'How's your day been?' asks Michelle.

'OK. Ivor March was found guilty. Did you hear it on the news?'

'I never listen to the news these days. It's always bad.'

'You've got a point there. What did you do today?' He follows Michelle into the kitchen and looks in the fridge for a beer. He is trying to avoid drinking, except at weekends, but feels that he deserves a small celebration. It is Friday, after all.

'I was working in the morning,' says Michelle. 'Then I picked George up from nursery and we went to the park. I met Cathbad there with Miranda.'

'Surely Miranda must be at school now. Want a drink?' Nelson proffers a wine bottle enticingly but Michelle shakes her head. She isn't much of a drinker and is very careful about her diet. She says it was harder to get her figure back after the birth of her third child and she's determined not to lose it for the sake of a glass of Prosecco in the evening. Nelson understands her reasons, and admires her self-control, but it would be nice to have someone to drink with sometimes.

'Cathbad said that Miranda hadn't been feeling well that morning,' says Michelle, 'but she looked fine to me. You know how soft he is with those kids.'

Cathbad, Judy's partner, looks after their children as well as teaching meditation and being, in his own words, a part-time druid. He is certainly more relaxed about school attendance, and rules in general, than Judy would be.

'Cathbad said that Ruth's enjoying her writing retreat,' says Michelle, not looking at Nelson. 'It's on the fens, in the middle of nowhere.'

'I don't know why she wanted to go a writing retreat in the first place,' said Nelson. 'Maybe that's what they do in Cambridge.' He puts a certain amount of scorn in the last word. He knows about the retreat because Ruth had asked him if he minded Frank looking after Katie for the week. Nelson *had* minded but knew that he couldn't say so.

'I hope Frank got Katie to school on time,' he says now.

'I'm sure he did,' said Michelle. 'He's not like Cathbad, he's very responsible.' She sees Nelson's face and says, 'He is her stepfather.'

'He isn't,' says Nelson. 'Because he's not married to Ruth.'

'They're living together,' said Michelle. 'It's the same thing.'

But, in Nelson's mind, it's not the same thing at all. Marriage is a union blessed by God and the law and it's the law that's uppermost in his mind at the moment. He goes into the sitting room with his beer and turns on the television. George brings over some building bricks for a game and Nelson joins in half-heartedly.

He no longer feels as if the evening is a celebration.

CHAPTER 3

Whatever Nelson might think, Ruth and Frank are conscientious about getting Kate to school on time. Ruth normally walks her there on the way to St Jude's, the college where she teaches forensic archaeology. If Ruth has an early meeting, then Frank takes her. He usually drives because his college is slightly outside the centre of Cambridge. Neither of them has taken to cycling, the most popular mode of transport in the city. Ruth hasn't been on a bike since her teens and thinks that, in her case, it's not true that the skill is never forgotten. Frank has an American distrust of anything on two wheels.

Ruth enjoys the walk with Kate. They talk about all sorts of things and pat every cat that they see. On this Monday morning, Kate wants to talk about Fortnite, the online game that has taken the pre-teen world by storm. Lots of Kate's friends play it but Ruth has told Kate that she has to wait until she's twelve, which is the official age rating. Kate doesn't seem too bothered about this but today she wants to start one of the endless circular arguments which make

Ruth think that her daughter will grow up to be a barrister. Or a master criminal.

'So what if you're twelve but you're not very clever. Is that still OK?'

'It's not about how clever you are. It's about what's appropriate.'

'I'm reading *The Subtle Knife*. Is that suitable for nine-year-olds?'

'Yes. It's a great book.'

'Will's fingers get chopped off. Is that OK because it's a great book?'

Ruth sighs and considers her answer. In her opinion, everything is all right if it's encased within the covers of a book. Well, almost everything. She wouldn't be that happy if she saw *Mein Kampf* in Kate's book bag. And it's true that Philip Pullman's books do contain some violent and disturbing scenes but, for Ruth, that is justified because they are well written. She can't imagine that Fortnite deals with the themes of life, death and organised religion. Or maybe that's just her prejudice.

'I love the dæmons in those books,' she says now, referring to the animal familiars that accompany the characters. 'What would yours be?'

Kate gives her a look as if recognising this obvious diversion tactic. 'A cat, of course. What's yours? You can't say cat too.'

Ruth had been about to say cat. She thinks about the animal kingdom as they near the school, a modern sixties block with a brightly coloured façade, incongruous amongst the ancient buildings surrounding it.

'An owl,' she says at last, 'because of Minerva. And Hecate.' Cathbad often calls Kate Hecate. She must phone him.

'And Athena,' says Kate, who also loves the Percy Jackson books. 'Not a bad choice, Mum.'

Kate says goodbye and skips away happily. She hadn't wanted to change schools but now, after two years, seems settled at St Benedict's. She has made lots of friends and the teachers all say how well she's doing, how quick and eager to learn. Ruth is always pleased when Kate is praised. She must get some of her brains from Ruth, surely? But Kate doesn't get her confidence from Ruth, or her ability instantly to become the most popular person in the class, arbiter of tastes and fashions. Goodness knows where she inherited this. Perhaps it's Nelson's professional arrogance translated into a subtler form. Or perhaps it's a gift from the gods invoked by Cathbad at her naming day.

Ruth walks on to her college, never ceasing to get a thrill from the sight of the grassy court with the Tudor buildings rising up around it. How did she, a south London girl, end up teaching at Cambridge? By being the best in her field, she tells herself. There's no room for false modesty in academia. She is an experienced lecturer who has published two well-received books. Soon to be three, with any luck. She has appeared on television and has been involved in several noteworthy digs. It was a wrench to leave the University of North Norfolk, even though she had always complained about the place, its lack of funding and ambition, its flimsy modern buildings and apathetic students. No, she made the choice to move on and, despite initial resistance from

Nelson, she and Kate now have a new life in Cambridge. There's nothing to be gained from thinking about the past.

But when she gets to her office, the past is there waiting for her in the shape of her old boss, Phil Trent.

DCI Nelson is standing looking at a long low building with marshland behind it. It's another beautiful day, the sun is already warm overhead and Nelson is in shirtsleeves, but, to him, the place still looks bleak and inhospitable. The marshes, variegated in shades of yellow and green interspersed with purple sea lavender, are, to him, an uncharted wasteland where an unwary traveller could take a wrong step and become mired in quicksand, a prey to the elements or worse. The building, with its battered sign saying 'Saltmarsh Community Centre', looks almost derelict, with its peeling paint and padlocked doors. But Nelson knows that it is still a thriving meeting place, with classes almost every night and events at the weekend. A sign on the noticeboard tells him that, this Saturday, Charlie Bennet, 'The Norfolk Elvis', will be performing. As he wanders around the centre, looking for signs of life, Nelson wonders idly how much someone would have to pay him to attend one of Charlie's performances. A hundred? Not a chance. A thousand? He might be tempted but the thought of 'Blue Suede Shoes' hardens his heart. You would have to pay him serious money to sit through that and, even then, he would leave before 'Are You Lonesome Tonight?' He feels sure that Charlie favours Elvis's white jumpsuit period.

'Can I help you?'

A woman is standing looking at him, holding a bicycle with a basket at the front. She is tall with blondish hair swept up in a bun. Something, maybe the hairstyle or the bike, gives her a rather old-fashioned air. He guesses her age to be about fifty but it's so hard to tell these days.

'DCI Nelson.' Nelson shows his warrant card.

'Ailsa Britain,' says the woman. 'I run the classes here.' She's casually dressed in a T-shirt and flowered skirt but is still a rather commanding presence. Her voice is commanding too, effortless upper-class vowels that sound as if they come from the days of the British Empire. Nelson runs through the case files in his mind. They must have interviewed Ailsa Britain when they were investigating the disappearances of Nicola and Jenny.

'Is it about Ivor March?' says Ailsa. 'I saw your press conference yesterday.'

'In a way,' says Nelson. 'Can we talk inside?'

He's not even sure in his own mind why he's there. He hasn't been to the community centre before. He'd visited the main locations in the Ivor March case – the garden, the suspects' houses, the places where the two women had supposedly vanished – but the initial interviews had all been handled by Judy, who had just passed her DI exams. She'd done a great job, everything meticulously checked and double-checked. Even the prosecuting solicitor had been impressed.

Ailsa props the bike against the wall, unlocks the main doors and ushers Nelson into a large room, empty except for a piano on a dais and a pile of stacked chairs.

'Would you like a coffee?' says Ailsa. 'It's only instant, I'm afraid.'

Nelson says yes to coffee. He doesn't mind instant, unlike Ruth who favours the proper bitter Italian stuff, preferably bought from a shop that pays its fair share of UK taxes. But he mustn't think about Ruth. Nelson takes two chairs and places them by a window that looks out over the marshes. God, what a desolate view, he thinks. Miles and miles of nothingness. And, when you get to the sea, that's bloody bleak too: no amusements, no cafés, just acres of grey sand. Nelson was born in Blackpool and still regards the Golden Mile as the perfect seafront.

'Beautiful, isn't it?' says Ailsa, appearing with two mugs and some custard creams on a tray. Nelson warms to her.

'It's a bit lonely for my taste,' he says.

'That's part of the appeal for me,' says Ailsa. 'I came here from London after my divorce and I just wanted to be in a place where I could see nothing but sea and sky.'

Ruth had come to Norfolk from London and she, too, loved the marshes. But not enough to stop her buggering off to Cambridge. Don't think about Ruth.

They sit looking out over the sea of grass and Nelson says, 'Were you working here when Ivor March was teaching?'

Ailsa takes a sip of coffee and looks at him coolly. 'Yes. I told all this to the policewoman who interviewed us.'

'Detective Inspector Judy Johnson.' Nelson knows that Judy detests the word 'policewoman'.

'Yes,' says Ailsa. 'She was very efficient.'

'So you knew March?'

'I knew Ivor quite well,' says Ailsa. 'He was a very charismatic man. I'm sure you've heard that before.'

'It has been mentioned.' Nelson distrusts charisma, which seems to him only another word for deceitfulness. He hates the way that the papers have dwelt on March's 'dark good looks' and 'fatal charm' rather than the fact that he strangled at least two women and buried them in his girlfriend's garden.

'He was a talented artist,' says Ailsa. 'His classes were very popular.'

This, too, has been covered by the papers with March's moody landscapes appearing on many inside pages. Apparently they are in great demand on eBay.

'He taught creative writing too,' says Ailsa.

'Talented writer as well, is he?'

'He hasn't had anything published,' says Ailsa, slightly defensively. 'But he has an artist's instinct for language.'

Nice work if you can get it, thinks Nelson. Maybe he should teach plumbing because he has an artist's instinct for running water.

'Did you know Nicola Ferris or Jenny McGuire?' he asks, wanting to bring the subject back to the victims, or probable victims.

'I knew Jenny,' says Ailsa. 'Such a nice woman. I was in the same class as her for a while. I knew Nicola by sight.'

'And what's your theory about what happened to Nicola and Jenny?'

For the first time, Ailsa looks troubled, a cloud passing over her pink-and-white features. 'I don't know. I mean, there are links to Ivor ... But I still find it hard to believe that he killed those other poor women.'

'He did,' says Nelson. 'And I'm convinced that he killed Nicola and Jenny too. I'm trying to find new evidence to tie him to the crime. It's difficult, without the bodies, but it can be done.'

'Are you sure that they're dead?'

'They haven't been seen since the night they disappeared. Both of them have friends and family, Jenny had a ten-year-old daughter. They are not the sort of people who just drop off the radar. I'm convinced that they're dead and that March killed them.'

'It's so awful,' says Ailsa. 'I mean, this is such a nice place, so friendly. And for this to happen ...'

But the classes are still continuing, thinks Nelson. Norfolk's Elvis is still performing at the weekend. Life at the community centre goes on but it has stopped, irrevocably, for four women. Because of Ivor March.

'Did you say that you were in the same class as Jenny McGuire?' he asks. 'Was that creative writing?'

'Yes,' says Ailsa. And for some reason she blushes. 'That's how I first met Ivor, actually. He used to run writing retreats.'

'Writing retreats?' An alarm is going off somewhere in Nelson's brain.

'Yes. At Grey Walls. It's a house in Cambridgeshire. In the middle of the fens. Have you heard of it?'

'I might have,' says Nelson.

CHAPTER 4

'This is a surprise,' says Ruth. It sounds better than 'what are you doing here?'

'I'm attending a conference on EU funding,' says Phil. 'Not that there'll be any after Brexit.'

Ruth feels her ears shutting as if they have flaps for this purpose. In the 2016 referendum, she had voted to remain in Europe and, now, the prospect of leaving fills her with such dread that she doesn't like to think about it. 'We have to fight,' Shona keeps telling her, as she prepares to go to London for yet another march. But Ruth fears that this is a losing battle.

'Just thought I'd pop in and see you,' Phil continues. 'Quite some office you've got here.'

Ruth's room is fairly small by St Jude's standards but is at least twice as big as the cubbyhole she had at UNN. It also has mullioned windows, a beamed ceiling and a small stone fireplace. Ruth's poster of Indiana Jones looks incongruous between two oil paintings of old Judeans, one of them wearing an Elizabethan ruff. Phil himself, in his studiedly trendy jeans and Converse trainers, looks as if he's wandered in from another century. Despite herself, Ruth thinks of the first time she met Nelson. He had come to the university to ask her advice about some buried bones. She remembers him standing in the corridor, looking too big, too serious, too *grown-up* for his surroundings. Well, Nelson is far away now and Phil is none of these things.

'How's Shona?' asks Ruth. She had been uncomfortable when Shona started seeing Phil, who was married at the time. Ruth was sure that the relationship would end badly and that she would be caught in the crossfire. But, ten years on, Shona and Phil still seem happy together, despite Shona's brief dalliance with a handsome Italian two years ago. They have an eight-year-old son, Louis.

'She's fine,' says Phil. 'As gorgeous as ever.' He can say things like this without blushing. 'She's part time now. She wants to be there for Louis. He's having a few difficulties at school. It's not easy being a gifted child.' Again, no blush. Ruth has never seen much sign of Louis being gifted, and has never really forgiven him for being rather rough with Kate when they were both toddlers, but she supposes it's nice that Phil is proud of his partner and son.

Ruth offers coffee which Phil declines, patting his waist-line. Goodness knows why, it's as flat as a pancake and how many calories are there in coffee, anyway? Ruth wonders why he has really come to see her and it's not long before he says, 'You know I was involved in the Ivor March case.'

'I read about it,' says Ruth. She feels ashamed of how jealous she had felt when Phil was referred to as 'the forensic archaeologist advising on the remains'.

'Rather an upsetting case,' says Phil, looking important. 'But quite straightforward technically. The bodies had clearly been buried using a handheld spade. The burials were obviously recent but the bodies must have been kept elsewhere for a period of time. One body was in fairly good condition but the other skeleton was completely defleshed.'

Spare me the details, thinks Ruth. She would use this phrase herself but it sounds particularly callous coming from Phil with his red-rimmed spectacles and teenager's shoes.

'I had to give evidence in court,' says Phil. 'Rather an ordeal. Have you ever done it?'

'A few times,' says Ruth. Nelson says that juries distrust expert witnesses but she always felt that they received her evidence with respect, even if they did look completely baffled.

'The thing is . . .' says Phil. Now we're coming to it, thinks Ruth. 'Nelson thinks that March killed two other women but their bodies have never been found. Well, on Saturday, I received this.' He holds out a postcard.

Ruth turns it over to look at the words. 'Call yourself an archaeologist,' reads the message. 'Ruth Galloway is worth ten of you. She will find Nicola and Jenny.' There's no signature. Ruth turns the card over to examine the image on the front, a black and white print that seems to show a ship's mast, or maybe a windmill.

Cley Marshes by Ivor March

*

Judy is also gazing at a sea view. Marion Prendergast, Jill's mother, lives in a bungalow in Cromer, high on the cliff, with a spectacular view of the pier and of the sea. It glitters behind Marion's head as she weeps, not for the first or the last time, for her daughter. Judy can only wait, knowing that her presence is probably a slight comfort. She has come to know Marion well over the past year. The Ferris and McGuire families too. Stacy Newman's parents are both dead and, whilst Judy has visited her sister in Newcastle, it's not the same. There is nothing so terrible as watching a parent grieve for a child. Yet it's a privilege too, in a way. Like a doctor or an undertaker, she is there at the worst times in people's lives, and that creates a bond, however hard she tries to preserve her professional detachment.

'At least that terrible man will go to prison for life,' says Marion at last.

'Yes,' says Judy. 'He will.' Sentencing has been delayed while the court waits for psychiatrists' reports on Ivor March. But he will surely be locked up for a long time, whether in a prison or secure mental institution. Judy thinks that he is as sane as she is although, as Cathbad often says, sanity is its own kind of madness.

'Do you think he stopped and offered her a lift?' says Marion, also for what feels like the hundredth time. 'Do you think that's what happened?'

'It seems likely,' says Judy. The trouble was that there were no traces of Jill in Ivor's car, or in Chantal's – Judy wouldn't have put it past him to use Chantal's. There was no CCTV at the lonely bus-stop but they were able to talk to a passing cyclist who remembered Jill standing there in her bright pink jacket ('She loved that jacket,' said Marion). He only saw a few vehicles on the road, two cars and a van. Without number plates they weren't able to go much further.

'She knew him,' says Marion. 'So she would have said yes. She liked him! That's what I can't forget. She liked him and his girlfriend. That Chantal. I blame her too.'

People do often blame the wives, mothers and girlfriends, thinks Judy. Usually it's deeply unfair. It's perfectly possible not to know that your son or husband is a serial killer. Psychopaths usually compartmentalise their lives very carefully. But, in this case, Judy finds it hard to believe that Chantal Simmonds didn't know about the murders. The bodies were buried in her back garden, for God's sake.

'Try to stop thinking about what might have happened,' says Judy. 'I know it's hard. Just try and remember Jill when you last saw her. When you had fish and chips. Hold on to that memory.'

Marion has told her about this evening several times. Jill came over once a week to have supper with her mother. On this occasion, neither of them felt like cooking so they bought fish and chips and went to the beach. They even shared a can of lager. 'Like teenagers,' said Marion.

'We did have a laugh,' she says. Her eyes flicker upwards, remembering.

'Hold on to that,' says Judy.

Driving back to the station, she thinks that she should

encourage Marion to continue to see the grief counsellor. This is a difficult time, when the excitement of the trial is over and the reality hits again. Ivor March is behind bars but Jill is still dead.

It's a strange time for Judy too. When she passed her inspector's exam two years ago, it had really felt as if her career was going places. Immediately afterwards she had been put in charge of the Ivor March investigation, one of the biggest the Serious Crimes Unit had ever tackled. It was a complicated and gruelling case but Judy felt that she had done well and, in last Friday's verdict, she had had her reward. But now, here she is, back at her desk – she hasn't even got an office of her own – doing the same old work, with Tanya breathing down her neck and new recruit Tony Zhang looking at her as if she's a relic from the days of the Bow Street Runners. She misses Clough. At least with Dave she had someone on her level, or rather someone with whom she was always vying for precedence. But they had some laughs together over the years and they both knew that, in a crisis, they would be there for each other. Now Judy is on her own.

Perhaps she should move? But Judy has lived in Norfolk all her life, her children were born and brought up here. She can't really imagine being anywhere else. Cathbad wouldn't mind moving, she knows that. He loves his adopted county – 'There's so much weirdness in Norfolk,' he often says happily, 'it's the perfect place for a druid to live' – but he also likes change and new horizons. He would seek out new weirdness wherever they went. 'It's all part of the great web,' he says, meaning that everything happens for a reason, but what if Judy is trapped in the web of some malevolent spider and needs to break free?

When she gets to the station, she is rather annoyed to see the boss sitting at her computer. He looks cross and baffled, as he often does when faced with technology.

'Can I help you?' she says.

'I was looking for the case notes,' says Nelson.

'Why?' says Judy. Though she thinks she can guess. Nelson is not going to rest until he has charged someone with the murders of Nicola and Jenny.

'I went to the community centre this morning,' says Nelson.

'Why?' says Judy again.

'I don't know.' The boss is obviously slightly embarrassed. He doesn't quite meet her eyes. 'It's the place that links Nicola and Jenny. I suppose I had some idea that there might be something more that we could get from talking to people there.'

'And who did you talk to?' Judy keeps her voice light but she's annoyed. She led the investigation, she interviewed everyone at the centre: teachers, students, cleaners, volunteers, even the headcase who calls himself the Norfolk Elvis.

'Ailsa Britain.'

'I remember her,' says Judy. 'She knew Jenny. And Nicola slightly. She has an alibi for the nights that they disappeared though.'

'Ailsa knew Ivor March too.'

'I think she did, a little. She'd been to one of his classes or something like that. It's in the files.' She leans over to find the relevant document.

'Ailsa mentioned that March used to run a writer's retreat. Did you know about that?'

'Yes,' says Judy. 'But neither Nicola or Jenny had been there, even though Jenny wanted to be a writer.' She taps on an icon called Grey Walls. Judy remembers visiting the house with Tanya. It was an autumn day and the porch had been full of leaves. A rather sullen-looking gardener was sweeping them away, looking as if this was a thankless and endless task. But, even in the middle of a murder inquiry, there had been a sense of real tranquillity about the place. Cathbad would have loved it.

'Grey Walls,' says Nelson. 'That's where Ruth was last week.'

'Really?' Judy turns to look at him. 'Cathbad said something about a retreat. I wouldn't have thought it was Ruth's thing.'

'Ruth's a Cambridge person now. It's what they do, going on retreats and . . .' Judy can see Nelson trying think of something appropriately decadent. 'Spa days and such. She loved it apparently. Who runs the place now?'

'Crissy Martin,' says Judy, selecting another file. A woman's face appears on the screen. Long pale hair, flowing dress, serene expression.

'Who's she again?'

'Don't you remember? She's Ivor March's ex-wife.'

Christina Martin. Back in his office, Nelson gets the files up on screen and reads through Tanya's interview with the woman who runs Grey Walls Artists' Retreat. Crissy was married to March from 2001 to 2010 and, during that time, they bought Grey Walls and renovated it, mostly using the money Crissy had received as a legacy from her dead parents.

'Why did you divorce?' Tanya asked. Nelson imagines her trying for an empathetic tone.

'Ivor met Chantal. We had an open marriage. We both recognised that it's unrealistic to expect monogamy. We're civilised creatures. But when Ivor met Chantal he realised that he wanted to be with her. It was all very amicable. And she's been a loyal partner to Ivor.'

Chantal Simmonds certainly has been loyal. When the bodies were found in her garden, the police had initially charged her with conspiracy to pervert the course of justice but there was no DNA link and they hadn't been able to make the charge stick. The bodies had been refrigerated before being buried in the garden but there was no large freezer in Chantal's cottage or March's flat. If Nelson could find the freezer, maybe he could prove that Chantal was involved. Maybe he should go and see her again? He will have to tread carefully. Chantal knows her rights and has a formidable lawyer. She would be quick to cry 'police harassment' and would greatly enjoy any subsequent publicity.

Judy has helpfully added a biography of Ivor March to the files. Born 1966 in Cambridge, only son of Sebastian and Susan March. He's a year older than Nelson. Nelson was fifty in November last year. His father had died at fifty and he had been dreading the milestone but in the end it wasn't too bad. His colleagues arranged a surprise party in the Lord Nelson pub (ha ha) and Jo and Cloughie had hogged the karaoke machine all night. Then, on the day itself, there had been a family meal with Michelle, George and his grown-up daughters, Laura and Rebecca. The one sadness had been not seeing Katie on his birthday. She'd sent a present and Ruth had added a rather ambivalent card with a picture of Pendle Hill and the words 'You're not over the hill yet, Nelson.' This seemed both comforting and almost threatening. Did it also suggest, though, that their personal journey was not yet over?

Ivor March had attended school in Cambridge where he had been a good student, excelling at art and English. He had studied art at St Martin's in London where he had met his first wife, Elizabeth Chandler. They married in 1987, when they were both twenty-one. Elizabeth had been pregnant but lost the baby. They divorced two years later. March moved back to Cambridge where he taught art at a private school. At the turn of the millennium March met Christina Martin, who seemed to have some private means. March and Martin married, bought Grey Walls and ran it as a writers' and artists' retreat until their divorce. March then moved to King's Lynn and continued his relationship with Chantal Simmonds. The couple didn't live together but, according to Chantal, they 'shared a spiritual bond'. This bond was apparently not broken by March's conviction for two murders.

There must be something there. Something that links March to Nicola and Jenny. Why can't he see it? Nelson should be attending a meeting about cuts to police funding but he keeps looking at the files, scrolling through witness statements and forensic reports. What is he missing?

When the phone rings he assumes it's Jo, asking why he isn't in some meeting or other, but it's a more welcome, and unexpected, voice.

'Nelson, it's Ruth.'

'Ruth! What's up? Is it Katie?'

A familiar sigh.

'*Kate's* fine. I was ringing because . . . well, Phil came to see me today.'

'Phil Trent? The dickhead you left in charge of forensic archaeology when you buggered off to Cambridge?'

Another, longer, sigh. 'I didn't "bugger off", Nelson. I left for a better job. Just like you did when you moved to Norfolk.'

'I've regretted it ever since.'

'I'm sure that's not true.'

She's probably right but Nelson is not in the mood to admit that there's anything good about any county south of Lancashire. He counters with, 'It was Katie I was worried about.'

'She's fine,' says Ruth. 'Doing really well at school. You came to her last parents' evening.'

'She's a little star.'

'She is. Anyway, about Phil . . .'

'What about him?'

'He was sent a postcard, one of Ivor March's paintings. On the back it said, "Call yourself an archaeologist. Ruth Galloway is worth ten of you. She will find Nicola and Jenny."'

'Jesus,' says Nelson. 'Postmark?'

'Ely.'

'Put it in a plastic bag. I'll be over in an hour.'

'I'm working.'

'Isn't term over? I thought the rule was: the posher the university the shorter the terms.'

'Teaching's over,' says Ruth patiently, 'but exams are still going on and students are handing in their dissertations. This afternoon I'm seeing two of my PhD students and then I've got an academic board.' She realises that this is a foreign language to Nelson.

'When are you free?'

'Not until five.'

'Who's collecting Katie from school?'

'Frank.'

Nelson grinds his teeth. A habit his dentist tells him he must try to break. 'I'll be there at five,' he says.

Ruth knows she shouldn't look forward to Nelson's visit but she does. She thinks about it all through the meeting, which is a dull affair about grade boundaries. Because of Kate, she still sees Nelson fairly regularly but something fundamental in their relationship changed when she moved to Cambridge. It wasn't the place – although Nelson claims to loathe the university town – it was the fact that she moved in with Frank. She surprised everyone with the decision, not least herself, but she knows, deep down, that it wasn't born out of passion but from a desire for something to change in her life. If she'd stayed in Norfolk, she would have carried on working at UNN, driving Kate to the childminder every morning, running digs in the summer and getting irritated with Phil. She would also have carried on seeing Nelson and occasionally, when they were a bit drunk or a bit emotional, they would have ended up in bed together. And there was a danger that she would have stayed just for this because sex with Nelson is so good that it effectively ruins sex with anyone else. Well, now she is living with Frank and they have sex and it's very nice, thank you very much. But she has only rented out her cottage on the north Norfolk coast. She's not quite ready to burn her boats yet.

At five precisely she gets a message from Larry in the porter's lodge to say that she has a visitor. She walks to meet him, thinking again of their first meeting at UNN.

These surroundings – the court, the ancient buildings, the sound of the organ playing in the chapel – couldn't be more different but there is still the sense that Nelson brings with him the excitement of being an outsider, a dangerous glimpse of the real world.

'What a place,' says Nelson, as they walk to Ruth's office. 'How much does all this cost the tax payer?'

'The college is independently wealthy,' says Ruth.

'Of course it is. As are most of your students, I bet.'

'Sixty per cent of our students are from state schools.'

'How many children go to state schools? Ninety per cent or more.'

'Your children didn't,' says Ruth. 'Your older children, that is. But you're right. Oxbridge should take more state school pupils. This place is elitist. I can't defend it.'

'But you still work here.'

'Let's not go through this again, Nelson,' says Ruth, opening the door that leads to her staircase.

Nelson subsides though he mutters something else about the taxpayer when he sees Ruth's office. She offers coffee, which Nelson refuses. Then she gets out the postcard, still in its plastic wrapping, and puts it in front of him.

Nelson puts on reading glasses to look at it, which gives Ruth a slight shock. Then he says, 'I'll take it to be analysed but I don't think it's March's writing. He's written to me a few times. Long letters about what a genius he is.'

'Who else could have written it?'

'Maybe the girlfriend, Chantal Simmonds. She's still obsessed with the case. Keeps writing letters to the local papers saying he's innocent. They don't print them but they do let us know.'

'But how could she have heard of me?'

'You're famous,' says Nelson. 'You've written books. You've appeared on TV.'

Ruth doesn't know whether he's joking or not. She says, 'You said in the news conference that you think March killed these other women, Nicola Ferris and Jenny McGuire.'

'Did you see it?' says Nelson. 'I hate that sort of thing. Jo says I'm too intimidating.' But Ruth thinks he looks rather pleased all the same.

'This letter says "She will find Nicola and Jenny". That assumes they're buried somewhere.'

'I think they are,' says Nelson. 'They both disappeared near the Cley marshes. I think they're buried in the area. They're not in Chantal's garden, that's for sure. We turned the place over.'

'If they're buried on the marshes, then their bodies will be well preserved,' said Ruth. 'Remember that first body we found? The Iron Age girl?'

'I remember,' says Nelson, and Ruth knows that he's thinking about the Saltmarsh and the hand emerging from the earth, still with honeysuckle rope twined about the wrist.

Nelson looks at the postcard again. His glasses are black and heavy-rimmed. They make him look older but they're also rather flattering. Ruth wonders whether Michelle chose them for him.

'How was your writing retreat?' he says.

Ruth is taken aback. 'What?'

'Your writing retreat at Grey Walls. Did you get your book finished?'

'Yes,' says Ruth. 'I did. Why are you interested in my writing, all of a sudden?'

'I'm interested in Grey Walls,' says Nelson. 'Because Ivor March used to work there.'

Now Ruth just stares at him. The light outside is bright but it seems as if the room has suddenly got darker.

'Did you meet a woman called Christina Martin?'

'Crissy Martin. Yes.'

'Like her?'

'Very much.'

'So did March. He used to be married to her.'

'You're joking.'

'I never joke about murder. March and Christina Martin were married for almost ten years. They ran this Grey Walls place together. I don't suppose that came up in conversation, even though March was on trial last week?'

'No, it didn't.' There were no televisions at Grey Walls and Ruth had deliberately avoided looking at the news on her phone. There had been three other guests but conversation in the evenings had tended towards art and poetry and the existence of God. They had not discussed the fact that Crissy's ex-husband was on trial for murder.

'Have you got any examples of Christina's handwriting?'

It so happens that Ruth has this very thing. When she left Grey Walls, Crissy gave her a box of home-made fudge, beautifully wrapped in green ribbon. With the present came a card, a woodcut of trees in winter. There's a note inside: *Dearest Ruth. It's been a joy to get to know you. Stay strong, stay angry, stay beautiful. Cxx.* Everything that is in Ruth shrinks from showing this message to Nelson. But she knows that it has to be done.

She has the card pinned to her noticeboard. Now she presents it to Nelson. His mouth twitches as he reads but he says nothing. Then he puts the card next to the postcard of the Cley marshes.

The writing is the same.

CHAPTER 6

It's still light when Nelson drives home along the Fen Causeway. In fact, it's a beautiful evening but, once again, the scenery gives Nelson no pleasure at all. He hates the way that the land drops away on either side of the road, the highest point in the landscape, and the way that the flat fields seem to wave and shimmer as they reach the horizon, giving the illusion of water and movement. It's an accident black spot, that's what it is. One wrong turn of the wheel and he would be in the ditch and, in this godforsaken part of the world, he'd probably lie for days before anyone found him. He thinks of Nicola Ferris and her abandoned bicycle. It was found the morning after her disappearance, lying by a gravel path that led across the marshes. Passers-by said that the wind was making the wheels spin as if the rider had only just dismounted. Jenny McGuire had been on a bike too. Hers was thrown into a hedgerow, about a mile from her home.

Nelson presses the hands-free option on his phone.

'Call Cloughie,' he growls.

Seconds later a voice says, 'Hi, boss.' Then it shifts into a different gear. 'Hi, Nelson.' Clough might be a DI now, in charge of his own patch in Cambridgeshire, but to him Nelson will always be the boss.

'Hi, Cloughie. How's the life of a DI?'

'Full of bloody meetings. I don't know how you've stood it all these years.'

'I never go to them if I can help it. I should be in one now but instead I'm driving home from bloody Cambridge.'

'Cambridge? Have you been to see Ruth?'

'Yes,' says Nelson. 'On business.' Clough knows about Nelson and Ruth, of course. The whole team knows but, by mutual consent, maintain the pretence that Ruth is simply a valuable expert witness. Now Nelson tells Clough about the postcard and the handwriting match. Clough had left King's Lynn by the time of the March case and often complains about missing out on the fun. But Christina Martin is on his territory. Nelson can't go charging in to interview her without checking with Clough first. It's come to this, he thinks, asking for Cloughie's permission before he acts. But, by and large, he's proud of his two protégés. Judy scored very highly in her inspector's exam and Clough is already heading up his own team. He has trained them well.

'So the ex-wife sent Phil a postcard,' says Clough. 'Why not just send it to Ruth?'

'I don't know,' says Nelson. 'But someone's playing games. I don't like it.'

'We'd better see this Christina Martin,' says Clough. 'Hadn't we?'

Nelson likes the 'we'. 'Tomorrow?' he says. He doesn't believe in wasting time.

'Yes, tomorrow,' says Clough. 'Meet you there at nine.'

It's true; Nelson has brought him up him well.

Ruth smells cooking as soon as she opens the door. She and Frank take it in turns to make supper. Neither of them is a particularly good cook but, over the two years they've been together, they have managed to amass a repertoire of edible meals. Frank brought up his three children alone after his wife died and he brings the same breezy competence to cooking that he does to everything else. It can't have been easy at the time, Ruth knows, but Fred, Jane and Sean seem to have grown up into admirably well-balanced adults. They all still live in America. Fred is married with a child (Frank is a grandfather! Ruth is sleeping with a grandfather!), Jane is a realtor, which apparently means an estate agent, and Sean seems to be a perpetual student. Frank's children have all visited them in England. They are all tall and athletic, with Frank's blue eyes and presumably their dead mother's fair hair. Fred and Sean were charming, expressing polite interest in archaeology and in Ruth, but Ruth liked Jane best because she took Kate rock climbing and taught her a number of Camp America songs, complete with gestures.

Today Frank is making chilli con carne. Ruth hopes that he hasn't put chocolate in it. He did this once because it was recommended in a magazine. For a historian, used to assessing primary and secondary sources, Frank has a touching faith in anything he reads in the cookery pages.

He overdid the chocolate, resulting in a claggy texture that had Kate racing from the room with her hands over her mouth. Ruth glances around the kitchen looking for an incriminating Green and Black's wrapper but there are only the usual ingredients, plus a stack of used utensils.

Kate is at the kitchen table, writing carefully in a lined notebook.

'Is that homework?' says Ruth, kissing her. She thinks that Kate's school sets too much homework. Several times she has been tempted to write to them citing evidence that homework set in the primary years has almost no effect on later attainment. Frank has always dissuaded her from sending the letter. He seems to enjoy helping Kate with her assignments, especially the history ones. Last year they made a model of a castle that was almost embarrassing in its historical accuracy.

'It's my reading journal,' says Kate. 'We don't have to do it but I want to keep up to date.' Ruth supposes that she can't really complain about self-imposed homework.

The chilli is successful and not in the least chocolatey. Afterwards, Kate disappears to watch television while Ruth and Frank load the dishwasher with what looks like every utensil in the house. Then Ruth makes tea. They are trying not to drink wine during the week.

'I saw Nelson today,' she says, putting mugs on the table.

She watches Frank hesitate before saying, 'Oh? Did he come to Cambridge?'

'Yes,' says Ruth. 'On sufferance. Complaining about elitism, snobbishness and too many bicycles.' She wants to make Frank smile, and succeeds, but in doing so feels oddly disloyal to Nelson.

'He didn't come here just to complain about the bicycles?'

'No,' says Ruth. She sits down, wondering where to start. Eventually, she says, 'You know the retreat I was on last week?'

'I sure do.'

'You met Crissy, the woman who runs it. I introduced you when you came to pick me up. She was really nice. I liked her a lot. Well, it turns out that she was married to Ivor March.'

'Ivor March? The man who killed those women in Norfolk?'

'Yes. He was on trial that very week and Crissy never mentioned it once. It was Nelson's case and Phil was the forensic archaeologist involved.' She tries not to let any residual resentment creep into her tone.

'Phil got a postcard last week,' she continues. 'It said that I should have done the excavation and that I was worth ten of him. It said that I would have found the other two women, the ones who are still missing. Well, it turns out that Crissy wrote the postcard. That's why Nelson came to see me.'

'Crissy wrote to Phil? She sounds as mad as her husband.'

'The thing is,' says Ruth, 'she seemed the opposite of mad. She's got this calm manner and this way of listening to you, really listening, that makes you tell her exactly what you're thinking. I thought she was amazing. I really did. And that's not like me.'

'It's not,' says Frank, smiling.

'And now I keep thinking – all that week, was she thinking about how her husband killed those women? And was she thinking about *me*? That I should be involved with the case.'

'It sounds as if you want to be involved with the case,' says Frank. His voice is casual but Ruth isn't fooled. She tries to examine her feelings honestly.

'I don't want to be involved with the case,' she says. 'It sounds horrible. Those poor women being killed like that. But I do miss being part of the team.'

'You have a new team now.' Frank looks her. It's the blue-eyed stare that makes women still write to him, care of the television company, offering to be the second Mrs Frank Barker.

'Team Rank,' says Ruth. It's an old joke, based on the time when Kate tried to put their names together in a Brangelina-ish way.

'Team Rank,' says Frank. 'With any luck you won't hear from this woman again.'

When Nelson gets home, he's pleased to see his daughter Laura's car in the drive. Quite apart from the pleasure of seeing Laura, her visit will distract Michelle from his late return. Michelle knows that he sees Ruth, of course. They often take Kate out together – George adores her – and, over the years, Michelle and Ruth have developed a cordial and respectful relationship. All the same, there's no sense in mentioning Ruth if he doesn't have to.

Laura is now a primary school teacher. She has a flat in

Lynn which she shares with two other teachers. There's no boyfriend at present or, at least, not one that she has introduced to her parents. When Nelson enters the sitting room, he feels his usual jolt of love at the sight of his first-born child now playing with his (surely!) last-born on the carpet.

'Hi, Dad.' Laura gets up and gives him a kiss. She'd been furious when she found out about Ruth and Kate two years ago but she has now forgiven him and, if she is sometimes slightly constrained in her manner, he manages to ignore this. He's lucky that Laura speaks to him at all.

'Hi, love. How's school?'

'Exhausting. The head thinks we're due an Ofsted inspection and keeps nagging us about data. Mine's up to date but he still nags.'

'Idiot,' says Nelson. He's not surprised to hear that Laura's paperwork is up to date. She's always been the conscientious daughter. Rebecca, now living in Brighton, is the one who leaves everything to the last minute.

'Laura!' George grabs his sister's hair. 'Laura. Becca. Katie.' He's a child of few words but he loves chanting his sisters' names. Hearing them together like that always makes Nelson feel happy and guilty in equal parts.

'Don't pull Laura's hair, Georgie,' says Michelle, coming in with a tray. Nelson doesn't know if she heard George say 'Katie'. 'You shouldn't let him, Laura.'

'It doesn't hurt,' says Laura. She pushes her long blonde hair, like her mother's used to be, back behind her ears. Michelle has brought soft drinks for her and Laura and a beer for Nelson. From this he deduces that he's not in disgrace.

'Are you staying for your tea?' Michelle asks Laura. With the family, she still says 'tea' in the northern way. With strangers, she'd say 'dinner' or even 'supper'.

'No,' says Laura. 'I'll have something back at the flat.' Nelson looks at her sharply. He often worries that Laura's not eating enough.

'I just popped in to say hallo,' says Laura. 'Your murder's in the paper, Dad.' Laura has always been the daughter who is most interested in Nelson's work. He's often thought that she'd make a good police officer.

She shows him the local paper, *The Chronicle*. It's folded back at an article headed, 'Jenny's last story.'

> *Ivor March, 51, was convicted last week of the murders of Jill Prendergast, 35, and Stacy Newman, 38, but police have always suspected that he was involved in the disappearances of Jenny McGuire, 36, and Nicola Ferris, 34. DCI Harry Nelson of the Norfolk Serious Crimes Unit confirmed in a press conference that police still suspect that March killed Jenny and Nicola, neither of whom have been seen since they disappeared from the Cley area of north Norfolk in the summer of 2016.*
>
> *Both women knew Ivor March. Nicola attended his art classes and Jenny was a creative writing student. Now Jenny's family have released the last story that Jenny wrote for the class where March was a*

> tutor. It's called 'The Lantern Men' and concerns
> the Norfolk legend of mysterious figures that prowl
> the marshes at night. It's said that travellers would
> see a man walking ahead of them and carrying a
> lantern. They would follow the light only to be led to
> their deaths on the treacherous ground. In Jenny's
> story, she sees the lights as she is cycling home across
> the marshes.

Underneath there's a brief extract illustrated with photographs of all four women and a rather crude drawing of
a man in a cloak carrying a lantern. There's also a photo
of Jenny McGuire that Nelson hasn't seen before. It shows
Jenny astride her bike with the marshes in the background.
She is smiling, strands of blonde hair blowing across her
face.

Nelson looks back at the article, focusing on the words
'cycling home'. He looks at the bottom of the page and sees
the by-line 'Maddie Henderson'. Maddie is Cathbad's eldest
daughter. She's not a great fan of the police but, nevertheless, Nelson plans to have a chat with her tomorrow.

CHAPTER 7

Nelson is surprised by his first view of Grey Walls. From its name, and from the sinister shadow of Ivor March hanging over it, he had imagined a Gothic monstrosity with towers at each corner. Instead, he sees a square stone house covered in ivy and purple flowers – he's vague about plants – with open windows and a distinctly friendly aspect. There is a covered veranda that runs the length of the house and on it two women sit, typing away earnestly. Clough is waiting for him by the gate, leaning on his car and eating a sandwich. Some things about Cloughie never change, thinks Nelson. He always has a smart car – this is a newish Land Rover Discovery – and he's always eating. But, despite that, Clough looks pretty fit. His wife has just had a second baby so maybe Clough is burning up the calories by pushing buggies. Nelson doubts it somehow.

'Hallo, Cloughie. How's it going?'

The two men shake hands, the formality covering a very real affection between them. After all these years, Clough is almost family and Nelson would defend his family with his life. He is fiercely tribal, which is why he still supports Blackpool after all these years.

'Can't complain,' says Clough. Which, if true, does imply a fairly drastic change of character. But Nelson thinks that Clough probably is pretty content at the moment. He has a new job, a promotion, a new house and a new baby. His wife is a glamorous ex-actress and his oldest child, Spencer, is a bouncing three-year-old. Life is treating him well.

'How's the baby?' says Nelson. He has a go at the name. 'Amelia.'

'Amélie,' says Clough. 'It's French. She's terrific. An angel. Doesn't sleep much, though. You forget what those days are like.'

'Tell me about it,' says Nelson. 'I was nearly fifty when George was born.'

There's a short silence while they both think about the difficult, tragic time when Nelson's first son was born. A birth and a death, a time none of them will ever forget. Then Nelson says, jerking his head towards the house, 'Does she know we're coming?'

'No,' says Clough. 'Sometimes a surprise is best.'

'Good thinking,' says Nelson.

They approach the veranda steps but, before they can make themselves known, a woman Nelson recognises as Crissy Martin appears in the doorway. At first sight she looks young and beautiful, with flowing blonde hair and a perfect oval face. But when she comes closer Nelson sees that she is older, about his age, in fact, and that the hair is more grey than blonde. Michelle has recently cut hers, thinking that forty-eight is too old to have long hair, but Crissy lets the white locks hang loose about her shoulders. Her dress is loose too, covering the fact that she is probably a lot larger than Michelle. But she is still good-looking, the pale hair, tanned skin and blue eyes making an arresting combination.

'Welcome,' she says. Her voice is attractive too, soft and low. 'Have you come about a retreat?'

'Morning,' says Clough in his most officious manner. 'I'm DI Dave Clough from the Cambridgeshire CID. This is DCI Nelson. We've come to talk to you about Ivor March.'

The smile doesn't falter but Crissy does glance quickly at the typing women. 'You'd better come in,' she says.

She leads them through a large sitting room, where a man is staring rather helplessly at his laptop, and into a room that seems more functional than the rest of the house. There are filing cabinets around the walls and the shelves hold, not leather-bound classics and Penguin originals, but files labelled: 'Bookings 15–16', 'Accounts April 12–April 13', 'Tax' and 'VAT'.

Crissy sits behind the desk and Nelson and Clough take the chairs opposite. Nelson waits, with some difficulty, for Clough to start the proceedings.

'Ms Martin,' he says, looking pleased with himself about the 'Ms', Nelson thinks, 'I believe you were married to Ivor March from 2001 to 2010.'

'You know all this,' says Crissy. Her voice is still even, although the fingers of one hand are tapping on the desk. 'I spoke to a policewoman. Tanya something.'

'DS Tanya Fuller,' says Nelson. 'We have the interview on file. Something else has come up.'

They both wait for Crissy to ask, 'What?' It takes some time but she eventually asks the question.

'Are you acquainted with Dr Phil Trent from the University of North Norfolk?' asks Clough.

'I don't think so,' says Crissy. 'I've never even heard of that university.'

Phil would be horrified to hear that, Nelson knows. He's always trying to raise UNN's profile, jealous of the fame of the nearby University of East Anglia.

'What about Dr Ruth Galloway, formerly of North Norfolk university, now senior lecturer at St Jude's College, Cambridge?' he says.

'Ruth Galloway . . . Ruth . . . yes, she was here on a retreat, only last week. A delightful woman.' She looks at Nelson when she says this and Nelson feels himself colouring. Has Ruth told Crissy about their relationship? Ruth is reticent about her private life but Crissy looks like the sort of person who is good at extracting secrets.

'Did you give this to Ruth with a parting gift?' Nelson passes over the card, now encased in plastic, open at the writing. Is it his imagination or does a spasm of fear cross the self-possessed face?

'Yes, I did,' she says. 'I like to give all my clients a parting gift. We become very close during retreats. Many secrets are shared.' This time she definitely looks at Nelson.

Clough reaches over with another clear plastic envelope.

'This was sent to Dr Phil Trent last week. Do you recognise the writing?'

Crissy says nothing.

'We believe it's your writing,' says Nelson, after another pause.

'You've no proof of that.'

'Not yet,' says Nelson. 'But we'll have a handwriting expert look at it and we'll examine the postcard for DNA and finger-prints. It's pretty hard to write a postcard without touching it.'

Another silence. Then Crissy says, 'I can explain.'

'Please do,' says Nelson.

'Ivor didn't kill Stacy and Jill,' says Crissy, speaking in a rush now, eyes glittering. 'I'm sure of it. A real forensic archaeologist would have found that out. Phil Trent isn't an expert in that field. I looked him up. When I met Ruth and found out that she used to work in north Norfolk, I knew that she should have been the person on the case.'

'Then why write to Phil? Why not contact the police?'

'I wanted to shake him. He sounded so smug on the stand.'

'How do you know? You weren't there. Ruth says you were here all week.'

'A friend was in court.'

'A friend? Who?'

Crissy is silent for a moment, still drumming her fingers on the desk. Then she says, 'Chantal.'

'Chantal Simmonds?' Nelson can't stop the incredulity showing in his voice. 'The woman your husband had an affair with? *She's* your friend in court?'

'We had an open marriage.' Crissy sounds more composed

now. She even managed a rather patronising smile, obviously pitying people with less civilised marriage arrangements. 'It was a spiritual union more than anything. I was a little angry when I found out about Chantal but I've come to appreciate her good qualities.'

Remind me what they are, Nelson wants to say. He's rather grateful when Clough cuts in, 'So Chantal thought that Phil Trent sounded smug in court and you sent him a poison pen letter?'

'Poison pen,' says Crissy. 'What an old-fashioned phrase. Chantal knows that Ivor is innocent. We're working together on this. I wrote the letter because I knew you'd recognise her handwriting.'

'Why do you both think that March is innocent?' says Nelson. 'His DNA was on the bodies.'

'DNA can lie.'

'I think you'll find that it can't,' says Nelson. 'Although witnesses sometimes do. The bodies were found in your friend Chantal's garden.'

'Phil Trent completely mismanaged that dig,' says Crissy, sounding wild again. 'Ruth is worth ten of him.'

It's what she said in her anonymous note. Nelson doesn't disagree with the sentiments but the words suddenly sound very sinister indeed.

When they leave the house, the two woman are still tapping away on the terrace. What can they be writing with such fury? thinks Nelson. He had an idea that writers spent most of their time staring dreamily out of the window.

'What do you think?' he asks Clough, as soon as they are out of earshot.

'We could charge her with impeding an inquiry or sending malicious messages.'

'Where would that get us though?'

'Or we could speak to Chantal Simmonds.'

'Now you're talking.'

They have reached Clough's car, its black paint gleaming in the sunshine. Clough looks at it proudly before reaching out and grabbing something from the windscreen.

It's a note, scrawled on a folded piece of lined A4 paper.

If u want to know more about Ivor March meet me at the Hanged Man on Newnham Rd tonite at 7:30. Ask for John.

'The Hanged Man,' says Nelson. 'Jesus wept.'

He decides not to tell Chantal that they are on their way. Clough is right about the value of surprise. They drive in convoy to Salthouse, a village on the north Norfolk coast. Nelson vaguely remembers Ruth telling him something about a Roman settlement nearby but, to him, there's nothing about the place that would have recommended itself to the homesick legions. There are fields, then a church with cottages clustered round it, then flat marshland intersected with pools and winding streams, then there's the sea. He can imagine how bleak it would feel on a winter's night when the wind (as Norfolk residents always tell you proudly) comes directly from Siberia.

'Beautiful spot,' says Clough, getting out of his car. 'I'd like to live somewhere like this.'

Nelson despairs of him sometimes.

Chantal's cottage is on the outskirts of the village, backing onto a meadow. And, it was in her garden that they found the bodies of Stacy Newman and Jill Prendergast. Today, the place seems a million miles from such horrors, but as they approach along the unmade-up path Nelson sees that Chantal's garden is still a building site with the earth churned up in great mounds. Why has she left it like that? So she can be reminded that two women were found there, women murdered by her boyfriend? What do the neighbours make of it? It's a small community and, at the time of the murder inquiry, people had seemed horrified that such evil could live in their midst. Do the same people now chat to Chantal when she goes to the shops or walks by the sea?

He gives Clough a quick biography as they walk. 'Chantal Simmonds, aged thirty-five, says she's an artist but I've never seen any evidence of it. Used to work in a local café but doesn't now. She was briefly married to a plasterer called Alan Simmonds, no children. She doesn't seem to have any close friends. Her parents are both dead. Chantal met Ivor March at a painting course in Cambridge. The rest is history.'

'I remember her in court,' says Clough. 'She never missed a day.'

'No,' says Nelson, pushing open a rickety-looking gate. 'She's certainly loyal. And tenacious.'

'You haven't got a warrant,' is Chantal's greeting.

'This is just a friendly visit,' says Nelson, 'just a chat.'

'A chat!' says Chantal. 'DCI Nelson wants a chat. I suppose you want to enquire after my health.'

'How is your health, Chantal?' says Nelson. 'All that prison visiting must take it out of you.'

'A lot you care,' says Chantal, but she steps back to let them in. That's one thing Nelson has learnt about March's girlfriend: she can't bear to be left out of things.

Chantal shows them into a small sitting room. The front room, Nelson's mother would call it. The cottage is a basic two-up, two down, made desirable by the setting – and by the large garden.

Chantal Simmonds is small with jet-black hair cut in a severe bob with a straight fringe. Journalists, who had used the words 'statuesque', 'beautiful' and 'blonde-haired' to describe March's victims, resorted to 'striking' for Chantal, which means, Judy says, that she looks foreign. She's the sort of woman who never dresses casually. Today she's wearing a red sleeveless dress and black high-heeled sandals. A strange outfit for sitting at home watching *Bargain Hunt* which, according to the frozen TV in the background, is what Chantal had been doing. A large ginger cat is sitting on the sofa. Apart from its flat face it looks very like Ruth's cat, Flint, and seems equally unimpressed by Nelson.

'We've just been to see Crissy Martin,' says Nelson.

'Bored of harassing me, are you? Well, good luck getting anything out of Crissy. She knows how to keep quiet.'

It's an interesting accolade, thinks Nelson. He says, still trying for a pleasant tone, 'We wanted to talk to Crissy about a postcard that was sent to Dr Phil Trent of the University of North Norfolk.'

Clough hands the plastic envelope to Chantal. She looks at it carefully, one red-nailed hand tapping on the arm of her chair.

'Phil Trent was the archaeologist who gave evidence at Ivor's trial, wasn't he?' she says at last.

'Yes,' says Nelson. 'Have you seen this postcard before?'

'No,' says Chantal. 'It's not my handwriting.'

'We didn't say it was,' says Nelson. 'We just wondered if you knew anything about it.'

'I don't.'

'That's funny,' says Nelson, 'because Crissy said that she sent it because you weren't impressed with Phil in court. She said you were working together on this.'

'Why ask if you already know the answer?'

'I just wonder why you and Crissy Martin would be working together.'

'Because Ivor's innocent,' says Chantal. 'And who would know better than the two women who loved him best?'

'Come on, Chantal,' says Nelson, 'you know he's not innocent. Ivor March killed those women and buried them in your garden.' Although the window doesn't face that way, all three of them instinctively look towards the back of the house. 'He killed Nicola and Jenny too and I'm going to prove it.'

'That's right,' said Chantal. 'Pin all your unsolved murders onto a man who's already in prison. That's what the police always do.'

'You knew Nicola Ferris, didn't you?' says Clough.

'Oh, this one speaks too, does it?' says Chantal. 'I knew her slightly. She was on Ivor's painting course. A nice woman.'

'And Jenny McGuire?'

'I've never met her. As I told bloody Judy Johnson and her sidekick a hundred times.'

Nelson thinks how much Tanya would hate to be described as Judy's sidekick.

'Jill Prendergast was your friend, wasn't she?'

'Yes,' says Chantal. 'And she was Ivor's friend too. That's why he would never have harmed her, not in a million years.'

'And Stacy Newman? Was she your friend too?'

'You know all this. Ivor knew Stacy from the old days in London. I met her once, at a party.'

Nelson decides to change tack. 'Why have you left the garden like that?' he asks. 'I would have thought you'd want to grass it over. Plant something.'

'I've left it like that so I can remember,' says Chantal. 'So I can remember you and your pal Phil Trent digging it up. And then framing Ivor.'

'You're not a fan of Phil Trent then?' says Clough.

'I'm not a fan of anyone connected with this witch hunt,' says Chantal. She turns to Nelson. 'I'm not a fan of Dr Ruth Galloway either. Though I know that you are.'

'What do you mean by that?'

Chantal smiles for the first time. 'Oh, DCI Nelson. What an innocent you are. Everyone knows that Ruth Galloway is the mother of your child.'

*

Outside, Nelson says, 'I don't like it. How did she know about Ruth?'

He has never discussed Katie's parentage with Clough, but he knows that his former sergeant knows, as do the other members of the team.

'It wouldn't be that hard to find out,' says Clough.

'I suppose not,' says Nelson. 'But I don't like the fact that Ivor's women all seem to know about Ruth.'

'Ivor's women,' says Clough. 'It's amazing how they all stay loyal to him.'

'Chantal Simmonds is just bloody-minded,' says Nelson. 'Crissy Martin though. I think she's more complicated.'

'Both good-looking women though,' says Clough. 'Not that it's relevant,' he adds hastily.

March's victims were all good-looking, something the press never fails to mention, which probably accounts for the endless public fascination with the case. Stacy and Jill were on almost every front page last week, smiling out from treasured family photographs, heartbreakingly unaware. Nicola and Jenny had been on many of the inside pages. *Are they victims of Ivor the Terrible too?* Ivor the Terrible. Nelson hates the nickname that the press have given to the killer, partly because he suspects that March loves it. What does the loyal Chantal really think about these women? She says that she was friends with Jill but Nelson doesn't see her as a woman's woman. There's a contempt in her voice when she talks about the members of her own sex, from Judy to Crissy Martin. Mind you, she's pretty contemptuous about him too. Chantal is a free-range hater.

Ivor March knew Jill, she'd even been at his birthday party. He knew Stacy from way back. Nicola and Jenny had been his students. Had he marked them out from the beginning or was he overtaken by a sudden evil impulse when he saw Jill waiting at the bus stop? Jill had been strangled. Nelson is sure that this was Stacy's fate too but she had been dead too long for there to be any forensic evidence. And this is probably what happened to Nicola and Jenny. Bastard. His hands clench on the wheel. He'll make March pay for those murders if it's the last thing he does.

He thinks about the newspaper article. *Jenny's family have released the last story that Jenny wrote for the class where March was a tutor.* On the outskirts of King's Lynn he takes a detour past the *Chronicle* offices, which are near the quay. He knows that reporters mostly work from home these days but he's in luck. Maddie is sitting on a wall outside the office talking into an unseen phone in a way that always makes Nelson want to call the men in white coats.

'Maddie?' he says.

She looks up. 'Sorry,' she says, to her invisible listener. 'Call you back later.' She looks up at Nelson, fixing him with her remarkable green eyes that always look slightly accusing. 'Hallo, Nelson. What brings you here?'

'Your article about Jenny McGuire.'

'You read that? I thought you hated the *Chronicle*?'

'Laura showed me.'

Maddie's face lights up. 'How is Laura?' She gets on well with Nelson's elder daughters, something that Cathbad calls 'emotional symmetry'.

'She's fine,' says Nelson. 'I was interested in the extract from Jenny's story, "The Lantern Men."'

'I didn't have you down as a fiction fan,' says Maddie.

'I'm full of surprises,' says Nelson. 'Do you have the full story?'

'Yes,' says Maddie. 'I've got it as a pdf.'

'How did you get hold of it? Did you talk to the family?'

'Yes,' says Maddie, rather defensively. 'I spoke to her parents. Nice people. They're looking after her little girl, Maisie. I think they were glad that someone was interested in Jenny's writing.'

'I'm interested,' says Nelson. 'Can you send it to me?'

'I suppose so,' says Maddie.

'Thank you,' says Nelson. 'How's your dad?'

Maddie now lives with Judy and Cathbad and their two children. Nelson knows that Cathbad is delighted to have his eldest daughter, from whom he was once estranged, living with them. He's not sure what Judy thinks about the arrangement.

'He's fine,' says Maddie. 'He's writing a book.'

Jesus, thinks Nelson, as he drives away. They're all at it. Ruth, Cathbad, all those people staring into their laptops at Grey Walls, not to mention Jenny McGuire and Ivor March with his creative writing classes. Why is everyone writing a bloody book? One thing's for certain, it's not something he would ever do. Maddie's right, he's not even much of a reader. He read a Jack Reacher book on holiday and, though he enjoyed it, that's probably it for another year. He parks in his usual place and takes the stairs two at a time.

'DCI Nelson!' Tom Henty calls from the front desk. 'I've got a call for you.'

Who can it be? thinks Nelson, descending the stairs. Most people now contact him directly or through his secretary. Who would ring the station's main landline? He picks up the phone, feeling wary.

'DCI Nelson? This is Sarah Hammond, Ivor March's solicitor.'

'Yes?' says Nelson, every nerve on alert.

'Ivor wants to talk to you.'

CHAPTER 8

Ruth gets the message just as she is leaving St Jude's. She is taking Kate swimming after school. They are meeting Cathbad and Michael at a sports centre just outside Ely. Ruth is running late, as ever.

Call me. N

Ruth sighs. Nelson always communicates like this. A 'please' or even a question mark would be nice. And why put 'N' when her screen is shouting 'Nelson'? She knows better than to wish for an x. She imagines he's ringing to tell her about his meeting with Crissy Martin. Should she leave it? It's not exactly urgent but, then again, she does want to hear about it. She presses 'call return' just as she reaches her car.

'Ruth.' Nelson answers immediately. She thinks he sounds odd, tense and almost excited. 'Something's happened.'

'What?'

'I got a call from Ivor March's solicitor.' Ruth can hear

voices in the background. Nelson must be at work. He mutters 'Not now' to someone then comes back to her. 'She said March wanted to see me urgently. I went to the prison this afternoon.'

'What did he want?'

'He said that he was willing to tell me where the other two bodies are buried.'

'My God. That's amazing.'

'Yes. I couldn't believe it. But he had a proviso. He always does. He can't resist playing games.'

'What was it?' asks Ruth.

'He wants you to excavate them.'

Ruth stops in the process of loading her bags onto the back seat. '*What?*'

'I tried to argue with him,' says Nelson, 'but he was adamant. He wants you to do the excavation and, unfortunately, he holds all the cards. He won't tell us where to look unless you do the digging. You don't have to agree though.'

Ruth stays frozen with her hand on the car door. Ivor March wants her to be involved in the case. A serial killer not only knows her name but is requesting her assistance. Should she refuse? This isn't her case, after all. She thinks of Frank's words last night. 'You've got a new team now.' But, of course, deep down, she wants to do it. She wants to be involved in the investigation. She wants to be the one to find the bodies.

'I'll do it,' she says.

She thinks that she can hear Nelson exhaling. 'Thank you, Ruth,' he says. 'Thank you very much indeed. Can I come and pick you up tomorrow?'

'Why?' says Ruth, momentarily confused.

'Ivor March wants to meet you.'

The sign for the Hanged Man actually shows a man with a noose round his neck. Admittedly, he looks rather jolly but it's not Nelson's idea of a joke. According to a noticeboard by the car park, the name refers to a boatman who killed himself from a nearby bridge after finding out that his girlfriend was unfaithful. This sombre story does not seem to have affected custom; the tables outside are full and people are sitting on the banks of the river, drinking Pimm's and making what seems to Nelson to be a lot of unnecessary noise. A boat comes by, crewed by an enthusiastic eight, and two swans pass in stately silence. Nelson scans the drinkers for a man on his own but he sees only braying students or families eating chicken and chips.

Nelson spots Clough's Land Rover entering the car park so he goes to meet him. He sees at once that Clough, in a tight blue T-shirt, jeans and fashionable-looking trainers, fits in perfectly with the crowd. He's sure that he, himself, looks exactly like an off-duty policeman. Perhaps it's the way his sleeves are rolled up? But Nelson despises short-sleeved shirts and he'd only wear a T-shirt if he were playing football.

'Any sign of our man?' says Clough, putting on a pair of sunglasses.

'He'll be inside,' says Nelson, 'in the dark. So you'd better take those off or people will ask where your guide dog is.'

The pub certainly does feel very gloomy inside. It's also

fairly empty so Nelson has no difficulty in spotting a middle-aged man sitting on his own by the fruit machine.

'John?'

The man jumps, as if he were not expecting the approach. 'Are you Nelson?'

'DCI Nelson. And this is DI Clough. I believe you have some information for us.'

'Yes,' says John, recovering his poise. 'Mine's a pint of Swedish Blonde.'

It's on the tip of Nelson's tongue to tell him to buy his own. Apart from anything else, he loathes beers with stupid names. But John is an informant and you always buy drinks for informants.

'I'll get it,' says Clough. 'What are you having, Nelson?'

'Coke, please. Jo would have a field day if I'm done for speeding.' He looks at John who already has two empty pint glasses in front of him. 'And I hope you're not driving.'

'Nah,' says John. 'I've got my bike.'

Clough gives Nelson a significant look, as if this explains everything. He goes to the bar and comes back with the drinks, including a half for himself.

'So, John,' says Nelson, 'you asked us to meet you. What have you got for us?'

John stares at him over the lip of his glass. He's a cadaverous-looking man with dark hair, greying slightly at the temples, and deep-set eyes. He looks so like a sinister retainer that Nelson is not surprised to hear that he's the gardener at Grey Walls.

'I've worked there for eighteen years,' he says, 'ever

since Ivor came. I've seen a few things in my time, I can tell you.'

You'd better tell us, thinks Nelson, or I've made this forty-mile trip to a pub with a tasteless name and pretentious beers for nothing. But he knows to keep silent.

'There were the four of them in the early days, you see,' says John, after a pause and some ruminative beer-drinking. 'Ivor, Crissy, Bob and Leonard. Ivor taught painting and writing, Bob was a printmaker and Leonard did sculptures. Crissy was the housekeeper. She did all the real work, all the cooking and cleaning and being nice to the guests. I did the gardening. It was good fun in those days. We all lived together at Grey Walls, teaching and working all day and eating together in the evening, staying up late drinking and talking. One winter we were snowed in and Ivor made all these snowmen, like an army patrolling our walls, he said. In summer we'd sleep on the lawn, looking up at the stars. I was part of it too, because I was the gardener and Ivor said that we had to listen to the land. He said that gardeners were the artists of nature.'

That sounds like something Cathbad would say, thinks Nelson. He wonders if John has called them there to reminisce about the good old days in the commune. But, after another pause for beer, John says, 'Then she came . . .'

'Who?' says Clough, who is obviously getting impatient too.

'Lisa. She was supposed to be an artist, but I never saw her draw anything. She was Bob's girlfriend but it was obvious that she wanted Ivor. Once, I caught them in bed together.

I was cutting back the wisteria and I saw them through the window. I didn't say anything though. Anyway, Crissy got pregnant and everyone was so happy. Ivor was ecstatic. He'd lost a baby with his first wife. He said that this was a new chance, a new beginning, an heir for Grey Walls. But then Crissy had a miscarriage and nothing was ever the same again. That's when it started.'

'What?' says Nelson.

'They'd go out at night, Ivor, Bob and Leonard. They had this van and they'd pick up women. They said that they were saving lost souls. The Lantern Men, they called themselves.'

Ruth is swimming, carving her way through the chlorinated water. She used to be quite a good swimmer, the only sport she ever excelled in, and even now she likes the feeling of moving fast, weightless and jet-propelled, something that never happens on land. Kate enjoys swimming too and is going to take part in a gala at the weekend. Cathbad is supervising the children in the smaller pool where Kate is probably challenging the long-suffering Michael to width after width, knowing that she'll win every time.

Three strokes, breath, three strokes, breath. Front crawl is Ruth's stroke, she has never worked out the legs in breast-stroke and veers wildly off-course if she attempts backstroke. But this is satisfyingly simple, overarm, breath, big kick every third stroke. She's in the middle lane, not aspiring to the fast track where everyone wears goggles and swimming caps, but much quicker than the steady breaststrokers in the slow lane. She likes it when she catches up with the swimmer in front, forcing them to go faster. God, it's easy to see where Kate's competitive streak comes from.

Then it happens. It's so sudden. Ruth is breathing under her raised arm, turning her mouth not her head, the way she was taught in the Eltham Centre, all those years ago, when she thinks, quite idly: what if I can't breathe any more? The next minute she is thrashing about in the water, sure that she is going to drown, sure that she no longer knows how to take air into her lungs. She goes under, panics, splashes wildly. Somehow her flailing arms take her to the side of the pool, cutting across the fast lane. She grasps the rail and tries to inhale the chorine-scented air. But her lungs don't seem to be working. She imagines them as one-dimensional, like the pictures in a book called *Flat Stanley* that she used to read to Kate. She puts her hands over her mouth and breathes into them.

'Are you all right?' The lifeguard, an anxious-looking teenager, is bending down to her.

Ruth keeps breathing into her cupped hands.

'What?' says Nelson, so sharply that Clough looks up from his lager in surprise.

'The lantern men. It's an old legend round these parts. Mysterious figures carrying lanterns that haunt the fens and the marshes. If you follow their lights, you're doomed. They can knock you down and leave you for dead. There are lots of stories of wherrymen being waylaid on their way home from the pub. The next morning you'd find their bodies floating downstream. They say that you must never whistle on a dark night or the lantern men will hear you. Ivor might have heard me talk about them – visitors often like to hear the old stories – but he meant the name in a good way. They were a light in the darkness, apparently. They were saving the girls from themselves, teaching them about art and life and all that. They'd bring the girls back to the house for a few days and make a fuss of them. Then they'd disappear.'

'What do you mean, disappear?' asks Nelson.

'I mean Crissy got rid of them. I'd see them in the morning, sitting in the kitchen thinking that they were part of this happy hippy family, then Crissy would make them break-fast and drive them to the station and they'd never be seen again. There was one girl, I think she was from Eastern Europe. They'd found her when she was lost on the fens. She stayed for months and then she just vanished. I asked Ivor where she'd gone and he wouldn't answer me.'

'Do you think something had happened to her?' asks Nelson. He's more jolted by this story than he cares to admit. The Lantern Men. The title of Jenny's story. The lights that lure unwary travellers away from the path. He thinks of the three men setting out in the van at night, the searchlight beam across the dark fens.

'I didn't think too much about it at the time,' says John, 'but then Ivor was arrested for the other murders and I started to wonder.'

'Can you remember her name?' asks Clough. 'The Eastern European girl?'

'Sonya, Sandra, something like that. Pretty little thing. Only young.'

'What happened next?' asks Nelson.

'It all stopped,' says John. 'The group broke up. Lisa and Leonard got married, right out of the blue. God knows why. I'd always thought that Leonard was the other way inclined, if you get my meaning. They moved away and Bob went too. Ivor met that Chantal and then he and Crissy broke up. Crissy carried on running Grey Walls as a writers' retreat. Like I say, she was always the one that did all the work. She's kept it together, even when she heard about Ivor. I mean, she couldn't believe it at first, but she carried on, almost as if nothing had happened.'

'Did you believe it?' asks Nelson. 'Did you believe that Ivor March killed Jill Prendergast and Stacy Newman?'

'I didn't want to believe it,' says John. 'I mean, I liked Ivor. He was always nice to me. But there was all that evidence . . .'

'Then why are you telling us all this now?' asks Clough.

'Because I met Lisa,' says John. 'She's back in East Anglia, running some sort of community centre. I think she means to get Ivor released. Crissy does too. Lisa told me that she wants to get all the gang back together. If that happens, I'm afraid that it'll all start up again.'

'What will start up again?' says Nelson.

'The killings.' John looks at Nelson, his face briefly illuminated by the bright lights of the fruit machine, red, orange and yellow.

'But Ivor March is in prison,' says Nelson. And he's going to tell us where the other bodies are, he reminds himself. Soon the case will be closed.

But John still looks at him with that haunted expression. 'Lisa's still free. Crissy too.'

'Can you tell us more about this Lisa?' says Clough. 'Her full name, for a start.'

'I can't remember it,' says John. 'But I've got a picture.' He draws an envelope from his pocket and brings out a photograph. It's the kind of slightly out-of-focus snap that used to fill albums before camera phones took over. Clough and Nelson peer at it. Five people are sitting on the terrace at Grey Walls. The wisteria is in flower so it must be early summer. Clough turns on his phone torch and, by its light, Nelson sees Ivor March, younger but unmistakable, with his arm round Crissy. There are two other men, one tall and thin, the other shorter, wearing glasses. And between the men is a woman Nelson recognises immediately as Ailsa Britain, from the community centre.

'Breathe deeply,' says Cathbad. 'In for four and out for eight.'

Ruth does as she's told, feeling stupid. They are sitting on a bench by the children's pool. Kate and Michael are queuing up for the slide. Cathbad is calm, almost detached, but Ruth knows that he is watching her intently.

'It must have been a panic attack,' she says. 'Why would I have a panic attack?'

'I don't know,' says Cathbad. 'Have you got anything to panic about?'

'Ivor March wants to see me,' says Ruth. 'I'm going to the prison tomorrow. With Nelson.'

'Well, going into a prison is stressful,' says Cathbad, 'all that bad energy and pent-up frustration in the air.'

'Have you ever visited one?' says Ruth.

'I've had a couple of friends who were sent to prison,' says Cathbad, 'and I spent a night in the cells once.'

'Really? Why?'

'It was at a demonstration,' says Cathbad. 'In my activist days. Getting arrested was one of our aims.'

Ruth wonders which of Cathbad's many causes this involved. She knows that he has lived in many places before washing up – his words – in north Norfolk.

'Was it the thought of prison that upset you just now?' asks Cathbad. 'You might have been projecting feelings of claustrophobia, of being trapped.'

'I don't know,' says Ruth. 'It was just that I suddenly couldn't breathe, as if the air was being squeezed out of my lungs.' She watches as Kate reaches the top of the slide and launches herself downwards with a yell of triumph. Michael hesitates for a moment before following her. Please, Goddess, keep Kate this brave for ever.

'You have to dig deep, Ruth,' says Cathbad. 'Reach down inside for the strength that is within.'

Is it there? Ruth wonders sometimes.

'I don't know why I'm having panic attacks, if that's what it was,' she says. 'I've got nothing to worry about.'

'That's the spirit, Ruthie,' says Cathbad.

Ruth repeats Cathbad's words silently all the way home. Kate is tired after her swim and sits quietly in the back seat, listening to music on Ruth's iPhone. Ruth has Radio 4 on but, for once, she isn't listening to *Front Row* as they talk soothingly about books she means to read but somehow never will. She is reliving the moment when her breath seemed to leave her body, the panic, the sense of darkness closing in. Dig deep, she tells herself, as she follows the signs to Cambridge. It's the perfect advice for an archaeologist. Dig down, excavate the layers, bring the past to the surface. Is there something in her past which is making her panic now? She has been through a lot in the past few years, one way and another: several disturbing murder cases, the death of her mother, relocation, a new job, a new relationship. Not to mention Nelson, which she isn't going to do, even to herself.

She parks in the underground garage they rent a few streets away from their house. This is one of the drawbacks of Cambridge; it's a town for bikes, not cars. When they get in, Kate goes straight up to bed. They had a vegan burger with Cathbad and Michael in Ely. Ruth wishes that she could follow Kate's example but she has to have a conversation with Frank first.

Frank is in his study but he comes downstairs when he hears Ruth's key in the door. He makes tea while Ruth tells him about swimming and about Cathbad's latest utterances. Frank claims to like Cathbad and, in turn, Cathbad opines that Frank is a 'serene presence'. But Ruth thinks that this conceals their true feelings. Frank distrusts Cathbad because of his connection to Ruth's past, and to Nelson. Cathbad might think that Frank is serene but he has often said that

Ruth, as a Cancerian, needs a partner who will disturb her peace of mind. 'You need fireworks, Ruth.' And no one is more disturbing and explosive than Nelson, a Scorpio, born within sight and sound of Bonfire Night.

When they are sitting in front of the television with their mugs of tea, Ruth says, 'I got a call from Nelson today.'

'Oh, yes?' says Frank. 'He seems to be in touch rather a lot recently.'

Ruth decides to ignore his tone. 'It's this Ivor March case,' she says, disliking the way her own voice seems to be pitched on a placatory note. 'Ivor March has said that he'll tell Nelson where the other two bodies are buried. You know the police think he killed two more women?'

She waits for Frank to say what a breakthrough this is but he remains silent. She ploughs on, 'It's a big deal. Up till now, March has refused to say where they're buried. He denies killing them, he denies killing Stacy and Jill too. Yet, suddenly, he says he'll tell Nelson where the bodies are. The only thing is, he wants me to do the excavation.'

'You? Why not Phil?'

'Because I'm the best,' says Ruth, bristling. 'Nelson says that March is so egotistical that he wants the best forensic archaeologist in the area.' Actually, Nelson had said 'in the country'.

'Nelson said that, did he?' Now the tone is unmistakable. Frank, normally so measured and reasonable, sounds positively snarky.

'Yes,' says Ruth, looking at him directly. 'Have you got a problem with that?'

'You're damn right I have.' It's almost a shout. Ruth is so surprised that she actually jumps, spilling some tea on her jeans. 'Nelson had no right to ask you,' says Frank. 'Ivor March is dangerous. He kills women. He shouldn't ask you to meet him.'

'Nelson will be with me,' says Ruth, before realising that this isn't the most tactful thing to say.

'I bet he will.'

'What do you mean?' says Ruth, flaring up in her turn. 'This is my job. It's his job too.'

'Your job is to be a university lecturer.'

'My job is to be a forensic archaeologist. This is why I've made a name for myself. Why I've written books. It's because I've been involved with cases like this.'

'And I've seen the toll it's taken on you,' says Frank. He takes a deep breath and runs a hand through his thick grey hair. When he speaks again, his voice is gentler. 'Look, honey, I know you're a terrific archaeologist. I just worry about you meeting a man like March. I think Nelson might be putting you in danger.'

'He would never do that,' says Ruth, but her tone is more conciliatory too. 'But this is important. Just think what it would mean to the families of those women if we find their bodies. That's why I have to do it.'

It's a fairly unanswerable argument. At any rate, Frank does not attempt to answer it.

'Just be careful, honey,' he says at last.

'I will,' says Ruth. 'I always am.'

CHAPTER 9

Nelson arrives punctually at eight a.m. Ruth would have preferred to be collected from the college but it's her day off and so her turn to take Kate to school. Predictably, Nelson jumps at the chance of dropping Kate off on the way. Ruth had also hoped to avoid an awkward encounter between Nelson and Frank but, of course, Frank is leaving just as Nelson is parking on the double yellow lines in front of the house.

'Hallo, Nelson,' says Frank. Ruth can see that it's an effort for him not to remind Nelson about the parking restrictions.

'Hallo, Frank,' says Nelson. 'All right?' He doesn't wait for an answer because, at that moment, Kate appears in the doorway and throws herself at him.

'Daddy!'

'Hallo, sweetheart.' He swings her into the air.

'Are you going to drive me to school today?'

'I certainly am.'

'Will you go fast? Can we have the siren on?'

'Of course not,' says Ruth. 'We'll go at twenty miles an hour just like everyone else.'

'Unless we have to chase a baddie,' says Nelson, opening the back door for Kate. She jumps in, neglecting to say goodbye to Frank. Ruth doesn't remind her because she is already dreading her own farewell. She normally kisses Frank goodbye every morning but she shrinks from doing so in front of Nelson. Ruth and Frank have made up after last night's almost-row but are still being overly polite to each other. Maybe they should just settle for a warm handshake? In the end, Ruth gives Frank a little wave. 'Bye, Frank.'

'Bye, Ruth,' says Frank. 'Be careful.'

'I will,' says Ruth, getting into the front seat. 'See you later.'

Nelson revs the car with unnecessary violence. Kate squeals with delight.

They drop Kate off at St Benedict's and then take the road for Thetford, where Ivor March is being held in a category C prison before being transferred to a Category A establishment for more serious offenders.

'It's lucky, really,' says Nelson, as they speed along the Newmarket Road. 'After sentencing he'll probably be transferred to Manchester, or even the Isle of Wight. That would be more difficult to get to.'

'Lucky me,' says Ruth. She's feeling very nervous, even about a category C prison.

Nelson laughs. 'Don't worry. It's not like a regular prison visit, with crowds of relatives, all crying and trying to smuggle in tobacco. We'll be in a private interview room, just you, me and a prison officer.'

'And Ivor March.'

'And March, of course.' Nelson swerves to overtake a caravan. Ruth shuts her eyes. She opens them; they are still alive and the road is clear.

'What's he like?' she asks.

Nelson is silent for a few seconds before replying. 'People say that he's charismatic but I have to say that I don't see it. He's clever, though, and conceited. He thinks that he's God's gift to women. I've seen that in a lot of villains.'

'It's not confined to villains,' says Ruth.

'No, it's not,' says Nelson. 'But March will try to manipulate you. He'll praise you and rubbish Phil, for a start. But you won't fall for that.'

'I'll try not to,' says Ruth.

'He obviously thinks that he can get you onside,' says Nelson. 'That's why he wants to meet you face to face. There are plenty of women who think he's innocent and want him released. Chantal Simmonds for one, Crissy Martin for another.'

'Crissy? Really?'

'Apparently so. I had a very interesting chat with her gardener last night.'

'John?'

'Yes, do you know him?'

'I talked to him a few times when I was staying at Grey Walls. He knows a lot about local folklore.'

'That doesn't surprise me. He sounded a bit like Cathbad at times. Well, according to John, Crissy, Ivor and their friends got up to a lot of very odd things at Grey Walls.'

'What sort of things?'

'Like picking up lonely women – God only knows what for – bringing them back to the house, letting them stay for a while and then chucking them out.'

'Chucking them out?'

'John said that Crissy got rid of them. He said that one day she'd just drive them to the station and they'd never be seen again. We've only got his word for that but there are no missing persons' reports that match the timeframe so I think we have to assume that March didn't kill them. There's one case I'm interested in though. An Eastern European girl who apparently vanished completely.'

'He could have killed her then?'

'Yes, and, if so, she could have been the start of it. That's how serial killers work. You get away with one and you think you're invincible. Then you get hungry for more.'

'Is that what Ivor March is? A serial killer?'

'You bet that's what he is,' says Nelson, taking the turn towards a sinister high wall with barbed wire along the top. 'He's killed at least four women, I'm sure of it.' Nelson stops at the gate and speaks into the entry phone. The doors open and, when they're through, shut firmly behind them. Ruth starts to feel even more nervous.

Nelson parks in a space designated for police and he and Ruth walk towards the main entrance. Once again they are buzzed in, then they walk through a scanner like the one at the airport that always protests at Ruth's under-wired bra. In the main lobby they are met by an officer who obviously knows Nelson because they exchange gruff greetings. Another guard with a sniffer dog approaches. Ruth hopes that the animal won't be excited by the smell of Flint. According to the 'Guidelines for Visiting Prisons' Ruth read online, women are advised not to wear 'revealing or provocative clothes'. This is not a problem for Ruth. She's wearing a black trouser suit with a white shirt, buttoned up to the neck. It's certainly not provocative but Ruth is pretty sure that it's covered with a fine layer of cat fur. But the dog passes them with the canine equivalent of a shrug. They are led into a small room and, once again, the doors clang shut. Ruth realises that she is shaking. The whole set-up, surely designed to make you feel alienated and unsettled, is working perfectly in her case. Oh God, don't let her have another panic attack. Breathe in for four, out for eight.

'Are you all right?' says Nelson.

'I'm fine,' says Ruth. 'Is this where we'll see March?'

'Yes,' says Nelson, who seems entirely unaffected by his surroundings. 'This room is set aside for interviews with lawyers or the police. It's nicer than the visitors' centre.'

Ruth looks around her. They are in a white box, windowless and featureless. There are four plastic chairs and a Formica table. A security camera whirrs in the corner. It's hard to see how anyone could describe the room as 'nice'.

A sound outside and Nelson looks at Ruth. 'That'll be him. Don't worry. Nothing can happen to you while I'm here.'

Ruth wishes that she could believe him.

The door opens and a man enters, wearing a blue prison overall, his hands handcuffed in front of him. He's accompanied by a prison officer. Ruth hadn't expected the handcuffs, they seem too dramatic, like something from a student production of *Crime and Punishment*. It's a few seconds before she looks up at March's face and finds herself meeting an amused smile.

'Good to meet you, Dr Galloway.'

How should she reply to that? 'Good to meet you, Mr Serial Killer?' She just says, 'Hallo.'

They sit down. March and the guard on one side of the table, Ruth and Nelson on the other. Nelson says, 'You wanted to see us, March.' His voice sounds harsher and more northern than usual. Ruth realises how comforting it is to have Nelson beside her. His leg, in anonymous dark trousers, is next to hers. She could, if she wished, just reach over and touch it . . .

'I wanted to see Dr Galloway,' says Ivor March. His voice is low and rather posh. There are no traces of Cambridgeshire or even London. He could be a Radio 4 continuity announcer.

'You said you were prepared to tell us where Jenny and Nicola are buried. Where *you* buried them,' says Nelson.

'DCI Nelson is very protective of you,' says March to Ruth. 'I wonder why.'

Ruth says nothing, hoping she isn't blushing. March is still staring at her with that half smile playing around his lips. Ruth supposes that he is fairly good-looking – dark hair and eyes, pronounced cheekbones – but she finds him creepy in the extreme. All that prolonged eye-contact, it's like something boys do in sixth-form before realising that it makes them look odd rather than sexy. Like serial killers, in fact.

'You said that you wanted me to excavate the bodies,' says Ruth.

'I've been following your career,' says March, still doing the stare. 'You're a very impressive woman, Dr Galloway. You found the Iron Age girl on the Saltmarsh. She's named Ruth after you, isn't she? That must have been some moment, when you pulled that arm out of the peat, almost perfectly preserved, with the honeysuckle rope still round her wrist.'

Ruth is shaken. The circumstances of her discovery are fairly well documented but there's something in March's voice that makes her blood run cold. Maybe it's the female pronoun and the detail about the rope.

March watches her to see if there's a reaction but Ruth keeps her face still. He goes on, 'You wrote a book about the Raven King in Lancashire. You were instrumental in clearing the name of an innocent woman accused of murder.'

Was I? thinks Ruth. Then she remembers: Mother Hook, the Victorian childminder, or 'baby-farmer', accused of murdering her charges. Ruth had excavated her remains and been involved in a TV programme that concluded that the children had died of natural causes. She prays that March hasn't seen it.

'I watched you on television,' says March. 'You have an excellent screen presence. I understand that you're now living with the presenter, Frank Barker.'

'Dr Galloway's private life is none of your business,' says Nelson.

'No,' says March. 'I can understand that this is painful for you, DCI Nelson. Can I ask you a question, Dr Galloway?'

'You can ask,' says Ruth. She notes that March calls her 'Dr Galloway'. This is her preferred form of address, she's proud of her doctorate and she doesn't see why near-strangers should call her Ruth, but is there something sinister in the way March keeps on using it? Has he heard that this is the way into her good favour?

March leans back in his plastic chair, cuffed hands around his knee. 'What do you think of Phil Trent?'

Careful, Ruth tells herself. 'He's a respected archaeologist,' she says.

'And your ex-boss?'

'Yes.'

'I thought he was an idiot,' says March. 'He was far too pleased with himself and he missed some vital clues. I want you to promise to do the excavation this time. Do I have your word, Dr Galloway?'

'I'll do the excavation,' she says, 'but I'll need some help from the field archaeology team.'

'But you'll oversee it?'

'Yes.'

'Thank you,' says March, leaning forward, 'thank you from the bottom of my heart.'

'Cut the crap,' says Nelson, 'and tell us where the bodies are buried.'

And, smiling, March does so.

Driving back along the A11, Nelson puts the windows down, as if to expel the stench of prison, and of Ivor March. The day had grown hotter. Ruth takes off her black jacket and rolls her sleeves up. There's a sense of escape, as if they've played their Get Out of Jail Free card.

'The Jolly Boatman,' says Nelson. 'That's been derelict for years.'

March told them that the bodies were buried in the garden of a pub on the Cley marshes that had once been owned by a friend of his. 'I used to drink there years ago,' he says, smiling as if at a pleasant memory. Nelson has already checked with the land registry and got permission to dig. Ruth has spoken to Ted from UNN's field archaeology team. They will start work tomorrow.

'He said it was near the church,' says Ruth. 'That's not far from where Nicola's bicycle was found.'

'I thought that immediately. It's near the community centre too, and the Dragon, which is where the art class went for end-of-term drinks.'

'Well, that all points to March,' says Ruth.

'It does,' says Nelson. 'I wonder why he's so keen to help, all of a sudden. There'll be a reason, if I know him.'

'He was horrible,' says Ruth, remembering.

'You weren't affected by the famous charisma then?' Nelson shoots a sidelong glance at her.

'No,' says Ruth. 'I can't see why anyone would be.' She thinks of Crissy, whom she had liked and rather admired. Crissy had liked Ivor March enough to marry him and, according to Nelson, she wants to get him released from prison. It makes Ruth doubt her own judgement. She, who doesn't make new friends easily, had confided in Crissy, trusted her. Had Crissy been talking to March about her all along, telling him about Ruth's relationship with Nelson? She remembers him saying, 'I can understand that this is painful for you, DCI Nelson.' Does March know all about Ruth and Nelson, and about Ruth and Frank too? Does he – God forbid – also know about Kate?

'Do prisoners get access to the internet?' she asks.

'No,' says Nelson, 'except under close supervision. Why?'

'I was just wondering how March knew all that stuff about me.'

'My guess is he got Chantal Simmonds, his girlfriend, to research you,' says Nelson. 'She seems to do everything for him. And she knows about you. About us. She said as much to my face.'

'About us' seems to reverberate around the car. Nelson has never used that phrase before. Ridiculously, Ruth feels herself colouring.

'I was thinking more about the archaeology,' she says, turning away until her face cools down. 'He seemed to know a lot about my previous digs. And he'd seen me on TV.'

'You're famous now, Ruth,' says Nelson. 'I expect you get stopped in the street and asked for autographs.'

Ruth ignores this. 'But he can't have watched *Women Who Kill* in prison. It was a few years ago now, must have been before he was arrested.'

Nelson is silent for a few minutes and Ruth thinks that he is considering this point. Then he says, 'Ruth?' in a completely new tone.

'Yes?' says Ruth, wondering what's coming next.

'There's a good pub near here. Want to stop for lunch?'

'Yes, please,' says Ruth, all thoughts of crime and punishment forgotten.

The pub is just off the main road but it looks as if it could be in a different world. It's in the middle of the Thetford forest, with trees all around, like a witch's house in a fairy tale. Inside it's almost empty. Ruth supposes this is normal for midday on a Wednesday. The only customers are a man at the bar who looks as if he's been there for many years and a Dutch couple in hiking clothes who appear to be lost, studying an ordnance survey map with worried faces. Ruth wonders how Nelson knows the place. Is it somewhere he comes with Michelle for pub lunches or for a cold beer on a summer evening? Don't think about that, she tells herself. She goes to the loo and is surprised to see that her reflection looks rather perky. She isn't wearing any make-up, in deference to 'Guidelines for Visiting Prisons', but her eyes look very bright and her hair is behaving itself for a change, waving slightly rather than falling limply to her shoulders. She rubs her cheeks to give them some colour and smiles at herself in the mirror. Be careful, Ruth, says her reflection.

They sit in the garden, a square of green overlooked by the forest. Ruth has a glass of wine but Nelson drinks Coke. How many times have they done this? wonders Ruth. Not many. The first time was in a quayside pub in King's Lynn, in the middle of the Scarlet Henderson investigation. Ruth remembers Nelson eating sausages and mash like someone refuelling, and talking about his daughters, who were then only names to her. Other than that, and apart from the dreamlike interlude in Italy, they haven't had many meals together. She can't imagine eating with Nelson every night, sharing the cooking like she does with Frank, discussing the day's events. She is sure that Michelle does all the cooking in the Nelson household. She remembers someone – probably Clough – praising Michelle's Yorkshire puddings. Of course, she would be a roast-meal-on-Sundays sort of person.

Sure enough, Nelson orders beef with all the trimmings. Ruth has fish pie, something that is beyond her culinary expertise.

'The prison seems miles away,' says Ruth, watching a black and white cat walk along the fence. It reminds her of her own much-loved Sparky, dead now for ten years.

'Prisons are grim places,' says Nelson, unconsciously echoing Cathbad. 'The idea of so many people locked up together, the claustrophobia, the unhappiness. A prison warder once told me that, at midnight on New Year's Eve, the inmates all shout and bang stuff against the walls. It's because another year has gone by. They're all just wishing the time away.'

'Will March get a life sentence, do you think?'

'There's no such thing as a life sentence any more,' says Nelson. 'In really serious cases the judge can make a whole life order which, in effect, means life. But, whatever happens, March should get at least fifteen years for each of the murders. He's fifty-one now. He won't be eligible for parole until he's in his eighties. If ever.'

'And if we find the other bodies that could mean thirty more years.'

'I hope so,' says Nelson.

Did March know this, wonders Ruth, when he smiled and told them where his other victims were buried? She assumes that he did. He's an intelligent man, after all, and one who has already been on trial for two murders. The thought which has been in her head all day finally comes to the surface.

'Then why did he tell us? If I find the bodies, if we find them, then he's never going to get out of prison.'

'He's a narcissist,' says Nelson. 'He loves to be the centre of attention. This way we all concentrate on him for a bit longer.'

'It's a high price to pay,' says Ruth. 'Is it possible that he actually feels some contrition?'

'No,' says Nelson shortly. Their food arrives and the land-lady asks whether they'd like more drinks. Ruth recklessly accepts a second glass of wine. She wants to forget Ivor March now but Nelson says, putting salt on his food in a way that Ruth suspects Michelle would not allow, 'Crissy wanted you to excavate because she actually thinks that March is innocent and that you'll find a way to prove it. I still can't get over the way these women all stand by him. Crissy, Chantal Simmonds. There's another woman too, Ailsa Britain, who's apparently campaigning for his release.'

What if he is innocent? thinks Ruth suddenly. But then she thinks of Ivor March saying, 'I've been following your career,' with that sinister stare, almost a leer. He is evil, she is sure of it.

They don't talk about March again. They finish their meal

and the landlady brings coffee and those gold-wrapped choc-olates that you only see on saucers in restaurants. They talk about Kate and the summer. Ruth mentions swimming with Cathbad but doesn't tell Nelson about the panic attack. Nelson says how good it was to see Clough again. Ruth says that she visited Cassandra and the new baby. 'They seem very happy, very settled. Amélie looks exactly like Clough.' Nelson updates Ruth on Laura and Rebecca. 'I still can't believe that my daughter's a teacher. I've never known a teacher, not in real life anyway.' 'I'm a teacher,' says Ruth. 'You're different,' says Nelson.

It's nearly three o'clock when the landlady – Sue – brings their bill. Ruth wants to split it but Nelson insists on paying.

'You must come again,' says Sue, pocketing her tip. 'You and your wife.'

It's a few moments before Ruth realises that the landlady is referring to her.

CHAPTER 10

Phil has had a trying day. Teaching is over for the term but he's had to take two revision groups and see half a dozen students. Undergraduates have got more challenging in recent years, he thinks, ever since they've started calling them 'clients' and charging them exorbitant fees. When Phil was an undergraduate at Sheffield in the eighties, you didn't expect to see your tutor unless you were ill or in danger of being kicked out. Now they seem to want his attention all the time. 'Can I have an extension on this essay?' 'I'm dyslexic, can I have more time on the exam?' 'My girlfriend/boyfriend/mother/dog doesn't understand me. Can I talk to you about it?' No, Phil wants to say, you can only talk to me about archaeology and then only if you really can't say it in an email. Better still, don't say it at all. A little repression never hurt anyone.

Phil is always busy these days. He can't afford to replace Ruth so has had to split her considerable teaching load between other members of staff. But the worst thing is, without Ruth, they can't run the MA in forensic archaeology.

Phil likes postgraduate students, especially when they come from overseas; they pay hefty fees and seem to have fewer essay/dyslexia/parent/dog crises. But now they've had to cancel their most lucrative course. What possessed Ruth to go off to Cambridge? OK, Oxbridge is prestigious but Ruth always claimed not to care about things like that. Shona says that it's all to do with Ruth's private life – something to do with getting away from Nelson – but Shona always thinks that everything's related to sex. It comes of teaching English Literature.

Today, Phil had to run a session on Human Evolution and was asked difficult questions about homo floresiensis. How can he be expected to keep up to date with every new development in anthropology, including hobbit-people in Indonesia? He'd told the student to google it but could tell by her face that she didn't think this represented good value for her tuition fees. Then he had a boring meeting about finance and now he has to go home and endure a dinner party, of all things. 'No one has dinner parties any more,' he'd protested to Shona but she'd been adamant. There is a new poetry lecturer that he simply *has* to meet and he's married to a really interesting woman who makes jewellery out of plastic found on the beach. It would do them good to have some intelligent conversation, Shona had said. She'll put Louis to bed early and Phil can make his special hummus. Damn, thinks Phil, he's forgotten to buy chickpeas. He'll have to stop at a shop on the way home. Wearily, he puts on his bicycle clips and hoists his backpack onto his shoulders.

In an effort to stay fit, Phil has recently started cycling into work. He enjoys it in the morning, freewheeling past all the traffic, the wind in his face. It's better than a double espresso for waking you up. But now he wishes that he was getting into a gas-guzzling car with air-conditioning and cruise control. He'd be home in a few minutes, there would be time to have a shower and a glass of wine before Mr Poetry and Ms Plastic turned up. Oh well, this way he's helping to save the world. He undoes the padlock, puts on his headphones – he's listening to a true crime podcast – and cycles through the campus. It's very quiet, the students are either revising or off-site. A light wind ripples over the ornamental lake and he can smell may flowers mingled with a pungent scent of weed. That must mean that there are students about somewhere.

The podcast keeps him entertained for the slog along the main round and the dance-of-death through the round-abouts. He passes the golf course and the industrial estate, immersed in the story of a serial killer who murders women and weaves clothes out of their hair. It makes him think of the poet's wife and her plastic earrings. When he reaches the outskirts of Lynn he takes a detour to pass a convenience store. He buys two cans of chickpeas, a lemon and a bottle of red, because you can never have too much booze at a dinner party. He adds a packet of After Eight mints because that's what his mother always offered guests with their coffee. He pays for his purchases and packs them all in his now-bulging backpack. Then he gets back on his bike, plugs in the Rapunzel Killer, and heads for home.

Phil and Shona have a Georgian town house off a square called Tuesday Market Place. Today Phil approaches via a backroad, a narrow alleyway where the houses lean in towards each other as if they are gossiping. But Phil is hardly concentrating on his surroundings now. He's nearly home. He can taste that first glass of wine as if it's already making its way down his throat.

That's why the attack comes as a complete surprise.

Something slams into him, knocking him off his bike. Phil hits the ground hard. He's wearing a helmet but the shock winds him for a moment. Then someone grabs him and seems to be pulling at his clothes. 'Get off,' says Phil, knowing that his voice sounds shaky and feeble. The figure leans over him and he thinks he sees the glint of a knife.

'Hey!' Another voice, loud, resonant and somehow familiar. The knifeman stops and looks round, then he takes to his heels. A new shape appears, clad in jeans, T-shirt and a billowing purple cloak.

'Cathbad,' says Phil.

Then his chest explodes.

Ruth is cooking. She's not really hungry after her pub lunch but she feels, in a vague sort of way, that she ought to make supper tonight. Frank hadn't wanted her to go to the prison but she had gone anyway. Not that Frank has any right to tell her what to do, thinks Ruth, chopping onions viciously, but, for the sake of a pleasant life, it's better if they aren't angry with each other. She knows, of course, why Frank hadn't wanted her to go. It was about Nelson. It's always about Nelson.

Frank knows that Nelson will always be part of her life, because of Kate. He's generous about this, he always talks nicely to Kate about her dad and is polite to Nelson when they meet. But he doesn't like it when Ruth works with Nelson. He'd never say so but it's evident in the way he talks about 'helping the police with their enquiries', in the slight roll of his eyes when Ruth shows what he considers to be an unnatural interest in serious crime. She had followed the Ivor March case from the start, for example, while Frank took refuge on the moral high ground. 'I'm afraid I don't like hearing about women being murdered.'

What will Frank say when Ruth tells him that tomorrow she'll be digging up the gardens of a pub, in the company of Nelson and most of the Serious Crimes Team? She's guiltily aware that this will also entail asking Frank to collect Kate from school. She remembers the delight on Kate's face today when she'd seen both her mother and her father waiting for her at the school gate. She'd flung herself into Nelson's arms jabbering about gold stars and netball matches and what Rosie said to Mrs Loomis in the lunch queue. Ruth had been forgotten but she didn't mind. She'd had to pretend that she had a cold to excuse her streaming eyes. It wasn't fair that Kate hardly ever saw her father in the week. Ruth didn't stop to think that Nelson was unlikely to have collected Laura and Rebecca from school very often. Just at that moment, she had felt that her situation was almost tragic.

Kate should see Nelson every day. Ruth should see Nelson every day.

But now she is cooking spaghetti bolognese to placate Frank. He's in the mood to be placated, that much is immediately clear. He says that the food is delicious and insists on clearing up afterwards. He chats to Kate about school and tells Ruth about an interesting manuscript that has just been discovered. It's only when Kate has gone upstairs to have her bath that Ruth mentions Ivor March.

'So he actually told you where the bodies were buried?'

'He told me where to dig. We're going to do an excavation tomorrow.'

'Tomorrow?'

'We have to move quickly.'

Frank doesn't query the 'we'. 'Do you think Ivor March was telling the truth?' he asks.

Ruth considers. 'I don't know. He kept smiling in this awful way. I wouldn't put it past him to play a trick on us. But that would make him look stupid too. I think he enjoyed having this information to taunt the police with. It would lower his status if it turns out to be a hoax. I'm pretty sure we will find something there.'

'In the back garden of a pub?'

'March said he used to know the landlord. He said it as if this explained everything.'

'Well, be careful, Ruth,' says Frank. 'I seem to keep saying that these days.'

'I'm just supervising,' says Ruth. 'I won't even get my hands dirty.'

'I bet you will.'

He smiles at her and Ruth remembers why she's here, in this Cambridge town house, trying to make this new life work. It's because Frank is a nice person and an extremely attractive man. He reaches out to take her hand. 'Ruth?'

'Yes?' Ruth smiles back at him. The moment hangs in the air, heavy with promise, but then Kate calls down that she can't find her pyjamas. Ruth gets up to help her and Frank opens *History Today*.

Nelson is also thinking about food. Michelle has made a mixed grill and, for once, he's having trouble finishing it. He keeps thinking about the roast meal in the pub with Ruth. It was delicious but it has left him less enthusiastic about his supper than usual. However, for many reasons, he is not going to mention the pub lunch to Michelle. She knows that he was seeing Ruth but he was careful to tell her the circumstances and to stress that the meeting was work-related. A pub lunch comes under a different category altogether. Not that there was anything in his behaviour towards Ruth that couldn't have been witnessed by his wife. They had both been careful to discuss neutral matters only and had not kissed hallo or goodbye, or even touched. But, even so, there had been something about eating in the pub garden, about the long, scented summer afternoon as they dawdled over the coffee, almost the only customers in the place, that felt illicit somehow. Nelson told himself that they had needed a respite after the horrors of the prison but that did not stop the thought that kept recurring during the lunch: if he was married to Ruth they could spend every day like this. Well, not exactly, because they'd both have to work, but even that is an intoxicating thought. Working together, talking about their cases over supper, arguing over the exact age of long-buried bones. Stop it, he tells himself.

'Are you feeling all right, Harry? You usually love kidneys.'

'I'm fine, love. I had some chips on the way home.'

'Oh, Harry. You promised you'd start eating more healthily. It's important when you're over fifty.'

'I'm not over fifty,' says Nelson. 'I'm fifty.'

'Fifty-one in November,' says Michelle. But she seems to accept the chips excuse. She clears his plate away – ignoring Bruno's hopeful glance – and tells Nelson that she doesn't suppose he wants any pudding. Nelson feels like he has to agree.

'Shall I make coffee?' he says.

'Not in the evening,' says Michelle. 'Or I won't sleep.' She's fanatical about getting a proper night's sleep. George is a good sleeper too, better than either of the girls. It's only Nelson who finds himself awake in the early hours, grinding his teeth and worrying.

Before he can slot in the coffee capsule that, according to Laura, is helping to destroy the planet, his phone buzzes. Judy.

'Sorry, love,' he says to Michelle, 'I have to get this.' But she too is looking at something on her phone and doesn't hear.

'Sorry to disturb you, boss,' says Judy, 'but I thought you'd want to hear this. Phil Trent has been attacked.'

'What?'

'Cathbad was on his way to the soup run in Lynn. You know, that volunteer work he does with the homeless? He heard an altercation and went to help. He found Phil on the ground with a man leaning over him. It looked like he had a knife. Cathbad shouted and the attacker ran away.'

Cathbad to the rescue again, thinks Nelson.

'Is Phil badly hurt?' he asks.

'He's had a heart attack,' says Judy.

'Bloody hell.'

'Doctors think it was the shock of the assault. Phil was knocked off his bike but he doesn't have any serious injuries from that. Cathbad said that he was lying in a pool of red liquid but that turned out to be a broken bottle of wine. Cathbad called the ambulance and waited with Phil until it came. Luckily he knows first aid.'

Of course he does, thinks Nelson. Cathbad knows everything. He's not at all surprised that Phil was on a bike and carrying a bottle of red wine. It fits all his prejudices about Ruth's ex-head of department.

'Is Phil going to be all right?' he asks.

'I don't know. He's in an induced coma at the moment. Shona's with him.'

'Poor bugger.'

'Yes,' says Judy. 'The thing is, the attacker ran off with Phil's backpack, which apparently had his laptop in it. And I was thinking, given the postcard that was sent to Ruth, could this be linked to the Ivor March case?'

'It's a coincidence,' says Nelson, 'and you know how I feel about coincidences.'

'Yes,' says Judy quickly, obviously not wanting him to tell her again. 'And I feel the same. Someone close to March clearly has it in for Phil Trent.'

CHAPTER 11

The Jolly Boatman is on the very edge of the marshes. The pub, a squat, white-walled building with boarded-up windows, still has a few wooden tables in its overgrown garden. There's also a piece of children's play equipment that now looks somehow ominous, like a half-built gallows, ropes swinging and wood rotting. Beyond this is a low wall and, beyond that, miles of undulating grass, green and yellow, with the wide, blue sky above. Ruth parks her car in the car park, deserted now apart from several police vehicles and the van belonging to Ted from the field archaeology team. For a second Ruth just sits and looks. The flat landscape is almost featureless but, in the distance, she can see the sails of a windmill. She can't see the sea but she knows it's out there. Seagulls fly high above them, white against the blue.

Ted, a bald giant in a high-vis vest, appears in her wing mirror. Ruth winds down her window.

'Hi, Ted.'

'Hi, Ruth. Admiring the scenery?'

'Yes,' says Ruth. It's very like the view from her beloved

Saltmarsh cottage and she feels her heart twist with longing. Don't look back, she tells herself, you've got a new life now. But the location in its lonely beauty, and the fact that she is about to dig for buried bones, reminds her of the first time that she and Nelson searched for human remains on the marshes.

'Marshland is very important in prehistory,' she had told him, as they followed the path across the uneven, treacherous ground, 'because it's a link between the land and the sea and between life and death.'

Nelson had been sceptical, she remembers, but that was before they had found a child's body buried there, an offering to faceless and vengeful gods. Had Ivor March chosen this spot for the same reason? He had certainly painted this landscape many times. Yesterday, when Nelson had dropped her back at home, she had googled 'Ivor March Art' and had spent almost an hour looking at watercolours and prints of grassland and waterways, boats on the shore, lighthouses and masts rising out of the mist.

Ruth gets out of the car. The pub is already cordoned off with police tape. Ruth expects to see Nelson but, when she nears the police cars, she finds Judy directing operations.

'Where's Nelson?' asks Ruth.

Judy steers her away from the others. 'He'll be along later. Did you hear about Phil?'

'No?'

'He was attacked on his way home last night. He's had a heart attack.'

'Oh my God. Is he all right?'

'He's in an induced coma. I'm going to ring the hospital later.'

'I must ring Shona,' says Ruth. 'Do you know what happened?'

'Well, Cathbad actually found him. He heard a noise and went to help. He saw the attacker bending over Phil. It was a man, he thinks. He ran off with Phil's backpack.'

'Was he a mugger then?'

'I don't think it was a straightforward mugging,' says Judy. 'Cathbad thinks the man had a knife, for one thing.'

'It's amazing that Cathbad was there,' says Ruth.

'He's here too,' says a voice behind her.

Ruth turns and sees Cathbad, dressed in shorts and a T-shirt and carrying a trowel. 'I thought you might need some help with the digging,' he says.

Ruth gives him a quick hug. Apart from being pleased to see Cathbad for his own sake, it will be useful to have another expert digger. Cathbad trained as an archaeologist before becoming a druid, shaman, house husband and all-round superhero.

'I was just saying how amazing it was that you were there when Phil was attacked,' she says.

'It's not amazing,' says Cathbad. 'It's all part of the great web.'

'The great web comes in handy sometimes.'

'It certainly does. Everything happens for a reason.'

'It's a bit tough on Phil though. Being attacked because of some cosmic plan.'

'Phil will survive,' says Cathbad, 'but this will have repercussions. We are all threads in the tapestry of life.'

Ruth can almost hear Nelson's voice saying 'bollocks'. Judy seems unmoved. She probably gets enough of this sort of thing at home.

'Where did it happen?' she asks.

'Near Tuesday Market Place in Lynn,' says Cathbad. 'Did you know that a witch's heart is buried in the wall there? She was burned at the stake and her heart flew out and into the side of a house.'

'It sounds pretty unlikely to me,' says Ruth. She thinks that Cathbad is looking at her a little too intently. He won't have forgotten the panic attack in the swimming pool. But Ruth doesn't want to talk about that now. Today she is Dr Ruth Galloway, calm, professional and detached.

'Shall we get started?' she says.

Ivor March said that the bodies were buried in the garden of the pub. It's gone wild now, the grass waist high in places. Ted has brought a lawnmower and a scythe as well as a hand-held magnetometer. If March buried Nicola and Jenny soon after they disappeared, they will have been lying in the soil for almost a year, enough time for the grass and weeds to have grown over them, but the magnetometer will sense magnetic disturbances in the earth, such as a burial. But, looking at the green space in front of her, Ruth thinks she hardly needs geophysics.

'Nettles,' she says.

'Yes,' says Ted.

There is a dense patch of nettles in the very centre of

the garden. Nettles thrive on nutrients from human waste and so their existence on a site usually means that people have lived there – or that there's a dead body buried in the vicinity. Ted passes the magnetometer over the area. There's an immediate reaction.

'Right,' says Ruth. 'Let's start here.'

Ted takes the scythe and, looking like the personification of Old Father Time or some more sinister folkloric figure, hacks back the vegetation. Then he, Cathbad and the police volunteers start to dig. Ruth stands back at this stage. She wants to get a sense of the land and to look at soil samples. Besides, digging gives her backache these days.

She knows. She knows as she watches the men dig, their shovels moving in unison, cutting through the chalky soil. She knows as she listens to a skylark singing high above and hears the distant roar of the tide. She knows what they will find.

They are hardly through the topsoil when Ted shouts, 'Stop!' He beckons Ruth over and she kneels to examine something embedded in the ground, as white as the chalk around it.

'It's a skull,' says Ruth. She kneels down and, with her pointing trowel, pushes away the earth. Ted helps her and, in a few minutes, they see a shred of cloth and a bone, still with leathery skin attached. Judy squats down beside them. Ruth knows that Judy is tough but she still wants to warn her about what she might see.

'It's OK,' says Judy, looking closer. 'But this looks very decomposed. Nicola and Jenny have only been dead two years.'

'Marshy soil can hasten putrefaction,' says Ruth, deliberately maintaining a detached, scientific tone. 'Sand or lime can retard the process.'

'Can you tell if the body is male or female?' says Judy.

'Not yet,' says Ruth, 'but when we excavate properly we should be able to tell. Male and female skulls look different. Male skulls have a more developed nuchal crest and larger mastoid bones. The female frontal bone is straighter and steeper. The long bones are different too because women are usually shorter. The pelvic bones are most definitive though. The female pelvis is much shallower and broader.'

'This skull is female,' says Cathbad. 'I can sense it.'

Ruth gives him a look, pushing sweaty strands of hair out of her eyes. She could do without Cathbad's sixth sense today. But, actually, she thinks that he is right. The chin, which she has just cleared, is pointed and delicate. Male chins are usually squarer. She thinks of the pictures she has seen of Nicola and Jenny, both attractive women with heart-shaped faces.

'Let's keep digging,' she says, 'but carefully. I think the other body must be nearby.'

By midday they have exposed the second body. A black van with the words 'Private ambulance' on the side now waits discreetly in the car park. A small group of reporters have gathered by the police lines, some with cameras trained on the archaeologists. Ruth spots Maddie's blonde head and wonders whether it was Cathbad who told her about the excavation.

'Did you see who's turned up?' says Judy, sounding exasperated. 'That's all I need.'

'Maddie?'

'Not Maddie. She's only doing her job, after all. No, Chantal Simmonds. The small, dark woman in the red dress.'

'Ivor March's girlfriend?' Ruth looks over and sees a figure in an incongruously smart outfit, like someone lost on their way to a wedding. She's standing a little apart from the press pack but there's also something separate about her, perhaps in the way she is holding herself, head up, arms crossed. She looks as if she is waiting for something.

'I suppose March told her we would be here,' says Ruth.

'I'm sure he did,' says Judy. 'Chantal will find some way of saying that the police have planted the bodies. She hates us.' And Ruth, looking at the small, tense figure, thinks that she can feel the hatred radiating from it.

They stop briefly for sandwiches and much-needed cold drinks. Then they start work again. Ruth is just brushing soil from the second skull when she hears the roar of a car's engine that can only mean Nelson's arrival. She keeps working though. She doesn't want Nelson to think that she was on tenterhooks waiting for him to turn up. In a few minutes she hears a familiar voice saying, 'You've found them then?'

Ruth looks up, conscious of her shiny face and untidy hair. She's wearing gloves but her bare arms are scratched and dirty and covered in nettle stings. She tries – and fails – to imagine Michelle ever letting herself be seen in such a state.

'We've found two bodies,' she says cautiously, 'and they look like they're female. We'll know more when we excavate them.'

'Any idea how long they've been there?'

'Again, I'd need to do some tests,' says Ruth, 'but it could be quite a recent burial. You can see the grave cuts in the soil.'

'If these . . .' Nelson gestures, obviously trying to think of a respectful word. 'If these remains are Nicola and Jenny, would you expect them to look like this? I mean, they've been dead less than two years.'

'It all depends on the soil,' says Ruth. 'This is marshland, so it's fairly alkaline, which preserves bones, but the soft tissue would decay pretty rapidly.'

'How long before you can excavate?' asks Nelson, one foot pawing the ground in a typically impatient way.

'We should get it done by the end of the day,' says Ruth, 'but it'll take some time. We'll need to clean the bones in the lab and then number and chart them.'

Cathbad is kneeling in a trench a few yards away. He has been working away assiduously, ignoring Nelson and Ruth. Now he says, 'Ruth!'

'Well, look who it is,' says Nelson. 'The hero of the hour.'

'Hallo, Nelson,' says Cathbad. 'Any word on Phil?'

'He's stable, apparently.'

'He'll pull through,' says Cathbad. 'It's not his time.'

'And you'd know, I suppose?' says Nelson.

'No one in this world knows anything,' says Cathbad. 'Me, least of all.' But he looks rather smug all the same, thinks Ruth.

'Have you found something?' she asks.

'Yes,' says Cathbad. 'I may not know anything but I think I've found a third body.'

Cathbad is right. There is a third body, buried a little bit away from the first two. It's lower down too, almost in the substratum. Cathbad's first sighting was of a femur, a thigh bone, and, as soon as she saw it, Ruth thought that she was looking at a woman. The so-called long-bone was relatively short, which either meant a female or an adolescent. By the time they reach the skull, Ruth is sure. The head is delicately shaped with no pronounced brow ridges. This body hasn't been buried as carefully as the others and the bones are a little jumbled but Ruth marks them carefully on her chart and sees that they are all present. There are three women buried in the garden of the Jolly Boatman.

'He's killed someone else,' says Nelson, watching as the sinister-looking black van drives away. It's evening now, the sun low over the sea, discovering the hidden streams that criss-cross the marshes. Geese fly overheard, their feathers pink and gold. The reporters are still there but Nelson has moved them further back so they won't have seen the third skeleton. The little red figure of Chantal Simmonds is still with them.

'March must have known that the body was here,' says Ruth.

'He knew, all right,' says Nelson. 'Now I'm wondering how many more victims there are. We need to get the cadaver dogs in.'

'I'll get the field team to come back tomorrow and dig up the rest of the garden,' says Ruth. 'But do you really think they'll find more bodies here?'

'I don't know what I think any more,' says Nelson.

'I think the third body has been there longer,' says Ruth. 'The bones were more discoloured and they were lower down in the earth. Mind you, the other two weren't quite what I'd expect for the context.'

'What do you mean?'

'Marshland is usually a good preservative. Think of Lindow Man or the Iron Age girl that we found on the Saltmarsh that time. But, from what I could see, some of these bones were cracked and flaky, almost porous.'

'Why would that be?'

'It could just be that there's a lot of groundwater. But soil with an alkaline pH higher than seven is meant to preserve bone.'

'Now you're starting to sound like Phil,' says Nelson.

'Poor Phil,' says Ruth. 'I hope he's OK.' Something is nagging away at her, something stuck at the back of her mind, like a bit of apple core lodged in your teeth. Nelson, though, has moved on.

'The problem will be identifying the third skeleton,' he says. 'Do you think we'll get some DNA?'

'It's harder with articulated skeletons,' says Ruth. 'The process of putrefaction seems to destroy DNA but alkaline soil is usually good for preserving DNA in bones because the bone apatite – the hard material – is protected from dissolution. I've taken samples from the surrounding soil too. There might be something there. Blood or hair or body fluid.'

'You got some material too, didn't you?' says Nelson. 'He must have wrapped the bodies up. Rope fibres too. There was DNA on the rope last time. And cat hair. Did you see any cat hair?'

'No,' says Ruth, 'but there could be traces in the soil.' She thinks of Flint and suddenly longs to be back with him. Her back is aching and her face feels as if it is sunburnt, despite liberal application of factor fifty. She wants to lie down with a flannel over her eyes. She also wants a long drink of water and something to eat. It's nearly six and Ruth's stomach is rumbling so loudly that she wonders if Nelson can hear it. He doesn't seem tired or hungry. He is full of the energy of the chase.

Ruth goes back to her car to drink from her water bottle. Rummaging in her backpack she finds her phone and turns it on to see if there's a message from or about Kate. Instead, the name Shona flashes onto her screen.

Have u heard about Phil? Can u come over?

CHAPTER 12

It's seven o'clock by the time that Ruth parks outside Shona and Phil's town house. She is so tired that she has had to have all the windows open to stop herself going to sleep. When she saw Shona's text she had briefly been tempted not to open it but to head for Cambridge, bath and supper. But it's quite rare for Shona to ask for her help and they have been friends for a long time. So Ruth rang Frank who said that Kate was fine and that he'd make sure she went to bed by nine. Kate herself came on the line to say that she came top in a grammar test at school. Ruth is against teaching grammar to nine-year-olds but she couldn't suppress a surge of pride at this achievement. She told Kate that she was proud of her and promised Frank that she wouldn't be too late home. 'Did you find the bodies?' asked Frank. 'Yes,' said Ruth, 'we found them.' It seems years ago. She doesn't tell Frank about the third skeleton, she's not sure why.

Shona meets Ruth at the door. She is red-eyed and her usually artfully disarranged hair is standing out wildly. Ruth hugs her.

'Any news?'

'He's stable, they say. The coma is just so they can ventilate him, apparently. I can't believe it. Phil's so fit. He's never had any heart trouble.'

'What happened?' says Ruth, following Shona into the kitchen, an open-plan affair with lots of chrome and exposed brickwork. Louis, Shona and Phil's eight-year-old son, is sitting at the breakfast bar playing a game on his phone.

'Why don't you go and watch TV in the snug?' Shona says to him. 'I'll make you some pizza in a bit and bring it in.'

Louis slouches away without making eye contact with either of them.

'He's very upset,' says Shona.

'He must be,' says Ruth. 'It's such a shock for all of you. Sorry I'm covered in mud, by the way. I've just come from a dig.'

'That's OK,' says Shona, but she puts a tea towel on the sofa before inviting Ruth to sit down. She pours them both a glass of wine without asking. Ruth sips it slowly, she still has to drive back to Cambridge.

'Someone just set on Phil when he was cycling home,' says Shona. 'He was knocked off his bike and the shock gave him a heart attack. Thank God Cathbad was there. He gave Phil mouth-to-mouth, apparently. He saved his life.'

'I saw Cathbad today,' says Ruth. 'He said it was all part of the great web.'

She hoped to make Shona laugh but her friend just gulps down some more wine. 'I can't believe it,' she says again.

Her eyes fill with tears. She really does love Phil, thinks Ruth.

'Judy says the man ran off with Phil's backpack,' says Ruth.

'Yes,' says Shona. 'I suppose he was just a mugger. Poor Phil. He'd bought chickpeas and wine because I was having a dinner party.'

'Is that what was in the backpack? Chickpeas and wine?'

'And Phil's laptop,' says Shona. 'They didn't take his phone. It was still in his pocket with the headphones attached. His wallet was there too.'

'So they just took his laptop?'

'Yes.' Shona looks at Ruth. 'What are you getting at, Ruth? Do you think it was more than just a mugging?'

That's the trouble; Shona knows her too well.

'It's probably nothing,' says Ruth. 'It's just that, after that postcard . . .'

'What postcard?'

'The one about the Ivor March case,' says Ruth, realising too late that Phil obviously hasn't told Shona about his mysterious correspondent.

'What? Oh, the man who murdered those girls and buried them in his garden. How can this have anything to do with that?'

'I don't know,' says Ruth. 'It probably doesn't.' She wants to ask what was on Phil's laptop but she's not a detective, her role is just to comfort her friend. She says, 'Why don't we put that pizza on? You should have something to eat.'

Plus, she's starving.

Nelson is briefing the team. It's late but everyone is energised by the thought that they might have found Nicola and Jenny, and possibly a third victim too.

Nelson takes his place at the front of the room and asks Judy to stand beside him. He wants to emphasise that she is his second-in-command, especially with Tanya Fuller in the front row, pen in hand, ready to show that she is every bit as good a detective as Judy. DC Tony Zhang sits beside Tanya. He's a new recruit, a recent graduate from the University of East Anglia. Tony is London born, of Chinese parentage. He explained this to Nelson in his interview, adding that Zhang means 'archer'. Nelson made the mistake of telling this to Superintendent Jo Archer, with the result that she regards Tony as her own special protégé. All the same, Tony's not a bad lad, hard-working but quick to have a laugh with his colleagues. Today, though, he looks rather apprehensive. This is his first murder inquiry and he's been in Tanya's company all day, which is enough to make anyone feel nervous.

'Three bodies were excavated from the garden of the Jolly Boatman pub in Cley,' says Nelson, 'which is the location given to us by Ivor March. Ruth is pretty sure that the bodies are female but we're hoping to be able to extract DNA. Apparently the putrefaction process can destroy DNA but there might be blood or waste matter in the surrounding soil. We also have hair and teeth which will help with identification. We can look at dental records but also teeth are good sources of DNA because the enamel protects them, or something like that. Is that right, Judy?'

'Yes,' says Judy, looking at her notes. 'Teeth are also useful for isotope testing which can tell us where someone grew up. Bones renew themselves but teeth don't, so we should be able to trace the victims geographically.'

A hand goes up. Tanya's. Of course.

'Did Ivor March say anything about a third victim?'

'No, he didn't,' says Nelson. 'He just mentioned Nicola Ferris and Jenny McGuire. Ruth thinks that the third body had been buried longer. It's almost certainly female, smaller and slighter than the other women but not a child. Ruth can tell by the teeth and the bones. Children's bones have growing ends on them but these were all fully fused.'

'Do we have any clues about the identity of the third woman?' asks Tanya.

Nelson hesitates. He has a theory but wonders if it's too soon to share it with the team. 'As Judy says, we'll know more when we've done DNA and isotope testing,' he says, 'but when I interviewed John Robertson, the gardener at Grey Walls, he mentioned a young Eastern European woman going missing about ten years ago. Apparently this girl was picked up by March and his friends when she was lost on the fens. She stayed with them for a few months and then she vanished. Robertson couldn't remember her name, thought it was something like Sonya or Sandra, but that could be a place to start. Judy will take you through the investigation strategy.'

He sits down and lets Judy continue, which she does very efficiently. She should really apply for a job as a DI somewhere else but Nelson dreads the thought of being left with

Tanya and Jo. But, then again, he'll retire soon and Judy can have his job. The thought makes him even more depressed.

'Our first port of call is obviously Ivor March himself,' Judy is saying. 'Did he know the third body was there? Is she another of his victims? If he's in a forthcoming mood – and, after all, he told us where to dig in the first place – he might tell us. DCI Nelson will talk to March because he's the one with the relationship.'

That's one way of describing it, thinks Nelson. He remembers March smiling at Ruth. *I want you to promise to do the excavation this time. Do I have your word, Dr Galloway?* Had he known what she would find?

Tanya has her hand up again.

'Ivor March wanted Ruth to do the dig, didn't he?'

'Yes,' says Judy. 'He asked for her specifically.'

'Why?'

Judy looks at Nelson before replying. 'He said that he wasn't impressed with Phil Trent. He knows that Dr Galloway is a bones expert.'

'So he must have wanted her to find the bodies?'

'Yes,' says Judy. 'I suppose, if he was going to confess, he wanted the thing done properly.'

'But he hasn't confessed, has he?' says Tanya. 'What if there's a particular reason why he wanted Ruth, and only Ruth, to do the excavation?'

She doesn't say what that reason might be and the question hangs in the air until Judy continues with the briefing. But Nelson thinks back to Ivor March smiling at Ruth: *DCI Nelson is very protective of you. I wonder why.* Why did March want Ruth to do the excavation? Was it because his egotism demanded that the best people be involved in the investigation, even if that meant that he was more likely to be found guilty? This has been Nelson's theory up until now. But what if Tanya is right and there's more to it than that? She's bright, Tanya, even if she can be a pain at times.

Judy continues. 'We also need to interview Robert Carr, known as Bob, Leonard Jenkins and Ailsa Britain, all of whom were living at Grey Walls when the Eastern European girl went missing. I can do that with Tony.'

Tony goes red, as he always does when addressed directly, but Nelson thinks that he looks pleased. It will be good if Judy can take Tony under her wing, teach him a thing or two.

He turns to Tanya. 'Can you take charge of the intel? See if anyone went missing at around the time of the girl's disappearance. You can have some civilian investigators to assist you. We also need to talk to the ex-landlord of the Jolly Boatman. Intel have traced him. He's called Simon Winsome, born in London, made some money in the city and moved to Norfolk to run a pub. He went bankrupt in 2004 and emigrated to Australia. March says that he and Winsome were friends so we need to find out if he knew anything about the bodies buried in his garden. If he does, we'll apply for an extradition warrant. The pub is still owned by the brewery but they've let it become derelict. Winsome was the last landlord.'

Tanya brightens at the words 'take charge' and at the thought of having civilians to boss around. All the same, intel can be a tedious job. Nelson is sure that Tanya will want some of the action. He's not surprised to see her hand go up again.

'Are we going to inform Nicola and Jenny's families?' she asks.

'They know we were digging,' says Judy, 'and I'll tell them that we've found the bodies, prepare them for the likelihood that they are Nicola and Jenny.' This will be a difficult task, Nelson knows. The families will be expecting that the bodies will be found, maybe even hoping for it, but the reality will still be hard to take. Nelson thanks his lucky stars that Judy is on his team.

'We need to prepare a statement for the press too,' says Judy. 'I assume you don't want to do the media, boss?'

'I'm too ugly for TV,' says Nelson. 'You do it.'

There's a polite laugh but Nelson sees Tanya looking at him seriously, as if she agrees with this assessment. She'd love to do the press conference.

'That's it,' he says, standing up. 'Thank you, everyone. We've got a busy few days ahead of us. But it looks as if we can at least bring some closure to the murdered girls' families. Go home and get some rest now.'

But Nelson himself finds it hard to rest. When he gets home George is in bed and Michelle is watching some endless cookery programme on television. Nelson is nodding off by nine but, when he goes to bed, he can't sleep. Michelle comes up at ten and is asleep as soon as her head touches the pillow. So no chance of sex either. By midnight Nelson decamps to the spare room. He's not much of a reader but he tries a few pages of one of Michelle's books and throws it across the room in disgust. Who writes this rubbish? If he met a man like Christian Grey he'd have him up on a charge before he could say 'safe word'.

He thinks about the bones lying in the earth, of excavating them while the birds called excitedly above them. He thinks of Ivor March smiling. He thinks of sitting in the pub garden with Ruth. He thinks of his children, in careful age order: Laura, Rebecca, Katie and George. Is Laura happy? Is Rebecca fulfilled? Where will Katie go to secondary school? Should George be speaking more? He tries to think calming thoughts, as once advised by Cathbad: 'Go back to a place where you were happy as a child.' But he can only think of playing football on a freezing recreation ground, his dad shouting from the touchlines. It was the only time that he ever heard his father raise his voice. His mother is another matter. Maureen is a great shouter. He must ring her at the weekend. The trouble is, Maureen doesn't know about Kate which makes conversation difficult. He should tell her, says Michelle, who is a great favourite with her mother-in-law. But will the truth kill Maureen? Will she want to kill him?

When he finally falls asleep Nelson dreams fitfully about buried bodies and disappearing girls. He is woken at five a.m. by his work phone.

'DCI Nelson. A girl has been found dead on the marshes near Cley. Looks like she's been murdered.'

CHAPTER 13

The sun is rising over the marshes. The reed beds are red and gold, the windmill a dark cross against the pale blue sky. As Nelson speeds along the narrow road, a flock of black-tailed birds rise up in front of him, noisy and indignant. He slows down, looking for the blue light of a police car. 'You have arrived at your destination,' says his satnav, a woman's voice chosen by Michelle to sound calm and unthreatening. But, as far as Nelson can see, he is precisely in the middle of nowhere. He thinks that he's near the community centre but something about the flat landscape is disorientating. You can't see where you're going or where you've been, there's just the present, the marshland and the sky. Nelson stops and gets out his phone.

'Where the hell is this incident?' he barks.

'I've given you the coordinates,' says the voice on the other end of the line, rather defensively.

'I'm in the middle of a bloody field.'

But, as he speaks, a figure rises up out of the grass. A

uniformed police officer. Nelson clicks off his phone and winds down the window.

'I'm PC Matthews,' says the uniform. 'You'll have to leave your car here, I'm afraid.'

Nelson parks his car and leaves the hazard lights on. It's blocking the road but he doesn't suppose there's much traffic at this time in the morning. He follows PC Matthews along a gravel path and across a wooden bridge over a ditch that is presumably sometimes a stream.

'Where does the path go?' asks Nelson.

'To the sea eventually,' says the policeman. He has a strong Norfolk accent. 'We're nearly there.'

They take a sharp turn and there, spread-eagled across the path, is a woman's body, long blonde hair merging with the sun-bleached grass. A racing bike lies on its side beside her.

Nelson approaches cautiously. The woman is obviously dead, her face is luminously white and there are livid marks around her neck.

'Who found her?' he asks.

'One of the nature wardens on an early morning walk,' says Matthews. 'He rang 999. I was the first responder with my partner, PC Hammond. He took the witness back to the visitor centre. I waited here for you.'

'Are you from north Norfolk?' asks Nelson. 'I don't think I know you.'

'Yes, sir. I work out of Cromer.'

'Did you call the crime scene investigators?'

'No, sir.'

'I'll do it now. Did you touch the deceased?'

'No. I mean . . . I could see she was dead.'

In the old days, thinks Nelson, as he waits for SOCO to answer the phone, the police would be all over the body checking for signs of life. They would pick up weapons, trample over evidence, even close the victim's eyes. Now the best thing that they can do is keep their distance and wait for the experts. He leaves a message for Mike Halloran, the chief investigator, calls Judy and asks her to meet him at the visitor centre. Then he leans over the body, careful not to tread on a strand of hair.

She's a young woman, dressed in exercise clothes, pink cycling shorts and a pink and black lycra top. And she's tall and blonde, like all of March's victims.

The visitor centre is a modern building of wood and glass that seems to rise out of the landscape like a spaceship. Inside, Nelson finds PC Hammond and the warden, a tall man who introduces himself as Liam O'Shea. They are sitting in the café which has windows all along one side, looking out over the marshes. The sun is up now and the sky is a pale, cautious blue. The café is closed but O'Shea has a flask of coffee and offers some to Nelson.

'I always take one on dawn walks.' He has a faint Irish accent, which makes Nelson predisposed to like him.

'Is this a regular thing, then?' says Nelson, accepting gratefully. 'Early morning walks?'

'Yes, I like to get out and hear the dawn chorus. It's a good time to check the footpaths and fences too.'

'So what did you see this morning?'

'I saw the bike first.' Nelson can tell already that O'Shea is going to be a good witness – he takes his time but is obviously remembering things carefully and in sequence. 'The bike was on its side so I thought that someone must have fallen off. Then I saw her . . . I thought she was just hurt at first but then I saw the marks on her neck . . .'

'Did you touch her?' asks Nelson.

'Just quickly. To see if I could feel a pulse. But there was nothing and her skin was cold.'

This must mean that the woman had been dead for several hours. This May is turning out to be unusually hot but, even so, the nights are cool. It wouldn't have taken long for rigor mortis to set in.

'I rang 999 immediately,' says O'Shea. 'The police came very quickly, considering it's such a deserted spot.'

'Nathan . . . PC Matthews . . . is a local boy,' says Hammond. His tone suggests that his colleague is to be pitied for this. Nelson sympathises.

'Do you often get walkers, or cyclists, on the marshes so early?' asks Nelson.

'We often get walkers,' says O'Shea. 'Like I say, it's a good time to see the birds. But cyclists are rare. It's a long way from the designated cycle path and the ground is uneven, not suitable for bikes really unless you've got a really good cross bike.'

'Did you recognise the dead woman?' asks Nelson.

'No,' says O'Shea. 'It's so sad. She looked very young.'

She did look young, thinks Nelson. The coroner and SOCO team will be on their way. They will take fingerprints and DNA which should help with identification. But, somewhere in Norfolk, a family will soon be missing a daughter.

'Did you see a mobile phone anywhere?' he asks. He had been struck that the dead woman had been without the headphones that always dangle from his daughters' ears whenever they do any exercise.

'No,' says O'Shea. 'I suppose it could have been thrown into the grass.'

'Yes,' says Nelson. 'We'll have a good look for it. The bike might well be marked too. It looked like an expensive one. '

'That's something that has been bothering me,' says Liam O'Shea. 'It was a road bike with thin tyres. More like a racing bike. Expensive, like you say. Who would ride a top-of-the-range racing bike over the marshes?'

By midday they have an identification. Heidi Lucas, aged twenty-five. She's a primary school teacher and lives with her boyfriend, Josh Evans, in Lynn. Josh was away last night, visiting his parents in London, and the last thing he heard from Heidi was a text saying that she was going out for a bike ride at eight p.m. When he arrived home at eight this morning, Heidi's bed hadn't been slept in and, after a flurry of phone calls to family and friends, he had called the police. He clearly hadn't expected the quick response and the blue light journey ending in the morgue.

'I know it's a terrible shock,' says Judy, sitting with him in the grim, windowless visitors' room. A box of tissues sits on the table between them. 'But do you feel up to answering some questions? We need to act quickly, you see, if we're going to catch the person who did this awful thing.'

'I understand,' says Josh, reaching for his water bottle and taking a long drink. He's a thin young man with red hair that is already receding. From his physique Judy is willing to bet that Josh is also a keen cyclist.

'Did you hear from Heidi after her text about going on a bike ride?'

'No,' says Josh. 'I texted to say good night but she didn't answer. That's a bit unusual but I thought her phone was just out of charge or something.'

'Did she say where she was going on her ride?' asks Judy.

'No, but she was doing road work,' says Josh. 'So I assumed it was around Lynn. She was training for a triathlon.'

'She didn't say that she was going to the coast? To Cley and the marshes?'

'No,' says Josh, wiping his eyes. 'Like I say, she was doing road work. Speed stuff. She wouldn't risk her bike on uneven ground. It's a Canyon Aeroad, cost near five thousand pounds.'

They'll know more when they have the forensics, thinks Judy, but, from what Josh says, it's seems clear that Heidi was murdered elsewhere and her body placed on the lonely footpath. Why? On the day after three bodies were found near Cley, a woman is killed in the near vicinity. A tall, blonde woman. Judy doesn't need the boss to warn her against the danger of coincidence.

'How did Heidi seem when you saw her last?' she asks.

'She seemed fine,' says Josh. 'Looking forward to the triathlon. We were going to do it together.' And, burying his face in his hands, he starts to cry in earnest.

CHAPTER 14

Judy leaves Josh with the family liaison officer. They will wait at the morgue for Heidi's parents, who are driving down from Leeds. Judy tries not to think about that journey, the initial shock and disbelief, the long motorway drive punctuated by tears, the horror that awaits them at the end.

Josh has given her an approximate route for Heidi's last bike ride and, by the time she gets back to the station, Nelson and Tanya are at the scene, organising door-to-door enquiries and searching for any CCTV footage. The SOCO team are still out on the marshes. The only people in the office are Tony Zhang, sitting moodily at a computer, and a civilian intelligence officer called Liz.

Liz greets her cheerfully. 'I've had some success with the intel.'

'What have you got?' asks Judy. She likes Liz, who brings a much-needed sense of the outside world into the police station. She also bakes amazing brownies.

'Robert Carr – Bob – and Leonard Jenkins are both living in Norfolk. Bob is living in Holt and Leonard in Cromer.'

'Both near Cley,' says Judy.

'Yes,' says Liz. 'Bob is still working as a printmaker. He lives above his studio. Leonard is a teacher.' Like Heidi Lucas, thinks Judy. Nicola Ferris too. She looks at her work phone, clicking through messages from Nelson. The Heidi Lucas case has precedence at the moment – the first twenty-four hours are crucial – but she wants to question Bob and Leonard before the news of the third body makes it to the press. She remembers the crowd of reporters at the excavation. It won't be long before they are on the trail.

'Good work, Liz,' she says. 'If you give me the addresses, I'll go and see them now. Tony, you can come with me.'

Tony jumps up immediately, obviously hoping for some action. Judy sympathises.

'Did you have any luck tracing the Eastern European girl?' Judy asks Liz.

'Not yet,' says Liz. 'We've been through all the missing persons reports and there are a couple of girls who might fit that description. I'll chase them up. You two have fun now.'

Fun is not quite the word that Judy would have chosen but she notes that Tony is looking distinctly more cheerful.

Bob Carr is a surprise. He looks much older than Ivor March, for one thing. Bob is tall but very thin and his grey hair is pulled back into a ponytail that reminds Judy slightly of Cathbad. But whereas Cathbad, though undoubtedly silver-haired, is brimming with energy and vitality, Bob seems rather frail. Judy can't see how he manages all the industrial-looking printing machinery in the studio. There is a metal press in the middle of the room plus several trays of what look like DIY tools: scrapers, files, chisels, brushes and rollers. The rest of the space is taken up by workbenches, kitchen cabinets, folded trestle tables, a tailor's dummy and an old bicycle on hooks. The room smells, not unpleasantly, of paint and linseed oil.

'It is hard work,' says Bob, 'though not as hard as it used to be in the old days when we used mainly lead and zinc. Nowadays you can print onto anything – glass, plastic, cardboard. This,' he indicates a print of a landscape overlaid with concentric circles of gold and silver, 'is done by sunlight, solar-plate etching. No acid or solvents required.'

'It's beautiful,' says Judy, looking closer. She can see the outlines of trees and houses, and traces of what looks like old-fashioned copperplate writing. She can just make out the words 'blue remembered hills'.

'I did art A-level,' says Tony, unexpectedly, 'but we never did anything like this.'

'Art is being squeezed out of the curriculum,' says Bob. 'Schools can't afford the equipment or the teachers. Everything is concentrated on English and maths – no music, no drama, no art. The creative spirit is dying. Sorry,' he says with a grin, 'don't get me started on my hobby-horse. I can get quite heated.'

But he doesn't look heated, thinks Judy. He just seems slightly sad.

Bob leads them up a wooden staircase to his apartment above the studio. It's a small space, part kitchen, part sitting room, and the overwhelming impression is one of colour:

every surface seems to be painted or covered with vibrant material. Prints and paintings cover every inch of the walls. Are some of them by Ivor March? It's hard to tell, although lots of them seem to show March's favourite themes: sea, sky, abandoned buildings. Even the door frames and window ledges are daubed with colour. The light shade is a metal colander, painted bright red.

'It is a bit much,' says Bob, apologetically, noting her look. 'I'm always experimenting and, well, I live on my own and there's no one to tell me to stop.'

They sit at a round table in the middle of the room, painted crimson with yellow dots and wavy blue lines. Bob offers them coffee, which he makes in a candy-striped cafetière. Judy's eyes are hurting.

'Mr Carr . . .' she begins.

'Bob, please . . .'

'Bob. We wanted to talk to you about the time that you lived at Grey Walls with Ivor March.'

Bob sighs. 'It wasn't just with Ivor.'

'I know,' says Judy. 'It was Ivor March and his wife Crissy, you, Leonard Jenkins and Ailsa Britain.'

'And John,' says Bob. 'John Robertson, the gardener.'

'Yes, my DCI has been talking to John. He says that you, Leonard and Ivor used to go out in a van finding lost women.'

Bob is silent for a moment, staring into his handmade pottery cup. 'You have to remember,' he says at last, 'we were trying to do something good. It was an artists' commune, a place where we could celebrate beautiful things.

Ivor painted, I made prints, Leonard sculpted. Students came and we taught them about life and art.'

'What about Ailsa Britain?' asked Judy. 'What did she teach?'

'She was an artist,' says Bob. 'She drew these amazingly intricate fairy pictures, a bit like Richard Dadd.' Tony nods solemnly although Judy had never heard the name. 'Ailsa was quite a talented printmaker too. Those are hers.' He points at some skeletal leaves over the mantelpiece.

'Wonderful use of colour,' says Tony. He has a serious art-lover expression on his face. Judy is impressed.

'Ailsa was your girlfriend, wasn't she?' she says.

'She was at first, yes,' says Bob. 'I met her when she came to one of my classes. She came to live with us at Grey Walls. It was a golden time even though things turned so dark later.'

'Tell us about the Lantern Men,' says Judy.

She thinks that Bob is going to pretend that he doesn't understand what she means but, after another brief pause, he says, still in the same calm, quiet tone, 'We called our-selves the Lantern Men after the legend of the lights that used to guide people across the marshes. We were a band of spiritual brothers, we wanted to help people. We'd find youngsters who were sleeping rough or who seemed lost in some way. We'd take them back to Grey Walls, Crissy would feed them, we'd talk to them about the beauty of life, they would draw pictures or write stories. Sometimes they'd just stay for a night or two, sometimes it was longer.'

'And then what happened to them?'

'They'd move on, spiritually refreshed.'

'John mentioned an Eastern European girl who stayed for some time. Do you remember her?'

'Sofia? Yes, of course. She was literally lost when we found her, wandering across the fens in search of a youth hostel. We took her home with us and she stayed for a few months.'

'Do you remember why she left Grey Walls?' asks Judy. 'Did you see her leave?'

'No,' says Bob. 'Crissy just said . . . or I think it might have been Ivor . . . they said that she'd decided to move on . . .' He stares at Judy, as if realising something for the first time.

'We found three skeletons yesterday,' says Judy, 'in the grounds of the Jolly Boatman pub near Cley. Ivor March gave us the location and we believe that two are the remains of Nicola Ferris and Jenny McGuire.'

'And the third could be Sofia?' Bob's voice is a whisper now.

'It's a line of enquiry,' says Judy.

'Ivor would never have hurt Sofia,' says Bob. 'He loved her. We all did.'

'Ivor March has murdered at least four women,' says Judy. 'He could well have more blood on his hands.'

She wonders if Bob, like Chantal Simmonds, is going to protest March's innocence but he says nothing.

'Are you still in touch with Ivor March?' asks Judy. She knows that Bob hasn't visited March in prison but she wants to know what he thinks about the man who was once his close friend and 'spiritual brother'.

'No,' says Bob, his voice very quiet now. 'It was such a nightmare. When I found out about Ivor, I couldn't believe it . . . He always seemed such a good man, holy almost. I couldn't bear to see him again.'

'What about Leonard Jenkins?' asks Judy. 'Are you still in touch with him? He doesn't live far away from you.'

'I wish Leonard well,' says Bob, 'but I've really got nothing more to say to him.'

'He married Ailsa Britain, didn't he?' says Judy. 'I thought she was your girlfriend?'

'She was,' says Bob. 'At one time I thought we were going to get married and start a family. But that didn't happen. Then she just announced that she was going to marry Leonard. I've never understood it to this day.'

'They're divorced now, aren't they?' says Judy.

'Yes, the marriage didn't last.' Is there a slightly satisfied note in Bob's soft voice?

'Are you in touch with Ailsa? She runs the community centre in Cley. Not far away.'

'Ailsa knows where I am,' says Bob. 'If she wants me, she can find me.'

Judy thinks that he still sounds hopeful.

Judy and Tony sit in the car outside the studio as tourists wander past, eating ice creams and looking in windows of chic boutiques and artisan bakers. Judy rings Liz to tell her that they have a name, 'Sofia. Bob thought her surname could be Novak or Novitch.' Liz promises to get on the trail.

'Bob seemed genuinely upset about Sofia,' says Tony.

'Yes,' says Judy. 'He did. He said "We all loved Sofia."
Maybe he was in love with her.'

'I thought he was still in love with that Ailsa.'

'He certainly seemed upset that she married Leonard.'

'Didn't the gardener chap – John – say that Leonard was
gay? I read it in the notes.'

Judy is pleased that Tony has read the case notes. She
wonders whether Tony himself is gay, not that she'd ever
ask. She certainly doesn't want to assume he is just because
he knows the right things to say about art. She realises
that she doesn't know much about the new recruit. He's a
graduate, fast-tracked to CID. He lives in Lynn and drives an
old VW Beetle that Judy rather admires. Beyond that, he's
a blank.

'He could be bisexual,' she says. 'We can ask him now.
If it comes up in conversation.' She starts the engine. It's
usually the lower-ranking officer who drives but Judy is a
terrible passenger.

School is over for the day but there are still plenty of students roaming around the modern academy. Judy supposes
that they are going to after-school clubs of some kind. It
seems a long time since her own schooldays, at a plate-glass
comprehensive very like this one. Judy had never wanted
to stay behind after school. She couldn't wait to leave and
hadn't wanted to go to university, although her grades were
good enough. 'Drama club,' says Tony. 'They're probably
going to drama club.'

Judy gives him a sidelong glance. 'Is that what you did at

school?' It can only have been about five years ago that Tony was a pupil. Some of the sixth-formers slouching past look slightly older than him.

'Yes,' says Tony. 'I wanted to be an actor once.'

Judy stores that one up.

Leonard meets them in the art room surrounded by papier-mâché faces, knobbly and grotesque, painted brown, yellow and bright pink. Leonard also looks older than March but he seems tougher-fibred than Bob. He is shortish but is tanned and fit-looking with crew-cut grey hair and black-rimmed glasses, the sort of teacher who has no problem keeping control in class. His voice is rather dry and sarcastic. Judy can imagine him making caustic comments about poor homework, if they even have homework in Art. Presumably Tony, ex-art student and aspiring actor, will know.

Judy asks Leonard about Grey Walls and he tells them much the same story about the Lantern Men saving lost souls. He remembers Sofia and says that her surname was Novak.

'Did you hear from her after you left Grey Walls?'

'No,' says Leonard, 'but I think Ailsa did.'

'Ailsa heard from Sofia?'

'Yes.' Leonard looks surprised at the urgency in Judy's voice. 'I think someone said that she had a postcard or something.'

That is something to ask Ailsa Britain when Judy interviews her tomorrow.

'I understand that you and Ailsa used to be married,' she says.

'Yes,' says Leonard, raising his eyebrows as if she is a pupil who has just asked him what his first name is. 'We were married for five years.'

'Ailsa was Bob Carr's girlfriend first, wasn't she?'

'Relationships were rather fluid in those days,' says Leonard drily. 'I gather that you've spoken to Bob?'

'We've just come from his studio.'

'He's a very talented printmaker.'

His tone implies that there is little else to be said for his former friend.

'Have you kept in touch with Ailsa?' asks Judy.

'Yes,' says Leonard. 'It's all very civilised. We meet occasionally and exchange cards at Christmas.' He gives her a rather sardonic smile. 'Ailsa gets on well with my husband, Miles.'

So Leonard *is* gay, which raises a few more questions about his first marriage. Judy asks if Leonard has been in contact with Ivor March.

'No,' he says. 'I've got nothing to say to a man who could do that to a woman.'

'You think he did kill them then?'

'Don't you?' says Leonard. 'I thought that you were the detective in charge of the case.'

Judy rather likes this description but thinks it betrays a certain interest in the police investigation.

'What about Crissy Martin?' she says.

'Ah, Crissy is a wonderful woman,' Leonard says, with sudden warmth. 'We too exchange cards at Christmas.'

Does anyone even send Christmas cards any more? Most

of Judy's friends post smug Facebook messages saying that they will be giving the money to charity instead. Cathbad bakes gingerbread men.

Leonard stands up and starts putting on his bicycle clips. It's a clear sign that the interview is at an end.

'We'll be in touch,' says Judy, wanting to end things on her own terms.

'I don't doubt it,' says Leonard.

CHAPTER 15

Nelson is to the point at the evening briefing.

'Heidi Lucas texted her boyfriend at seven fifty-five on Thursday night saying that she was going on a bike ride. This was a regular habit for her, and the boyfriend, Josh Evans, has given us a map of her usual route. He says she would have stuck to roads because she was training for events and because her bike, an expensive model, wasn't suitable for rough terrain. Evans thinks that she would have gone along the Lynn Road towards Torrington St Clement. It's about eighteen kilometres, there and back. I've put a Red Route in place and we'll go door-to-door at every house along it. Tanya and I have been organising that today. The likelihood is that Heidi was ambushed somewhere along the way, killed and her body taken to the Cley marshes.'

Someone puts up a hand. 'Is this a copycat killing?'

Nelson sighs. 'There are superficial similarities to Ivor March's killings. The location, the mode of killing and the fact that Heidi was tall and blonde, like all of March's victims. But we mustn't let ourselves get obsessed with this theory. It's possible that there was another motive altogether. Josh Evans has an alibi, he was with his parents in London all evening. He has surrendered his phone and the text from Heidi is on there. There are witnesses who saw Heidi on her bike so we know that she was alive after eight p.m. The last sighting was near Marsh Road at about eight twenty. Evans looks to be in the clear but we are also investigating Heidi's friends and work colleagues. She was a good-looking girl, someone might have had an obsessive crush on her. Strangulation usually implies intimacy. We haven't got the post-mortem results yet so we don't know if there was a rape or not.' He stops, thinking of the young woman, younger than his daughters, going out for a ride on a summer evening. It's an effort to keep his voice steady so he compensates by being more deadpan than ever.

'We haven't found Heidi's phone either. Young people usually take their phones whenever they leave the house and Evans says that Heidi liked to listen to music when she cycled. It seems likely that the killer took her phone and we're making every effort to trace it. Tanya, do you want to take us through the door-to-door?'

Tanya is on her feet immediately. It would take more than a brutal murder to damp down her ambition, but ambition's not a bad thing and she was a real help on the investigation today. She takes the team through the various sightings until the last one, on the corner of Marsh Road, where a woman walking her daughter home from Brownies remembered seeing a pretty girl on a bike. 'My daughter spotted the pink cycling shorts. She loves anything pink.'

Judy fills them in on the interviews with Bob Carr and Leonard Jenkins. It seems that they have a possible name for the third body buried in the pub garden: Sofia Novak.

'I'll talk to March tomorrow,' says Nelson. 'In the meantime, Judy, you continue with that investigation. Tanya, you lead on Heidi Lucas. Both of you keep me informed every step of the way. Tony,' he finds the new recruit in the circle of faces, 'you can choose.' He is interested to see what the young man will say. It's at times like this that he misses Cloughie.

'Can I work with Judy? DI Johnson?' Tony says immediately.

Interesting that Tony has chosen the cold case over the ongoing investigation, or maybe he just prefers Judy to Tanya. 'OK,' says Nelson, 'you work with Judy. Tanya, you can pick your team. That's all for tonight. We need to start work bright and early tomorrow.' He has been on the go since five but he isn't tired. He won't rest until they have found Heidi's killer.

It's nearly nine by the time Nelson gets home and, as he turns into the cul-de-sac, the first thing he sees is a young woman on a bicycle, her hair flying out from beneath her helmet. He slams on the brakes.

'Hi, Dad.' Laura comes to a stop.

'What are you doing?' asks Nelson.

Laura looks surprised. 'Visiting Mum and George. You're late home.'

'But why are you on a bike?'

'I've joined a cycling club,' says Laura. 'Trying to keep fit and all that.'

In Nelson's view Laura is quite fit enough already and she has a tendency to become obsessive about exercise. And he doesn't like to see her on a bike. He doesn't like it at all.

'Be careful,' he says. 'Stick to places where there are people. Put your lights on. It'll be dark soon.'

'Stop fussing, Dad,' says Laura. 'Cycling's great. You should try it.' And, with a wave of her hand, she pedals off into the twilight.

When Nelson gets in, he asks Michelle why Laura has joined a cycling club.

'I don't know,' says Michelle. 'But I thought it was a good idea. She can meet people.'

Michelle means 'meet a nice boy'. Laura hasn't had a boyfriend since she finished with Chad more than two years ago, unless you count a brief liaison with a Norwegian called Lars, which Nelson doesn't. He knows that Michelle would like to see both girls in steady relationships – she was married at twenty-three – but Nelson thinks he prefers it when they're single.

'What's the club called?' he asks.

'Lynn Wheels.'

After supper Nelson goes into what was once the den and is now called his study. Before he searches 'Lynn Wheels', he clicks on his emails. There's a new one from Maddie Henderson.

'Hi Nelson! You said you wanted to read Jenny's story. Well, here it is. And, if you want to give me an exclusive about the excavation at the Jolly Boatman, you know where I am!'

She signs off with a smiley face.
Nelson clicks on the story and begins to read:

The Lantern Men by Jenny McGuire

The first time she saw the lights she thought that it was a trick of the eye, one of those strange flickers that heralded the start of a migraine or the beginning of a more distressing episode. She had been working late, marking student essays that seemed to believe that Of Mice and Men was really a comedy of manners, and, when she looked out towards the marshes and the sea and saw the flash – on, off, on, off – she thought that it was a sign that she should take a break, watch some undemanding TV and forget about the complexities of her life.

Then, two days later, she saw it again. This time she was cycling home after her creative writing class, full of a slightly muddled belief in the power of words. She was freewheeling along the Rumble Road and saw the light right on the horizon, a flickering orb that moved unsteadily as if was floating, or being carried. She came to a halt. It was a summer's evening, still half light at ten o'clock, a liminal zone between day and night, a deceitful, untrustworthy time. But, as she sat there, astride her bike, she had the strangest desire to follow the marsh light, to let it lead her over the uncertain ground, neither land nor sea, even though the path might lead to her death.

She met him a week later. He was an author, brought in to

speak to her creative writing class. He was mildly famous, a name that frequently occurred in Guardian reviews, though not often on bestseller lists, a tall, angry-looking man in horn-rimmed glasses.

'The muse catches you working,' he told them. 'Don't wait for inspiration, that might not come until the end. I'm an artist which means that I have to create, whether I want to or not.'

Most of the group had thought him pretentious. 'I'm an artist,' mocked Barry in the tea break. 'His last book is number 25,420 on Amazon.' But I knew that The Artist was not talking about Amazon rankings but something altogether more profound. And maybe he knew that I knew because, at the end of the evening, he asked for my phone number.

The first time that he came back to the cottage, I told him about the lights. I had seen them several times by then.

'The lantern men,' he said. 'Demonic beings who carry lanterns across the marshes. You never see their faces even though they are carrying a light. But, if you follow them, if you leave the path, they will lead you to your death.'

'You do know a lot of strange things,' I said.

'I know everything,' he said, looming above me. 'Which is why you must do exactly as I say.'

And I did . . .

Nelson's phone vibrates. 'Cathbad', says the screen. Trust him to ring just when Nelson is reading about myths, legends and what seems like a very dangerous sexual fantasy.

'Hallo, Cathbad,' he says. 'What is it this time?'

'Just ringing for a chat.'

'Pull the other one.'

Cathbad laughs. 'I was thinking about Ivor March.'

'Me too.'

'So you think he might be innocent as well?'

'What?' Nelson's shout is so loud that Michelle appears at the door of the study. He mouths an apology and she points upwards, indicating that she's going upstairs to bed.

Nelson tries for a more reasonable tone. 'Two women were found buried in March's girlfriend's garden and covered in his DNA. He had just told us where two other victims were buried and we have probably found a third. No, Cathbad, I don't think he's innocent.'

Cathbad ignores this. Nelson imagines him sitting in his wizard's chair, his animal familiar beside him, giving full rein to his inner nutcase. Judy is probably putting the kids to bed.

'It came to me when I was helping to excavate the bodies,' he says. 'I suddenly thought: Ivor March is innocent. I know that he didn't kill these women. I thought I should tell you.'

'Thanks a lot. Did you mention it to Judy?'

'Yes.' Even Cathbad sounds slightly abashed. 'She said it was nonsense.'

Good old Judy.

'It is nonsense,' says Nelson. 'But while I've got you on the line, you might as well make yourself useful. Have you heard of the lantern men?'

'The lantern men of the marshes? Of course I have. They lead unwary travellers to their deaths. They're linked to will-o'-the-wisps, spirits who are shut out of heaven and hell. Some say that the original was a blacksmith called Will who was so evil that he was condemned to walk the earth for ever, never ascending to heaven or descending to hell. The devil gave him a single coal from hell to keep him warm and he carried it in a pumpkin. That's where jack-o'-lanterns come from. You know, the lighted pumpkins that children make on Halloween.'

Like The Artist in the story, Cathbad does know a lot of strange things. Nelson remembers John, the gardener at Grey Walls, talking about the lantern men. *Visitors often like to hear the old stories.*

'In Scandinavia, they are said to be the souls of unbaptised children,' Cathbad goes on. 'In South America they are "luz mala", evil light, or "la candileja", spirits who carry ghost lights after death.'

Cathbad always overdoes foreign pronunciations. It's very annoying.

'They're also called "ignis fatuus", that's Latin for foolish fire. Then there are the glowing owls too.'

Glowing owls. Jesus wept.

'Thank you, Cathbad. You should go on *Mastermind*. Specialist subject: General Weirdness.'

Cathbad laughs, obviously taking this as a compliment.

'Glad I could help. And you will think about what I said about March, won't you?'

'Goodbye, Cathbad.'

Nelson goes back to the story.

And then it seemed that I was part of his story and he was a part of mine. Or I was a picture that he had begun to paint, sketching the outline, flooding it with colour. I was only really alive when I was with him. Strange then that my thoughts began to be about death. When, in bed, he carried me to ecstasy, I began to wish that he would carry me further, to the end of life itself. Who knows what lies beyond, at the place where the marsh meets the sea?

Jesus, thinks Nelson, how much more of this is there? Just a page to go. The woman meets The Artist several more times and has sex with him in which S&M is coyly implied. Then he tells her to follow the lights on the marshes. 'I thought they would lead me to my death,' she says. 'Maybe that is a consummation devoutly to be wished,' replies The Artist in his insufferable way.

The story ends like this:

So she followed. The lights led her up hill and down dale until she came to the place where He was waiting. He was holding his lantern aloft and it was as if this was the first time that she had seen his face.

'Are you ready to die?' said The Artist.

'I am,' she replied. And, smiling, he put his hands around her neck.

'Bollocks,' says Nelson.

CHAPTER 16

Nelson makes an appointment to see Ivor March at nine the next morning. On the way he calls Maddie from his hands-free phone.

'What is it?' she says. 'It's Saturday morning. I was asleep.'

'I thought journalists never slept,' says Nelson, though he knows that his daughter Rebecca, who is the same age as Maddie, would sleep all day if she didn't have some nebulous marketing job to attend.

'Did you want something?' says Maddie.

'I read Jenny's story and I just wondered if you had anything else of hers. You said something about her parents giving you a box of her things. In that article of yours there was a photo that I hadn't seen before. Do you have any others?'

'There was one more pic, I think,' says Maddie. 'Jenny with March and some other men. I thought it might be a little insensitive to print it. '

It's news to Nelson that Maddie ever considers such things. 'Can you send it to me?' he asks.

'OK. What's the news on the excavation? Did you find the bodies? I saw the coroner's van.'

'Bye, Maddie,' says Nelson. 'Go back to sleep.'

'You've ruined it now,' says Maddie. 'I might as well get up. I've got to go to some stupid agricultural show later.'

Nelson drives on to the prison. He waits in the interview room, thinking about his last visit with Ruth. Was Tanya right and was there something strange about March's insistence that Ruth should take charge of the excavation? March must have known that Ruth, who is the best forensic archaeologist around, would find the bodies and that must point to March's guilt. March has always pleaded his innocence. Why is he suddenly telling them where to find his victims? And, furthermore, he must have known that Ruth would find the third body. If March is convicted of three more murders then the chances are that he will never be released from prison.

Nelson decides not to mention Heidi Lucas. If March isn't involved, then he won't have heard about the murder. If he is somehow involved, then this is a whole other conversation. Besides, Nelson finds himself badly shaken by the young woman's death. Not only is she a similar age to his eldest daughter, she was also a primary school teacher. There's even a superficial likeness to Laura, especially in the pictures provided by Josh Evans: Heidi as a bridesmaid, flowers in her long blonde hair; Heidi riding a City Bike in Brighton; Heidi at a beach bar, suntanned and happy, surrounded by friends. And now this glowing young woman is dead and Nelson has another killer to catch.

March, when he appears, seems as unconcerned as a man can be when handcuffed and attended by a prison officer. He sits opposite Nelson and smiles. Nelson remembers the last line in Jenny's story. *And, smiling, he put his hands around her neck.*

'Hallo, Ivor,' says Nelson. 'How's life imprisonment treating you?'

March still hasn't been sentenced but Nelson wants to remove the smile.

It doesn't work although the grin starts to look slightly forced. Surely March must know that he'll spend the rest of his life behind bars, whether in a prison or a psychiatric hospital?

'We excavated the garden at the Jolly Boatman,' says Nelson, 'and we found two skeletons which we believe to be female. Dr Galloway is confident that enough DNA will be retrieved to allow for a formal identification.'

This isn't quite what Ruth said but Nelson knows that she is hopeful that DNA plus dental records and isotope testing will give them a result. March just smiles some more and says, 'I told you Dr Galloway was the best.'

'She certainly is,' says Nelson, watching March closely, 'because she found a third body.'

Not a flicker.

'Well, well, well,' says March, leaning back. 'Fancy that.'

'It's a woman,' says Nelson, resisting the temptation to hit March across the room. 'Do you have any idea who she might be?'

'I'm sure you have an idea, DCI Nelson.'

'I asked you,' says Nelson.

'You asked me about Nicola and Jenny,' says March, 'and I told you where to find them.'

What does he want, thinks Nelson, a good citizenship medal?

'It's a bit of a coincidence,' he says, 'a third woman's body turning up. I don't like coincidences. Who is she, Ivor?' He doesn't like using March's first name but Madge Hudson (Queen of the Bleeding Obvious) says it's important, to reinforce their so-called 'special relationship'.

March continues to smile at him, handcuffed hands clasped as if in prayer. The warder watches impassively from the doorway.

'I met John Robertson recently,' says Nelson. 'I gather he's a friend of yours.'

'Not exactly a friend,' says March. 'More of an acolyte. John's a simple soul.'

'John was telling me about the fun and games you used to get up to with your friends Bob and Leonard. He mentioned an Eastern European girl who went missing.'

'Did he?' March examines his fingernails.

'What was her name?'

No answer. March looks at him steadily, although the smile has almost gone.

'Is it Sofia Novak, Ivor? She stayed at Grey Walls, didn't she?'

No answer.

'Did you kill her, Ivor? Did you bury her in the pub garden?'

In the cognitive interviewing technique, as practised by

Judy, you are meant to offer the suspect alternative scenarios, but Nelson is too angry by now. He glares at March who stares coolly back before saying, 'Have you spoken to Bob and Leonard?'

'We've been in contact with them.'

'They haven't visited me, you know,' says Ivor. 'Only the women are faithful, Chantal, Crissy and Ailsa. It was the same with Jesus. It was the women who stayed at the foot of the cross.'

'So you're Jesus now, are you?' says Nelson. He might be a lapsed Catholic but, right now, he's praying hard for a thunderbolt.

'It is you who say it,' says March. The line sounds oddly familiar. Nelson has a feeling that it comes from the Good Friday service.

'I was reading a short story by Jenny McGuire,' he says. 'There's a character in it called The Artist who reminded me of you.'

'Ah, Jenny,' says March. 'She was quite an effective writer, if rather derivative.'

As far as Nelson knows, Ivor has never written a book so he wonders what qualifies him to judge, or to teach creative writing at all. He remembers Ailsa Britain saying that March had 'an artist's instinct for language'. The A word again.

'The story's called "The Lantern Men",' he says. 'That's what you used to call yourselves, isn't it? You, Bob and Leonard. When you went about abducting women.'

'We weren't abducting them,' says March. 'We were saving them.'

'Did you save Sofia Novak?'

'Yes.' March meets his gaze squarely. 'We saved her. She stayed with us for a while and then she went on to a better life.'

That's what people say when someone has died, thinks Nelson. They've gone to a better place.

'I don't think she did,' he says. 'I think you killed her and buried her in the garden of the Jolly Boatman. It was owned by a friend of yours, wasn't it? Simon Winsome. You used to drink there.'

'You seem confused, DCI Nelson,' says March. 'Why don't you talk to Dr Galloway? I'm sure she'll have the answers.'

'She'll have answers that'll convict you for three more murders,' says Nelson.

But March just continues to smile at him.

Ivor March is also in the forefront of Judy's mind. This is because Ailsa Britain, aka Lisa, is describing her feelings for the serial killer. They are sitting in a room at the community centre while, next door, the Italian Culture Class listens to Grand Opera. Tony Zhang seems to be finding it hard to keep a straight face as Puccini wafts through the walls.

'He was so charismatic,' says Ailsa dreamily. 'He made you feel as if you mattered, as if you were the most important person in the world. And he was a brilliant teacher too. He made you look at everything. I mean, really look.'

'You didn't mention this the first time I asked you about March,' says Judy. 'You just said that you'd been on one of his courses. You forgot to tell me that you were part of a commune at Grey Walls.' This is rather a sore point with Judy who feels that recent revelations have made her original investigation look less than thorough.

'It wasn't a commune,' says Ailsa. 'It was just a few like-minded souls living together.'

What is that if it isn't a commune? thinks Judy. It makes her feel nervous when the Grey Walls set start to sound like Cathbad.

'John Robertson thought that you and Ivor March had an affair,' says Judy. 'Even though you were in a relationship with Bob Carr.'

'John knew nothing,' said Ailsa. 'He was just jealous because he loved Ivor too.'

'Did you have a sexual relationship with March?'

'No,' says Ailsa, lifting her chin. 'It was a marriage of minds only.'

'John says that he saw you and Ivor in bed together. '

'And you believed him?'

'Are you saying it wasn't true?'

'Of course it wasn't true. Ivor was married to Crissy who was my best friend. I adore Crissy. I'd never hurt her. I would never do that to another woman.'

'Tell me about Bob Carr,' says Judy. 'How long were you two together?'

'Two years,' says Ailsa. 'It was one of the happiest times of my life.'

'But then you married Leonard Jenkins, didn't you?' says Judy.

Un bel di vedremo, sings Madame Butterfly. One fine day we shall see.

Ailsa hesitates before replying. She puts her hand up to her bun. How does she get it to stay so smooth? Judy can never do anything with her own curly hair, except occasionally tie it back. Maybe she should get it cut. It might make people take her more seriously. Who ever heard of a DI with a ponytail?

'Leonard is a lovely man,' says Ailsa.

'And he's gay.'

'Do you really think that things are so simple, DI Johnson? Gay and straight? Good and evil?'

Maybe not, thinks Judy, but some things are simple. Ivor March is evil, he has killed at least four women. She tries not to think about Cathbad and his sudden assertion that March is innocent.

'When you were living at Grey Walls,' she says, 'do you remember a girl called Sofia Novak?'

'Sofia? Why are you asking about her?'

'So you do remember her?'

'I think so. She stayed for a few months.'

'Did you hear from her after she left?'

'No, I don't think so.'

'Leonard thought that you had received a postcard from Sofia.'

Now Ailsa does look rattled. 'I might have. I can't remember.'

'If you could remember, it would be a great help,' says Judy. 'Do you know where Sofia was from originally?'

'Hungary, I think. She was a lovely girl.'

'Was?'

'I just meant . . . I haven't seen her for so long . . .'

'When was the last time?'

'One evening, I think. Over supper Sofia said that she was leaving soon. It was a surprise but she was backpacking, after all. We knew she'd move on eventually.'

'And you didn't see her again?'

'No, I was feeling sick the next day and stayed in bed. I assumed that Crissy took her to the station.'

'You assumed?'

'That's what normally happened when girls . . . people . . . wanted to move on. Why are you asking about Sofia?'

'I'm not at liberty to say,' says Judy. 'One last question: do you know a woman called Heidi Lucas?'

'I don't think so. Oh . . . was she the poor girl who was killed yesterday? Why are you asking about her?'

Judy lets Ailsa's question answer hers.

Back at the station, Judy finds Tanya giving a rather self-important briefing. 'Last confirmed sighting of Heidi Lucas was at approximately 20.20 on Thursday night. Stella Patten, aged thirty-eight, walking her daughter home from Brownies, noticed Heidi cycling past. That was on the corner of Marsh Road. But we've had another possible sighting that came out of today's door-to-door. A man called Ted Avery said he saw a woman answering Heidi's description near Churchgate Way at 20.30. The woman was on a bike but stationary, talking to another woman who was also on a bike.

We don't have much of a description, I'm afraid, apart from the fact that they were both wearing helmets and were in cycling clothes. We'll be talking to Heidi's bike club to see if anyone else was cycling that route on Thursday night.'

'What's the cycling club called?' asks a familiar voice at the back of the room. Judy turns to see that Nelson has come in. He looks like a thundercloud but that could just be because he's been to see Ivor March.

'Lynn Wheels,' says Tanya.

Nelson gives an exclamation. Tanya looks at him quizzically but Nelson nods at her to go on.

'We've spoken to Heidi's colleagues at Byways Academy. She taught PE and was apparently very popular. So far we haven't turned up any jealous ex-boyfriends or potential stalkers. Heidi has been in a relationship with Josh Evans for five years, ever since they met at Loughborough University. Evans also teaches PE at Byways and has a solid alibi for Thursday night. He was with his parents in London and CCTV at the station shows him boarding the 16.44 train from King's Lynn to London King's Cross.'

'Why was he going to see his parents mid-week?' asks someone.

'Apparently his mother has been ill,' says Tanya. 'He was back in time for school on Friday – he caught the 5.42 and was at the flat by eight. That's when he found that Heidi was missing.'

Tanya finishes off by telling everyone that they're doing a great job. She knows it's the weekend but the first forty-eight hours are crucial, et cetera, et cetera. She'll be a DI by this time next year, thinks Judy. She has even produced an information pack complete with maps and thumbnail sketches.

Nelson beckons Judy to come into his office. She follows him, knowing that Tanya's eyes are following her.

The boss sits at his desk and starts stabbing at his keyboard in a random way that makes Judy want to elbow him aside and take over. She thinks again that he looks tired and rather angry.

'How did it go with March?' she asks.

'Waste of time,' says Nelson. 'The man's just playing games with us. He admitted to knowing Sofia Novak though. He said that they'd saved her and that she'd gone on to a better life.'

'Ailsa Britain said the same thing,' says Judy. 'But she was a bit vague about having heard from Sofia once she'd left Grey Walls. Leonard said that Sofia had sent a postcard to Ailsa but Ailsa didn't seem to remember it.'

'March killed her,' says Nelson. 'I'm sure of it. His latest is that he's like Jesus. All his male disciples have deserted him and only the women are loyal.'

'Like Christ on the cross?' says Judy, who was also brought up a Catholic. 'Bloody hell.'

'Precisely,' says Nelson. He jabs at the keyboard once more and turns the computer screen to face her. 'I want you to look at something,' he says. 'It's a short story that Jenny McGuire wrote. I'm emailing it to you. And this is a picture that Maddie sent me this morning.'

He turns the screen so that she can see. The picture shows

Jenny McGuire with four men. She thinks that the community centre is in the background.

'That's March next to her, of course,' says Nelson. 'But who are the others? Bob Carr and Leonard Jenkins? But who's the fourth?'

'Yes, that's Bob and Leonard,' says Judy. 'I don't know who the other man is.'

'Maddie says that on the back it says "July" and "Bill". Who's Bill?'

'I don't know. The fourth man?'

Judy looks at the picture. Ivor March has his arm round Jenny. Bob is looking at the camera but Leonard is looking at March. The fourth man, who is small and heavily built, has his arms crossed and stares ahead belligerently.

'Where did this picture come from?' she asks. 'Ivor always swore that he didn't know Jenny that well. This proves otherwise. Why didn't her parents show me this photo?'

'I think it's only just come to light,' says Nelson. 'Apparently Jenny's parents found a box with some of her stories in it. The photograph was in the box, along with another one of Jenny on her bike.'

'Maddie has obviously got in with the parents,' says Judy, trying not to sound as disgruntled as she feels. She had worked hard on gaining Jenny's parents' confidence. She genuinely liked them too and it's for their sake – and that of the other families – that she is still working so hard on the case. But she had seen the McGuires yesterday, to tell them about the excavation, and they had never mentioned the photograph. Instead they had given it to Maddie, whom they had only just met. And Maddie hadn't mentioned it either, thought Judy bitterly, although she'd had plenty of opportunities as she sat eating meals that Judy had cooked for her.

'Maddie can be persuasive,' says Nelson. 'Just like Cathbad.'

Judy sighs. 'Did Cathbad tell you that he's decided that March is innocent?'

'He did say something of the sort. Why has he got that idea into his head?'

'I don't know. Apparently it was when he saw the bodies in the pub garden. He suddenly felt that March hadn't killed them. I wasn't very patient with him, I'm afraid. We had a bit of a row.'

'I don't blame you,' says Nelson.

'The thing is, though, boss,' Judy stares at the computer to avoid looking at Nelson, 'what if March *is* innocent? I mean, we've got this other murder, Heidi Lucas, that looks like all the others. What if the killer is still out there?'

Nelson doesn't answer for a few seconds and Judy thinks that he's going to explode but, when he does speak, his voice is unexpectedly gentle. 'Don't beat yourself up, Judy. March is guilty. His DNA was all over Stacy and Jill's bodies, he told us where to find Nicola and Jenny. He knew Sofia Novak and probably killed her too. We mustn't let ourselves start imagining patterns where there aren't any. Ten to one Heidi was killed by someone she knew, a jealous ex or an online stalker. March didn't kill her.'

'I know you're right,' says Judy. 'It's just that she was blonde, like the others, and riding a bike, like Jenny.'

'That shook me too,' says Nelson. 'This story,' he points towards the computer, 'it's about a girl on a bike seeing weird lights out on the marshes. It's called "The Lantern Men". Cathbad was telling me all about the legends, ghost lights and what have you. He's better than Wikipedia.'

Cathbad knows all about mythology, thinks Judy. It's just everyday life that seems to confuse him. Aloud she says, 'The Lantern Men? That's what Ivor, Bob and Leonard called themselves.'

'Yes, it makes me wonder what they really got up to in that van. In the story the girl has an affair with a man called The Artist and he eventually kills her.' He says, in what sounds like a deliberately casual voice, 'I sent the story to Ruth.'

'Did you?' says Judy, trying not to sound too surprised.

'Yes,' says Nelson. Now he seems to be avoiding her eyes. 'I thought she might be interested in it, being a university lecturer and a writer and everything.'

'If you want literary criticism, you should send it to Shona,' says Judy. 'She's the one who teaches English.'

'Shona's got enough on her plate,' says Nelson. 'Have you heard how Phil's doing?'

'He's out of the coma,' says Judy. 'I rang the hospital this morning. They wouldn't tell me anything else. We should go and talk to him when he's strong enough.'

'I still think there's something suspicious about Phil being attacked,' says Nelson.

Phil was attacked, thinks Judy, then they found the three bodies, then Heidi was killed. The boss might say not to look for patterns but something is going on. You don't have to be an expert on mythology to think that dark forces are at work. She recalls a favourite quotation of Cathbad's. She can't remember where it's from but she always finds it both ominous and depressing.

The things we fear in secret always happen.

CHAPTER 17

Liz calls Judy just as she is getting ready to go home.

'I think I've found her,' she says.

'Sofia Novak?'

'Yes. Sofia Maria Novak, born 1989 in Debrecen, Hungary. She left school in 2007, after which nothing. No university records, no marriage certificate, no death certificate. It's as if she disappeared. Her parents are dead but her mother was English so it's probable that Sofia spoke perfect English which could be why she was backpacking here rather than mainland Europe. There's a brother and a sister but I haven't been able to trace them. I've got a photograph from her identity card and, this is the best bit, I've managed to find her old dentist so we can get hold of her records.'

'We've got the skull,' says Judy. 'That should be enough for an identification. Great work, Liz. Can you email me the picture?'

It comes through a few minutes later but the passport-sized photo gives little away. Like students the world over, Sofia is staring truculently into the camera. Black shoulder-length hair, dark eyes, one of those Arabic-looking scarves. There's nothing that gives you any sense of the person who vanished eleven years ago, but Judy is sure that she is looking at the girl who was buried in the garden of the Jolly Boatman.

She thinks about Sofia Novak all the way home. She can only have been eighteen or nineteen when she met the Lantern Men. What was she thinking when she got into their van? Was she relieved when they took her back to Grey Walls and she met Crissy and Ailsa? At what point did she start to become afraid? Judy thinks of her daughter Miranda, who is only five. Will Miranda want to go backpacking when she's eighteen? Cathbad will probably want to let her. He's all for children being free spirits and studying at the university of life. Whereas Judy realises that she has a far more pessimistic view of the world, which probably comes from being in the police. She'd like to keep Michael and Miranda at home for ever, except that's what she did. She didn't go to university, she married her childhood boyfriend and now lives in the same place where she grew up. OK, along the way she swapped the boring, dependable husband for a druid but, even so, it's not the most inspiring of CVs. Shouldn't she want better – *more* – for her children?

When she opens her front door, Michael is playing the piano and she can smell vegetable curry cooking. Her senses are instantly calmed. Michael only started lessons last year but he is now finding his way through Walter Carroll with something like brio. He never needs to be reminded to practise and even seems to enjoy scales. Judy likes them too, up and down, up and down, every note in its place. It's very soothing. She thinks she'll get Miranda lessons when she's older, though she has a suspicion that her daughter will favour a louder and more raucous instrument.

She listens at the sitting room door for a moment and then goes into the kitchen where Cathbad is cooking and Miranda is at the table colouring in a dinosaur picture. Thing, the bull terrier, is sitting watching Cathbad, hoping something edible falls on the floor. He wags his tail when Judy comes in but doesn't get up.

Judy kisses her daughter on her curly dark head.

'That's nice,' she says.

'I saw a dinosaur today,' says Miranda.

'Did you?' Ridiculously, Judy looks towards the window as if she might see a stegosaurus munching the leaves of the cherry tree.

'We went to the dinosaur park at Lenwade,' says Cathbad, adding coriander to the sauce. 'The dinosaurs are rather anthropomorphised but there's a nice walled garden with goats and donkeys.'

'I saw Dippy,' says Miranda, 'and I got wet.'

'Dippy Diplodocus's splash zone,' explains Cathbad.

'Did you bring her a change of clothes?' asks Judy.

'Yes,' says Cathbad patiently. 'Plus a towel and some healthy snacks.'

Judy thinks of her day: trying to identify one dead woman, talking to the relatives of another. She imagines herself splashing happily in the shadow of a giant plastic dinosaur and, for a second, feels so jealous that it actually hurts.

'Why don't you go and watch TV?' she says to Miranda. 'I want to talk to Daddy.'

'I don't like the noise Michael's making.' Perhaps she won't get piano lessons for Miranda after all.

'He's just stopped,' says Judy, as 'The Little Brook' trickles to an end. 'You can watch *Britain's Got Talent.*'

Miranda heads off eagerly (another indication of poor musical taste?) and Judy sits down at the kitchen table. Cathbad puts a glass of wine in front of her.

'Tough day?'

'You could say that.' Judy takes a deep swig of Winbirri white. 'Though I might have a lead on the third body.'

'Really?' says Cathbad. She knows that he takes a proprietorial interest in the remains that he discovered.

'I think she might be a Hungarian girl called Sofia Novak. March befriended her about ten years ago, after which she disappeared.'

She shouldn't really give Cathbad the name but she finds herself wanting to discuss the case with him. If only to make him see that March really is guilty.

But Cathbad just says, stirring busily, 'That doesn't mean he killed her though.'

'Cathbad!' Judy stands up to face her partner. 'You can't really think that he's innocent. He told us where to find those bodies. His DNA was all over the first two.'

'I'm sorry, Judy,' says Cathbad. 'I know it's not what you want to hear but, when we excavated those bones, those women, I had a strong presentiment that March hadn't killed them.'

'I suppose you didn't have a presentiment about who did?'

'No,' says Cathbad, sounding genuinely regretful. 'But I will tell you if I do.'

'Thanks,' says Judy.

If Cathbad gets the irony, he doesn't remark on it. Thing's tail starts wagging again and Judy hears the front door open.

'Maddie,' she says. Though there's no one else it can be.

Cathbad's oldest daughter comes into the room. She has been covering a local agricultural show and is, Judy notices, still wearing her muddy wellingtons.

'What a day,' she says. 'I'll be happy if I never see another cow or pig again.'

'Well you won't find any in this kitchen,' says Cathbad. Judy pours Maddie a glass of wine. She used to resent her quasi-stepdaughter's presence but now they have a friendship that almost amounts to love, helped by the fact that Maddie saved Judy's life a few years back.

'And bloody Nelson woke me up at the crack of dawn,' says Maddie, sitting at the table and draining half her glass. It always irritates Judy that Maddie drinks wine like lemonade. Her tipple of choice is vodka and lime.

'He was going on about some short story,' says Maddie. 'You'd think he'd have other things on his mind, what with this new murder and everything.' She looks at Judy speculatively, her green eyes bright and mischievous.

'It's no good, Maddie,' says Judy. 'I don't know anything about it. I'm still on the Ivor March case.'

'Is Tanya in charge then?' says Maddie. 'Good. She always talks to the press.'

'I bet she does,' says Judy. Tanya's craving for publicity is almost unhealthy.

'It's a funny thing, though, isn't it,' says Maddie. 'The murder seems so much like one of March's but he's in prison.'

'I wouldn't call it funny,' says Cathbad.

'Nor would I,' says Judy. She swallows the rest of her wine and pours herself another glass.

Ruth is also working, alone in her office at St Jude's. She has papers to mark and she can't really do it at home with Saturday night TV blaring and Kate wanting her to listen to her rendition of the latest song from drama group. She has a study in the attic, that was one of the things that first attracted Frank to the house. 'We'll be a two-study family, honey.' She hadn't liked Frank calling them a family though she knows that's what they look like from the outside. But she had liked the study, with its sloping roof and its view over the Cambridge rooftops. She had imagined herself working there but, somehow, that has never really happened. Frank can work quite happily in his next-door room, headphones on, reading accounts of Victorian housing and sanitation. But Ruth gets too easily distracted, especially when Kate is in the house. Even if Kate is watching TV downstairs or playing with friends, Ruth feels herself on Mother Alert. Will her daughter fall and hurt herself? Will she argue with her playmate? Will something unsuitable appear on TV, like a Conservative party broadcast? Ruth can never really relax in her study eyrie. Hence the writing retreat at Grey Walls.

She used to be able to work when Kate was in bed but these days, and especially at weekends, Kate seems to stay up as late as they do. Ruth has a sneaking suspicion that she would be stricter about bedtimes, and about everything really, if it was still just her and Kate. It's almost as if she has to put on a good show in front of Frank: look how well Kate and I get on, no need for pesky rules, we're as carefree as characters in an American sitcom.

Besides, she loves being in the college at night. There's a palpable sense of industry and purpose, the ancient building heavy with centuries of study and learning. From her open window she can smell the trees and the newly mown grass outside. There's just one other light, on the other side of the court, and Ruth likes to think of her fellow night-worker, a white-haired scholar poring over some obscure text or adding a footnote to the definitive book on Byzantine Art. Actually, it's more likely to be a student studying for finals. Only third years have rooms in the old block. Exams end next week and then it's more marking and more meetings, until graduation in July. The college is hosting a conference in August so Ruth will take that month off. Maybe she, Frank and Kate will go away somewhere. A family holiday.

She goes back to the paper that she is marking. When she started at St Jude's she had been rather surprised that her students didn't, at first, seem any cleverer than her postgraduates at UNN but they do have a spurious confidence that will, no doubt, take them a long way in life. 'We know that Stonehenge marked a shift in the Neolithic psyche from solar to lunar allegiance ...' What does this mean? No one has any idea what Neolithic people thought of the sun or the moon. We can theorise that monuments like Stonehenge had some sort of astronomical significance but we can't *know*. Ruth resists the temptation to put a red line through the sentence. Instead she just writes in the margin, 'Really?'

She thinks of her visit to the stone circle at Stanton Drew two years ago. When she and Cathbad arrived, the stones had loomed out of the mist, like sentinels or some-thing altogether more sinister. It had been a strange, sullen place, not welcoming to outsiders, or maybe that's just Ruth's memory playing tricks on her, because of what happened afterwards.

She looks up from the candidate's almost insultingly neat handwriting. Is it her imagination or did the door to her staircase just open? Ruth sits completely still, listening. Then, unmistakably, she hears footsteps on the stone stairs. A Classics professor has the room below hers but she knows that he's gone to Rome for the weekend because he has promised to bring back some limoncello – he's rather a good neighbour. The footsteps seem to have stopped. Was she mistaken? But the door is made of oak, it wouldn't open by accident. And she was sure that she heard something. Some*one*.

Ruth goes to the window and looks out. The court is empty, the one lighted window casting a golden rectangle on the dark grass. The paths are gravel. Surely she would have heard the person approach? She walks to her door but doesn't open it. Suddenly she is really afraid. She imagines her mysterious visitor standing waiting on the other side of her door. She even starts to believe that she can hear them breathing. For one crazy moment she thinks of Ivor March, his shadowed eyes and half-smile. *I've been following your career. You're a very impressive woman, Dr Galloway.*

'Who's there?' she says, her voice sounding high and, despite her best efforts, scared.

There, there, there. Her voice echoes around the panelled room. The two old Judeans look down on her. Interloper, their painted faces say. You're not welcome here. It's no concern of ours if you're murdered at your desk.

'Get stuffed,' says Ruth, aloud. She opens the door. The landing is empty. Ruth runs down the stairs. The door at the bottom is firmly shut. She opens it. Larry, the porter, is passing on his rounds, keys jingling at his waist.

'Did anyone come in just now?' asks Ruth.

'No,' says Larry. 'They'd have had to come past the porter's lodge and I didn't see a soul.'

A soul. The word sounds strange and rather spooky. Body and soul. The Holy Spirit. The Holy Ghost. Ruth thinks of her parents, evangelical Christians who enjoyed talking about their souls. Her mother is dead now and her father, in his eighties, has taken up with a woman at his church, a spritely sixty-year-old called Bella Parkinson. Has Ruth's mother decided to pay her a visit from beyond the grave? But Ruth is an atheist who doesn't believe in life after death.

'Everything all right, Ruth?' says Larry.

'Yes, fine,' says Ruth. 'I just thought I heard something.'

'Probably just the building creaking,' says Larry. 'That

happens at night sometimes when the wooden beams cool down and contract.'

'I'm sure you're right,' says Ruth. She goes back to her office and finds that an email has appeared on her computer screen. It's from Crissy Martin.

'Ruth,' says the message, 'I need your help.'

CHAPTER 18

Ruth ends up taking Kate with her to Grey Walls. It isn't ideal but, for some reason, she doesn't want to tell Frank about the email from Crissy. Besides, she tells herself, Frank has done enough babysitting – despite Kate's protests that she's *not* a baby – over the last few days. Kate has her swimming gala in the morning so Ruth spends a few chlorine-heavy hours trying to follow Kate's red cap as it ploughs up and down the lanes. Kate is a good, if splashy, swimmer. Ruth remembers how keen she used to be on swimming. When did it stop? When she became embarrassed to be seen in a swimming costume? Well, that won't happen to Kate, she tells herself. Her daughter is as slim as a reed now but, even if she fills out later, Ruth will fill her with self-confidence and body positivity and all those things that sound so easy on paper. Ruth has a sudden flashback to a beach in Italy and the look Nelson had given her when she emerged from the changing room in a black one-piece. It had, unmistakably, been a look of approval.

The smell of chlorine and the shouts and splashes of the

swimmers reminds Ruth of her swim on Tuesday. Why had she suddenly been unable to breathe? Was it a panic attack or something more serious? What if it had been an actual heart attack? She remembers reading somewhere that heart attacks are harder to spot in women and that many people have them without knowing it. After all, Phil had one and he's a million times fitter than Ruth. She tries to practise her breathing, sitting on the wooden bench with Kate's hoodie in her lap. In for four, out for eight. The woman next to her gives her a suspicious look and moves away slightly.

Kate comes second in her race and St Benedict's comes third overall, so honour is satisfied. Ruth gives Kate a drink and a KitKat (you get so hungry swimming, Ruth has had to eat a KitKat herself just from the stress of watching) and tells her that they are going for a drive.

'Where are we going?' asks Kate, getting into the passenger seat and dumping her wet towel in the back.

'You remember that place where I went for the writing retreat? Well, I've got to go and talk to the lady who runs it. Just for a few minutes.'

Kate seems to accept this. Ruth is always talking to strange people 'just for a few minutes'. She settles back in her seat and favours Ruth with a stroke-by-stroke analysis of the gala. All Ruth has to do is agree that Kate was best, that the girl who beat her was clearly older than nine, and that Miss Redding has very big feet, almost flipper-like in her poolside slides.

The fens are lush and green in the midday sun. Although the weather is staying hot, the countryside is still far from the parched look of August. There are dog roses in the hedges and the lanes foam with cow parsley. They pass beet fields and wind turbines, motionless in the still air, birds sitting on wires, a horse and rider ambling along, 'Please pass wide and slow'. Kate laughs at a sign for 'Pidley Sheep Lane', but then becomes bored and searches for pop music on the radio. Pharrell Williams's 'Happy' fills the car and they sing along, although Ruth still can't see what's so happy about a room without a roof.

Grey Walls looks serene in the sunshine, softened by light purple wisteria. Crissy is waiting for them and she, too, looks tranquil in a long, white dress with her ash-blonde hair loose. She greets Kate enthusiastically and suggests that she sits on the veranda and draws a picture. As Crissy also supplies a wealth of coloured pencils and paper, plus a chocolate brownie, Kate is happy to agree.

Crissy kisses Ruth on both cheeks. 'It's so good of you to come.'

'You said it was urgent,' says Ruth. She's feeling slightly constrained in Crissy's presence. On the one hand, Crissy is still the same warm, empathetic person she was a few weeks ago. On the other, Ruth has since found out that she used to be married to a serial killer and writes anonymous notes to expert witnesses. Ruth also can't forget the way Ivor March looked at her, as if he knew her intimately. Did that knowledge come from Crissy?

Crissy takes Ruth into her study, a room she has never seen before. It has none of the carefully casual charm of the rest of the house. There are steel cabinets and shelves full of lever-arch files. A yearly planner fills one wall. There's just one small window but, through it, Ruth can see Kate's dark head with its untidy, après-swimming ponytail, and feels reassured.

'Thank you for coming,' says Crissy again, as she takes her seat behind the desk. 'I didn't know where else to turn.'

'What is it?' says Ruth. She feels at a disadvantage sitting in the visitor's chair. Previously, when she talked to Crissy, it was at the kitchen table or swinging gently in one of the porch seats.

'You've heard about the girl who was killed? Heidi Lucas. Her body was found on the marshes near Cley.'

'Yes,' said Ruth. She saw it on the evening news the day after the excavation and the location, the Cley marshes, had given her a tiny shock of recognition and fear.

'It's him,' says Crissy, staring at Ruth with eyes that look almost wild.

'Ivor March?' whispers Ruth.

'No.' Crissy waves this aside as if it's a buzzing mosquito. 'Ivor didn't kill anyone. I know. I know Ivor. I was married to him for almost ten years. I know the things he's capable of and cold-blooded murder isn't one of them. No. It's him. The Lantern Man.'

'The Lantern Man?' echoes Ruth. She realises that she's still whispering.

'Ivor, Bob and Leonard used to call themselves the Lantern Men,' says Crissy. 'They used to go out and rescue girls who were lost or in danger. Ivor didn't have any children. His first wife had a late miscarriage and they knew the baby was a girl. I got pregnant once but I lost the baby too. Ivor was inconsolable, he was convinced that it was his fault. Afterwards I think he was always looking for daughters to care for.'

Her tone is affectionate but Ruth feels her flesh creep. She does not like the thought of Ivor March roaming the countryside 'looking for daughters'. She also notes that Crissy talks about losing that baby as if this was only a tragedy for Ivor. How did it affect Crissy, who always seems the most motherly of women?

'Bob and Leonard used to live here, didn't they?' she says.

'Yes,' says Crissy. She reaches onto a shelf behind her and shows Ruth a picture in a cheap, clip-on frame. It shows Ivor with two other men, one tall and thin, one shorter and wearing glasses. They are all smiling and someone has written across the bottom, 'All for one and one for all.'

'The three musketeers,' says Crissy. 'In those days when we were all one happy family. Me, Bob, Leonard and Ivor. Ivor taught painting, Bob printmaking and Leonard sculpture. I was the housekeeper.' She laughs suddenly. 'It sounds menial but I think it's the happiest I've ever been. I looked after the house and John looked after the garden.'

'And who was this Lantern Man?'

'That's what I'm trying to tell you. I don't know. Ivor, Bob and Leonard called themselves the Lantern Men. They'd go out at night, looking for girls to save. They wanted to teach them that there was more to life than drinking and sleeping around. They wanted to teach them about Art and Beauty.'

Her voice gives capital letters to these last words. There's a fanatical gleam in her eyes that chills Ruth still further. She remembers Nelson telling her about these trips to 'save' girls. It was the day that they had visited Ivor in prison. She remembers asking what happened to the girls and Nelson replying that Crissy 'got rid of them'. She realises how little she really knows about the woman sitting in front of her.

'You mentioned a Lantern Man, in the singular,' she says.

'Yes. Ivor talked about *the* Lantern Man. He said that he came with them at night sometimes and that he was dangerous. He was their dark side, he said. When Ivor was arrested for the murders of Stacy and Jill, I went to see him in prison. He said that he'd murdered them. The Lantern Man.'

'He didn't give you a name?'

'No. He said that he didn't know his name. He'd only joined them a few times and he'd used an alias.'

'Did Ivor tell this to the police?'

'They wouldn't listen. You know what the police are like.' She gives Ruth a strange, rather crooked, smile. 'DCI Nelson is a hard man. He was convinced that Ivor was guilty. So was DI Johnson. Where DCI Nelson leads, she follows. DS Fuller too. All the women are in thrall to him.'

Now Ruth definitely doesn't like her tone. 'As I recall,' she says stiffly, 'there was a lot of forensic evidence linking Ivor to the crimes.'

'Forensic evidence can be planted,' says Crissy.

'It can,' says Ruth, 'but it hardly ever is. Ivor's DNA was on the bodies. Even his cat's fur.'

'Mother Gabley.' Crissy smiles. 'He loved that cat. You know she was named after a sixteenth-century woman from Wells who was accused of witchcraft. Chantal's got her now.'

This heart-warming story doesn't exactly reassure Ruth.

Crissy leans forward, not smiling any more. 'And, if the Lantern Man doesn't exist, who killed Heidi Lucas? It sounds as if she was killed in the exact same way as the others.'

Ruth shifts her chair backwards. 'What do you want me to do about it?' she asks.

'I want you to talk to DCI Nelson,' says Crissy. 'Convince him that Ivor is innocent and that the real murderer is still out there. That's why I wanted you to do the excavation. I knew you'd find something and that, if you had doubts, Nelson would listen to you. He loves you.'

'I never said that he loved me,' says Ruth, speaking with difficulty. 'I just said that we'd had a brief affair and that he's Kate's father. Nelson's married to another woman.'

'I know he loves you,' says Crissy. 'And he loves Kate. He'll listen to you. Talk to him.'

And, as much to escape as anything else, Ruth agrees.

When she gets outside Kate is sitting at the wrought-iron table, surrounded by pictures. A dark man is leaning over her.

'Kate!' says Ruth, more sharply than she intended.

Kate looks round and so does the man. Ruth recognises John the gardener and her heart-rate returns to something like normal.

'Hi, Ruth,' says John. 'Your daughter's an artist.'

And Ruth thinks of the short story Nelson sent her yesterday. The story entitled 'The Lantern Men'.

'Are you ready to die?' said The Artist.

Nelson and Michelle are eating Sunday lunch. As usual, Michelle has made a roast but Nelson thinks that there's something sad about the small piece of pork ('Serves two') and the empty chairs around the table. George is in his high chair, smearing his face with apple sauce, but he doesn't compensate for the absence of Laura and Rebecca and their spirited chat about people he has never met and TV programmes he has never watched. They invited Laura but she said that she was going out on a bike ride. 'Perhaps she's met someone at the club,' said Michelle. Nelson kept his fears to himself.

Rebecca lives in Brighton where she has a big circle of friends and a boyfriend called Asif. Nelson is wary of any man around his daughters but he rather likes Asif, who is respectful and surprisingly good company. Rebecca hasn't been home for a while. She took the revelation about Katie better than Laura but Nelson wonders if she has since distanced herself a little from the family unit. Maybe this is only to be expected. And it's a long drive from Brighton to Norfolk. That won't stop Nelson ringing her tonight and playing the guilt card though. 'When are you coming to see us, love? Georgie misses you. Bruno too.'

'Why don't we go for a walk this afternoon?' says Michelle. Bruno, who is lying in the doorway, pricks up his ears at this. 'It's a nice afternoon. We could go to the park and take George on the swings.'

'Swings!' shouts George.

'All right,' says Nelson. It's not his preferred way of spending a Sunday afternoon but there's no football on TV and he might as well get some exercise. After all, as Michelle is always reminding him, it's important to stay fit after fifty.

Despite threatening to make them give up sugar, Michelle has made apple pie for pudding. Nelson is just finishing his second slice when the doorbell rings. Bruno barks once, in case they have missed it. Nelson and Michelle look at each other. George laughs delightedly.

Nelson sees blonde hair through the rippled glass of the door and, for a moment, his heart leaps. But it's someone else's daughter.

'Hallo, Maddie. This is a surprise.'

'I'm not interrupting, am I?'

'No, we're just finishing lunch.'

Michelle gives Maddie some apple pie. Maddie once lived with them for a few weeks and both Nelson and Michelle got into the habit of treating her like a third daughter. Fourth, in Nelson's case.

'I just popped round,' says Maddie, 'because I was going through that box of Jenny's and I found some more photos. They were in an envelope and it was caught between the pages of a manuscript. Delicious pie, Michelle. Can I have another bit?'

'Can I see the pictures?' says Nelson, trying not to sound too impatient. Michelle gives him a look.

Maddie gets out a plain white envelope and tips two pictures onto the table. One shows Crissy Martin with two men, both of them looking at her with what seems like adoration. The second is a group photograph showing a crowd of people gathered round a bonfire on the beach. Nelson's attention is immediately drawn to Ivor March, the dark hair, the supercilious expression visible even from a distance. There's Crissy Martin too and Chantal Simmonds. Two other women are crouching at the front, one of them poking the fire. This is Jenny McGuire. Maddie points to the other one.

'That's her, isn't it?' she says. 'Heidi Lucas. The girl who was killed.'

CHAPTER 19

'So Ivor March did know Heidi Lucas.' Judy is examining the photographs. Nelson is rather envious of the fact that she doesn't have to hold them at arm's length to do so.

'Apparently so. Do you know who all these other people are?'

'That's March, obviously. Crissy is on one side, Chantal on the other.'

'I bet he loved that,' says Nelson. 'His ex-wife and his mistress both all over him. But it's interesting. Chantal told me that she'd never met Jenny.'

'Well, she obviously had. This is quite a gathering. Next to Chantal is Bob Carr, the printmaker. That's Leonard Jenkins, the sculptor who's now a teacher. I'm not sure who that is . . .'

'That's John Robertson, the gardener at Grey Walls. I don't recognise the man next to him.'

'Nor do I. That's Jenny McGuire at the front next to Heidi.'

'And who are the men with Crissy Martin in the other picture?'

'Bob and Leonard.'

'Looks as if they're both in love with her. Their tongues are practically hanging out.'

'Leonard called her a "wonderful woman" but he's gay.'

'Doesn't stop him being in love with her.'

'You're learning,' says Judy.

Nelson ignores this. 'What about Bob Carr? Wasn't he in a relationship with Ailsa?'

'Yes, but she married Leonard. It's all very confusing.'

'That's one word for it. Anyway, we need to ask all these people about Heidi. This is a coincidence too far.' He squints at the picture. It's too small for him to see Heidi's face clearly but she looks relaxed, one hand pushing back her hair, the other holding the stick with which she's poking the fire. But what is Heidi doing here with these people?

'You heard that we got the forensics back from the lab,' says Judy.

'Yes,' says Nelson. 'That's good news.' They have managed to retrieve enough DNA from the first two bodies for a positive identification. It is now beyond doubt that it is Nicola Ferris and Jenny McGuire who were buried in the garden of the Jolly Boatman.

'Nothing on the third body?' he says.

'Not yet,' says Judy. 'It was in the ground longer so the DNA has deteriorated too much. But I've got Sofia Novak's dental records. We should soon know if it's her or not.'

'Are you going to tell the families?'

'Tony and I are just off now.'

'OK,' says Nelson, 'but we need to ask Heidi's boyfriend and family about these pictures.'

'That's Tanya's patch.'

'I suppose it is,' says Nelson.

Nelson briefs Tanya who immediately sets off to see Josh Evans, Heidi's boyfriend. Judy and Tony head out to visit the Ferris and McGuire families. Nelson disappears into his office to avoid talking to Super Jo, who is hovering on the edge of the briefing, the words 'press conference' forming on her lips.

He has hardly closed the door when his phone starts to buzz. 'Ruth' says the screen.

'Ruth,' says Nelson, 'is it —'

'It's not about Kate,' says Ruth. She sounds harassed and rather tense. Nelson imagines her in that depressing-looking office with the panels and the oil paintings. That place would be enough to make anyone feel stressed.

'I got a message from Crissy Martin,' says Ruth.

'What?' Nelson is on alert now.

'She said that she wanted to see me urgently. That was on Saturday night. I drove over to Grey Walls yesterday. Crissy is convinced that March is innocent.'

'Not another one,' says Nelson.

'What do you mean?'

'Just that Cathbad has got some lunatic idea in his head that March didn't kill the women. He said that it came to him during the excavation at the pub.'

'Have you had the forensics results? Does the DNA match? Are they Nicola and Jenny?'

'Yes,' says Nelson. 'We've had a positive identification. Judy's gone to see the families now.'

'It's a shame about the DNA on the third body but isotope analysis seems to show that she grew up in Eastern Europe. I'll send you a simplified version.'

'A simplified version is definitely what I need. Judy's managed to get hold of some dental records for our potential victim. I'm hoping for a result later today. Carry on telling me about Crissy Martin. Did she have any evidence for suggesting that March didn't do it?'

'She said that there was a fourth man, besides Ivor and his friends. She called him the Lantern Man. She said that he killed the four women. She seemed to think that he'd also killed that poor girl who was found on the marshes the other day.'

'The Lantern Man? What's she playing at? Did she have a name or anything useful like that?'

'She said that Ivor didn't know his name. Apparently this man only joined them a few times and he used an alias.'

'Ivor doesn't know his name because he made him up. Does this Crissy think we're idiots?'

'No,' says Ruth, 'she says that you're a hard man. She thinks that you want to frame Ivor and that Judy and Tanya do everything you say.'

'I wish. Did Crissy say anything that might actually be useful?'

'Not really. She just wanted me to convince you that Ivor

is innocent. She seems to think that I have a lot of influence over you. I told her that was rubbish.'

Ruth's voice is bland but Nelson suspects that she's making a point of some kind. 'Ivor March is guilty,' he says. 'He was the one who told us where to find the bodies, for God's sake. Did you see anyone else at Grey Walls?'

'Only John, the gardener. He was talking to Kate when I came out of the house. It gave me quite a shock at first.'

'Talking to Katie? What was she doing there?'

'I took her with me. We went after her swimming gala.'

Now Ruth really does sound defensive but Nelson can't stop himself saying, 'What possessed you, Ruth? That place is full of weirdos.'

'Weirdos? What does that mean?'

'It means people who are friends with serial killers, or married to serial killers. I don't want Katie going back there.'

'Well luckily it's not up to you,' says Ruth. And she terminates the call.

Nelson sits there for a few minutes, drumming his fingers on the desk. He feels deeply aggrieved. He is surely within his rights to tell Ruth not to take Katie, *his* daughter, to a house that once belonged to a murderer? How dare Ruth hang up on him like that? Does she know what it's like for him, trying to identify one killer's victims, while another madman is out there, strangling innocent women? And how come all these people are suddenly convinced of March's innocence? Cathbad, Crissy, Ruth (by association), even Judy had sounded doubtful. What's the matter with everyone?

But, after a few minutes, he starts to calm down. He

knows that he can't interfere in Katie's upbringing, though he suddenly wonders, with a fresh surge of rage, whether Frank knew all about the trip to Grey Walls. But he can't take his frustrations out on Ruth. He's about to press call back when he changes his mind and writes a text.

Sorry. N.

After a good ten minutes – he wouldn't expect it earlier – Ruth texts back.

That's OK.

Encouraged, Nelson texts, *Sending email. N.* Then he finds the photo of Jenny with the four men and emails it to Ruth with the message, 'Jenny with Ivor, Bob and Leonard. Don't know who the fourth is? Do you recognise him? Is it the Lantern Man?'

Seconds later, Ruth emails back. 'I don't know if it's the Lantern Man, but I do know who it is.'

Tanya and DC Bradley Linwood, her sidekick of choice, catch Josh in a free period. He's still in his tracksuit and has a whistle round his neck. They sit on a bench looking out over the playing fields. For Tanya, the whole scene – the newly mown grass with the lanes marked out, the girls wearing running vests, the sound of tennis balls being hit – reminds her exhilaratingly of school. She excelled in sport as a teenager, athletics and rounders in summer, hockey and netball in winter, and studied sports science at university. Her wife Petra is also a PE teacher, though at a private school, something that occasionally affords them both a twinge of conscience.

'Do you play cricket here?' Bradley asks Josh. 'I loved cricket at school.'

This is why Tanya likes working with him.

'Yes,' says Josh. 'Lots of state schools don't play cricket but we've got a good team. A boys' team and a girls' team,' he adds, with a glance at Tanya.

'I'm surprised to find you back at work,' she says.

'They offered me compassionate leave,' says Josh, 'but . . . I don't know . . . I found that it helped being back at work. It's a busy term and we're short-staffed . . .'

His voice trails away. They are short-staffed, Tanya knows, because Heidi Lucas taught PE here too. She wonders what it can be like for Josh, being reminded of his girlfriend at work and at home. Two girls pass carrying javelins, giggling.

'Hallo, Mr Evans.' They gaze at him soulfully.

'Hallo, girls. Be careful how you carry those.'

More giggling.

Tanya waits until the students are out of earshot. 'I'm sorry to trouble you again,' she says, 'but we've found this picture of Heidi. I wondered if you knew anything about the people in it.'

She shows Josh a colour copy of the photo. It has been enlarged which makes the faces slightly blurry. Only Ivor March seems to be in focus.

'I don't know,' says Josh, sounding distracted. He rubs his short, ginger hair. He's the sort that will be bald by forty, thinks Tanya. 'Maybe it's the cycle club.'

'The cycle club? Lynn Wheels?'

'Yes, I don't recognise the others but that man,' he points, 'he's a member. Len something.'

Tanya looks at the key thoughtfully provided by Judy. Leonard Jenkins.

'Did Heidi know Leonard Jenkins well?'

'I don't think so. We had a drink with him once. He seemed like a nice bloke. Good cyclist too.'

'Do you remember anything about this barbecue?' asks Tanya. 'It was only last year. July.'

'I think so. I remember Heidi saying that some other people from the club were going.'

One other person, thinks Tanya.

'Why didn't you go?'

Josh blushes. He has the complexion that goes with red hair. 'I don't think I was asked.'

'Did you think that was odd?'

'Not really. I mean . . . we didn't do everything together. Anyway . . .' A rather pleading look. 'I thought Len was gay.'

'Leonard Jenkins is gay, as far as I know.'

Josh exhales. 'It doesn't matter now, I know, but I'm sure Heidi would never have cheated on me. We were happy together. Ask anyone.'

Tanya believes him.

*

Judy and Tony sit facing Steven and Denise Ferris. Denise is holding a picture of Nicola as if this is the nearest that she can get to her daughter.

'I'm so sorry,' says Judy. She has got to know the couple well over the last year. Steve is a taxi driver and Denise an ex-nurse. They have two younger children, Louise and Joe. Louise is married with a baby and Joe still lives at home. Nicola was the 'career girl', the one who wanted more from life than a husband and children. She went to university, spent a year in Paris, qualified as a French teacher and worked hard on her art. And now she's dead.

'At least we can have a funeral,' says Steven, with a bravery that tugs at Judy's heartstrings. 'At least we can do that for her.'

'We knew really,' says Denise, looking at Nicola's photograph. It's a grand studio affair, showing Nicola looking mistily glamorous in a black evening dress, her blonde hair piled up. Judy wonders what the occasion was. 'We knew that she was dead, that he'd killed her. Were you there when they . . . when they dug her up?'

'Yes,' says Judy. 'Dr Galloway, the archaeologist, was very careful, very respectful. Everyone on the site felt the same. My partner said some prayers when we . . . when we found them.'

'Is he a vicar?' asks Denise.

'No,' says Judy, feeling inadequate at the thought of describing Cathbad. 'But he's very spiritual.'

'Will he be charged with her murder?' says Steven. The couple always avoid saying Ivor March's name.

'Yes,' says Judy. 'I mean, he told us where to look. We're hoping for some more forensics too.' This is a problem, one that Judy doesn't dwell on now. So far there has been no sign of March's DNA on any of the bodies found in the pub garden. Instead she says, 'You ought to know that a third body was found.'

'A third body?' echoes Denise. 'Did he kill another girl?'

'It seems so,' says Judy, ignoring the voice in her head – Cathbad's – saying that there's no evidence to link March to this third victim. 'Does the name Sofia Novak mean anything to you?'

'No,' says Steven. 'Novak like the tennis player?'

'Yes,' says Judy, who is a big Andy Murray fan. 'Except that it's her surname.'

'I'm sorry,' says Denise. 'It doesn't ring a bell.'

'That's OK,' says Judy. She is convinced, in her own mind, that the dental records will show that the third body is Sofia but as she was obviously killed before the others, it's unlikely that Nicola would have known her.

'Just to prepare you,' she says, 'there'll have to be an inquest. It'll be quite short and the family liaison officer and I will be with you throughout. Dr Galloway will give evidence, and the pathologist too. You can ask them questions if you want to. The coroner will then pass a verdict, which I expect will be "unlawfully killed". We need that if we are going to trial. I'm so sorry that you have to go through this.'

'It's all right,' says Steven, though clearly nothing will

ever be all right again. 'We just want justice for Nicky.'
Judy's heart contracts, as it always does when the family
use this abbreviation. Nicola, it seems, was only Nicky to a
few people.

Judy says goodbye and stands up to leave. Tony shakes
hands with the couple and then says, suddenly, 'I'm so sorry.
My sister died when I was ten. I know what it's like.'

Judy stares at him but Denise puts a comforting hand
on his arm. 'I'm so sorry, love. You never get over it, do
you?'

Nelson rings back immediately. This is not something that
can be discussed over email.

'What do you mean, you know who it is?'

Ruth says, slowly, 'I think it's Larry. One of the porters
at my college.'

'Jesus,' says Nelson. 'Are you sure?'

'Pretty sure. I mean, he's younger in the picture but he
hasn't changed much and I see him every day.'

'Did you have any idea that he knew Ivor March?'

'None at all.' Nelson thinks that Ruth sounds rather
shaken. After a brief pause, she says, 'I was here alone the
other night and I thought I heard someone outside my door.
I went to look and there was no one there but Larry was
in the court. I thought he was just doing his rounds. I was
relieved to see him actually. But now . . .'

'I'm coming over,' says Nelson. 'I want to talk to this
Larry.' He knows that this isn't his job. He should relay the

information to Judy and let her interview Larry. And it isn't a good use of his time, Cambridge is over an hour's drive away. But he is already gathering up his car keys.

'Thanks, Nelson,' says Ruth.

In the car, Tony says, 'Sorry'.

Judy says, 'I'm sorry about your sister but . . .'

'I know,' says Tony. 'I shouldn't have said anything.'

He's looking straight ahead but his colour is up slightly. Judy feels sorry for him. She says, 'It's just . . . I know you wanted to empathise and that's great but Denise and Steven have enough on their plates without having to feel sorry for you too.'

'I know,' says Tony. 'I don't know why I said it. I usually never talk about Lily.'

'Do you want to tell me?' says Judy.

'There's not much to tell,' says Tony. 'Lily died of men-ingitis when she was five and I was ten. Nothing anyone could do. She felt ill one evening and was dead the next morning. But nothing in our family was ever the same again. Everything was either before or after, if you know what I mean.'

'I know,' says Judy, thinking of all the families that she has visited with bad news. And, even as she asks them to sit down and begins her careful statement, she knows this: nothing will ever be the same again.

'Life is bloody unfair sometimes,' she says. 'Do you feel up to visiting Jenny's family?'

'Of course,' says Tony, sitting up straighter. 'You can count on me.'

Judy is starting to think that she can.

Patrick and Mary McGuire live in Holt. Jenny lived with them after her divorce and her ten-year-old daughter, Maisie, still does so. Maisie is at school today but there's evidence of her everywhere: a scooter in the hallway, her artwork stuck on the fridge, her photo, grinning in school uniform, on the mantelpiece.

'Our lives revolve around Maisie now,' says Mary. 'It's such a comfort. Sometimes it's as if we have Jenny back.'

'God rest her soul,' says Patrick. There's evidence of the couple's faith everywhere too: a holy water stoup by the front door, a painting of Jesus pointing accusingly at His Sacred Heart, palm crosses poking out from picture frames, a candle from Lourdes in front of Jenny's picture. It reminds Judy of her childhood home, her parents are also Irish Catholics, but she wonders what Tony makes of it.

Judy tells Mary and Patrick about the excavation and the third body. She prepares them for the inquest and a possible further trial. They both cross themselves often but say little. Like Steven and Denise Ferris, they were prepared for this.

Tony doesn't mention his sister but his manner is empathetic and kind. Judy asks if Jenny might have known Sofia Novak.

'I don't remember the name,' says Mary. 'But Jenny saw lots of people in her work. And at her evening classes at the community centre.'

Jenny had worked in the gift shop at a stately home. Judy imagines that most of the people she met there were harmless National Trust types. The community centre is another matter.

'I've seen the short story Jenny wrote,' says Judy. '"The Lantern Men". It was very good.' Actually, she has no idea whether it was good or not. She has no patience for literary analysis, which is one of the many reasons why she has never joined Cathbad's book club.

But Mary seems pleased. 'She was a talented writer. Everyone says so.'

'Maisie writes stories too,' says Patrick. 'They're so good. I've kept them all in a special folder.'

Stop writing stories, Maisie, Judy wants to say. It can only lead to trouble. Aloud, she says, 'The story mentions someone called The Artist. Do you have any idea who that was meant to be?'

'I couldn't bear to read it,' says Mary. 'I just gave the box to that nice reporter, Maddie Henderson. Do you know her?'

'She's my stepdaughter,' says Judy. It seems the closest explanation to the truth. She gets out the photograph of the group around the campfire.

'This was in the box with the short story,' she says. 'Do you recognise any of the people?'

'There's Jenny,' says Mary, pointing to the figure at the front. 'I don't recognise anyone else.'

'That's him,' says Patrick, in a hard, tight voice. 'That's Ivor March. And that's his girlfriend. I recognise her from court.' Patrick had attended every day of the trial, against Judy's advice.

'Oh yes.' Mary drops the picture. 'That's him.'

'Do you recognise this girl?' Judy points at Heidi.

'No,' says Mary. 'She looks nice. She looks a bit like Jenny.'

'Yes, she does,' says Judy.

'Maddie reminded me of Jenny too,' says Patrick.

Suddenly Judy has a powerful desire to cross herself or mutter a prayer or light a candle. Anything to ward off the evil eye.

CHAPTER 20

Ruth is with one of her PhD supervisees, an anxious woman called Cho, when Nelson appears at her door. Cho becomes even more confused than usual and stops her rambling account of variations in the human cranium.

'Thanks, Cho,' says Ruth, glancing at the clock. 'I think that's enough for today. Are you clear about what to do now?'

Cho mutters something and scuttles past Nelson as if he's the devil incarnate. To be fair he is scowling and looking at his most intimidating.

'Didn't you see the sign on the door saying that I was with a student?' asks Ruth.

'No,' says Nelson. 'I haven't got time to read signs.' Ruth is willing to bet that he walked on the grass too.

Nelson sits in the chair vacated by Cho. 'Larry Hanson, that's his name,' he says. 'I've got an appointment with him in ten minutes.'

'You didn't mention me on the phone, did you?'

'No. I just said that his name had come up in connection with the Ivor March case.'

'I bet that terrified him. It would terrify me.'

'He didn't sound scared,' says Nelson. 'He was very polite and pleasant. Of course, he may not even have known Ivor that well. One photo isn't evidence of anything.'

'No,' says Ruth. 'It's just ... with Crissy going on about this fourth man and everything ... I suppose I just freaked out a little.'

'That's understandable,' says Nelson, in his 'good with women' voice which always makes Ruth want to throw something at him. 'I've been thinking about this fourth man that Crissy mentioned. On the back of the picture was the word BILL, in capitals. I thought it was a name but now I'm wondering whether it's initials. Bob, Ivor, Leonard and Larry.'

'Who wrote that?' says Ruth. 'Jenny?'

'I assume so since the picture was found with her things. Her parents found a box with some old photos in, plus printouts of her short stories. Maddie went through it and found this, plus a picture that shows Ivor March with Jenny and Heidi Lucas.'

'Was that the girl who was killed the other day?'

'Yes. It's the first evidence of any link with Ivor March and the Grey Walls mob.'

Ruth notes the word 'mob'. She would have called them a group, a cabal, a sect. Something infinitely more sinister.

'There's this picture too.' Nelson produces it with something like a flourish. The print shows Crissy Martin, laughing in a halter-neck dress, while two men stare at her adoringly. Ruth is almost certain that she's seen them before.

'Leonard Jenkins and Bob Carr,' says Nelson. 'The other two Lantern Men.'

Now Ruth remembers. The picture Crissy showed her on Sunday. Ivor, Bob and Leonard. The three musketeers. All for one and one for all. She thinks about the writing on the back of the other photograph. BILL.

'If Jenny kept these pictures,' says Ruth, 'it suggests that she knew all these people quite well. Ivor, Bob, Leonard and Larry. Any one of them could have been The Artist in her story. Crissy said that Bob was a printmaker and Leonard was a sculptor.'

'Larry isn't an artist. He's a college porter.'

'He told me once that he used to make pots,' says Ruth. 'Potters are artists. Look at Grayson Perry.'

Nelson looks as if he would rather not do this. 'What did you think of the story?' he asks.

'It was a bit odd,' says Ruth. 'And I find all that S and M stuff rather boring. But some parts were good. She obviously did some research into local folklore. I hadn't heard of the lantern men before but it's a popular legend around here.'

'Cathbad gave me a lecture on them,' says Nelson. 'Something about the devil putting a light in a pumpkin. Biggest load of bollocks you've ever heard.'

'The narrator didn't have a name,' says Ruth. 'I wondered why that was.'

'I didn't notice that,' says Nelson. 'I just noticed that she had some very funny ideas.'

'The story suggests that the narrator wants to die,' says Ruth. 'That's the most disturbing part. Do you think that's what Ivor did? Convince the women that they wanted him to kill them? It doesn't seem possible.'

'It's not possible,' says Nelson. 'What is possible is that Ivor lured these women onto the marshes and then murdered them. He may have convinced them that he was in love with them. Some women obviously find him attractive. Look at Crissy Martin. Chantal Simmonds too. And Ailsa Britain. All of them still carrying a torch for him.'

The old-fashioned phrase makes Ruth think of the lantern men, the lonely light moving shakily across the horizon. 'What about Heidi?' she says. 'Do you think her death's linked to the others?'

'Well, Ivor March didn't kill her,' says Nelson. 'I know that much. But what worries me is that someone might be wanting to link the cases. Heidi was strangled, her body was found on marshland but she was obviously killed elsewhere. I don't want that to get out, by the way.'

'I won't tell anyone,' says Ruth.

'Not even Frank.'

'I don't discuss my work with Frank,' says Ruth with dignity. She doesn't like Nelson's tone. 'Shouldn't you be seeing Larry now?'

Larry Hanson is friendly, if slightly defensive. He's a solid-looking man, rather below average height, who looks as if he could handle himself in a fight. Larry says that he did some boxing in his youth and used to work as a bouncer. He moved to Cambridge after his divorce and saw the job at St Jude's advertised in the local paper. 'I thought it sounded peaceful,' he says, with a rather sardonic grin. 'A bit like that *Morse* series that used to be on TV on Sunday nights.' As far as Nelson remembers, Morse's Oxford was a hotbed of gruesome murder, but he thinks he knows what Larry means.

He doesn't seem a very likely potter but Larry says that he was always good with his hands, managing to make this sound very sinister. He attended 'two or three' pottery courses at Grey Walls. They were run by a woman called Tamsyn. He has no idea where she is now. He kept in touch with Ivor and Crissy. 'They seemed like nice people. I wasn't to know, was I?' This is said with a certain amount of truculence but Nelson agrees that Larry wasn't to know. Nelson takes out of the photograph of Jenny McGuire with the four men.

'Do you remember when this was taken?'

Larry examines the photo. He has a complicated tattoo on one hand, star and moon and tendrils like a plant, or a snake.

'It was last summer,' he said. 'Some of the old Grey Walls crowd met up for a barbecue on the beach. A sort of reunion.'

The words 'Grey Walls crowd' strike a chill to Nelson's heart, as does the thought of a reunion. He produces the other photograph. 'Was this taken the same day?'

'Yes,' says Larry. 'Ivor was always keen on building camp fires. He said that they were beacons in the wilderness. Something like that.'

Nelson has heard Cathbad say something very similar. Strange how Cathbad now seems almost normal and Ivor March sounds deranged.

'That's Jenny McGuire, isn't it?' he says. 'Did you know her well?'

'I think I only met her that once,' says Larry. 'She was one of Ivor's students at the community centre. Nice girl.'

'What about this woman?' He points at the figure holding the stick.

'I can't remember,' says Larry. 'Helga? Helena? One of those names. She came with one of the other blokes.'

'Which one? Can you remember?'

'Maybe Len or Bob. I think it was Len. They belonged to some sort of cycling club. I remember thinking it was odd. I mean, Len's gay. Live and let live, that's what I say, but what was he doing with such a pretty girl?'

What indeed, thinks Nelson.

'Tell me about that day,' he says. 'What did you do? Where did you all meet?'

'We met at the community centre. Ailsa runs it. That woman there.'

'Do you know Ailsa well?'

Larry shrugs. 'I met her a few times. She's OK. A bit stuck-up.'

'So you all met at the community centre. Then what did you do?'

'We walked down to the beach. I collected driftwood with John. We had some beers in a cool box. The others all sat around chatting. One thing I remember, Ivor spent a lot of time talking to Jenny. Chantal wasn't happy about that at all.'

'Really?' says Nelson. 'How did you know?'

'Well, Chantal was with Bob and I saw them looking at Jenny and Ivor. Then Bob went over, I think he was trying to break them up, but Ivor took no notice. He stayed sitting with Jenny until it was time to eat. I think they were talking about books. Ivor taught creative writing.'

Were they discussing Jenny's short story? wonders Nelson. The story that features the sinister artist. Whatever the topic he can imagine Chantal being annoyed that Ivor's attention was focused on another woman.

'Wasn't it awkward at the picnic,' he says, 'what with Crissy and Chantal both being there? I mean, Chantal was Ivor's girlfriend and Crissy used to be married to him.' To say nothing of Ailsa Britain and her relationship with Ivor, whatever that was.

'They seemed to get on OK,' says Larry indifferently. Nelson does not have Larry down as a great student of human nature. Surely there would have been tensions with not only Chantal and Crissy, but also Jenny and Ailsa amongst the party. Ivor had been married to Crissy, Ailsa had been in a relationship with Bob and was briefly married to Leonard, Jenny clearly had feelings for Ivor, Chantal was his fanatically devoted girlfriend. Nelson also wonders if Larry, recently divorced, was interested in any of the women present.

'What about Heidi?' he asks. 'Who did she talk to?'

'I can't remember,' says Larry. 'Maybe to the women, Ailsa and Crissy. John and I built the fire and Len did most of the cooking. Bob was with Chantal, trying to calm her down, I think, and Ivor was with Jenny.'

'Can you remember the exact date of the barbecue?' he says. 'It says July on one of the pictures.'

'July the fourth, I think, because someone made a comment about the fourth of July being Independence Day and Crissy said that her divorce had made her independent from men.'

That sounded like rather a barbed comment for such a supposedly happy occasion. By the end of July Nicola Ferris was dead. In August Jenny McGuire left home for the last time. What had happened to prompt this killing spree?

CHAPTER 21

Tanya arrives at the community centre just as the French conversationalists are leaving and the cyclists are starting to arrive. She spots Ailsa Britain, who she remembers from the first investigation, packing some boxes into the car.

'Hallo.' Tanya strolls over.

'Oh, hallo.' She doesn't think that Ailsa looks exactly delighted to see her but, then, the woman always was a bit of a cold fish.

'Are you off for the day?'

'Yes,' says Ailsa. 'Lynn Wheels always lock up after themselves.'

'Do you know them well, the Lynn Wheels lot?'

'Not really. I know Douglas, the organiser.'

'Did you know Heidi Lucas, the girl who was killed?'

'I met her a few times. I was so shocked when I heard what had happened to her.'

Tanya gets out the photocopy, looking a little creased now.

'Do you remember this evening? I think it was last July. There's you with Ivor March, isn't it? Heidi's in the front.'

Ailsa looks at the picture in silence. Her face is composed but Tanya thinks that she can sense a feeling of unease. *You see, Judy, I can do feelings too.*

'I remember the evening,' says Ailsa. 'I don't really remember Heidi.'

'Who invited her?'

'Leonard, I think.'

'Your ex-husband?'

'Yes.' Ailsa gives her a straight look. She has blue eyes, emphasised by navy mascara that is, in Tanya's opinion, a mistake. 'I don't know how he knew Heidi.'

'Probably Lynn Wheels,' says Tanya. 'They were both members.'

On cue, a worried-looking man approaches them. 'DS Fuller? I'm Douglas Foster, the club secretary.'

'Hi.' Tanya shakes hands. 'Let's go inside and talk. See you later, Ailsa.'

Ailsa Britain does not reply.

Tanya and Douglas sit in one of the classrooms. Outside they can see the cyclists arriving for their evening meeting. They are chatting and laughing, probably comparing racing saddles and spokes. They don't seem devastated by Heidi's death but, to be fair, that might not show on the outside. The members seem an eclectic bunch, some are grey-haired and others, to Tanya's critical eye, look at less than peak fitness. But there are young people too. Tanya spots a slim blonde woman in stripy shorts who looks vaguely familiar. She's very attractive too but Tanya is married now and shouldn't be noticing such things.

'I'm so sorry about Heidi,' she says to Douglas.

'We're all devastated,' he says. 'Heidi was a lovely girl. A talented cyclist too.'

'We're anxious to find a woman who was seen chatting to Heidi on Thursday evening,' says Tanya. 'Do you know if any of your members were cycling that route?'

Douglas shakes his head. 'I don't, I'm afraid. It's not a club night and that wasn't an official route. A lot of members have cycling apps like Strava. They can post a time for the distance and compare themselves to other riders. Heidi may well have chosen her route that way.'

They still haven't found Heidi's mobile phone but her bank statements will show if she had downloaded any apps. Not that this gets them very far.

'Heidi was seen chatting to a woman with long greyish blonde hair, dressed in black cycling clothes riding a blue bike,' says Tanya. 'Does that description ring any bells?'

Douglas shrugs helplessly. 'It could be anyone. There are lots of cyclists on the road.'

'Do you have a list of members?'

'Yes, I printed one out for you.'

'Thank you.' Tanya scans the list quickly and sees the name Leonard Jenkins. She doesn't think that she saw Leonard outside but she's only seen him in photographs so can't be sure.

'Does Leonard Jenkins come to meetings regularly?' she asks.

'Yes,' says Douglas, sounding surprised at the question.

'He's one of our veterans but he's very fit. He's done lots of racing, here and abroad.'

'Did he know Heidi?'

Now Douglas looks positively worried. 'I'm not sure. I think so. It's a very friendly club.'

'We know that Leonard and Heidi attended a barbecue together last year,' says Tanya. 'Did you know anything about that?'

'No,' says Douglas. 'But there can't have been any funny business. I mean, Leonard is gay.'

Depends what you mean by funny business, thinks Tanya.

'Was Heidi particularly friendly with anyone else at the club?' she asks.

'I think she had lots of friends,' says Douglas. 'Like I say, everyone's very upset. We're going to have a candlelit vigil for her.'

When Tanya leaves, making her way through the assembled cyclists, she sees that some of them are, in fact, in tears, and others are standing around rather helplessly. She is also rather disconcerted to realise that the attractive blonde in striped shorts is the boss's daughter, Laura.

Tanya starts the evening briefing without waiting for the boss but he strolls in halfway through. Probably been in Cambridge with Ruth.

'We've spoken to the witnesses who saw Heidi on her last bike ride,' she says. 'Stella Patten, the women walking home from Brownies, saw her at twenty past eight. She can only really remember the pink shorts but we're pretty sure it was Heidi. Ted Avery saw a woman answering to Heidi's description talking to another woman near Churchgate Way at eight thirty. The description of the second woman's a bit vague, I'm afraid. Ted spoke to a police sketch artist but all he really got was that the woman had long hair, "greyish or blonde". Other than that, he can really only remember the bike. He says it was blue and brown.'

'Weapons bias,' says Judy.

'Probably,' says Tanya. To show that she understands the term, she explains to Tony. 'When faced with an assailant holding a gun, the witnesses can usually only remember the gun. That's known as weapons bias.'

'And in this case the bike's the weapon?'

Tanya ignores this. She has already noticed a regrettable tendency towards levity in Tony Zhang.

'I've spoken to Douglas Foster, who runs Lynn Wheels, and he confirms that Leonard Jenkins is a member. He doesn't know if Leonard knew Heidi but he says that the club is very friendly.'

The boss makes an exasperated noise. 'It's highly suspicious that Leonard took Heidi to that barbecue. Why would an older, gay man socialise with a young woman? What if he was procuring her for Ivor March?'

'Procuring her?' says Judy.

'Maybe Leonard thought that Ivor would find Heidi attractive. Maybe that was the deal. Leonard and Bob found women for March.'

'That's quite a stretch,' says Judy. 'There's no reason why a young woman can't socialise with an older man. It's irrelevant whether Leonard is gay or straight or bi. They were probably just friends.'

Tanya agrees really but she doesn't want Judy to get any brownie points for political correctness.

'It does seem a little odd,' she says. 'DC Linwood and I spoke to Josh Evans, Heidi's boyfriend. He remembered the barbecue but said he wasn't invited. Josh and Heidi both knew Leonard from the club and they had a drink with him once so it does seem a bit strange that Josh didn't get an invite. Josh says that he and Heidi were happy together and all their friends and relatives seem to agree.'

Nelson points at the group photograph, which is enlarged on the big screen. 'Ivor March, Chantal Simmonds, Crissy Martin, Ailsa Britain, Bob Carr, Leonard Jenkins, John Robertson. All the major players were there. A few weeks later the killings started, first Nicola then Jenny herself. Something happened that evening, I'm sure of it. I've just been talking to this man here, Larry Hanson. He's a porter at a Cambridge college and the fourth man in the picture with Jenny. Bob, Ivor, Leonard and Larry. B.I.L.L.'

'You went to see him?' says Judy. Tanya thinks that she sounds pissed off. 'When?'

'This morning,' says Nelson. 'He works at Ruth's college.'

That figures, thinks Tanya.

'Ivor, Leonard and Bob used to live together at Grey Walls,' says Nelson. 'At nights they would go out in a van "saving young women".' He puts caustic quotation marks around the phrase. 'They may well have "saved" Sofia Novak, who could be the third body found in the garden of the Jolly

Boatman. Crissy Martin also mentioned someone called the Lantern Man. She says he was responsible for the murders.'

'Why didn't I know about this?' says Judy. Definitely pissed off now.

'Crissy just told Ruth at the weekend,' says Nelson, 'but it's all bollocks. She couldn't give a name or a description. Crissy just wants March to be released and that's not going to happen.'

'Did this Larry Hanson say anything useful about the barbecue?' says Tanya. She wants to remind everyone that she's in charge of this meeting.

'He said that Ivor and Jenny spent a lot of time together and that Chantal was jealous.'

'Did he say anything about Heidi?'

'No, he hardly remembered her. Said that she seemed to talk mostly to Ailsa and Crissy.'

They all look at the projection of the group on the beach. The faces are indistinct but the sky behind them is dark blue, the tide is out and the sand is in bands of brown and yellow. The bonfire is bright in the foreground, casting what seem like ominous shadows across the faces of Jenny and Heidi.

Someone speaks. Nelson looks round in surprise. Tanya has to check twice before she realises who it is. PC Roy 'Rocky' Taylor, a man who, according to Clough, needs to be watered twice a week.

'Who took the photograph?' he says.

CHAPTER 22

Early the next morning DC Bradley Linwood is walking across the marshes at Cley. A line of crime-scene investigators moves slowly towards him. They have organised a fingertip search of the place where Heidi Lucas's body was found. It's difficult because the land's uneven and there are little streams everywhere but DCI Nelson is convinced that there is more to find. The scene hasn't yielded much so far. They haven't even found Heidi's phone. According to the CSIs, the victim was killed elsewhere and her body deposited on the footpath. But forensics can't tell them why. They never can, in Bradley's opinion.

He's glad to be working on this case though. It's a chance to prove himself and he's grateful to Tanya for picking him as her number two. 'She fancies you,' say his friends in the pub. 'She's gay,' Bradley told them, but that only made them worse. He had tried flirting with Tanya, in an experimental way, when he first joined the team, but he was rather glad when he found out about Petra and realised that he could stop. But he needs to impress her on this case. He got his promotion after being first on the scene when a woman priest was murdered in the grounds of Walsingham Priory a few years ago. Since then he feels that he's been treading water. What he needs is a breakthrough. He realises that Mike Halloran, the leading crime scene investigator, is waving at him. Thank you, God. Or thanks to whatever gods are in charge. He once had a chat with that druid husband of Judy's and now he's not sure what he believes, if anything.

'Have you found something, Mike?'

In answer Mike holds out something in a plastic evidence bag. Bradley sees a glint of orange.

'What is it?'

'It's a badge,' says Mike. 'A child's badge.'

Bradley looks closer and sees a grinning pumpkin head.

'Where did you find it?'

'About fifty metres away,' says Mike. 'It could be nothing but could be linked to the scene. It's possible that a bird picked it up and then dropped it again. Gulls are attracted to shiny objects.'

'It's a Hallowe'en badge, isn't it?' says Bradley.

'Jack O'Lantern,' says Mike.

The name sparks a memory. DCI Nelson talking about Ivor March. Apparently he'd been part of a gang who'd called themselves the Lantern Men. Bradley gets out his phone and a few googles takes him from Jack O'Lantern to will-o'-the-wisps to lantern men.

Satan mockingly tossed him a burning coal which he put in a pumpkin to light his way as he endlessly wandered the earth looking for a resting place . . .

He dials Tanya's number. 'Ma'am, I think we've got something.'

'It could be nothing,' says Nelson. But it's obvious from his expression that he doesn't think so.

They are all crowded into the briefing room. Judy's team, Tanya's team and the sundry experts who make up the investigation: crime-scene investigators, civilian analysts, data specialists.

Tanya takes her time describing the find, enjoying the fact that everyone is looking at her and a few people are taking notes. But she gives full credit to DC Linwood and the search team. She's not a monster, whatever Judy thinks.

'Let's not get too excited,' says Nelson, looking angrier than ever, which for him counts as excited. 'Someone could just have dropped it.'

'It's May,' says Tanya, trying, not entirely successfully, for a neutral tone. 'Why would anyone be wearing a Hallowe'en badge in May?'

Nelson doesn't answer, which Tanya takes as acceptance of her point. She turns to Mike Halloran.

'Mike, can you tell us where the badge was found?'

Mike speaks from his seat. 'It was in the long grass about fifty metres away from the place where Heidi's body was found. It's possible, though, that it was left at the scene and picked up by a bird. Gulls, like magpies, are attracted to shiny objects. The bird would have soon realised that the badge was inedible and dropped it. It's hard to see, otherwise, why it ended up so far from the path.'

'And you're pretty sure that Heidi wasn't killed at the scene?' says Nelson, speaking across Tanya in what she considers to be a rather impolite way.

'Yes,' says Mike, 'the ground wasn't disturbed and her body was lying on the grass as if it had been placed there. No soil or grass on her shoes.'

'So someone transported Heidi and her bike to the middle of the marshes and left them there?' says Nelson.

'That's what it looks like,' says Tanya. She goes back to her notes. 'Death was by manual strangulation. The pathologist thought she had been grabbed from behind. The finger-marks were indicative of this. No sexual assault and her clothes weren't disturbed.'

'Heidi wasn't wearing her helmet,' says Nelson. 'I remember that her hair was loose.'

'She was wearing it when she was spotted on the bike in Lynn earlier,' says Tanya. 'The killer must have taken it, along with her mobile phone.'

'That could suggest that the killer is attracted to women with long blonde hair,' says Judy. 'He may have arranged her hair deliberately. I've seen the pictures. It was fanned out on the grass, almost like a photo shoot.'

'March killed women with long, blonde hair,' says someone.

'Except Sofia Novak,' says Nelson. 'If the third body at the pub is hers.'

'Even so,' says Judy. 'There are definite similarities, the victim's physiology, the marshland setting. And then there's the badge. That's a clear reference to the lantern men.'

'It's *possible*,' says Nelson, stressing the word. 'Lighted pumpkins are sometimes linked to the legend of the lantern men.'

'And Jenny wrote a story called "The Lantern Men",' says Judy.

This is news to Tanya. She wants to bring the conversation back to Heidi. After all, they know who killed Jenny McGuire. Now they have to find out who murdered Heidi Lucas. For her family's sake, she tells herself.

'We need to talk to everyone who was at that barbecue,' she says. 'That's the link between Heidi and Ivor March. Judy,' she turns graciously to her colleague, 'maybe you should talk to Bob Carr and Leonard Jenkins, as you know them.'

'What about Chantal?' says Judy. She doesn't look delighted to be given an assignment by Tanya. 'She hates us both.'

'You talk to Chantal,' says Tanya. 'I'll take Crissy and the gardener bloke. Someone must know something.'

Ruth is staring at her computer screen, on which two rather annoying emails are displayed. The first is from the tenants of her cottage saying that for 'personal reasons', they will have to leave immediately, three months before their lease is up. The second is a group message from Shona containing a picture of Phil in his hospital bed giving the thumbs up sign.

Ruth sighs. The rental thing is a pain because it means that she'll have to get new tenants and it's difficult finding anyone interested in a rather shabby cottage on the edge of a lonely marsh. The second email just makes her feel guilty. She should have rung Shona. She should have visited Phil. She decides that she can rectify the first omission.

'Hi, Shona. Is this a good time?'

'Yes, fine,' says Shona, sounding really pleased to hear from her, which makes Ruth feel even worse. 'I'm at the gym.'

'Really?' Guilt is now pouring off Ruth, or maybe it's just a hot flush. She used to be a member of a gym and used it ten times in ten years, which amounts to almost five hundred pounds a swim. Since moving to Cambridge, she hasn't bothered to join another. Her only exercise is walking and the occasional swims with Kate.

'I was just wondering how Phil was.'

'Really good,' says Shona, panting in a rather off-putting way. 'He's on the normal ward now and he might even come home at the weekend. In a way this heart attack has been a wake-up call. Phil's determined to take things easier, not to work so hard, to eat more healthily and to take more exercise. We're going to go on a yoga retreat together.'

'Sounds great.' It's news to Ruth that Phil has ever worked too hard but she's pleased that he's on the road to recovery.

'Give him my best,' she says. 'Give him my love' would be overdoing it. 'I'll try to pop in and see him one day this week.'

'Please do,' says Shona. 'He's getting so bored. I think that's a good sign, don't you?'

'Definitely. Shona?'

'Yes.' More panting.

'Do you know where Phil kept his notes on the excavations at Ivor March's girlfriend's house? Were they on the laptop that got stolen?'

'Yes, I'm afraid they were,' says Shona. 'Why?'

'I just wanted to check something. I've read Phil's report. I just wondered if there was anything else in his notes.'

'I suppose they might have been stored to the Cloud. Shall I check?'

'If you've got a moment that would be great,' says Ruth. 'I'd better let you get on with your exercise now.'

'OK,' says Shona. 'Ciao.' Ruth can hear her feet pounding on the treadmill.

'Judy,' says Nelson. 'Can I have a word?'

He can tell Judy is angry with him. Her face is expressionless but he doesn't have two older sisters for nothing. Judy follows him into his office and sits down, carefully crossing her legs and her arms.

'I'm sorry I didn't tell you about Larry Hanson,' he says. 'When Ruth told me about him, I just rushed straight over.'

Judy's reaction tells him two things. One, he has clearly never apologised to her before. Two, she hasn't forgotten something he told her two years ago about his feelings for Ruth.

'That's OK,' she says. 'Do you really think that there's a link between the Grey Walls lot and Heidi?'

'It's possible. Look at the people who were there. Ivor, Bob, Leonard, Ailsa, Chantal and Crissy.'

'God, what a cast list.'

'Yeah. The party from hell. See what you can get from Bob and Leonard.'

'I will.'

'What do you think about Leonard Jenkins? There's a link with Heidi through the cycling club.'

'I'm keeping an open mind,' says Judy, 'but I can't see it. I mean, he's a teacher. I know ...' She sees that Nelson is about to speak. 'Never assume and all that. But I can't see why Leonard would kill Heidi. I mean, he can't have been obsessed with her. He's gay, for one thing.'

'He was married to Ailsa though. Sometimes these things are complicated.'

'I know. There could be a work link as well. Heidi was a teacher. Nicola Ferris too.'

'That's a possibility,' says Nelson. Judy is silent for a minute and he knows that she is thinking. He also thinks he knows what she's going to say next and he wishes that he could stop her.

'Boss? What if Ivor March is innocent?'

'You're kidding.' Nelson tries for bluster. 'Has Cathbad got to you at last?'

Judy colours. 'No, of course not. He just had a feeling, a presentiment, when we excavated Nicola and Jenny. But this last death has made me think. Whatever you say, Heidi's murder does look like the others. And there's the badge too. The link to the lantern men legend. And now Crissy's talking about some mysterious fourth man. Is it possible that someone else has been responsible for the killings all along?'

'No,' says Nelson. 'Ivor March killed Stacy, Jill, Nicola and Jenny. Sofia Novak too.'

'But how can you be sure?'

'Look, Judy,' Nelson tries for an understanding tone. 'This case has put a lot of strain on you –'

'Don't try that one on me,' says Judy, sounding rather less than respectful to a senior officer. 'I'm not cracking up. I'm just keeping an open mind, the way *you've* always taught me. Four women are killed, maybe five. A man is put in jail. Then another woman is killed in the same way. You're the one who says that you don't believe in coincidence.'

'It's not a coincidence,' says Nelson. 'That's what worries me.'

'You mean it might be a copycat?'

'It worries me how many people know about the lantern men thing,' says Nelson. 'Jenny McGuire even wrote a story about it. John Robertson tells those stories to everyone who comes to Grey Walls. It wouldn't be difficult for someone to stage this killing so that it looks like one of March's.'

'But why?' says Judy. She no longer sounds resentful, she just sounds as if she wants to know.

'So that we'd think that he was innocent,' says Nelson.

'Who would do that?' says Judy. But Nelson can think of several names. He's pretty sure that Judy can too.

When Ruth gets home, she finds that she has another athletic visitor. Laura's bike is propped against the garden wall and Laura herself is on the sofa with Kate watching a Nickelodeon series about a teenage girl who inexplicably runs a Hollywood studio.

'Laura's here,' says Kate.

It's unnecessary information but Ruth is always glad to see the sisters together. For years they were unaware of each other's existence and the revelation was painful in the extreme, but the upshot is that Kate has gained two adored older siblings. Laura, in particular, is very fond of Kate and often takes her out for thrilling jaunts to sacred places like Topshop or the Silver Shoes Bowling Alley.

'I saw your bike outside,' says Ruth. 'Don't say you cycled all the way from Lynn?'

'No,' says Laura, 'but I'd love to do it one day. It's a lovely ride along the Long Causeway. I left my car at the station and cycled over here. It's the only way to get around in Cambridge.'

'You're right there,' says Ruth. 'I live in dread of running over a cyclist one day.'

'You call them rude names,' says Kate primly.

'Only sometimes,' says Ruth. 'Do you want anything, Laura? Tea? Cold drink? Can you stay for supper?'

'Frank's making me some tea,' says Laura. 'And I can't stay to supper, I'm afraid. I just popped in to see Kate and to give you this.'

She hands Ruth a flyer with the word 'Sportive' printed in large green letters.

'It's a bike race,' explains Laura. 'This Saturday, along the coast. Titchwell, Wells, Stiffkey, Blakeney, the Saltmarsh. I was wondering if you might like to come and cheer me on. My first race. Twenty-five miles. I'm very nervous.'

Frank comes into the room with two mugs of tea. He gives one to Laura and hands the other to Ruth.

'What do you think, honey?' he says. 'Might be fun.'

'Please can we go?' says Kate. She's not bothered about bikes, she would plead for anything if it meant spending time with Laura. But Ruth has already decided that they will go. She decided the moment that Laura mentioned the Saltmarsh.

CHAPTER 23

This time Judy and Tony meet Leonard before school and their welcome is markedly less warm.

'This is bordering on harassment,' says Leonard. They are in his office in the art department and he is very much in teacher mode, packing blue notebooks that look like reports into his bag.

'It's just a few questions,' says Judy, sitting down to show that, nevertheless, the questions are serious. 'I wanted to ask you about Lynn Wheels.'

'What?' A very teachery eyebrow raise.

'Are you a member of a cycling club called Lynn Wheels?'

'Yes, I am,' says Leonard and his eye flickers towards the cycling helmet on his desk.

'How often do you go there?' she asks.

'Most weeks. It's a nice way to relax after work.'

Judy can't see what's so relaxing about cycling for miles but she always envies people who have hobbies. She really ought to get one.

'Heidi Lucas, the woman who was murdered last week, was also a member of the club. Did you know her?'

Judy pushes a picture of Heidi across the desk. Leonard picks it up and examines it, squinting behind his black-framed glasses.

'I think I recognise her,' he says. 'I don't really know the younger members.'

'Heidi was a teacher at Byways Comprehensive. That's quite near here. Did you ever meet her at a training course or something like that?'

'What did she teach?'

'PE.'

'I'm unlikely to have met her then.' There's a slight sneer in his voice and Judy remembers the way other teachers always seem to look down on the sports staff, perhaps because they wear their tracksuits all day long.

She gets out the photograph of the barbecue and the bonfire.

'Do you remember this evening?' she says. 'July the fourth last year.'

Leonard adjusts his glasses as if this will help him answer the question. Judy waits.

'Is that Heidi Lucas in the front of the picture?' she says at last.

'I think so. Yes.'

'Several people say that you brought Heidi to the barbecue. That she was your guest.'

'I . . . I may have done.'

'You may have done?'

Another silence. 'She was very pretty,' says Tony.

Leonard turns on him. 'What are you trying to imply? That I was interested in Heidi? Is that how you think it was?'

'Why don't you tell us how it was?' says Judy.

Leonard takes off his glasses and rubs them. 'I liked Heidi,' he says at last. 'She was interesting and intelligent. I thought that she'd like the group.'

'The group? You told us that you weren't in touch with Ivor March.'

'I said I hadn't been in touch since he was convicted of murdering those girls.'

That might be true but Judy had the distinct impression, from their earlier interview, that Leonard hadn't seen Ivor for years. She will have to check her notes.

'What about Jenny? Did you know her too?'

'I only met her that once. She was one of Ivor's students. Seemed a nice woman. I was very shocked when she . . . when she disappeared.'

'She was murdered,' says Judy. 'Her body has been found.' It's in today's papers including a piece in the *Chronicle* by Maddie entitled, 'The lost girls of the marshes'.

'Heidi was murdered too,' she continues. 'Two of the women in that picture are dead. You can see why we're interested in your Independence Day party.'

Leonard rubs his eyes. 'I can't believe that anyone in the group would . . .' He stops.

'What where you doing on Thursday night?' asks Judy.

'I was at home with my husband.'

'What time did you get home?'

'About six. I was invigilating a GCSE art exam so it was a bit later than usual.'

'Did you go out again after that?'

'No.'

Heidi was still alive at eight thirty so this, theoretically, puts Leonard in the clear. Judy gets out her phone and finds the picture of the pumpkin badge.

'Have you see this before?'

'What is it?' Leonard peers closer. 'It's a child's badge, isn't it?'

Judy repeats, 'Have you seen a badge like this before?'

'I don't know. Maybe at Hallowe'en. The students here wear all sorts of stuff on their blazers. It's a kind of fashion. Why are you asking me?'

Judy doesn't answer. Leonard didn't seem to react to the Jack O'Lantern with anything other than bemusement but he could be a good actor. The best teachers usually are.

'Tell us about the barbecue,' she says.

'Ivor spent a lot of time with Jenny,' says Leonard. His voice is different now, dreamy and reflective. 'They were sitting on the beach a little way from the rest of us. I don't think Chantal was too happy about it. I saw Chantal talking to Bob and then Bob went over to try to break them up but Ivor and Jenny stayed there chatting until it was almost dark. As we walked back I could hear Ivor and Chantal arguing.'

Having been on the receiving end of Chantal's anger a few times, Judy is sure that she wouldn't have held back. But, a few months later, Chantal Simmonds was passionately defending her partner against the charge of murdering two women. Women who were later found buried in her garden.

'What about Heidi?' says Judy. 'Who was she talking to?'

'Ailsa, I think. I remember that they went down to the sea shore to paddle. It was a warm evening.'

'What were you doing when all this was going on?' she asks.

'What do men always do at barbecues? I was cooking the meat.'

Judy has a sudden craving for barbecued ribs. She wonders how many of the Grey Walls set were vegetarians like Cathbad. Maybe cooking the meat wasn't such a time-consuming job after all.

'Did you see Heidi again after the barbecue?' she says.

'Just at the cycle club. Oh, I think I had a drink with her and her boyfriend once.'

'Why wasn't Josh, the boyfriend, invited to the barbecue?' asks Judy. 'Wasn't he "interesting and intelligent" too?'

'No he wasn't,' says Leonard coolly. 'I found him rather dull, since you ask.'

Is it really that simple, thinks Judy. The boss always thinks the worst of everyone but could he be right and was Leonard somehow offering Heidi to Ivor March? But March had spent the whole evening talking to Jenny McGuire.

'One last question,' she says. 'Who took the photo?'

'The photo? Oh . . . that was Miles. My husband.'

Judy wonders if he's lying.

As they descend the stairs, the students start swarming

upwards. They seem impossibly loud, their feet thundering on the stone steps. Judy could never be a teacher.

In the playground Judy gets a message from the forensic dentist.

The third body is definitely that of Sofia Novak.

Ruth doesn't like hospitals. Still, she tells herself, as she negotiates the labyrinthine parking system at the Queen Elizabeth, she doesn't suppose anyone really *loves* them. But the last few years have had their share of medical trauma: first Nelson nearly dying in this very hospital, then Ruth's mother actually dying in London, then Ruth and Cathbad's near-fatal car crash. Just the smell, a potent mix of antiseptic, instant coffee and hand sanitiser, has the power to make Ruth feel slightly sick. She tries to ignore it and sets off along the endless corridors in search of Phil's ward.

Her ex-boss is sitting up in bed doing the *Guardian* crossword. Just the quick one, Ruth is relieved to notice. She can do the quick crossword in fifteen minutes but the cryptic is still beyond her. Frank often suggests that they do *The Times* cryptic together on a Saturday but something in Ruth shies away from that kind of intimacy. She's happy to sleep with Frank but solve two down (*Teach about swindler (5)*)? No, it's too much. Besides, he's better at it than her.

'Ruth!' says Phil sounding genuinely pleased. 'Shona said that you might come.'

'How are you?' says Ruth.

'Better,' says Phil. 'Feeling pretty bored, to tell you the

truth. I've got a TV but it only seems to show *Antiques Roadshow*.'

Ruth glances along the ward, where every TV seems to show the same cracked Toby jug. 'I've brought you a book,' she says. She's brought him an Ian Rankin hardback, one that she wants for herself. She realises that she has no idea what sort of books Phil reads, if any.

'Thank you,' he says. 'I don't normally read crime fiction.' A black mark to him, in Ruth's opinion.

'Shona says that you might be home at the weekend,' she says.

'I hope so,' says Phil. 'I'm really missing Shona and Louis.' He looks quite human, sitting there in his striped pyjamas, with his red-rimmed specs on top of his head. Ruth feels quite warmly towards him, even though she notes that he rarely mentions missing his two sons by his first wife.

'At least term is nearly over,' she says. 'You can have a proper rest over the summer.'

'Yes,' says Phil. He picks up the Rebus book and seems absorbed in the cover. Then he says, 'I'm not sure I'll be going back.'

'What do you mean?' asks Ruth.

'This was a wake-up call,' says Phil, putting the book down. 'I'm fifty-five, Ruth. I don't want to die in my office looking at paperwork. I've got twenty, thirty more years to spend with my nearest and dearest. I want to travel, walk the Inca trail, go to a full moon party in Thailand, see the sun rise over the pyramids. I want to write a book.'

Several thoughts rush into Ruth's head. Phil is fifty-five?

He must dye his hair. His travel plan sounds a bit like a belated gap year. She imagines that full moon parties are full of drunk eighteen-year-olds marking the transition from public school to Russell Group university. She can't see Phil scaling Machu Picchu, he often complains about the non-existent hills in Norfolk. And has Phil forgotten that he has a school-age son? What will Louis be doing while his father is watching the sun rise in Egypt? Plus, Nelson is right. Why is everyone writing a book?

But, then, crowding out these rather mean-minded reflections, is this thought: there will be a vacancy for Head of Archaeology at UNN. Is this what Cathbad meant about the attack on Phil having repercussions?

Phil is looking at her shrewdly but not without affection. 'You should go for it, Ruth,' he says, as if she has spoken the thought aloud. 'You're a really good archaeologist. A good leader too.'

'I only moved to Cambridge a couple of years ago,' says Ruth.

'But your heart is still here,' says Phil. 'Isn't it?'

Bob Carr is friendly but slightly on the defensive, Judy thinks. He has two students working in his studio. They are busy dabbing a waxy substance onto sheets of metal and hardly look up when Judy and Tony enter.

'Can we talk in private?' asks Judy.

'Of course,' says Bob. 'Sara and Jo are just applying hard-ground before they draw out their designs prior to exposing the plates to the corroding medium.' It's a whole other language.

They climb the wooden stairs to the psychedelic apartment. Bob makes coffee in the candy-striped cafetière. Judy drinks gratefully. Leonard had hardly been in the mood to offer refreshments.

'Do you remember this?' Judy shows him the photograph. 'It was taken in July last year.'

Bob smooths out the photocopy. His hands are stained with ink so he is careful only to touch the edges.

'It was a lovely evening,' he says. 'The tide was out and the sand stretched for miles.'

'Do you recognise these women?' Judy points. She's not in the mood for reflections on the beauties of Norfolk. She gets enough of that at home.

'That's Jenny,' says Bob. 'Oh dear.' He rubs his eyes with an inky hand.

'And the other woman at the front?'

'I can't remember her name but she came with Leonard. A sweet girl, as I remember.'

'That's Heidi Lucas. She was murdered last week.'

'Oh dear,' says Bob again. His hands are shaking slightly.

'We're interested in anything that you can remember about the barbecue. Who was Jenny talking to, for example?'

'I think she talked to Ivor for a while. And to Ailsa and Crissy.'

'We've heard that she talked to Ivor for a long time and that Chantal Simmonds was angry about it.'

'Chantal's a lovely woman.' It's the first time that Judy

has seen Bob look annoyed. 'She and Ivor had the perfect relationship. She's above petty jealousy.'

'So you didn't go over to try to break up Ivor and Jenny?'

'I may have gone over just to chat to them. I certainly wasn't trying to break anything up. It was a perfectly happy evening, Detective Inspector.'

Lovely, perfect, happy. Judy finds Bob's adjectives interesting, especially in the light of what came later.

'What about Heidi? Do you remember who she spent time with?'

'She collected driftwood with John and I remember her going to the water's edge with Ailsa. They made quite a picture, silhouetted there. I wished I'd brought my sketchbook.'

'What about Leonard? Did he spend much time with Heidi? After all, she was his guest.'

'Leonard spent most of his time cooking. He always makes such a production out of it.' A definite note of sourness there. 'Miles was running around being his commis chef.'

'Miles? Leonard's husband?'

'Yes. He always tags along to these things.'

An interesting way of putting it, thinks Judy. She gets out copies of the other photographs.

'Do you remember these being taken?'

'No, but people take so many photos these days.'

People take photos on their mobile phones, thinks Judy, but the interesting thing about these is that they were printed out, annotated, preserved.

'Who's the fourth man in this picture?'

'Larry something,' says Bob. 'He came to Grey Walls a couple of times. A good man. A simple soul.'

'What about this picture? You and Leonard with Crissy. You're both looking at her very affectionately.'

'Everyone loves Crissy,' says Bob. 'I love her, Leonard loves her, John loves her. Ivor never stopped loving her.'

'Even though he had a perfect relationship with Chantal?' says Tony.

'Love is complicated,' says Bob. 'You'll find that out one day.'

'One last thing.' Judy shows the pumpkin badge on her phone. 'Do you recognise this?'

'A Jack O'Lantern,' says Bob immediately. 'It's an interesting legend. Linked to the lantern men, of course.'

'So we've heard,' says Judy.

'I've done a few prints of the lantern men,' says Bob. 'They're for sale downstairs.'

'We'll have a look on our way out,' says Judy. She's certainly not going to part with hard cash for one of Bob Carr's etchings.

As they descend the stairs she asks Bob where he was on the evening of last Thursday.

'Here,' says Bob. 'Where I always am.'

'On your own?'

'Chantal dropped in around eight. We had a lovely chat.'

Nelson is in his office when there's a knock on the door. No, not a knock, more of a whimsical tattoo, an irritating series of tiny taps.

'Come in,' he barks.

'It's only me,' sings a light soprano.

He might have guessed. Madge Hudson, supposed expert on criminal profiling. He's willing to bet that he has Super-intendent Archer to thank for this visitation.

Sure enough. 'Jo suggested that I pop in to have a chat about Ivor March.'

'Very kind of you.'

Madge takes the seat opposite. She's a tall woman, usually trailing scarves and shawls. It's as if she has a tail, like a dragon. She disentangles a piece of gauze from the arm of the chair and smiles at Nelson.

Or a crocodile.

'I understand that Ivor has disclosed where the bodies are buried.' 'Disclosed' is a very Madge word and she is always on first-name terms with suspects.

'He told us where to dig, yes.'

'He asked for Dr Ruth Galloway by name, I hear.'

'That's right,' says Nelson, keeping his face expression-less.

'Why do you think he did that?'

It's always a danger signal when Madge starts asking ques-tions, especially with her head on one side like this.

Nelson says, still not cracking a smile, 'I assume it's because Dr Galloway is the best in her field.' There's a joke there somewhere (Ruth often seems to spend her time dig-ging up fields) but he's not going to attempt it. Madge would only think it was a deflection tactic anyway.

'Or because he thinks that Ruth is a way to get at you.'

'I'm not sure I follow.'

'Ivor knows you're close to Ruth. This is a way of manipulating you.'

Nelson wonders what she means by 'close'. Does Madge know about him and Ruth? He wouldn't put it past Jo to tell her.

'What did Ivor say when you asked him about the bodies Ruth excavated?' asks Madge, head so far to the side that a dangling earring gets caught in her scarf.

'He said that he was like Jesus on the cross, abandoned by his followers.'

'That's very significant,' says Madge, untangling herself. 'It means he has a god complex.'

You don't say, thinks Nelson.

'And a saviour complex too. Didn't he say that he was saving these women?'

Jo had briefed her well. Nelson is rather impressed.

'Yes. Apparently March and his friends went out in a van picking up women and supposedly saving them. I think one of those women is buried in the pub garden.'

'The Jesus thing is interesting,' says Madge. 'Jesus sacrificed himself for his followers, didn't he?'

He sacrificed himself for all mankind, thinks Nelson, remembering catechism lessons at his old school, St Joseph's, or Holy Joe's as it was known locally. Jesus died on the cross so that we could be freed from original sin and ascend to heaven. The gates of purgatory were opened.

'So . . .' Madge fixes him with an unusually direct look. 'Who is he saving this time?'

'What do you mean?'

'Ivor asked Ruth to excavate. As you say, she's the best in the business. Ivor must have known that she'd find the bodies. He's always professed his innocence and now, by telling you where to find the victims, he seems to be admitting his guilt. Why would he do that?'

'You tell me,' says Nelson. But, in fact, this question has been niggling at him for days. He thinks of Tanya saying, 'But he hasn't confessed, has he?', of Ruth asking if March really was a serial killer, even of Cathbad's lunatic belief that March is innocent.

'There are two possibilities,' says Madge. And somehow she seems more solid and less floaty. She crosses her arms in a businesslike way. 'One, March is guilty but he wants to confess. That could account for the religious imagery too. Well, I don't need to tell you about confession, do I?'

Nelson stares at her stonily. He regrets ever telling Madge that he was brought up as a Catholic.

'So one possibility is that he wants to confess but he wants to do it in the showiest way possible, hence calling Ruth in. He enjoys a drama, he likes to take centre stage. He might even think that it would embarrass you, having a woman come up with the conclusive evidence, especially a woman that you're . . . well, close to. Another possibility is that he's innocent but he's protecting someone.'

'Who?' says Nelson, really wanting to know what her answer will be.

'Someone he loves, of course,' says Madge, head on one side again.

CHAPTER 24

Tanya arrives at Grey Walls to find Crissy Martin leading a meditation session. It's quite embarrassing, the front door is open so Tanya and Bradley walk straight in to find four women lying on their backs on the sitting room floor, slowly waving their legs in the air. Tanya hesitates in the doorway, assailed by whale music and the scent of patchouli oil.

Crissy is sitting cross-legged at the front. Her eyes are closed. Tanya clears her throat.

'I'll be with you in a second, Detective Sergeant,' says Crissy.

Tanya wonders how the hell Crissy identified her so easily. They have met before, of course, when Tanya interviewed Crissy but, even so, it's quite something to recognise a person with your eyes shut. She got her rank right too.

Crissy takes her time winding up the session. The women are told to imagine their bodies filling with light and then to feel their earthly bonds breaking and their souls floating up into the ether. 'You will leave your corporeal worries behind you. How small they look from the heavens.' Tanya knows that Bradley is trying not to laugh. She just feels deeply irritated.

When the women have floated out of the room Crissy offers herbal tea or water. Tanya doesn't drink caffeine but she has a sudden compulsion to ask for a double espresso. They both ask for water. It's another hot day and Bradley's air conditioning wasn't working on the drive over. Crissy fetches a jug and glasses and leads the way onto the veranda.

'We won't be interrupted here. The clients are working in their rooms.'

'Are they all writers?' asks Tanya.

'This group are but the retreats are open to anyone who requires spiritual refreshment.'

'How much does a retreat cost?'

Crissy tells her and Tanya rapidly changes her opinion of the guests from 'mugs' to 'mugs with money'. Judy told her that Ruth had spent a week here. Who knew that archaeology was so lucrative?

'I wanted to ask you about this photograph.' Tanya puts her photocopy down on the wicker table. Crissy puts on a pair of gold half-moon spectacles to look at it. Tanya wouldn't be surprised to find out that they were plain glass.

'We believe this was taken in July last year,' says Tanya. 'Do you remember the event?'

'I think so,' says Crissy. 'We've had many evening gatherings on the beach.'

'Can you remember anything about this specific evening?

This woman, for example.' Tanya points at Heidi. 'Do you remember her?'

'Yes, she came with Len, I think. A lovely girl. She had a beautiful aura.'

'That's Heidi Lucas, who was murdered last week,' says Tanya. 'So you can understand why we're anxious to speak to anyone who knew her.'

'I didn't realise . . .' Crissy looks shaken now. She raises her hand to her hair and Tanya notices the liver spots on the back on it. An old woman's hand. 'I don't think I ever knew her name. I never realised that this was the girl . . .'

'Can you remember anything that Heidi did at the barbecue? Who did she speak to? Who did she spend time with?'

'She talked to Ailsa. I remember them walking down to the sea to immerse their feet in the water.' Tanya supposes that 'paddling' is too mundane a word for Crissy Martin. 'Heidi talked to me too. She'd spent some time in Germany, which is where I lived as a girl. We discussed the Black Forest and its legends.'

'Speaking of legends, you talked to Dr Ruth Galloway about the Lantern Man. You said that he killed Heidi Lucas.'

'I spoke to Ruth in confidence.' Crissy is definitely rattled now.

'There are no secrets in a murder inquiry,' says Tanya. 'Do you know who this Lantern Man is?'

'No,' says Crissy. 'That's the whole point. Ivor himself didn't know his name or anything about him.'

A likely story, thinks Tanya. She points again at the photograph. 'What about Jenny McGuire? She was there that day too. Can you remember anything about her?'

'She talked to Ivor for a while. She was one of his creative writing students. Like Ailsa. I think they were discussing a short story she had written.'

'Was that the story called "The Lantern Men"?'

'I don't know,' says Crissy. 'I don't teach creative writing. I just provide a safe space so that others can create.'

'Did you see Heidi again after the barbecue?'

'No. I told you, I didn't even know her name. It's so sad. She seemed a lovely soul.'

'You're very close to Leonard Jenkins and Bob Carr, aren't you?'

'I used to be.' Crissy folds her hands in her lap, serenity restored. Tanya thinks that she detects a note of complacency in her voice. She produces the picture of Crissy with the two men. 'Do you remember this picture being taken?'

'Yes, it was the same evening.'

'They're looking at you very admiringly.'

'We were very close once,' says Crissy. 'This was an enchanted place. We lived here so happily, me, Ivor, Bob and Leonard. Even now, it makes me happy to think of those days.'

Tanya notes that Ailsa Britain is not in this list. She thinks that Crissy is the sort of woman who only values admiration when it comes from men. This is even true of some gay women, in Tanya's experience.

She shows Crissy a photograph of the pumpkin badge.

'Do you recognise this?'

'It's a Hallowe'en thing, isn't it? I don't like Hallowe'en as a holiday. Why dwell on the darkness in life?'

Don't ask me, thinks Tanya. You're the one who was married to a serial killer.

'Have you seen a badge like this before?'

'Maybe. Hallowe'en is so commercialised. It's the kind of thing children wear, isn't it? Do you have children, Detective Sergeant?'

'No.'

'Nor do I. It's a sadness in my life.'

Tanya doesn't think that she can stand much more of this. She says, 'I won't take up any more of your time. John Robertson works here, doesn't he? Is it possible to talk to him?'

'Why?'

Tanya feels like telling Crissy to mind her own business but she says, 'We're anxious to interview everyone who was at the barbecue on July the fourth last year.'

'It's John's day off,' says Crissy. 'I think he's gone to visit his brother in Yarmouth.'

At first, Chantal Simmonds refuses to let Judy in.

'You've interviewed me about a hundred times already. I've got nothing else to say.'

'New evidence has come to light,' says Judy.

Chantal looks past her to Tony. 'This is a new face,' she says, rather rudely in Judy's opinion.

But Tony gives Chantal his best smile. 'Hi. I'm Tony Zhang. Pleased to meet you.'

Somehow this gets Judy and Tony over the threshold and into the sitting room. Chantal's cat purrs at them from the sofa.

'She sheds,' she warns Tony, who goes to stroke the animal.

'I don't mind,' says Tony. 'I love cats.'

Tony is definitely proving to be an asset. Chantal brushes imaginary cat hair off her black skirt. As usual, she is dressed rather formally: pencil skirt, silk blouse, high heels.

'What's all this about?' she says, when they take their seats opposite her, on either side of the cat.

Judy hands over the photograph. 'Do you remember this being taken?'

Chantal examines the picture for some time. Her nails are perfect too, shiny and red. 'No,' she says at last, 'I can't say I do.'

'It was at a barbecue on Cley beach on July the fourth last year. Is that you next to Ivor?'

'It's not a good one of me.'

'But it is you?'

A shrug. 'Yes.'

'You told me several times that you'd never met Jenny McGuire but she was there, at the barbecue, with you.'

'I must have forgotten,' says Chantal. 'She was rather forgettable.'

'I've heard that she spent the evening deep in conversation with Ivor.'

Chantal's face is immobile but her nostrils flare slightly. 'Who told you that? Bob? Leonard?'

'Both of them.'

'They were probably jealous. They both adored Ivor. Lots of repressed homosexuality in that group.'

There's little trace here of the lovely person and perfect relationship described by Bob Carr.

'Leonard also said that you and Ivor argued that night. Was it about Jenny?'

'We didn't argue,' says Chantal. 'We never argued.'

'Do you know this man?' Judy points. 'Larry Hanson?'

'I met him a few times,' says Chantal. 'He was a potter, I think.'

'What about this woman?' Judy points. 'Do you remember meeting her?'

'Not really. She was another forgettable one.'

'That's Heidi Lucas. The woman who was found dead on Cley Marsh last week.'

'Are you going to try and pin this one on Ivor too?' says Chantal. 'Well, good luck with that.'

'What were you doing last Thursday night, Chantal?'

Chantal examines her nails. 'I was here. On my own. As usual.'

'Funny, Bob Carr says you popped in to see him.'

'That's right.' Chantal meets Judy's eyes without embarrassment. 'I was in Holt seeing some friends so I dropped in on Bob on my way home. We talked about Ivor.'

'What time was this?'

'About seven thirty or eight.'

'Which?'

'Eight.'

So, in theory, it would be possible for Chantal to have had a lovely chat about Ivor and still have killed Heidi. Unlikely though, Judy has to admit.

Judy holds out her phone showing the Jack O'Lantern badge.

'Have you seen this before?'

Chantal takes the phone and enlarges the picture.

'I don't think so,' she says. 'Why?'

Judy doesn't answer. They don't want the whereabouts of the badge to become public knowledge. Nobody seems to have reacted with horror at the sight of the pumpkin but maybe this too is only to be expected.

'You've heard that we found Jenny and Nicola's bodies,' says Judy.

'I'd heard,' says Chantal. 'I heard there was a third body too.'

This news hasn't been made public but Judy isn't surprised that Chantal knows. The boss saw Ivor March on Saturday. It's Wednesday now. Chantal will have had plenty of time to communicate with her boyfriend. At any rate, Judy can't see any point in denying it.

'We haven't had a formal identification yet,' she says, which is technically true. She hasn't updated the files yet. Judy watches Chantal closely as she says this. As ever, Chantal is hard to read but Judy thinks that she can see several emotions crossing the carefully made-up face. And the strongest of these is anger.

The evening briefing is a rather tense affair. Judy and Tanya lead it together which means that Tanya nods annoyingly whenever Judy is speaking and tries to cut in at the earliest possible opportunity.

'Leonard Jenkins didn't admit to knowing Heidi at first,' says Judy. 'But when we showed him the picture he admitted that he had taken her to the barbecue. He said it was because she was "interesting and intelligent".'

'Or because Ivor March would think she was interesting and intelligent?' says Nelson.

'I did wonder about that but Leonard says that March spent the evening talking to Jenny McGuire.'

'That's what Larry Hanson said,' says Nelson. 'He also said that Heidi spent most of her time with Crissy and Ailsa.'

'Leonard and Bob said that too. Apparently Heidi went paddling with Ailsa.'

'Ailsa told me that she hardly remembered Heidi.' Tanya jumps in. 'Crissy Martin did though. She said that Heidi had a beautiful aura. She also claimed that she had no idea that Heidi was the woman who was killed last week.'

'Of course she knew,' says Nelson. 'I wouldn't trust Crissy Martin further than I could throw her.'

'Which wouldn't be very far,' says Tanya. 'She must weigh over eighty kilograms.'

'What has that got to do with anything?' says Judy. She doesn't know what eighty kilograms is in stones but it annoys her when Tanya goes all 'war on obesity' on them.

'Did anyone have anything significant to say about the barbecue?' says Nelson.

'Leonard said that Chantal was angry because Ivor spent so much time with Jenny,' says Judy.

'Crissy said that too,' says Tanya. 'But she said that Jenny was just asking Ivor's advice about her short story.'

'That wouldn't take all evening,' says Nelson. 'I read it in ten minutes and a load of crap it was too.'

'Bob Carr said that Jenny and Ivor were talking too,' says Judy. 'But he denied that Chantal was upset. He said that Ivor and Chantal had the perfect relationship. According to him, everyone in the group is lovely and in love with everyone else.'

'But Bob and Leonard haven't visited Ivor in prison,' says Nelson. 'What about the pumpkin badge? Did anybody recognise it?'

'Nobody admitted to it,' says Judy. 'Bob said Jack O'Lantern at once though. And he's done some prints of the lantern men. Tony and I had a look when we were at his studio. I couldn't really make head or tail of them, lots of overlapping shapes and colours.'

'I liked them,' says Tony brightly.

'Thanks for the artistic appreciation,' says Nelson, 'but none of this gets us anywhere. However, we do have a positive identification for the third body found at the Jolly Boatman. Judy?'

'Yes,' says Judy. 'Dental records show that the body is that of Sofia Novak, who was aged eighteen when she disappeared in 2007. We're still trying to trace the family. I thought I'd see Ailsa Britain again. I'm sure she knows more about Sofia than she let on.'

'Good idea,' says Nelson. 'I'm going to see March tomorrow. I'll push for a confession. He killed Sofia, I'm sure of it. And he must have known that we'd find her body if we dug in the grounds of the Jolly Boatman. As Tanya said, why ask for the best archaeologist if he didn't want the bones to be found?'

Tanya looks delighted to be quoted. Judy says, 'The inquest on all three women is set for tomorrow. I'll attend with DC Zhang.'

'I'll be there too,' says Tanya quickly.

'I'll try and make it,' says Nelson. 'Depends how long it takes with March. Is Ruth giving evidence?'

'Yes,' says Judy. 'Chris Stephenson too.' She knows that the pathologist, unlike Ruth, is not one of Nelson's extremely small group of favourite people.

'Let's hope for "unlawfully killed",' says Nelson. 'That'll help with bringing March to trial.'

'His DNA isn't on the bodies though,' says Judy.

'Not yet,' says Nelson. 'But something might come up. Remember Ruth found that plant last time, something that only grew in one garden in Norfolk.'

Nelson is exaggerating, but only just.

'I have a feeling that March will confess,' says Nelson. 'This is his moment. You know how he likes to be centre stage. He's got a god complex.'

Judy looks at him sharply. This doesn't sound like the boss at all. He distrusts anything with the words 'complex' or 'syndrome' attached, as she knows to her cost.

'What if he doesn't confess?' she says.

'We'll get him,' says Nelson. 'We'll get him one way or another.'

He sounds confident but, right at this moment, all Judy can hear is Cathbad's voice.

Ivor March didn't kill those women.

CHAPTER 25

Ruth is always nervous before an inquest. It's like a mini courtroom, with a witness stand and dais for the coroner. But, unlike a court, the family are usually just a few feet away, hearing you talk about putrefaction and the preservation of bones. Today there are two sets of families, the Ferrises and the McGuires. They seem to know each other, exchanging hugs and the occasional tight smile, but sit apart. The pathologist, Chris Stephenson, is at the front, smiling around the room as if he's at a cocktail party. There are four police officers present: Judy, Tanya, Maggie the family liaison officer, and a young man Ruth doesn't recognise. No Nelson though.

Judy comes over to talk to Ruth.

'Have you heard?' she says. 'We've got Mother Hubbard.'

'Oh no.' Phyllis Hubbard is an old-style coroner. She's apparently an ex-solicitor but Ruth has never seen any sign of legal expertise in her rulings. Phyllis Hubbard is most notable for almost always getting the name of the deceased wrong. 'I really hoped we'd have someone better,' says Ruth. 'This is such a high profile case.'

'I know,' says Judy. 'Lots of press here. Outside too.' The other seats in the small, panelled room are taken up with people Ruth assumes to be journalists. She spots Cathbad's daughter Maddie in the back row, blonde head bent over her notepad.

Judy leans closer. 'Did you see who else is here?'

'Who?'

'Chantal Simmonds. March's girlfriend.'

Ruth tries to scan the room in a casual manner. She remembers Judy pointing Chantal out to her at the excavation. Then she'd been dressed in red but today she's entirely in black. Again, her clothes are formal, almost like fancy dress. She's even wearing a hat with a tiny veil.

'What's she playing at?' says Judy. 'I hope the families haven't spotted her.'

'This must be awful for them,' says Ruth.

'Yes, it is,' says Judy, 'but I'm hoping that, once this is over, we can release the bodies for burial. That will give them some closure, at least.'

Ruth often hears people talking about closure but it always sounds a bit simplistic to her. She is still haunted by Scarlet, the child she found buried on the marshes all those years ago. God knows what the parents are still going through. Well, Maddie knows. Scarlet was her half-sister.

The assistant coroner calls the room to order and asks everyone to stand for Mrs Phyllis Hubbard. Mother Hubbard enters, wearing a tweed suit despite the heat, her glasses on a chain around her neck. She greets the families and tells them that they are welcome to ask questions of any of the witnesses. She then expresses sympathy for the deaths of Nicole, Jane and Sonya. Judy exchanges a look with Ruth.

Chris Stephenson is the first to give evidence. He says that he examined the three skeletons. They were of adult females with all teeth erupted and all bones fused. It was impossible to tell cause of death. No one has any questions.

'Dr Ruth Galway,' says Mrs Hubbard.

Nelson sits facing Ivor March. The photograph is on the table between them. The picture has been enlarged which gives it the blurred beauty of an Andy Warhol poster. Sofia Maria Novak. She stares up at them, dark-eyed and unafraid, reminding Nelson of all those times that he photographed his daughters and they refused to smile for the camera. How old was Sofia in this picture? Sixteen? Seventeen? By eighteen she had left home and was back-packing round Europe. Shortly afterwards she met the Lantern Men.

For a long time Ivor March doesn't even look at the picture. He stares at Nelson with an intensity that is obviously meant to be intimidating. Nelson isn't scared though. He knows that he has March on the ropes.

Eventually March looks down at the photograph. And then, it seems, he can't look away. He stares and stares, raising one handcuffed hand to push his hair out of his eyes. Nelson says nothing. Even the prison guard stands as still as an effigy. The windowless room quivers with something that seems more than tension. Nelson almost expects to see little pluses and minuses of electricity floating in the air.

Eventually, March says, 'She was such a beautiful girl. This doesn't do her justice.'

Nelson says nothing.

March touches the image of Sofia's face. 'Sofie,' he says.

Nelson says nothing.

March looks at Nelson. There are tears in his eyes and he wipes them away with the back of his hand.

'I really loved her, you know,' he says.

Nelson says nothing.

'She was so ... fierce. So young and sure of herself. She was miles from home and, yet, she wasn't scared of anything. I think we were all in love with her. Me, Bob, Leonard, Ailsa and Crissy. Even John. She was like a breath of fresh air. No, something infinitely more bracing. The west wind raging over the Urals. She blew my mind. She really did.'

Nelson keeps silent. March's tears are nauseating but they are the only genuine signs of emotion that Nelson has ever seen in him. And he's pretty sure that the Urals aren't in Hungary.

'We were in love.' March looks defiant now. 'It was a real love affair, even though I was so much older than her.'

'Did you kill her, Ivor?' says Nelson.

Ruth opts to take the humanist oath. 'I solemnly, sincerely and truly affirm that the evidence I shall give will be the truth, the whole truth and nothing but the truth.' She thinks that Mother Hubbard, supposedly a devout Baptist, gives her a disapproving look.

'Dr Galway, can you tell us what happened in the grounds of the Jolly Boatman pub?'

Ruth describes how she organised the dig and how the bodies were found. First Jenny, as they know now, and then Nicola.

'They were articulated,' she says. 'In one piece,' she adds, for the families' benefit, hoping that this will be comforting in some way. 'They had clearly been laid in the earth and hadn't fallen there organically. We excavated the bodies and, later on, I examined the bones in the lab. I also took samples from the surrounding earth in the hope that we might be able to extract some DNA.'

'Is it likely that you would get DNA from a skeleton?' asks Phyllis Hubbard, although she must have heard this before.

'DNA deteriorates after death,' says Ruth. 'The strands become shorter. And it deteriorates more quickly in an articulated skeleton. By taking samples from the soil there's always a chance that you can find DNA in bodily fluids or hair. And this was the case here.' She hopes that Mrs Hubbard won't ask what sort of fluids.

She doesn't. Instead she says, 'And then you found the third body? Is that correct?'

'Yes,' says Ruth. 'It was found by a member of the team.' She exchanges another glance with Judy. 'It was clear that this body had been in the earth longer because it was completely skeletal. The bones were more discoloured and they also seemed to have been placed in the ground with less care. We were unable to extract DNA from these remains but dental records later allowed us to make a formal identification.'

'The body was that of Sonya Novak?'

'Sofia Novak. Yes.'

'Was there anything in the way these bodies were buried that could suggest cause of death?'

'We did find traces of rope which could indicate that the bodies were tied up before or after death,' says Ruth. 'There was no DNA on the rope.' She knows this was disappointing to Nelson and his team. March's DNA had been all over the ropes that had bound Stacy and Jill, his first victims.

'Was there anything else that struck you as noteworthy?' asks Mrs Hubbard, one of her stock questions.

Ruth hesitates. She had thought there was something slightly strange about the bones but it's hard to put into words and difficult to know if it will help the coroner come to a verdict. Still, she has sworn on her own atheism to tell the whole truth. 'The remains of Jenny and Nicola were slightly atypical for bodies buried in alkaline soil,' she says. 'Some of the bones were cracked, almost honeycombed in places.'

'Why would that be?'

'I'm not sure. It could be due to the presence of groundwater in the soil. This would make it acidic, which damages bone. But general weathering and root action, plants growing along and into bone, can also change the appearance of skeletal remains.'

'Thank you, Dr Galway. Is there anything you want to add?'

'Just to express my profound sympathy to the families of Nicola, Jenny and Sofia. And to reassure them that we treated their daughters' remains with the utmost respect.'

'Are there any questions for Dr Galway? No? You may step down.'

As Ruth does so she sees a movement at the back of the room and glimpses a black-clad figure heading for the door. A clatter of high heels, a slam. Chantal Simmonds has left.

'Did you kill Sofia?' says Nelson.

March touches the picture again. 'We had a love affair,' he says. 'Crissy understood. We always had an open marriage. I wasn't Sofia's first lover. She was a wild child. She liked all sorts of things. Some of them . . . dangerous.'

'Dangerous?' says Nelson.

'She liked to be strangled,' says March. 'Auto-erotic asphyxiation. I looked it up. It's quite common apparently. The blood vessels constrict and you get an incredible high. I didn't want to do it but she begged me. The first time she said I didn't do it hard enough. So I tried again. And it went wrong.'

'What do you mean?' says Nelson. He's pretty sure he knows what March means but he wants him to say the words.

'I killed her,' says March. 'It was terrible. The worst moment of my life. We were in my bedroom at Grey Walls and she just went limp. I didn't know what to do. I knew she was dead. There was no point calling an ambulance.'

Nelson clenches his fists but says nothing. Surely any

decent human being would have called an ambulance? But this is Ivor March. Such rules don't apply to him.

'What did you do next?' he asks.

'I didn't know what to do,' says March. His voice is low, expressionless, lacking its usual assurance and mocking edge. 'There was no one in the house. Everyone else had gone for some kind of nature hike. Eventually I wrapped the body up – I wrapped *her* up – and put her in the van. I drove around for hours. Then I remembered that my friend Simon had been digging up the garden of his pub to put in a swing or something like that. So I went there.'

'Did Simon know?' asks Nelson. They have been in touch with Simon Winsome, who now runs a pub in Melbourne. He claimed to know nothing about the bodies in the garden of the Jolly Boatman. If he was lying, Nelson will drag him back to England to face trial.

'No,' says March. 'The pub was closed while they did the work in the garden. The earth was all churned up. It was easy to bury Sofia. I put her in the ground and I said a prayer. It was all I could do.'

'Did you tell anyone else?' asks Nelson.

'No,' says March. 'No one knew. I think Crissy may have suspected something. She knew something was wrong. She could always read me like a book. But I kept it a secret from her. I told her that Sofia had sent Ailsa a postcard saying that she was back in Hungary. I don't think she believed me though. It destroyed our marriage. I met Chantal shortly afterwards. She offered the chance of a new life and I took it.'

There are many things Nelson could say. March was offered a new life with a new young girlfriend. Sofia had no such opportunities left. Her life was over, killed in a sex game and buried in the garden of a rundown pub, miles from home. Nelson will make sure Ivor pays the price for his crime. Crissy Martin too, if it turns out that she did know about it.

'I'll be back later to take a proper statement,' he says to March. 'You'd better have your lawyer present.'

March bows his head. 'That's why I wanted Ruth to dig there. I told Crissy to write to Ruth too. I knew she'd find Sofia. I'm glad she did. Sofia deserves a better resting place.'

'They all do,' says Nelson. 'What about Nicola and Jenny? Are you ready to tell me what happened to them?'

March turns to the guard. 'I want to go back to my cell now.'

CHAPTER 26

Nelson drives back to the station in high spirits. They have a confession at last. He can forget all this talk of Ivor March being innocent. They will be able to charge March with the murder of Sofia Novak and possibly Nicola Ferris and Jenny McGuire too. Back in his office, he telephones Sarah Hammond, March's solicitor, and asks her to meet him at the prison in an hour. Then he hesitates. He should wait for Judy, she's in charge of this inquiry after all, but he's desperate to get the confession on record in case March changes his mind. He looks in the open-plan area but the only person there is PC Rocky Taylor. Rocky waves happily at Nelson. Nelson nods back.

He's just thinking that he'll have to take Rocky with him when Judy appears at the door.

'Inquest over,' she says. 'It was Mother Hubbard but she wasn't too bad.'

'Did she get the names wrong?'

'Of course, DCI Naylor. Verdict was unlawful killing. On the balance of probability, et cetera, et cetera.'

'That's good. I was worried she'd leave it open. Juries hate an open verdict.'

'Better for the families too. Ruth was good on the stand. Very clear but steered away from anything too graphic. Chantal Simmonds was there.'

'Was she? Spying for March, I suppose. Anyway, speaking of March, I have news.'

'Don't tell me he confessed?'

'Only to Sofia Novak but it's a start. Want to come with me to charge him?'

'Do I?' Judy looks as if he has offered her a rare treat. Which he has. They sweep out of the station, leaving Rocky watching them, open-mouthed.

Ruth is left feeling rather flat after the inquest. Judy disappeared as soon as Mother Hubbard gave her verdict and so Ruth was left to exchange a few stilted words with Tanya. She congratulates Tanya on her marriage, which took place earlier in the spring.

'Thank you,' says Tanya. 'I hate the word wife though. Neither of us is a wife.'

Ruth doesn't think that she used the W word. She's not a fan either but, then, she has never been married.

'How's Kate?' asks Tanya. Ruth is rather touched that she has remembered the name.

'She's fine,' she says. 'She's nine. She'll be in secondary school in a year.' Ruth is rather dreading the inevitable rows with Nelson about this choice.

'If you want advice, you can always ask Petra,' says Tanya. 'She teaches at Heath House.'

'Thank you,' says Ruth. 'That's very kind.' She has already crossed Heath House (private, selective) off her list.

Tanya leaves with the new, young officer in tow. Ruth gathers up her papers and heads to the door just as the next family comes in, white-faced and shell-shocked.

She is hurrying to be back in time for her parking meter when a voice says, 'Dr Galloway?'

Ruth turns. It's Chantal Simmonds, the black dress and hat looking even more incongruous in the daylight.

'Hallo,' says Ruth. She doesn't want a cosy chat with Ivor March's girlfriend but she can't see any point in pretending that she doesn't know who Chantal is.

'You did the excavations, didn't you?' says Chantal. She is puffing on one of those vape things. There's a sickly sweet smell of mango in the air. It makes Ruth feel rather nostalgic for the days when smokers gathered outside offices for cigarette breaks, companionably coughing their lungs out.

'Yes,' says Ruth.

'You didn't find Ivor's DNA on the bodies, did you?'

'You heard me give evidence,' says Ruth.

'Yes, I heard you. I was impressed. You're a definite improvement on Phil Trent.'

Ruth can't help being rather pleased to hear this. Praise is always welcome, whatever the source. But then she thinks of Phil in his hospital bed watching reruns of *Antiques Roadshow*.

'Phil's in hospital,' she says. 'Someone attacked him.'

'I know,' says Chantal, waving the vape pipe as if it's an old-fashioned cigarette holder. 'But he'll get better. It'll all be for the good in the end, you'll see.'

This sounds uncomfortably like Cathbad. Ruth doesn't want to think that she might benefit from her colleague having a heart attack. 'I'd better be going,' she says.

Chantal ignores this. 'You met Ivor, didn't you?'

'Yes,' says Ruth. She can see a traffic warden approaching her car.

'Do you think he's guilty?' says Chantal.

'Yes,' says Ruth. 'I do.' She remembers Ivor's voice. *You're a very impressive woman, Dr Galloway.*

'I don't think you do,' says Chantal. 'Look at the forensics again, Ruth.'

Call me Dr Galloway, Ruth wants to say. Except this is the way Ivor March had addressed her.

'What do you mean?' she says.

But Chantal just laughs. 'Is that your car?' she says. 'I think you're about to get a ticket.'

Nelson is still in a good mood when he gets home. He had been worried that March would change his mind when confronted with his solicitor but he tells the same story again, still in that subdued monotone. The only disappointment was that, however hard he tried, Nelson was unable to get March to confess to killing Nicola and Jenny too. He might be able to push for a prosecution on the grounds that three dead bodies in the same place looks like rather a coincidence but, without forensic evidence, it's a long shot. Still, a good day's work.

The garage door opens with satisfying ease. Both his son and his dog greet him at the door. And, in the sitting room, he finds his wife and eldest daughter.

'Hallo, Dad,' says Laura, who is dressed in her cycling clothes. There is a map spread out on the table and various healthy snacks scattered around.

'Hallo, love.' Nelson is carrying George but leans over to kiss his daughter.

'Be careful, Harry,' says Michelle automatically.

'What are you looking at?' Nelson lowers himself onto the sofa with George still clinging round his neck.

'It's a map of Laura's race,' says Michelle. 'Laura's doing a cycling race on Saturday, starting at Titchwell. We'll be there, won't we? Unless you have to work?' There's a definite edge to these last words.

'It's just a sportive,' says Laura. 'Nothing serious. Only twenty-five miles.'

'That sounds a long way to me,' says Nelson. 'On a bloody bike too.'

'That is kind of the point of a bike race,' says Laura, leaning across to make a face at George. He laughs and grabs at her hair.

'Of course we'll be there,' says Nelson. He has always tried to support his daughters in their various interests, spending hours watching Laura play netball or applauding Rebecca in some God-awful play. It makes him sad that, although he watched her stellar performance as the innkeeper in last year's school Nativity, he will never be able to perform the same service for Katie. He is also slightly ashamed of how much he is looking forward to taking George to football.

'I invited Ruth and Katie too,' says Laura, not looking at either of her parents. 'They said they'd come. Frank too.'

Nelson waits for Michelle to say something. He can only see her leg but he can tell by the way it's jiggling that she's annoyed.

'When did you go to see Ruth?' she says.

'On Monday,' says Laura. 'After school.'

Nelson had also seen Ruth on Monday but he knows better than to mention this. He feels his teeth grind at the mention of Frank.

'Are you getting keen on cycling, then?' he says to Laura. He's always been in favour of sports but he worries that his eldest daughter is too thin and cyclists always seem to be little more than sticks. He thinks of Heidi Lucas, her wandlike legs and fragile arms, her hair spread out across the grass.

'It's great,' says Laura, with worrying enthusiasm. 'I love the club too.'

'One of the members was murdered recently,' says Nelson. 'You need to be careful. Don't go out on your own at night.'

'I know,' says Laura. 'I never spoke to Heidi but some of the members are really upset. They're holding a candlelight vigil for her tomorrow.'

'Poor girl,' says Michelle, standing up. 'Will you stay for supper, Laura?' She tries for a casual tone but Nelson can hear the tension in her voice.

He thinks Laura will refuse but she suddenly laughs and swings George up into the air. 'Yes,' she says, 'that would be lovely.'

'I'll drive you home,' says Nelson. 'The bike can go in the back.'

Laura doesn't say no to this either. Nelson and Michelle exchange glances behind Laura's back as she plays with her brother. So many emotions but the predominant one is relief.

Ruth arrives home feeling slightly shaken by the day's events. The inquest had been stressful and upsetting as always and the conversation with Chantal had been oddly disturbing. What did she mean: look at the forensics again? Does Chantal really believe that Ruth will find evidence that Ivor March is innocent? *Could* he conceivably be innocent? The recent murder has raised that question in Ruth's mind but it is outweighed by March's previous conviction and general creepiness, plus Nelson's belief in his guilt. But Nelson has been wrong before. All in all it's been a confusing day. Plus, she got a bloody parking ticket.

When she gets in Frank is making supper and Kate is drawing at the kitchen table. Ruth is grateful to Frank for cooking. She doesn't feel like preparing food, although she suspects that it might be her turn. What she really wants is an hour on her own in her study but that's the thing when you live with someone. You can't always do what you want. She gives Kate a hug and stands on tiptoe to kiss Frank on the cheek.

'Can I do anything to help?'

'No. It's shepherd's pie. Even I can't mess up shepherd's pie.' He gives the pan a rather anxious stir.

'Shall I open some wine even though it's Thursday?'

'Why not?' says Frank. 'Let's live dangerously.'

Ruth opens a bottle of red and pours them both generous glasses.

'How was the inquest?' says Frank.

'OK,' says Ruth. 'Death by unlawful killing which is the verdict Nel— the police wanted.'

'That's good,' says Frank. 'Must be a stressful experience though.'

'It's not pleasant,' says Ruth. 'What with the families sitting there and everything.' She glances at Kate but she seems absorbed in her picture.

'What are you drawing?' asks Ruth.

'It's very complicated,' says Kate. 'I can't explain now.'

Ruth knows how she feels. She doesn't much want to talk about her work either.

'How was your day?' she asks Frank.

'OK. Two progression boards and three students wanting dissertation extensions.'

'The usual then.'

'Yup. I'll be glad when this term is over.'

'Me too,' says Ruth but there's something in Frank's tone that makes her slightly uneasy. Does he sound a little sad? Maybe wistful is a better word. It's OK for her to feel these things sometimes but it shakes her to think that steady, reliable Frank might also have moments of self-doubt. She realises that she has drunk half her wine. Frank fills up her glass.

'We did alcohol in PSHE,' says Kate. 'It's very bad for you.'

'Mmm,' says Ruth non-committally.

'And I don't like shepherd's pie,' says Kate.

'Yes you do,' says Ruth. She thinks that she can sense irritation emanating from Frank. Kate isn't usually a fussy eater but she has recently become rather squeamish about meat. Ruth fears that the day is approaching when Kate will announce that she wants to be vegetarian, like Cathbad and his children. Ruth has nothing against vegetarians, she just thinks that it would put a strain on her already limited culinary repertoire.

The shepherd's pie is quite good though. Like all of Frank's cooking it lacks salt but Ruth doesn't add any because she knows how annoying this is. She eats enthusiastically to show her appreciation. Kate picks at hers.

'I'm quite looking forward to the weekend,' says Frank. 'It'll be good to see the Saltmarsh again.'

What's he talking about? Oh, Laura's bike race. Ruth can't believe that Frank can mention the Saltmarsh so casually. He must know what it means to her. It was both her beloved home and the place where she endured some of the worst experiences of her life. How can Frank say he's looking forward to seeing it, like it's the Golden Gate Bridge or some other tourist attraction?

'I don't know how much of the Saltmarsh we'll see,' she says. 'The race starts at Titchwell, in the Briarfields car park.'

'They have stops along the way where they give out water

to the competitors. Bananas and jelly beans too, energy food. Jane used to do some road racing when she was in college.'

'Americans say jelly when they mean jam,' says Kate.

'I know,' says Frank. 'When will we learn? We say biscuit when we mean cake too.'

'It's not your fault,' says Kate. 'Miss Blake says it would be boring if we were all the same.'

'Miss Blake is right,' says Frank. 'Look at your mother and me. We're very different but we get along just fine.'

What's he getting at? thinks Ruth. It suddenly feels very important to change the subject.

'Team Rank.' Frank is smiling at her.

'Is there more shepherd's pie?' says Ruth.

'You can have mine,' mutters Kate.

After the meal, Kate escapes to watch television. She left a Matterhorn of mashed potato on her plate but Ruth decides against demanding that she finish it. There will only be an argument which will probably give Kate food issues for life. She'll eat again when she's hungry. Ruth appreciates the way that Frank doesn't comment. All the same Ruth feels strangely nervous at being left alone with her partner, if that's what Frank is. She starts a bright conversation about Victorian mourning rituals, one of Frank's areas of interest.

'Ruth,' says Frank.

Ruth's monologue on jet jewellery trails away. Frank fills up her glass again.

'Ruth,' says Frank. 'Shall we go on holiday, just the two of us?'

'Without Kate?'

'You know Nelson and Michelle want to take her to Cornwall in the summer. We could go to Europe. To Rome or Barcelona. The Amalfi coast.'

Ruth can't resist a slight thrill at the names. She loves Italy and Spain. But she is far from sure that she wants to let Kate go on holiday with her father and stepmother, to say nothing of Baby George. And she's worried that the proposed romantic break means something ominous. At least Frank can't want another child. Ruth is fifty in July.

'I don't know,' she says. 'I've never been away without Kate.'

'We won't be far away,' says Frank, with an American's expansiveness towards distance. 'Only a couple of hours on a plane. And I think it could be good for us. Give us a chance to chill, to relax, to talk.'

Ruth is worried that the Us has a capital letter. She's not sure that she wants time to talk. In her experience, talking can lead to trouble. Why can't they just go on with their lives, going to work every day, taking Kate to school and picking her up, watching box sets in the evening?

'Maybe,' she says at last.

'Great,' says Frank, taking this for agreement. 'I'll get some brochures. It'll be fun, honey.'

When she finally escapes to her study, Ruth stares at her computer screen. Her emails scroll in front of her. St Jude's. Kate's school. Publishers wanting her to recommend their books. Various shops where she can't ever remember buying anything. Why is she so frightened at the thought of going on holiday with Frank? After all, they have been living together for two years and they get on very well. It's a civilised, respectful relationship where they both do their share of housework and childcare. They have two studies, for goodness' sake. What could be more civilised than that? But the last two summers have been spent in Cambridge, with the odd day trip to the coast. Ruth and Frank have never gone on a plane together, they have never shared hand luggage, they have never stayed in a hotel. The thought of this, signing in as Dr Ruth Galloway and Dr Frank Barker, makes Ruth feel as if she's hurtling downhill in a roller-coaster.

Flint appears in the doorway and meows accusingly. From the sitting room Ruth can hear the *Simpsons* theme tune. She imagines the opening credits, that blue sky with the perfectly shaped clouds. And then it happens again. One minute she is breathing normally, the next she can't remember how to do it. She is sucking at the air, unable to take it in. It's a horrible feeling, like being trapped in her own body. She grips the edge of the desk. You're safe, she tells herself. You're in your own house. Frank and Kate are downstairs. Breathe in for four, out for eight. Her hand flails and touches blissfully familiar fur. Flint. She strokes him, head to tail, scratching at the base of his tail, the way he likes it. She realises that she is breathing again. Thank you, healer cat.

Her phone is buzzing. Shona. Shall she let it go to voice-mail? No, it might be something about Phil.

'Hallo.'

'Hi, Ruth. Are you OK? You sound a bit strange.'

'I'm fine. A bit breathless, that's all. Just walked up the stairs.'

'You should come to spin classes with me.'

When hell freezes over, thinks Ruth.

'How's Phil?' she says.

'Much better,' says Shona. 'It was really nice of you to visit him yesterday. He was very touched. He said you had a lovely chat.'

'It was good to see him,' says Ruth. She realises, to her surprise, that they did have rather a nice chat.

'The doctors think he can come home at the weekend.'

'That's great news.'

'Yes, it is. I've told him that he has to have a proper rest. No worrying about work.'

'Phil mentioned that he was thinking about taking early retirement.'

'That's right.' Shona's voice sounds as if she knows exactly what Ruth is getting at. 'There might be a vacancy at UNN.'

'That's not what I meant,' says Ruth. 'I was just thinking about Phil. About you and Phil. He said that you wanted to go travelling . . .'

Her voice trails away.

'That's nice,' says Shona. 'Actually, the reason I was ringing is that I think I've found Phil's notes. The ones about the excavation. They were on the Cloud. Shall I send them over?'

'Yes please,' says Ruth.

'Doing it now. How are you, anyway? How's life amongst the dreaming spires?'

From Ruth's study window she can actually see the spires. It's a beautiful evening, the ancient buildings golden in the twilight. Ruth strokes Flint, who is now lying on the desk.

'Fantastic,' she says. *Apart from not being able to breathe.* 'We must get together soon.'

'Yes, we must,' says Shona. 'We'll have a girls' night out.'

And with that threat, she rings off. Ruth refreshes her screen and the new email is there. She clicks onto the attachment and starts to read. Flint puts a fat orange paw on the keyboard. A row of Ps appears on the screen. Ruth deletes them.

Notes on the excavation at 5 Church Lane, Salthouse. Phil is meticulous, even in his preliminary work. Coordinates, the day's weather, wind direction, the number of people on site, soil pH, the initial appearance of the bones. Ruth stops. *Look at the forensics again.* This is it. The thing that has been bothering her ever since the day Phil visited her at St Jude's. A church bell rings, somewhere across the rooftops. Eight o'clock. Ruth picks up her phone and sends a text to Crissy Martin.

And then she goes on reading.

CHAPTER 27

Ailsa Britain does not look overjoyed to see Judy. She stands in the hallway of the community centre, as if she wants to stop Judy from coming any further in.

'I've got a class in a minute,' she says.

'What do you teach?' says Judy.

'Painting.'

Bob had also said that Ailsa was a gifted artist, in the style of someone Judy had never heard of. But she remembers that Ailsa has actually known Jenny – and March – through creative writing classes. What sort of thing does Ailsa write? She has never thought to ask.

'I'm trying to trace Sofia Novak's family,' she says. 'I wondered if there was anything more that you could tell me about her.'

'She was Hungarian,' says Ailsa. 'I got the impression that her parents were rather stuffy. They didn't approve of her interrailing. Her father was a civil servant and her mother was a housewife. I remember because we talked about women needing to liberate themselves from domestic tasks.'

As far as Judy can make out, all the domestic work at Grey Walls was done by Crissy Martin. Judy can't imagine Ailsa helping out much.

'Any other family?' she says.

'She sometimes talked about a brother and a sister. I think Sofie was the youngest, the baby.' She smiles when she says this and Judy realises that Bob might have been telling the truth when he said that everyone loved Sofia, or Sofie as Ailsa has just called her. What would she say if she knew that Ivor March had confessed to killing Sofie? But Nelson wants to keep that information confidential for a while, in case he can get March to confess to the other murders.

'Anything else?' she says. 'The smallest thing might help.'

'I don't know . . .' Ailsa sounds rattled now. 'It was all so long ago.' Her phone buzzes. 'Excuse me, I must take this . . .'

She goes into one of the classrooms but Judy hears her saying, 'Crissy. What is it, darling?'

Crissy Martin. Interesting. She hadn't known that Crissy and Ailsa were on darling terms. But Ailsa had told Judy that she adored Crissy. They have clearly kept in close touch over the years.

Ailsa has left her portfolio propped up by the door. Judy opens it carefully. What she sees is an extraordinarily detailed picture, in ink and what looks like delicate water-colour. At first she can't make sense of the intricate shapes and swirls but then she sees that it's a house, but one that is almost entirely covered in brambles. Each branch is studded with deadly-looking thorns and the occasional blackberry blooms, swollen and sinister, the sort of fruit that would send you to sleep for a hundred years. There are people caught up in the brambles too, men and women with luxuriantly curly hair, as if that too has been growing unchecked for years. Judy hears Ailsa saying goodbye and hastily shuts the portfolio.

The picture has left her strangely shaken. Partly because the bramble-covered house is so obviously Grey Walls.

'I keep having panic attacks. At least I think they're panic attacks.'

The doctor, a pleasant woman who looks as if she's in her early thirties, doesn't laugh or reach for a hotline to the nearest mental hospital. In fact, she doesn't look very interested. Ruth is her last patient of the morning and she has probably used up her store of empathy. Ruth knows that she is lucky to have got an appointment at such short notice but she, too, is now rather bored by the whole business. The loo in the waiting area had a sign on it saying, 'Patient Toilet'. Well, the WC must be the only thing around here that isn't feeling frustrated.

'Describe them to me,' says Dr Kahn. She looks at Ruth with professional kindness. In the two years that Ruth has been living in Cambridge, she has only visited the doctor once, when Kate had tonsillitis. At least it won't say 'malingerer' on her medical notes.

'The first one happened when I was swimming,' says Ruth. 'I panicked. I suddenly felt as if I couldn't breathe. I thought I was going to drown. Then I had another one last night, just out of the blue.'

'Do you have any other symptoms?' asks Dr Kahn. 'Increased heart rate? Dizziness.'

'It's more like vertigo,' says Ruth. 'I feel as if I'm going down in a lift, very fast.'

Dr Kahn looks at her meditatively before reaching for her blood-pressure cuff. Ruth is relieved that she isn't going to be dismissed with a 'think positive thoughts and drink more water' but she always feels stressed at these tests which, of course, makes her blood pressure soar. 'White coat syndrome' someone called it when Ruth was pregnant with Kate and constantly under surveillance. She also has a constant nagging fear that doctors will tell her that she needs to lose weight. She gets this even when she goes to the dentist. Another example of white-coat neurosis.

'It's a little high,' says Dr Kahn a few minutes later, 'but nothing to be too worried about. You're probably just a bit anxious about being here.'

Ruth, who has been trying to conjure up images of tranquil seas and tropical islands, exhales.

'What do you do for a living?' asks the doctor.

'I'm a university lecturer.'

'That must be stressful at times.'

'Sometimes,' says Ruth. 'I'm been involved with a police case recently, as an expert, and that can be a bit, well . . . difficult . . .'

'I can imagine,' says Dr Kahn, looking as if she can. 'I think it was probably a panic attack,' she continues, 'and the best thing you can do for that is try to control your breathing. I've got a pamphlet here somewhere.' She searches on her desk.

'I've got a friend who has taught me some meditation techniques,' she says.

'That's good,' says Dr Kahn. 'Try to take it easy. It's the holidays soon. I imagine that you get nice long holidays.'

'I wondered if it could be the menopause,' says Ruth, registering the slight resentment in the last remark.

'Any other symptoms?' asks the doctor.

'Not really.'

'Perimenopause can make women anxious,' says Dr Kahn. 'There are some herbal treatments that might help. I've got another pamphlet somewhere . . .'

'It's OK,' says Ruth, standing up. 'Thank you for your time.'

'Is there anything else that might be worrying you?' says the doctor. 'Anything at home?'

'No,' says Ruth. 'Everything's fine at home. We're just planning our summer holiday.'

As she says this, she feels a band tightening around her chest.

'Crissy Martin rang when I was with Ailsa,' says Judy.

'Did you hear what it was about?' says Nelson. They are in his office but Nelson is late for another meeting. His PA, Leah, is standing accusingly at the door.

'No,' says Judy, 'but I thought it was odd. I mean, I didn't think that the two women were that close. Why would Crissy be ringing Ailsa?'

'John Robertson, the gardener, said something about Crissy and Ailsa,' says Nelson. 'Implying that there was something going on between them. Mind you, he implied that about almost everyone in that house.'

'Chantal Simmonds said that both Bob and Leonard had feelings for Ivor.'

'She thinks everyone's in love with Ivor. But Ailsa was in a relationship with Bob and married Leonard.'

Judy thinks of Ailsa's picture, of the brambles choking the house, of the bodies – dead? Or asleep? – lying amongst the poisonous fruit. She thinks of the tangled relationships in the house. Of Sofia being welcomed in, and then disappearing without trace.

'We should keep an eye on all of them,' she says. 'It's the bike race tomorrow.'

'I know,' says Nelson. 'We're going to cheer Laura on.'

'I checked the entries,' says Judy. 'Leonard's in the race as well. I think I should come along too.'

'Good idea,' says Nelson. 'OK, Leah. I'm coming. Bloody hell. Who'd be a DCI?'

'Probably not me,' says Judy.

'Don't be daft. You'll be a DCI one day. A bloody good one too.'

Judy knows that she's blushing. To cover it up, she says, 'See you at the bike race.'

'Jesus wept,' says Nelson, gathering up what looks like a random pile of papers, 'what a way to spend a Saturday.'

CHAPTER 28

The first person Ruth sees is Nelson. He is with Michelle and George is up on his shoulders. Why do men always carry children in this way? she thinks irritably. Is it to make themselves even taller? Or is it to present their child as a trophy, like a footballer with the FA cup? She pretends not to see him until Kate shouts, 'Daddy!'

Ruth always wonders what Kate thinks when she sees Nelson with George. Does she resent the fact that George has his father with him all the time, ready to hoist him on his shoulders at a moment's notice? If so, Kate never shows it. She's always pleased to see Nelson but never complains when she has to leave him. Suddenly, this makes Ruth feel sad.

'Hallo, Nelson,' she says.

Nelson puts George down and the toddler makes a bee-line for Kate, whom he adores. It's all very complicated.

Nelson and Frank shake hands.

'The little guy is really growing,' says Frank. 'How old is he now? Two?'

'He was two in February,' says Michelle. She is wearing skinny jeans and a white T-shirt and looks almost like one of the competitors. Ruth doesn't know Michelle's exact age, she's younger than Nelson but not by much. George was definitely a surprise. Sadly there's not by much sign of Michelle succumbing to middle age and elasticated waists. Suddenly Ruth's own jeans (not the skinny variety) seem uncomfortably tight.

'Where's Laura?' says Ruth.

'Over there.' Michelle points. Laura is with a group of other riders. She's wearing a pink lycra top and cycling shorts with stripes down the side. Her hair is in a plait and she's carrying her helmet. A wave of pure affection washes over Ruth. Yes, it's complicated all right.

Kate is playing with George, making him laugh by swinging him round. Suddenly she stops and shouts, 'Cathbad!'

It's almost too much, thinks Ruth. A reunion here, within sight of the Saltmarsh. Ruth, Cathbad and Nelson, the same three people who crossed the marshes one treacherous night ten years ago, trying to save a kidnapped child. Please don't let Cathbad be wearing his cloak.

The gods are on her side. Cathbad is disguised as a normal person, wearing shorts and a black T-shirt advertising some obscure band. Michael is with him and he, too, rushes over to Kate. Judy follows, holding Miranda by the hand.

It's obvious that Judy is not here purely for the pleasure of watching a cycle race in the sun. Letting Miranda join the other children, she turns to Nelson. 'Leonard's over there,' she says.

'Where?' says Nelson.

'Talking to Ailsa Britain, wearing all black.'

Leonard Jenkins, one of the three Lantern Men mentioned by Crissy. Ruth follows the direction of Judy's pointing finger and sees a middle-aged man holding his bicycle and talking to a woman and two other men. Even from a distance, there seems to be something intense about their conversation. The three musketeers, thinks Ruth. All for one and one for all.

'And that's Bob Carr,' says Judy. 'Leonard told me that they never see each other these days. Well, they certainly seem pretty friendly today.'

'Who's the other man?' says Nelson.

'I think it must be Leonard's husband, Miles.'

'Keep an eye on them,' says Nelson. 'When's the first stop?'

'Burnham Overy Staithe,' says Judy. 'There are timing mats at each stage. The riders have stickers with metal chips on the seat posts of their bikes. It's all very organised.'

'You go to Burnham,' says Nelson, 'I'll go to the next one. Where is it?'

'Wells, then Stiffkey, then Blakeney. It ends in Cley, by the visitor centre.'

'All the fun places. Well, they can't get up to much on a bike race.'

Ruth moves away so it doesn't look as if she's eavesdropping. They are in the car park of Briarfields, a charming hotel where Ruth once had a meal in the company of six female priests. At one end of the car park is a wooden gate and beyond that, Ruth knows, is a path leading to the dunes. They are only about a mile away from Ruth's cottage. It's a hot day and so the race has been scheduled to start at six p.m. when, it is hoped, the temperature will be cooler. It's still sultry though and Ruth feels too hot in her jeans. God knows what it would be like to cycle in this weather.

'Hallo, Ruth.'

Ruth turns but can't at first place the man addressing her. He's wearing a number, so he must be in the race, but his shorts and T-shirt look more like gardening clothes than race gear. That's who he is. John Robertson, the gardener at Grey Walls.

'Hallo,' she says. 'I didn't realise that you were a cyclist.'

'I'm not a professional like this lot,' says John. 'But I ride my bike everywhere. And I thought it would be a nice route along the coast. Didn't expect it to be this hot though.'

'It is hot,' says Ruth. She's rather thrown by the sudden appearance of John Robertson. She remembers sitting on the veranda in the evening listening to the gardener telling stories of spectral shapes, sacred springs and restless spirits, of green children lost in a forest and ploughmen who discover fairy gold. He has lived at Grey Walls a long time, he must have known Ivor March well. Bob and Leonard too. Ruth thinks of John bending over to talk to Kate. *Your daughter's an artist.*

'Five minutes,' shouts someone through a megaphone.

'I'd better be going,' says John. 'Nice to see you again, Ruth.'

'Good luck in the race,' says Ruth.

'Thanks,' says John. 'I'll need it.'

Kate is still playing with Michael and Miranda. Judy and Michelle are nearby. Frank is there too. Ruth watches him chatting easily to the two women. Michelle laughs, putting her hand up to her hair.

Ruth moves closer to the starting line. She can see Laura in her pink top and stripy shorts. The man Judy pointed out as Leonard is just behind her.

A klaxon sounds and the race is on.

'Good luck, Laura,' shouts Ruth, surprising herself.

'Is that your stepdaughter?' says a voice close beside her. Crissy Martin.

'No,' says Ruth. She's trying to remember exactly what she told Crissy about Nelson and Frank and her relationship with them. She remembers Crissy calling Frank her husband and the shock it had given her. 'Laura's the daughter of a friend,' she says at last.

'Friends are important,' says Crissy. She's giving Ruth her sympathetic stare but Ruth is no longer taken in by the eye contact and the hand on the arm. This is the woman who sent an anonymous letter to Phil, who believes that Ivor March is innocent.

'Yes,' says Ruth, 'they are. Did you get my text?'

'About the bones? Yes. I've been thinking about it and . . .' She stops. The woman called Ailsa is walking over, accompanied by the two men. From Judy's description earlier Ruth thinks they are Bob Carr and Leonard's husband, whose name she didn't catch.

'I can't talk about it now,' says Crissy. Her voice has an urgency that surprises, and rather frightens, Ruth.

Nelson doesn't know why Frank Barker annoys him so much. Just the sight of him with Ruth and Katie, looking as if he's the husband of one and father of the other, makes Nelson's teeth ache. Now he's chatting away to Michelle, Judy and Cathbad, just like they're best friends. Everything about Frank grates on him: his grey hair (who does he think he is, George Clooney?), his polo shirt and chinos, his American accent. *The little guy is really growing.* OK, he *is* American but it sounds so pretentious. He actually heard Frank call Ruth 'honey' once. Michelle always says how charming Frank is and now she's flicking her hair and laughing at something he's said, just because he's said it in that phony accent. Of course, Michelle likes Frank because, if Ruth's with him, then she can't have designs on Nelson. In his heart, Nelson knows that he dislikes Frank for the same reason.

Who is Ruth talking to? Bloody hell, it's Crissy Martin. All the gang are here today. Except Ivor March and he's been unavoidably detained by prison. Nelson doesn't know what the two women are talking about but they look serious, heads together, Ruth frowning in the way she does if she's trying to work out a forensics problem.

Michelle glances over and must have seen Nelson glowering because she detaches herself from the adoring group around Frank and comes towards him. 'What's the matter?'

'Nothing. Were you having a nice time chatting to Frank Sinatra?'

'Frank Sinatra? You're so old-fashioned, Harry. No one listens to Frank Sinatra any more.'

But Nelson does. He has a particular fondness for 'My Way' and all those clichéd songs about being a bastard and getting away with it. The trouble is that Nelson has never been able to get away with anything. He thinks that it comes of being a youngest child.

'That woman Ruth's talking to,' he says. 'That's Ivor March's ex-wife.'

'Really?' says Michelle. 'You'd never think it. She looks quite nice. But March's girlfriend seemed normal too. I suppose you can never tell. Look at George playing with Katie and Michael. He's so sociable.'

Nelson looks over to where Katie and Michael are running in and out of the bushes with George at their heels. Miranda is telling them to stop, clearly upset that no one is paying attention to her. Frank looks over but it's Cathbad who joins the children and initiates a game of grandmother's footsteps.

'Cathbad should be a nanny,' he says.

'He is good with kids,' says Michelle. 'What are we doing now? Going on to the next stage?'

'I told Judy that we'd go on to Wells,' says Nelson. 'I want to keep my eye on Leonard Jenkins.'

'And on our daughter,' says Michelle.

'Oh yes,' says Nelson. 'Of course.'

'Ailsa, darling, have you met Ruth?' Crissy is employing her best hostess voice. 'Ruth, this is Ailsa and Bob and Miles.

We've all come to support Miles's husband, Leonard, who's riding in this race.'

'Ruth,' says Ailsa. 'Are you the archaeologist?'

Ruth steels herself for some comment about the recent excavation but Ailsa says, 'You're the woman who found the Iron Age body on the Saltmarsh, aren't you? The lost girl of the marshes.'

'That was ten years ago,' says Ruth. 'It was the police who found her but I did the excavation, yes. Not far from here, actually.'

The girl had indeed been found on the Saltmarsh. The police had initially thought that they had found the body of a missing child but Ruth can never forget the moment when she saw the Iron Age torque that had lain in the grave, the dull sheen of metal, the honeysuckle rope that had tied the victim to the earth.

'Ruth teaches at Cambridge,' says Crissy.

'Do you know Larry Hanson?' says Bob, who is a soft-spoken man with grey hair in a Cathbad-like ponytail. 'He's a porter at one of the colleges.'

'He works at my college,' says Ruth. 'I know him a little.'

'He's in this race,' says Bob. 'Did you know?'

'No,' says Ruth. 'I didn't know.' She's surprised, and a little shaken, to think that Larry is here today. He didn't strike her as a cyclist either.

'John is too,' says Crissy. 'My gardener.'

'I know,' says Ruth. 'I saw him.'

It sounds very feudal, thinks Ruth. *My gardener*, not my friend, or even 'the man who does the gardening'. It occurs to her that Crissy has always acted a little like the Lady of the Manor.

Kate detaches herself from the group of children and runs over to Ruth.

'Mum! You said we could go to the beach!'

'Yes, I did,' says Ruth. 'Bye, Crissy. Bye.' She waves a general farewell.

Crissy inclines her head graciously.

Laura tries to concentrate, to get into a rhythm. That's the secret to all exercise, she finds, to focus on what your body is doing. Cathbad says this in his meditation classes too. Be aware of your breathing, empty your mind, let yourself become one with the universe. Maybe this is why she likes exercise – and meditation – so much. It's a way of escaping. She knows that she won't forget seeing a man die in front of her three years ago – she actually saw his soul leave his body although no one except Cathbad believes this – but, if she is concentrating on propelling a bike forward, or lifting weights, or doing lengths in the pool, then somehow the memory loses the power to hurt her. She sometimes wonders how her mother copes. After all, Michelle was there too, she knew the man well. But maybe having George has made Mum forget everything else. And, in any case, Laura's mum was never one for brooding on her emotions. She was always a good person to tell your troubles to because she listened carefully and never tried to solve them. Dad always wanted to sort things out, if necessary by getting your geography teacher fired because he gave you detention, but Mum just listened and then encouraged you to move on, to have a cup of tea, to go for a walk or to the cinema with friends. Is that what Michelle has done? Has she moved on?

Laura increases her speed. Four riders have pulled ahead and she's in the chasing group, the *peloton* it's called in the Tour de France. Eventually they'll draw in the four escapees but then others will pull away and the whole thing starts again. It's surprisingly tactical, another reason Laura enjoys cycling. Laura knows that she won't win the race but she hopes to do well in her class, age eighteen to thirty. Funny to think that she's now closer to thirty than eighteen. Some of the older riders are really good. Like Leonard Jenkins, the guy in the glasses who teaches at Cromer Academy. He won a time trial the other week, beating lots of the younger members.

They are on the coast road now, passing caravan parks and signs for lavender picking. Occasionally, between the caravans and the pubs promising Sunday lunch for a fiver, there's a tantalising glimpse of the sea. 'At least you'll see some nice countryside,' Mum had said earlier but really you can't see much when you're racing. It is pleasant though to smell the sea and feel the sun on your face. It's humid today, not ideal racing conditions, but there's a slight breeze on this stretch. Laura is pedalling next to Sasha, a cycling friend who is almost a real friend and that makes it nice and companionable.

She puts her head down and concentrates on the here and now.

*

They go through the gate and take the path over the rough grass towards the dunes. It's hard going. The afternoon has become hot and airless, the light is hard and almost unreal, throwing every blade of grass into sharp relief. Ruth thinks that there will be thunder before nightfall.

But, despite the sweaty climb up the shifting sand, it's always a thrilling moment when you reach the top and then, suddenly, there's the sea, glittering like a Christmas present. Kate runs forwards, arms outstretched as if she'd like to hug it. She has always loved the sea. According to Cathbad this is because she's a Scorpio, but Nelson's a Scorpio too and he views all beaches, except the Golden Mile at Blackpool, with extreme distaste. Ruth's Cancer the Crab but she has never seen a single Cancerian trait that seems to apply to her. Artistic, domesticated, sentimental, emotional. No, no, no and maybe. It is a water sign, though, and Ruth too loves the sea, although she approaches it now in a rather crab-like, tentative way.

'Take your shoes and socks off if you want to paddle,' she shouts. Too late, a wave splashes over Kate's favourite pink trainers.

Frank also approaches warily. In his blue shirt, beige chinos and deck shoes he looks like he belongs on a yacht and not striding across a Norfolk beach. Kate takes off her shoes and socks and Ruth does the same, feeling the familiar firm, wet sand under her toes, enlivened by the occasional razor clam shell. It reminds her of walking across this self-same beach with Erik and Peter years ago. They had been excavating a Bronze Age henge. Erik was the archaeologist in charge and Peter was a volunteer, shortly to become Ruth's lover. She remembers the moment when they had first seen the henge timbers rising from the earth, Erik falling to his knees in the centre of the sacred circle. The memory is so strong that she can almost see Erik's shadow on the sand and feel Peter's hand in hers.

Ruth and Kate run in and out of the shallow waves. The water is still very cold, it won't warm up until July, maybe August. Now, in early June, it's like standing in melted ice. Frank sits on a clump of sea kale and watches them.

Suddenly Kate stops with her back to the sea and points. 'Mum, look!'

Ruth looks. Across the sand dunes and the marshes, spotlit in this strange sunlight, she sees a glint of white. Three cottages standing very close together, like tiny boats on a sea of pale green. Ruth hadn't realised that they had walked so far.

'Look, Mum! That's our house.'

'Yes,' says Ruth. 'Yes, it is.'

Judy watches the riders go past with something like envy. What must it feel like to be in a pack like this, surrounded by friends and rivals? Judy has never been one for team sports, unless policing counts, but suddenly she wishes that she was wearing a T-shirt with 'Lynn Wheels' written on the back surrounded by a stylised bike wheel, that she was shouting 'keep it up' to the competitors and handing out fig rolls.

Laura grabs a drink from the stand and then is on her way, waving to Judy as she passes. Judy, too, is very fond of Nelson's eldest daughter, especially after all they went through three years ago. Cathbad says that Laura is a strong soul, a 'warrior', but she always seems rather fragile to Judy. Mind you, Laura seems to cope with being a primary school teacher, which surely must mean that there's a warrior, or a saint, in there somewhere.

Judy waits until Leonard Jenkins passes. He's not far behind, which is impressive considering that he must be at least twenty-five years older than Laura. He looks intense, wearing a red bandana and a sporty version of his black-rimmed spectacles, frowning at the road ahead.

'Go on, Len!' Judy looks in the direction of the shout and sees Ailsa Britain waving her silk scarf in the air as if she's at Ascot. Her voice is surprisingly strong. Next to her Crissy Martin laughs and says something to Leonard's husband, Miles. What does he think about Leonard's ex-wife cheering him on in this way? She scans the riders for John Robertson but she can't pick him out of the lycra-clad throng. It makes her feel rather twitchy to think that so many of the Grey Walls set are here today. *What a cast list*, she'd said to Nelson when he told her about the barbecue on the beach. Well, almost the same people are here today. Except Jenny McGuire and Heidi Lucas, of course.

Michael is standing with Judy. He has his Polaroid camera, a new obsession, and is busy taking paparazzi-like shots of the race. Cathbad has gone to the ice-cream van with Miranda. It's not Miranda's idea of fun, watching adults on bikes, and she's made it clear that she can only be recompensed by regular infusions of E numbers.

Judy is just going to join them – she feels a sudden urge for a 99 – when a voice says, 'You're nicked.'

Judy spins round and then a smile spreads slowly across her face.

'Hallo, Cloughie,' she says.

George is growing restless so Michelle takes him to look at the boats in Wells Harbour. Nelson waits for the first group of riders to appear. He's pretty sure that Laura will be up with the leaders. She's always been competitive in sport. In other things too but she often disguises this by pretending she doesn't care who wins at Monopoly or does the best in exams. This used to drive Rebecca mad.

The riders appear around the corner, the sea on one side, flint-fronted cottages – one of them Cathbad and Judy's – on the other. Nelson strains his eyes for Laura's pink top. Maybe she's fallen behind. This is her first race, after all. The first group whizzes past, spokes gleaming in the sunlight. Nelson waits, not very patiently, for the second wave. Here they are, with Leonard Jenkins, wearing a ridiculous red bandana, out in front. The third group passes, then the fourth, then the people who are just there for a day out, breathless but still game.

Nelson is left staring at the empty road, barriers at each side, the sea sparkling away as if it hasn't a care in the world.

Laura has vanished.

CHAPTER 29

Ruth ends up driving to Cley on her own. They brought two cars in case Frank wanted to leave early but Kate seemed tired after their visit to the beach and Frank offered to drive them both home.

'Thanks, Frank,' says Ruth. 'Are you sure?'

'Sure I'm sure,' says Frank. 'I know you want to see the end of the race.' Is this said with a slight edge? Ruth decides to let it go. She does want to see the end of the race but she knows, and she knows Frank knows, that she also wants to see Nelson. When is this going to end, this desperation to see him and the subsequent despair when she does? She had hoped that it would end with the move to Cambridge but, although that had helped for a time, working together on this case has brought all those feelings back, as painful and inconvenient as ever. She thinks of Dr Kahn. *Is there anything else that might be worrying you?* Nelson had looked so happy with Michelle and George, the perfect family, toddler in their arms, watching their adult daughter taking part in a healthy outdoor activity. Ruth could never be a wife in skinny jeans, sunglasses on top of her head, perfectly dressed for every occasion. If she and Nelson were together they'd probably argue all the time and she'd turn up at work functions covered in mud from a dig. But Nelson once said that he wanted them to be together. Is that what Ruth wants? But she can't ask herself that question any more.

It's even more humid when she arrives in Cley. She almost thinks that she can smell thunder in the air, hot and metallic. The visitor centre is a modern building that looks at home in the landscape, its curving lines following the hillside, grass growing on the roof. It's meant to be eco-friendly and has its own wind turbine, totally still today. The road had been closed for the race but most of the spectators haven't arrived yet, they're probably still at Stiffkey or Blakeney. There are just a few officials in Lynn Wheels T-shirts setting out the water bottles and energy snacks on trestle tables. There is also a banner that says 'Finish Line'. In twenty minutes or so the leaders, hopefully including Laura, will cross that line, tired but happy, toasting their success with jelly beans.

Ruth parks her car and goes to visit the grave of four airmen who crash-landed here in 2014. The four Americans chose to bring their helicopter down in this deserted location rather than endanger life. It's a regular pilgrimage spot for Ruth and Kate. Kate likes to pick flowers and put them on the granite slab dedicated to the tragically named 'Jolly 22'. Ruth picks a few daisies and scatters them on the faces of the smiling pilots, one carrying his child. 'Rest in peace,' she says, as she always does. Then she looks out over the marshes. There's a path in front of her, gate firmly closed, with a note saying, 'No Entry. Sensitive Wildlife.' Ruth thinks she knows how the wildlife feels.

The sky is now electric blue and the grass a strange luminous yellow. Here and there Ruth can see stretches of water, the same unearthly blue as the sky. They are not far from the Jolly Boatman pub, not far from the place where the last poor girl was found, Heidi Lucas. Ruth thinks about the bodies that she excavated. Has she discovered an oversight in Phil's initial findings? She confided as much to Crissy Martin and now she is worried about having done so. She should really have told Nelson first but she wanted to be sure.

Her phone buzzes. Is it Nelson, who often seems to know when she's thinking about him? Telepathy, Cathbad would say, but maybe she just thinks about him all the time?

It's not Nelson, it's a text from Laura.

Got a puncture and can't reach Dad. Can u help? I'm at the car park on the Saltmarsh. Near your old cottage X

Nelson is on the phone to Judy immediately.

'Did you see Laura?'

'Yes, she was one of the leaders. Doing really well.'

'She hasn't arrived at Wells.'

'Well maybe she had a puncture or something.'

'Maybe. I'll call her now. Can you drive along the route to see if she's by the side of the road somewhere?'

'OK, boss. Don't worry. I'm sure she'll be fine.'

Nelson stands in the middle of the road to call his daughter. Her phone goes immediately to voicemail. He leaves a message, trying to sound jaunty rather than worried. 'Where have you got to, love?' He presses send and turns round to see Michelle approaching, carrying George, who looks tired and cross and sticky.

'Where's Laura?' says Michelle, depositing George in Nelson's arms. 'Did I miss her?'

'She didn't finish,' says Nelson.

'Oh dear,' says Michelle, 'and she was doing so well.' She seems to be thinking only of the sporting disappointment whereas Nelson is consumed by a darker fear. He thinks of Jenny McGuire's story. How did it go? *She had the strangest desire to follow the marsh light . . . even though the path might lead to her death.* Had Laura seen the lights of the lantern men? Were they, even now, leading her to her doom? He tells himself to calm down, to get a grip. Ten to one Laura has had a puncture or fallen off her bike. Dangerous things, bicycles. He's always been wary of them, seeing them as middle-class and smug. No one cycled in Blackpool in the seventies. He thinks of all the people he has seen on bikes recently: Ailsa Britain, John Robertson, Leonard Jenkins . . .

'Harry!' He realises that Michelle has been talking to him for some time.

'Sorry, love.'

'I was saying why don't you track Laura's phone? You can do it on Find My Phone.'

Nelson has always been vague about technology. Super

Jo is threatening to send him on a course called 'IT for Older Officers'. He knows, of course, that mobiles can track location. They use it on half their cases these days. But he never bothers much with his own private phone. Michelle is much better at this sort of thing and recently she has linked all their family mobiles so that they can share calendars and photos. Or they could if Nelson knew where to look. Michelle takes his phone from him, manipulating it like a young person, using only her thumb.

'There you are,' she says. 'There's Laura's phone.' She shows him a map with a glowing icon at the centre of it. Nelson swipes, impatiently and clumsily, to make the picture bigger. Sea on one side, houses on the other.

'She's not far away,' he says. 'She's on the coast road.' He starts walking, still carrying George.

'Harry,' says Michelle, 'get the car. We'll need to put the bike in the back. And George is tired.' Nelson looks down at his son, whose head is lolling.

'Yes,' he says. 'The car. I'll get it. You wait here.'

He hands George over and Michelle sinks resignedly to the side of the road, her sleepy child in her arms.

'The boss is panicking,' says Judy.

'Nothing changes,' says Clough. He's looking very pleased with himself, thinks Judy. Slimmer, fitter, wearing clothes that are only slightly too young for him. Promotion obviously agrees with Clough. Maybe she should try it. She's a DI too, of course, but Clough is now in charge of his own team. She must start to think seriously about moving.

'Nelson wants me to drive along the route to see if Laura's fallen off her bike,' she says.

'Aren't the roads closed to traffic?'

'Do you think the boss cares about that?'

Clough laughs. 'You're right. Shall we go in my car? Cathbad might want to take the kids home.'

Judy looks over to where Cathbad is sitting on a wall with Michael and Miranda, all three of them eating ice creams. Judy never did get her 99.

'You're right,' she says. She walks over to Cathbad and explains the situation. He says that he'll drive the children home.

'I'm sure it's nothing,' says Judy. 'Laura has probably just had a puncture.'

'She's a strong soul,' says Cathbad, 'but I think you're right to be careful.'

Judy turns back to Clough.

'Let's go.'

'The dream team back together,' says Clough. 'Starsky and Hutch.'

'Cagney and Lacey,' says Judy. But she can't help smiling as they get into Clough's testosterone-charged car.

Ruth texts back, *On my way.* Then she texts Frank. *Laura has puncture. Near Saltmarsh. Going to get her. See u later x.*

The air is now so heavy that she feels as though she's swimming through it. Nevertheless, she's happy to think that she can help Laura and happy to be driving towards the Saltmarsh. *Near your cottage,* Laura says. It's empty now and Ruth has the keys. At least she thinks she has. She rummages in her organiser handbag, which actually seems to make things harder to find, hiding them in secret zippered compartments. Eventually her hand closes on her cat key-ring. She puts the keys in the pocket of her jeans. Maybe they can call in? Suddenly she has such a longing for her old home that it almost takes her breath away. Her book-lined sitting room, her bedroom with its view of the sea, the blue garden gate leading to the path through the wild grass. She gets in her car and sends a quick further text to Laura.

Won't be long xx.

CHAPTER 30

Nelson is driving too fast and Michelle tells him to slow down. 'We won't see Laura if you go so quickly.' She has Laura's location on her phone now and is studying it intently. George is asleep in the back seat.

'Here it is!' she says suddenly. Nelson screeches to a halt. They are halfway between Wells and Burnham. On their left is a high hedge, on their right the sand stretches away and the sea is a blue line against the horizon.

'We're near Holkham beach,' says Michelle. It was a favourite place when the girls were young.

'Let's see.' Nelson takes the phone. 'It says she's here,' he says, 'right here.' The phone icon is vibrating urgently as if it senses his frustration. Nelson gets out of the car. There are a few people on the beach, trekking home across the sand with deckchairs, buckets and spades. But, other than that, the road is deserted, still closed off for the race. The tarmac shimmers and Nelson realises that it's very hot. As he watches a car appears on the horizon, a black jeep that looks somehow sinister until he recognises the driver.

'Cloughie!' The car stops and Nelson strides towards it. Clough opens the door and jumps down. Judy follows.

'What are you doing here?' says Nelson.

'Came to watch the race. Thought Judy might need a hand.'

'I didn't,' says Judy. 'But it was good to see you. Your driving hasn't improved though.' She turns to Nelson, 'Any sign of Laura?'

'No,' says Nelson. 'But this app thing says she's here.'

Judy takes the phone and walks towards the side of the road. Suddenly she gives an exclamation and bends down to pick up something that is lying in the shallow ditch alongside the grass verge.

'What is it?' says Nelson.

Judy holds up a shiny black rectangle.

'I think it's Laura's phone.'

Ruth has trouble getting to the Saltmarsh because the coast road is still closed for the race. She has to take a circuitous route that leads her back inland where she ends up getting stuck behind a tractor for what seems like hours. She hopes that Laura isn't getting worried but she doesn't like to stop to text again. Eventually she manages to overtake the tractor and then she's on her way, passing landmarks so familiar that they seem like friends: the boarded-up pub, the caravan park, the strawberry picking sign, the field where a donkey and goat seem to co-exist happily, the house with a mural of Rupert Bear.

Now she is driving over the Saltmarsh, the road that she

took every day for more than ten years. Even now it's hard to believe that she isn't driving back from a hard day at UNN, looking forward to relaxing with Kate and Flint and listening to *The Archers*. The light is still very strange – now the sky has a yellowish tinge and every reed in the reedbeds looks as if it is outlined in ink. She has the air-conditioning on in the car – she gets so hot these days – but she can tell that, outside, the temperature is rising.

To get to the car park she actually has to drive past her cottage. There are the three white houses, close together, that they saw from the beach earlier. Bob Woonunga is away, enjoying an Australian winter, but she can see Sam and Ed's car outside their house. Sam and Ed are weekenders. In the fifteen years since they've lived on the Saltmarsh, Ruth has probably seen them as many times. She has avoided many invitations to barbecues and 'kitchen sups' and, barring one memorable New Year's Eve, has been able to find reason not to attend their parties. But now she feels an unexpected surge of affection for the couple who have, it's true, only ever been extremely nice to her. They have been coming to Norfolk since their children were small, they must love the place. Ruth suddenly wishes that she could call in and drink coffee with Sam in the kitchen which is exactly like Ruth's, only a hundred times classier. But Ruth has to rescue Laura first.

She drives slowly past her blue gate. Her tenants haven't mowed the lawn and the grass reaches as high as the ground-floor windows. Flint would love lurking there, waiting for unsuspecting wildlife to wander into his waiting jaws. He has his own cat gym in Cambridge, a two-storey structure of wood and sisal, bought by Ruth in a frenzy of guilt, but he has never played in it. He likes the sights and smells of the Saltmarsh. So do I, thinks Ruth. She realises that she is very nearly crying.

The car park is almost empty. It's late now, almost eight, and this part of the marshes is not on the tourist trail. There's just one old car without its wheels and, leaning up against the sign describing the birds and telling you not to drop litter, a bicycle. Is that Laura's? It looks vaguely familiar. Ruth parks by the car and gets out.

'Laura?' she calls.

Close by, a flock of birds rises up out of the undergrowth, calling loudly and angrily. Ruth jumps. She walks around the car park although there's nowhere that anyone could hide. Hide. A few feet away is a wooden hide, a hut used by birdwatchers. It's raised on stilts and camouflaged so that it blends into the landscape. Is that where Laura is? Ruth has reasons of her own for not wanting to approach the hide but she can't think what else to do.

As she sets out along the gravel path, she hears the first, ominous, rumble of thunder.

Nelson stares at the phone. The screen is dark, a web of cracks spread across it. He pokes at it hopefully but nothing happens. He goes back to his car where Michelle is sitting in the passenger seat, unwilling to leave George.

'What's happening, Harry? Is that her phone? Where's Laura?'

'I don't know,' says Nelson.

He taps the broken screen again and for a second it flickers, then dies.

Nelson swears. George wakes up and begins to cry. Michelle leans across to comfort him but Nelson can hear the fear in her voice. 'It's OK, Georgie. It's OK.'

Judy appears at his side. She too looks worried but her voice is as calm as ever. Too calm, Nelson thinks. 'It's possible she just dropped it, boss.'

'Then where is she now?' says Nelson.

Clough has been walking along the verge. Now he comes towards them. 'I can't see any signs that anyone's fallen. There's no glass or brake marks on the road and no disturbance in the undergrowth. Also it's hard to see how Laura's phone could have got in the ditch if she dropped it when cycling past.'

Nelson thinks of the Jack O'Lantern badge and Mike O'Halloran's theory that it had been carried away by a curious seagull. Well, a bird couldn't carry an iPhone 10, those things are almost as big as a small TV.

'I'm going to put out a MISPER,' says Nelson.

Judy and Clough look at each other. Nelson knows that they are thinking that it's overreacting to put out a missing persons' report for an adult who has only been missing an hour. But these things are discretionary – something the public often doesn't understand – and he, Nelson, is still is charge. He gets out his phone just as George shouts, 'Laura!'

They all look at George and then in the direction of his fat, pointing finger.

There, on the horizon, is a small figure in pink and black, pushing a bike.

'Laura!' Nelson starts to run towards his daughter.

Ruth approaches the hide. 'Laura?' she calls. A bird calls, high above, and then there's another crack of thunder, this time very near. She'd better get inside, if only to shelter from the rain that must surely be coming. Ruth climbs the wooden steps and looks inside.

'Hallo, Ruth,' says a man's voice.

CHAPTER 31

It has started raining but Nelson hardly notices. He stops in front of Laura. She looks hot and cross and about twelve.

'I got a puncture and I lost my phone,' she says. Her lower lip is trembling.

Nelson wraps his arms round her, making her drop the bike. 'Thank God you're all right.'

'Dad!' Laura extricates herself. 'Look what you've done. I was up in front too. I might have got a really good time. And I've lost my *phone*.' This almost seems the biggest disaster of all and Nelson knows how to fix it. He holds up the precious black rectangle.

Laura gapes. 'Where did you find that?'

'It's a long story. Let's get you out of the rain.' He picks up the bike and they walk to the car. Laura expresses amazement at, in turn, the presence of her mother, George, Judy and Clough.

'It's a welcoming committee,' says Clough, giving her a hug.

'But how did my phone get here?' says Laura. 'I had it with me at the last stage. I took a selfie.'

This is another youth phenomenon that Nelson doesn't understand but he doesn't say so. He is also trying to think of an innocent explanation for why Laura's phone ended up by the side of a road that she hadn't yet cycled along. Nothing springs to mind.

'Did anyone approach you at the last stage?' he asks. But Laura has got into the back of his car and pulled George onto her lap. He is delighted to see his sister, tears and tiredness forgotten. Michelle twists round in her seat to talk to them.

Nelson is left with the bike.

'I'll put it in my car,' says Clough. 'I've got the room.'

'So that's why you drive a farm vehicle,' says Judy.

'I'll drop it off at your place, boss,' says Clough.

'Can you drop me off first?' says Judy. 'It's only up the road.'

'Just call me Dave the taxi,' says Clough.

'Always good to have a back-up career in case the policing doesn't work out.'

Nelson hardly listens to the familiar cross-talk act. Who took Laura's phone? Why had they then abandoned it? How did it get broken? It's a new one, worth a bob or two. Why does he feel that, in some dark and unfathomable way, it's all tied up with Ivor March?

'Did you see Ailsa Britain at the last stage?' he says to Judy. 'What about Crissy Martin?'

'They were all there,' says Judy. 'I remember Ailsa shouting good luck to Leonard.'

'Remember the woman who was talking to Heidi in the

road,' says Nelson, 'just hours before she died. Could that have been Ailsa or Crissy? They've both got long, greyish hair.'

'I suppose so,' says Judy, 'but it was such a poor description. The witness only saw them from the back.'

'There's something going on,' says Nelson. 'Too many of the Grey Walls crowd were here today.'

'Never trust a grown man on a bike,' says Clough. He takes Laura's and heaves it into the back of the Land Rover. 'Ready, Judy?'

'Yeah,' says Judy. She taps on the car window and waves goodbye to Laura, Michelle and George.

Nelson gets into his car.

'You're soaking, Harry,' says Michelle, sounding, as she always does, as if the rain is entirely his fault.

'Home,' says Nelson. 'Home and hot baths. Bruno will be missing us.'

'Bruno!' shouts George. It's another name that he knows.

Ruth swings round. She doesn't recognise the man and yet, somehow, she does. He's tall and thin with grey hair in a ponytail.

'Where's Laura?' she says.

'On her bike,' says the man. 'Or off it by now. I rather think that she's got a puncture.'

'I know,' says Ruth. 'She sent me a text and told me to meet her here.'

'Oh no,' says the man, 'I sent you the text.'

'You did?' Ruth turns to look at him properly. He has a mild-looking face with faded blue eyes. She knows immediately that she doesn't trust him. The rain is thundering on the roof. Ruth realises that she's very scared.

'Speaking of which,' the man reaches out and grabs Ruth's phone, which is in her hand. 'I'll have that.'

'What are you doing?' Ruth grabs at her phone and, at the same time, the man raises his hand and strikes her very hard with something that feels like an iron bar.

The room tilts and spins. With a shock Ruth realises that she's looking up at the wooden ceiling. And then, darkness.

Bruno is delighted to see them. He runs around the house looking for a welcome gift and comes back with one of Michelle's bras.

'Drop!' says Michelle, wresting it from his jaws. She looks embarrassed though Nelson can't think why. He knows all her bras by heart.

Laura goes to have a bath. Nelson gets a beer from the fridge. He offers one to Michelle but she puts the kettle on for tea. When Clough arrives a few minutes later he accepts a beer and the two men sit in the kitchen drinking while the rain sluices the conservatory windows. There's a loud clap of thunder almost directly overhead. Bruno barks.

'Dexter hates thunder too,' says Clough. Dexter is his bulldog. Nelson sometimes wonders how Clough's wife, Cassandra, copes with two small children and a hyperactive dog. Clough is a devoted father but, as a new DI, he works long hours. Nelson knows that Michelle found it difficult in the early days. Well, he knows it now. At the time he was probably blissfully unaware of anything except that he had the perfect family waiting for him at home.

'What's going on?' says Clough. 'You obviously thought that something had happened to Laura.'

That's the thing about Clough. He's not as dense as he makes out.

'I think the Grey Walls lot are mixed up with the murder of Heidi Lucas,' says Nelson. 'You know, the girl that was found dead on the marshes recently? Well, we've got photographs of Heidi at a barbecue last year with Ivor March and co. And Heidi belonged to Lynn Wheels, the cycling club that organised today's race. Laura's a member of the club and, well, she looks a bit like Heidi and all of March's other victims. Tall, blonde, good-looking. I thought someone might have abducted her.'

Clough frowns into his beer. 'You say "all of March's other victims" but March is in prison. He couldn't have killed Heidi.'

'I know,' says Nelson, 'but I still feel that he's pulling the strings. The women, Ailsa, Crissy and Chantal, they'd do anything for him.'

'You think they'd kill for him?'

'You saw what Chantal Simmonds was like. She's obsessed with him.'

'She's obsessed with something, all right.'

'The last person to see Heidi alive was a woman with long hair. What if March told one of the women to kill her just to show that the Lantern Men were still at work? You know he confessed to killing Sofia Novak, the Hungarian girl they picked up?'

'No,' says Clough. 'I didn't know that. But he hasn't con-fessed to the others, has he?'

'No,' says Nelson. 'But he killed them. I'm sure of it.'

'Are you?' says Clough. His tone is casual but he's looking at Nelson with an uncomfortable degree of understanding.

Nelson stands up to avoid answering. 'Another beer?'

'I'd better not. I'm driving.'

Nelson opens the fridge and stares at its blue-lit contents: milk, juice, beer, a bottle of Prosecco with a fizz-containing cork, salad tray, yoghurts, two pork chops encased in plastic, Tupperware containers. Does he, in fact, think March killed all the women?

'Your phone's buzzing,' says Clough.

Nelson picks it up. Unknown number.

'DCI Nelson,' he barks.

'Nelson, it's Frank. Ruth's . . . Frank Barker. Is Ruth with you?'

Judy feels oddly restless. Maybe it's the thunder. By the time she gets home it is rumbling around the house, circling it like a tiger.

'Thor the Thunderer,' says Cathbad. He is sitting on the sofa with Michael, Miranda and Thing. Michael and Thing are obviously slightly scared. Miranda loves it.

Judy looks out of the window. Lighting is flashing out at sea, illuminating the strange yellowish sky.

'It's fun, isn't it?' she says, for Michael's sake. She doesn't think it's fun at all. She can quite see why ancient religions both worshipped and feared the elements.

Another crash, right overhead. Michael moves nearer to Cathbad. Thing seems to be trying to burrow into him. Miranda screams with laughter.

To distract Michael, Judy kneels down to look at his Polaroid photos, which are spread out on the coffee table.

'Good pictures,' she says, squinting at the tiny rectangles. 'There's Laura and there's Kate. There's Ruth talking to Crissy. The boss scowling. And there's Laura on her bike. Great shot, you've caught her just as she's leaning over to get some water. Oh my God . . .'

She goes over to a side table to look at the picture under a lamp. Outside the lightning flashes like a distress signal. On off, on off.

'What is it?' says Cathbad.

CHAPTER 32

Dark, light, wooden beams, a cobweb, pictures of birds, their outlines black and shaky. In a moment of clarity Ruth realises two things: she is drifting in and out of consciousness, and a man has his hands around her neck. From somewhere inside her own head she hears Cathbad's voice. 'Dig deep, Ruth.' She makes an almighty effort, pushes the man away and staggers to her feet. He comes towards her again. He's like some malevolent spirit, an elemental, unknowable and unstoppable. His hands are on her neck, their grip superhumanly strong. He pushes her against the wooden wall of the hut. She gasps and tries to kick out but her strength is fading. In a moment she'll pass out and then he'll kill her. She can feel the man's breath on her face, she smells sweat and something sharp and chemical. Dig deep, she tells herself. Then the ground comes up to meet her.

'What do you mean, is Ruth with me?'

Frank's voice is anxious and for a moment Nelson forgets

how much Frank annoys him. He even forgets the pretentious American accent.

'She texted me at six twenty to say that Laura had a puncture and she was going to pick her up. At the Saltmarsh. It's past eight now and she's not answering her phone.'

'She texted you?'

'Yes.' Frank is obviously reading from his phone. '"Laura has puncture. Near Saltmarsh. Going to get her. See you later."'

'Laura's home,' he says. 'She did have a puncture but it was nowhere near the Saltmarsh. What time did Ruth send her text?'

'Six twenty-two.'

Twenty-two minutes past six. Laura went through the Burnham stage at six sixteen, he had asked her in the car. She had hoped to be in Wells by six thirty. Nelson found her at ten past seven. It's eight fifteen now. Someone took Laura's phone at Burnham, left a message for Ruth and then abandoned the phone by the side of the road, from which position it could issue misleading messages to Nelson. Why?

So that Ruth could be lured away.

'I'm going to the Saltmarsh,' he says to Frank.

'I'll meet you there.'

'No, you stay there in case Ruth calls. Besides,' a slight pause, 'you need to look after Katie.'

'OK.'

'Ruth didn't say where on the Saltmarsh? It's a big place.'

It's a godforsaken bloody wasteland, in Nelson's opinion.

'No. Sorry.'

'I'll find her,' says Nelson. He nearly says 'don't worry'
but thinks better of it. He ends the call to find Cloughie
staring at him.

'Trouble?' says Clough.

'Trouble,' says Nelson grimly.

Ruth is lying on wooden boards. She can hear someone
breathing, very close to her. What has happened? Is she actually dead? But her throat hurts. Surely she wouldn't be feeling
pain in the afterlife? But she can hear the rain drumming on
the roof and, very faint and far off, the rumble of thunder.
She opens her eyes and sees rafters. She's still in the hide and
the killer is with her. She can see him sitting, hunched over,
beside her. His back is towards her and she can see a long,
white ponytail. He's panting, as if he's exhausted. Maybe he
thinks she's dead, or at least unconscious. Now is her chance.
She moves her hand to the side and touches something
metallic. Just the feel of it seems to give her strength. She
wraps her hand around the metal bar and, very slowly, raises
herself up. Then she hits out at the white head with all the
power in her body. She must have made contact because the
man gives a kind of grunt and falls forward. Ruth gets to her
feet and staggers towards the door. The trouble is that she's
unsteady after her ordeal. She hardly knows how to put one
foot in front of the other. The man is groaning, so she knows
she hasn't killed him. The room tilts and sways. And then,
suddenly, there's a space in front of her. She falls through
it and finds herself on the ground. She's on her hands and
knees in the mud and the rain is still falling. Somehow she

gets herself upright. She has to get away. Dig deeper, Ruth. She lurches forward, into the storm.

'Let's go in my car,' says Clough. Nelson hates being driven but he concedes that the Land Rover might be more able to cope with the rough terrain of the Saltmarsh. He climbs into the ridiculously high seat and tries Ruth's number again. 'Hi, you've reached Dr Ruth Galloway.' Trust Ruth to put the Dr in there. Clough performs a neat three-point turn and heads for the main road. Nelson's phone rings. Judy.

'Have you heard?' says Nelson. 'About Ruth?'

'No,' says Judy. 'What about Ruth? I just rang because I saw something weird on Michael's pictures.'

Nelson seems to be having trouble processing information. Michael. Pictures. Something weird.

'I was looking at his Polaroids,' Judy goes on, 'and I saw one of Laura getting her drink from the pit-stop place. And guess who was in the background? Bob Carr.'

'Bob Carr? Why is he even here?'

'I saw him in the crowd earlier but in the picture he's kind of hovering over Laura. It's possible that he took her phone. And stuck a pin in her tyres too. It's hard to tell in a Polaroid but his expression is odd. Malign.'

Malign. It's an unusual word but it sounds like the right one.

'Someone texted Ruth from Laura's phone,' says Nelson. 'The message was that she'd had a puncture and was at the Saltmarsh. We're on our way now. Cloughie and me.'

'I'll meet you there,' says Judy. 'In the car park.'

*

Ruth runs, zigzagging across the path. Her throat hurts and, when she puts her hand up to her head, she realises that it is bleeding. Don't worry about that, she tells herself. You just need to escape. You need to get home to Kate. The thought of her daughter spurs her on. She stumbles through some reeds and finds herself knee deep in water. Wrong way. She stumbles again and falls, face down this time. Suddenly, overhead, there's a tremendous crash of thunder. It seems to shake the whole world on its axis. The sky turns white. Ruth has a dim feeling that it's a bad idea to be submerged in water during an electrical storm. Somehow, she wades forward and finds dry ground, heaving herself upwards by hanging onto the long grass. Where is she now? The trouble is that the rain has reduced everything to a grey no-man's land, a place that seems neither land nor sea, a waiting room between the worlds. She turns and starts running in the opposite direction.

And finds herself facing the man.

Judy is already at the car park when Nelson and Clough arrive. She is sheltering under the awning of a kiosk advertising ice creams. It's still raining hard.

'Ruth's car is here,' says Nelson.

'And a bike,' says Judy, pointing. 'An old one, not a racer.'

'I've been tracking Ruth's phone,' says Nelson. 'Katie must have linked it to mine. Clever little thing.'

'What does it show?' asks Judy.

'Not much. She's in the middle of the marsh somewhere. Bloody green all round.'

'And he could have planted her phone somewhere to put us off the track,' says Clough. 'Like he did with Laura.'

'Who?' says Judy. 'Bob Carr?'

'It's possible,' says Nelson. 'He was one of the so-called Lantern Men. Anyhow, the priority now is to find Ruth.' He looks at his phone. 'This way.'

The blue dot that is Ruth seems to be fairly near them. Nelson prides himself on knowing his compass points but actually marches several steps in the wrong direction before rectifying his mistake. Neither Clough or Judy says anything.

The phone takes Nelson along a gravel path with reeds high on either side. Ahead is a small wooden hut and within it, apparently, the blue dot. Nelson is there in an instant. There's no door and, inside, just a window with a wooden bench below it and a poster describing various birds. But there, in the middle of the muddy wooden floor, is a mobile phone.

Nelson snatches it up. He knows immediately what the passcode will be. Katie's birthday. 011108. The last text message was one to Laura, *Won't be long xx.* There are several missed calls from 'Nelson'.

Judy is examining the floor which is a mess of footprints. Nelson should probably have been watching where he put his feet.

'Boss,' says Judy, crouching down. Her voice is quiet but Nelson knows that she's found something important.

'What is it?'

'Blood.'

*

Ruth stares at the man, almost too tired to go further.

'It was harder to kill you,' he says. 'Perhaps because you're so much bigger than the others.'

Great, that's all Ruth needs. Insults about her weight.

'You don't want to kill me,' she says, trying for a rational, soothing tone. Dig deep, Ruth.

'I do,' says the man. 'Because you guessed. You asked Crissy about the acid. I use it in my printmaking, you see. That's why it was on the bones.'

That was the thing that had been bothering Ruth ever since she had excavated the bodies in the pub garden. The porous, cracked appearance of the bones was the result of acid damage. Phil had just assumed that this was due to unexpected acidity in the soil but Ruth was puzzled by the fact that only two of the bodies were affected. After reading Phil's notes Ruth had texted Crissy to ask if any of the Grey Walls artists used acid in their work. Crissy hadn't replied but she must also have shown the text to Bob Carr, the printmaker, who is now trying to kill Ruth.

'Phil Trent didn't guess,' says Bob. 'I looked through his report and, even though he spotted the anomaly, he didn't make the connection. Just kept waffling on about soil pH.'

'You were the person who attacked Phil,' says Ruth. 'You took his laptop.'

'I just wanted the notes,' says Bob, as if this is perfectly normal behaviour. 'I didn't know that he'd have a heart attack.'

'You killed all those women,' says Ruth. Her clothes are drenched, blood and rainwater are running down her face, she feels as if she's been put through a mangle, but she has a vague idea that she should keep him talking. She doesn't feel as if she could walk another step.

'Not Sofia,' says the man. Bob. 'I wouldn't have killed her. She was so young, just a child really.' He sounds almost self-righteous. 'But I knew Ivor had killed her and I knew where he'd buried her too. That's what gave me the idea.'

'Why?' says Ruth. She should just turn and run but she's no idea where she is. The grey, drenched marshes are all around them, visibility has shrunk to a few metres. Ruth has the crazy idea that Nelson will come and save her but Nelson has no idea where she is. She thinks that she's crying, tears mixing with blood and rain.

'I was saving them,' says Bob. 'Saving them from themselves. They were so beautiful. So tall, blonde and beautiful. Too good for this world. And then Leonard took Ailsa from me. I realised that this was my mission. To be like the lantern men. To save women from the evil that's in this world.'

There are many things Ruth could say. Saving people doesn't usually include murdering them. The lantern men were deceivers, evil spirits, they weren't cold-blooded killers. Instead she says, as loudly as she can, pointing behind Bob's head, 'Look!'

He looks. Ruth turns and runs.

'Look at this,' says Judy. On the wooden floor there's a metal file with a long handle. There's a definite blood smear on one edge.

'Looks like something a printmaker might use,' says Judy.

'I remember all the equipment in Bob Carr's studio. I wondered at the time if he was strong enough to use it. But he's obviously stronger than he looks. Fitter too, if he's ridden his bike all the way here.'

'We have to find Ruth,' says Nelson. He can feel his heart beating as if it is outside his body. Ruth is somewhere out there in the storm, injured, perhaps badly. He goes to the door and sees Clough kneeling in the mud. He is soaked, his dark hair plastered to his head and Nelson is pretty sure that he's in the same state. Only Judy has the sense to be wearing waterproofs.

'Someone's fallen here,' says Clough.

Nelson looks down. The gravel has stopped and here it's just earth. Earth that seems to be stirred into a quagmire.

'There's a handprint,' says Clough. 'Looks like someone was trying to break a fall.'

Nelson imagines Ruth staggering and falling, wounded and terrified, a murderer close beside or behind her. He has to find her. Where are they? He seems to remember that, from here, one path leads to the sea and the other, via a circuitous and treacherous route, to Ruth's cottage.

'You go that way,' he says to Clough. 'I'll take this path.'

'We should stay together,' says Judy.

'No,' says Nelson. 'You stay here in case they come back. Radio for back-up. I'm going on.'

He runs along the path, wishing he was fitter, wishing that he wasn't fifty. It's still light but the rain makes it impossible to see anything. One foot off the path and you can find yourself in water or, worse, quicksand. He remembers taking this route with Cathbad years ago. One moment Cathbad had been next to him, the next he had just disappeared. Nelson had hauled him out of the mire, had saved his life, according to Cathbad. Well, today there's no one to save Nelson. He must tread carefully.

Ruth runs into the rain. Compass points are important for archaeologists. 'The most important thing is the direction,' Erik used to say. Christians are buried with their feet towards the east. In China dying is called 'going west'. Churches often face towards the east and baptismal fonts are placed by the north door, the door into the world. The Egyptian pyramids were mapped according to cardinal points. East is rebirth and renewal, according to Cathbad, the west is autumn, winter and harvest.

But Ruth has no idea where she is going. She thinks that she can smell the sea which means that she is going away from the hide, the car park and safety and into the unknown. But, then again, Bob has probably made his way back to the hide. At any rate, he doesn't seem to be following her. Ruth thinks of the game that Cathbad was playing with the children earlier. Grandmother's footsteps. She always found it rather scary as a child. You look round and your pursuer is right behind you, breathing down your neck. Is that what will happen with Bob? Will he suddenly appear, hands reaching out for her? Hands that have already killed at least four women.

Ruth stops. The rain is directly in her face and she seems to remember that the storm was coming from the sea. She puts her hand to her head and it comes away red with blood. She needs help, quickly. Should she turn round? The lightning flashes, silently this time, illuminating the grey marsh leading to the grey sea. She is lost in the liminal zone between life and death. 'Help me, Erik,' she whispers.

Then she hears something. A low, sonorous call that sounds somehow familiar. She remembers tales told by Cathbad and Erik, of the souls of lost children calling from the sea, of nixes and sea sprites and sirens singing unwary sailors to their doom. That sound again. Is it the call of a bird? It's very near now.

Then she sees the light, a flickering unsteady orb, the same height as a lantern carried in a human hand. It's moving in front of her, bobbing and swaying. The bird calls again. Ruth thinks of Jenny's story, of the lantern men leading you to your death. But, for some reason, this manifestation seems comforting, like a lighted window on a dark night.

She steps forward, following the light.

Nelson hears the sound too. It strikes a chord in his memory. Something that has to do with that terrible chase on the marshes, with finding a lost child and seeing a man drown in front of his eyes. He stops, momentarily disorientated. Then it comes again, an undulating note that seems to reverberate in the air.

Nelson moves forward, hardly knowing whether he is following the strange cry or not. He just knows that he has to get to Ruth. He thinks of Jenny's story, of following the light across the marshes. He hears John Robertson's voice.

They say that you must never whistle on a dark night or the lantern men will hear you. The rain is falling so heavily that he can hardly see a few yards in front of him. He stops again to look at his phone, trying to keep it under cover of his jacket. All he can see is a pulsating blue dot in the middle of a sea of green, with the real sea a blue void to the north. He clicks onto Ruth's phone, abandoned back in the hide. At least that is some way away and he isn't going round in circles. He keeps walking, trying to move away from the blue and towards the tiny yellow road that represents civilisation. He prays that Ruth has gone this way too and not stumbled into a stream or the treacherous quicksand. 'Hang on, Ruth,' he tells her, 'I'm coming.'

The light is always just ahead, illuminating the long grass interspersed with dark water. Occasionally Ruth treads in a shallow stream but, on the whole, the ground remains miraculously firm beneath her feet. She's exhausted now, sick and unsteady, but she carries on, putting one foot in front of the other, trusting in whatever is leading her. Then, suddenly, the glowing orb disappears and Ruth is staring at a tarmacked road and three small white houses.

She is home.

Ruth runs up to Ed and Sam's house and batters on the door. No answer. She realises that their smart Audi is missing. They must be out, they've probably gone for a meal somewhere, escaping the bad weather. But there is her own house, her dear familiar house. She puts her hand in her jeans pocket and there's the cat key ring. It's like *Alice's*

Adventures in Wonderland. The door into the walled garden. Eat me. Drink me.

She has to push the door because it often sticks in wet weather but then she's inside, in her own sitting room. Some of her books are still on the shelves, though she took most of them with her to Frank's, but there's her blue sofa with a new throw over it to impress the tenants, there's her John Sell Cotman print, her woodcut of trees in winter, the table where she used to sit to mark essays and dream about Nelson. Ruth locks the front door and then goes into her kitchen. It's unnaturally tidy but she finds a tea towel, wets it and puts it to her head. There aren't that many mirrors in the cottage but there's one in the downstairs loo, decorated with seashells in a fit of Cancerian creativity. Ruth examines her reflection. She looks completely mad, drenched, covered in mud and blood, eyes staring. There's a cut on her hairline. It's still bleeding sluggishly but doesn't look too deep. She presses the tea towel to it again and goes into the kitchen and puts the kettle on. She will have a cup of tea in her own kitchen. Despite everything, it feels wonderful to be back in the cottage. Perhaps she is a true Cancerian after all. She'll drink the tea and then she'll work out how to ring the police. There's no landline at the cottage any more. 'Tenants don't expect it,' said the agency. Maybe Sam and Ed will be back soon. She looks at the clock over the cooker, always covered with a film of grease. It's only nine o'clock. It feels like midnight.

She makes her tea and goes back into the sitting room. A crack of thunder makes her jump but it seems to be moving further away. She wishes that Flint was with her, kneading the sofa and shedding hairs over her. She drinks her tea and puts her head back on the throw. Surely now's the time for a panic attack but Ruth is surprised to find that she's completely calm. In fact she's nearly asleep. That must be the effect of the head wound. She should try to stay awake. The rain batters against the window, Ruth's head drops.

Suddenly she's wide awake. The rain seems to have stopped but there's another sound.

Someone is rattling the door handle.

CHAPTER 33

Ruth freezes. The rattling continues. She can see the handle pressing down and this evidence of an unseen hand scares her more than ever. She stands up, dropping the blood-soaked towel. Thank God she locked the door. What about the back door? The cottages are terraced, with Ruth's in the middle, but it would be easy to climb through the gardens, especially as both neighbours are out and Ruth is, as ever, completely in her own.

She makes her way slowly into the kitchen and tries the handle of the stable-type door that leads into the garden. Locked and bolted. She stands in the kitchen, listening. It's horribly quiet. The rain and the thunder seem to have stopped completely. She can hear her breathing, shallow and ragged. She hears Cathbad's voice again, 'in for four, out for eight'. She tries it and it does calm her. She can see her Phillips radio on the window ledge. It had been a wrench to leave it behind but Frank had bought her a new one for her Cambridge study. If only she could hear the soothing tones of Radio Four. What would be on now? *The News*, perhaps, Corrie Corfield making even the Brexit negotiations sound comforting. Ruth edges towards the radio just as a window shatters and she hears the unmistakable sound of someone climbing in. Ruth looks round wildly and grabs a wooden spoon hanging from a rack. Fantastic, she tells herself, what are you going to do? Stir him to death? But the feel of the wood in her hand steadies her. Wood is life, Erik used to say, stone is death.

The kitchen door is kicked open and Bob stands there, wild-eyed and terrifying. But he's breathing deeply too and Ruth can see cuts on his hands. He's unarmed, surely she can escape. She makes a dash for the back door but Bob grabs her arm as she passes. He's far stronger than he looks, she knows that now. Ruth hits at him with the spoon but he hardly notices. He has her pinned to the floor now. She can smell him, sweat and turpentine.

'Looks like I'm going to have to kill you here,' he says, his face close to hers. 'It's not how I like to do things, but still.'

'Oh no you don't, sunshine,' says a voice. The next minute Bob has been pulled away and Nelson has knocked him to the ground. Bob struggles up and Nelson hits him again.

'Nelson!' shouts Ruth, half in relief, half in warning.

Nelson stops. Bob is lying at his feet, one eye blackened. He looks as if he's unconscious.

'Don't kill him,' says Ruth.

'All right,' says Nelson, 'if you say so.' He takes out his phone and barks a few words, then he says, 'Have you got any rope?'

'Haven't you got handcuffs in your pocket?' says Ruth. She feels strangely light-headed and euphoric.

'No,' says Nelson, who is bending over Bob, 'get some rope.' From the kitchen, Ruth hears Nelson reading Bob his rights. 'Robert Carr, I'm arresting you for the attempted murder of Ruth Galloway . . .' It sounds like something from a TV show but it's happening here, in Ruth's cottage. She finds some green garden twine and presents it to Nelson who rolls his eyes but uses it to tie Bob's hands together. Bob is lying face down on the rug but he seems to be alive, making slight groaning sounds. Ruth moves backwards until her legs hit a chair and she sits down. Her head is swimming but she still has that sense of unreality, as if this is all happening to someone else. She has to tell herself: someone has just tried to kill me. It's so absurd that she almost wants to laugh.

Judy and Clough appear before Nelson has finished his efficient-looking knots. Was he a boy scout? Ruth bets that he was.

Clough and Nelson get Bob onto his feet. Judy comes over to give Ruth a hug. 'Are you all right?'

'Yes,' says Ruth. She is pretty sure that she's grinning foolishly. 'Fine. Never better.'

Judy gives her a concerned glance. 'You ought to get that head wound checked out.'

'I'll call an ambulance,' says Nelson. 'You take Carr to the station. How did you get here?'

'Clough's car.'

'Good. Leave me your keys and I'll drive yours back.'

Judy looks like she wants to say more but she hands Nelson her car keys.

'Are you sure you're all right?' she says to Ruth.

'I'm fine,' says Ruth. 'Nelson will call an ambulance.'

'OK then.' Judy and Clough manhandle Bob to the door. He looks pathetic now, shuffling along, his grey hair loose and stringy. Did he really kill all those women? It seems impossible.

When the door shuts behind them, Nelson comes over to Ruth.

'Let me see your head,' he says. He pushes her hair back gently and she can feel his hands on her forehead.

'It's not too bad,' he says. 'Looks clean enough.'

'I'm fine,' says Ruth.

'So you keep saying,' says Nelson. He kneels down in front of her. Ruth looks at the top of his head. His hair is really very grey now. She has an insane desire to stroke it. She realises that she is stroking it.

'Ruth . . .' Nelson takes her hand and looks up into her face. 'We shouldn't do this.'

'You're right,' says Ruth. She leans forward just as his lips touch hers.

Judy rings Tony and tells him to meet her at the station. He sounds very excited. 'I'll come at once.' Judy can remember the days when catching the perpetrator was purely a thrill, the culmination of the chase. These days everything seems much more complicated.

Clough waits while Judy reads Bob Carr his rights again and asks whether he wants a solicitor. Carr shakes his head, he still seems slightly dazed. One eye is closed and purple.

Judy hopes that the boss didn't hit him. There are some very incriminating knuckle marks there.

'I'd like to ask you some questions now,' she says. 'Do you need anything? Tea? Coffee? Water?'

'Just some water, please.'

Tony goes to fetch it. Judy has a whispered conversation with Clough.

'Do you need me to stay?' says Clough.

'No, it's fine. Thanks for everything.'

'I enjoyed it,' says Clough. He surprises Judy by giving her a quick kiss on the cheek as he leaves.

In the doorway, Clough meets Super Jo head on. Judy hears her give an exclamation of surprise and, she thinks, delight.

'Hallo, Dave. Have you come back to us?'

'No. I just happened to be on the scene.'

'That's what good coppers do.' Jo gives him a pat on the back. She's always had a soft spot for Clough, thinks Judy. She hopes Nelson will forgive her for calling the superintendent but she really couldn't let Jo find out about Carr's arrest on the evening news.

Judy barely has time to appreciate Jo's Saturday evening attire of leggings and oversized Ramones T-shirt when Tony arrives with the water. After a brief consultation with Jo, Judy ushers Bob Carr into interview room one. There's no time to talk to Tony about strategy. She just hopes that he'll have the sense to follow her lead.

'This is an interview under caution with Robert Carr. Present DI Judy Johnson and DC Tony Zhang.' Judy presses record. Jo is watching through the two-way mirror.

'Why did you attack Dr Galloway just now?' asks Judy.

'I wanted to keep her quiet.' Bob looks at her out of his mild blue eyes.

'Why?' Wait, Judy tells herself, give him time to answer.

But Bob doesn't seem to need time. 'She knew,' he says. 'About the others.'

'Which others?'

'Stacy and Jill. Nicola and Jenny too. There were signs of acid damage on the bones, you see. I didn't do it on purpose but I kept them at the studio. There must have been traces of acid on the material I wrapped round them. Phil Trent didn't spot it. He just thought that they had been buried in acidic soil. But Ruth knew better and she made the link. She texted Crissy to ask if any of the artists at Grey Walls used acid.'

'Did you kill Stacy, Jill, Nicola and Jenny?' Wait, she tells herself again. Let the suspect incriminate himself.

'I was saving them,' says Bob, leaning forward earnestly as if he is explaining the theory of solar-plate etching. 'They were too beautiful to live. I got the idea from the Lantern Men. We were a light in the darkness, guiding women onto the right path. Sometimes the kindest thing is to save the women from the world.'

'How did you kill them?' asks Judy.

'I knew Stacy from the old days in London,' says Bob. 'She was beautiful, tall and blonde like Crissy and Ailsa, like all of Ivor's women. I met her again at a party at Ivor's house. There was a definite spark between us. We started sleeping together and, one night, I just put my hands round her neck and that was that.'

'You strangled her?'

'I didn't mean to. Ivor had told me that some women like being choked during sex. That's all it was at first. A game. But afterwards, she looked so beautiful and at peace, I realised that I'd done her a favour.'

'What did you do with her body?'

'I kept it in the freezer at my studio. I almost forgot about her. Then I met Nicola at the community centre. She was beautiful too. I knew she was going to the end-of-term drinks at the Dragon so I waited for her on the way home and I killed her. It was easier that time.'

I bet it was, thinks Judy. She is temporarily lost for words so Tony says, in exactly the right even tone, 'What about Jenny?'

'I met Jenny at the barbecue on the beach. I knew where she worked. It was easy. I waited for her as she cycled to work. It was almost as if she was waiting for me. Like in her story. The Artist was me, you see. I buried Jenny and Nicola in the garden of the Jolly Boatman because I knew that Ivor had buried Sofia there.'

'You knew that Ivor had killed Sofia Novak?' says Judy.

'I guessed. I knew all of Ivor's secrets. He told me about the choking game. I knew he was sleeping with Sofia. Then, one afternoon, I came back early from a hike and I saw him drive off as if the hounds of hell were after him. I followed him and saw him burying something in the pub garden. I never saw Sofia again. So sad. She was a lovely little thing.'

Bob sounds genuinely upset about Sofia whereas, in his view, his own victims were lucky to have been saved. Judy grips her hands together and keeps her voice steady.

'What about Jill Prendergast?'

'I met her at Ivor's fiftieth. We got talking and she told me that she had a boyfriend. I knew that she needed saving from him. Jill was too good for some electrician, someone who had probably never thought about art and beauty in his life. I wasn't sure how to do it but then, one night, I was driving home and I saw Jill waiting at the bus stop. I offered her a lift. She said yes immediately. It was almost as if she knew what I was going to do and she accepted it. I drove her to a lay-by and strangled her. It was as easy as that.'

'What did you do then?'

'I put her in one of the freezers at the studio while I worked out where to bury her.'

'You buried her in Chantal Simmonds' garden. Why?'

'Well, I didn't think I could use the Jolly Boatman again,' says Bob, as if explaining a technique to a particularly slow student. 'Three bodies are enough, don't you think?'

'Is that why you buried Stacy there too?' says Judy. 'After all, you had kept her in the freezer for a long time. Why did you suddenly decide to bury her?'

'No comment,' says Bob. Rather too late, in Judy's opinion.

'Did Chantal Simmonds know that you'd buried Jill and Stacy in her garden?'

'No comment.'

Judy looks at Tony. 'What about Heidi Lucas?' says Tony. 'What happened to her?'

For the first time, Bob sounds slightly quavery. 'I thought it was over. I thought I wouldn't have to save any more women. But then you dug up Jenny and Nicola. It was all in the papers. Their photos too. And I thought of Heidi. I remembered her from the barbecue, you see. I knew the route she'd take because I've got the same cycling app. We discussed road racing that evening. I met her on the way, persuaded her to come to my van and I strangled her. I left her on the marshes and put the badge beside her so that you'd know it was the Lantern Man.'

The Lantern Man, in the singular. Isn't that what Crissy Martin had said? Did she know all along?

She knows she has to get permission from the CPS first but, after she has sent Bob back to his cell, she says out loud, in her best DI voice, 'Robert Carr,. You are charged that you did murder five women, Stacy Newman, Nicola Ferris, Jenny McGuire, Jill Prendergast and Heidi Lucas contrary to common law . . .'

It's almost eleven o'clock by the time that Nelson appears at the station. Super Jo and Tony have gone home. Bob Carr is in the cells and Judy is watching a video of her interview with him.

'Hi, boss,' she says. 'He confessed. To all five of the women. Stacy, Jill, Nicola, Jenny and Heidi.'

'Heidi too?'

'Yes. He says that the publicity about finding Nicola and Jenny made him want to "save" another woman. I've been thinking about the witness who saw Heidi chatting to a woman on a bike. I think that was Carr. He's got a ponytail and the witness only saw him from the back. He has a bike too. I saw it when I was in his studio. Chantal called round to see Bob that evening but she left at eight. Afterwards, Bob went out on his bike to kill Heidi.'

'Bloody cyclists,' says Nelson. Judy thinks that he sounds strange. Normally, at this stage of an investigation, Nelson would be full of energy, hardly staying still for a second, barking orders and slamming doors. But, as he sits down next to her, she thinks that he looks calm and almost light-hearted. She never thought that she'd say this about the boss but he looks . . . peaceful.

'How's Ruth?' asks Judy.

'OK. I took her to hospital in your car. No concussion. The cut wasn't serious but it needed a few stitches.'

'Did Frank come to collect her?'

Nelson meets her eyes blandly. 'Yes. I phoned him from the hospital. I left before he arrived though.'

I bet you did, thinks Judy. Aloud, she says, 'Carr declined to have a lawyer present. He was full of crap about saving the women from themselves but it was clear that he got a sexual thrill out of the murders. That's why the women all looked the same, tall and blonde and beautiful.'

'That's why Sofia Novak looked different. She was the only one that March killed.'

'Bob found out about Sofia. He followed March and saw him burying her. That's what gave him the idea about the pub garden. Ruth spotted traces of acid on the bones. She asked Crissy if any of the artists used acid in their work. Bob Carr did. He told us that day we visited his studio.'

'Crissy must have told Bob that Ruth was asking,' says Nelson. 'Idiot woman. That was what made Bob go after

Ruth. He used Laura as a decoy. She was his type, after all. Bloody nutcase.' That sounds more like the old Nelson.

'I still don't understand about Stacy and Jill,' says Judy. 'Bob killed Stacy before the others and kept her in a freezer at his studio. I don't understand how Jill and Stacy came to be buried in Chantal's garden and covered with March's DNA.'

'Did Chantal know that Bob had killed them?'

'I don't know. Bob wouldn't say. Came over all "no comment".'

'I'll talk to Chantal tomorrow,' says Nelson. 'Crissy Martin too.' He tries to smother a yawn.

'It's been a long day,' says Judy.

'It has,' says Nelson. 'It seems years since we were watching that bloody bike race. It was good to have Cloughie in on the hunt again.'

Normally this would irritate Judy. She knows that Nelson misses Clough around the station. He probably thinks that there are too many women on the team now. But it *had* been unexpectedly good to see Clough again.

'Clough's really upset that he's missed out on this case,' she says.

'Serves him right for moving to Cambridge,' says Nelson. 'Right. Shall we call it a day? Can you give me a lift home?'

'Sure,' says Judy, standing up and turning off her computer. 'You know what the worst thing is though?'

'What?'

'Cathbad will say that he was right about Ivor March.'

'Cathbad's always right,' says Nelson.

Now Judy is really worried about him.

CHAPTER 34

Even Nelson has to admit that Salthouse looks beautiful in the morning sun. Yesterday's rain seems to have washed everything clean. The sea glitters and the houses look as if they have been newly painted. By Ivor March perhaps. The church bell is ringing and Nelson realises, with a slight shock, that it's Sunday.

The path to Chantal Simmonds' cottage looks overgrown and picturesque, wild flowers blooming in the hedges, the nettles almost waist high. When Nelson gets to the house he sees that the garden is still a building site, the banks of earth looking somehow sinister, as if a coffin is about to be buried.

Chantal opens the door before he knocks. As usual, she looks as if she is dressed for a party in a tight pink dress with a black jacket. She invites Nelson into the sitting room where the ginger cat is on the sofa, in exactly the same place as before.

'That's March's cat, isn't it?' says Nelson.

'Yes,' says Chantal, stroking the orange fur. 'She's called Mother Gabley.'

Chantal sits beside the cat and Nelson takes the chair opposite. For a minute they look at each other in silence and then Nelson says, 'Why did you frame Ivor March?'

Chantal takes a deep breath, as if she is about to embark on one of her famous rants, but then she shrugs, a tiny movement that makes her look like a completely different person.

'He killed my sister,' she says.

'Sofia Novak?'

'Yes. Sofie was my little sister.' Chantal is still stroking the cat but so hard now that its fur is flattened. That's why the papers implied that Chantal looked foreign, thinks Nelson, because she was, in fact, Hungarian. Or, rather, half-Hungarian. Wasn't her mother English? It accounts for the perfect accent, if so. And, far from being attracted to tall, blonde women, March was clearly drawn to small, dark women, like Chantal and her sister. Except for Crissy, of course, and hadn't Crissy said that theirs was more of a 'spiritual union'.

'My real name is Kiri,' says Chantal, and even her voice changes slightly. 'Kiri Novak. I changed my name when I came to England and married Alan. His surname's been useful to me at least.'

'Did Sofia follow you to England?'

'No, she came here after she left school,' says Chantal, her voice softer than Nelson has ever heard it. 'She was going to backpack round Europe, staying at youth hostels. She wanted adventure, she said. Dad begged her not to go alone. I was back in Hungary by then. Sofia came to England in July 2007. That was the last anyone saw of her. My parents were devastated. They both died within a few years. The grief killed them, I'm sure of it. I came back to England to look for Sofie. We only had one letter from her and it was postmarked Cambridgeshire. No address, just "Grey Walls". It wasn't hard to find the place though. I decided to befriend Ivor, to find out what he knew. It wasn't difficult. Ivor's so vain, he thinks every woman is after him. Ivor and I became lovers and then I met Bob and Leonard. Eventually Bob told me that he thought that Ivor had murdered a "foreign girl". Bob said he didn't know where she was buried. I know that's a lie now. He didn't tell me because he'd buried two other women there.'

'You were at the excavation,' says Nelson, 'and at the inquest.'

'Yes,' says Chantal. 'I wanted to see my little sister laid to rest. I must say that Dr Galloway was very respectful. I owe her for that.'

'Why didn't you go to the police? Why go to all the trouble of framing Ivor?'

'There was no proof,' says Chantal, 'and I didn't even know where she was buried. But then I got friendly with Bob and I realised how weird he was. Even I didn't realise how weird, until he told me that he'd killed Jill. I was horrified at first – Jill was a friend of mine – but then I realised that it was a way to get my revenge on Ivor. I told Bob that I would help him. That's when he told me that he'd killed Stacy five years earlier. She was still in a freezer at his studio. I told him to bury them both in my garden.'

'Why would you do that?' says Nelson. Even when, early that morning, he had realised the truth about Chantal, it still seemed too fantastical. He still hardly believes it even though he is hearing this account from her own lips.

'I wanted Ivor to suffer,' says Chantal and now her eyes gleam with the familiar fervour. 'I wanted him to go to prison for crimes that he didn't commit because he'd never be charged with the one he was guilty of. It was easy to get Ivor's DNA – I had his comb, his toothbrush, I even saved some semen from a condom. Oh, and I used your fur too, didn't I?' she says to the cat. 'You didn't mind. You always preferred me to Ivor.' Mother Gabley purrs, eyes shut, as if agreeing.

'But why did you pose as the loyal girlfriend?' says Nelson. 'Why not say that you suspected March?'

'That was clever, don't you think? You'd never suspect me of planting the evidence, though it was the obvious solution, because I loved Ivor *so much*.' She puts her hands over her heart and rolls her eyes heavenwards.

'Did you suggest to Ivor that he get Ruth involved?'

'Yes, I knew she was the best. I told Ivor that she might find evidence that he was innocent but really I wanted her to find Sofie. I guessed that Ivor would tell her where she was buried.'

She did find evidence, thinks Nelson, and it nearly killed her. Chantal's face, when she talks about her sister, stirs his pity but then he reminds himself that she let a known murderer go free.

'How could you have guessed that?' he asks, though he himself guesses at the answer.

'Because of you,' says Chantal, smiling beatifically. 'I knew that Ivor would tell Ruth, if he told anyone, because of her link with you. Crissy told me all about your affair with Ruth.

I knew that Ivor would tell Ruth because he wanted to get to you. It suited his sense of drama to have your ex-girlfriend digging up his victims. Plus, I honestly think he felt guilty at the end. The bastard.'

Nelson thinks of Madge saying 'he enjoys a drama'. Never ignore the bleeding obvious. 'Was that why you got Crissy to send that anonymous note to Phil Trent,' he says, 'because you wanted Ruth involved?'

'That's right. Crissy was easy to manipulate. She thinks she's so wonderful, drifting round that big house being patronising to everyone. She didn't even mind when I seduced Ivor. She still thought that she was the Queen of the May and that all the men were in love with her.'

'I thought she was your friend. I thought you were working together.'

'No,' says Chantal, her face darkening. 'I wouldn't trust that woman. She was part of it. She befriended Sofie. She would probably never have stayed at Grey Walls if there hadn't been a woman there. A woman pretending to be all kind and motherly. I hate Crissy. Ailsa too. They enabled Ivor.'

This might be true, thinks Nelson. Nevertheless, Chantal let a murderer go free to kill again.

'I'll need you to make a statement,' he says.

'OK.' That shrug again. 'I don't care about anything now that I've found Sofie.'

'I think Ivor guessed,' says Crissy Morgan, sitting on her veranda, sipping herbal tea like the heroine of one of the films Michelle likes to watch. 'That's why he told me about the Lantern Man. He must have suspected Bob all along. And he must have suspected that he'd buried the bodies in garden of The Jolly Boatman. They both used to drink there.'

'It would have been more helpful if he'd told you straight out,' says Nelson. But, even as he says this, he knows that telling things straight out is not Ivor March's style.

'That must have been why he wanted Ruth to excavate,' says Crissy, still musing on March's perspicacity. 'He knew that she'd understand about the acid. A mordant, it's called in printmaking. That means "to bite".'

Nelson wishes that he had Bruno with him and that he would bite Crissy, hard. But, if Bruno were here, he'd be rolling over so that Crissy could stroke his stomach. He's a bad judge of character sometimes.

'And he was right,' says Crissy. 'Ruth did work it out.'

'And you told Bob Carr and he tried to kill her.'

'I didn't mention Ruth's name. I just asked if he used acid in the process.'

'Carr knew why you were asking,' says Nelson. 'He's not stupid.' A deranged, psychotic murderer, yes. Stupid, no.

'I never wanted to put Ruth in danger,' says Crissy, wide-eyed. 'I love Ruth.'

Do you, thinks Nelson. He distrusts this new modern trend of saying 'I love you' at every opportunity. His daughters sign 'Love you!' at the end of texts as if it's a substitute for 'goodbye'. But he knows that love is a serious thing. Love is dangerous.

'If Ivor had told you his suspicions about Carr,' he says, 'would you have informed the police?'

'Of course,' says Crissy.

Nelson doesn't believe it for a moment. Chantal didn't tell the police that Bob Carr had killed four women. He feels sure that Crissy too would have kept the information to herself or maybe used it in some tortuous way that would end up complicating things still further. He thinks that Crissy likes to know secrets, likes to sit here in the sunshine, her country house behind her, imagining herself at the centre of a web of tangled relationships and passions. She was the housekeeper, that's what John had said. And the keeper of much else besides.

'Bob always was strange,' says Crissy. 'Ailsa said that, when she was with him, she'd wake up in the night to find him staring at her. He'd put his hands round her neck sometimes too. He said it was something Ivor had told him about. Some erotic game. I think that's why Ailsa married Leonard, even though she must have known that he was gay. It was to get away from Bob. Ivor must have guessed. Bob used to follow him round like a lapdog.'

There's contempt in her voice. Bob Carr did shadow Ivor, thinks Nelson, and that's how he saw him driving off one night with Sofia's body in the boot of his car.

'I just knew that Ivor couldn't have killed them,' Crissy is saying. 'He's a gentleman, he wouldn't harm a woman.'

'He killed Sofia Novak,' says Nelson. 'He confessed to it.'

Now Crissy really does looked shocked. Her face changes and, to Nelson, it looks as if she has suddenly aged ten years.

'I don't believe it.'

'Ask him,' says Nelson, 'on your next visit.' He stands up to leave.

Crissy remains sitting. In her white dress with her long white hair she looks as if she has been turned to stone.

'Why did he tell you to dig at the Jolly Boatman then?' she whispers. 'He must have known that you'd find her.'

'I think he felt guilty,' says Nelson. And, as he drives away, the stone house growing smaller in his rear-view mirror, he thinks that he does understand part of this case. March might not have been guilty of all the murders but he was guilty of one. He must have known, as Chantal said, that he deserved to suffer. He knew, when he told Ruth to dig in the grounds of the Jolly Boatman, that Sofia's body would be discovered. He didn't have to confess though. It was guilt that prompted March to do that. March killed Sofia and Nelson hopes that he serves a long time in prison for his crime. March killed a teenager, a young woman on the very threshold of her life, and he deserves to pay for that. Nelson will never really understand why March did it or why Bob Carr murdered Stacy, Jill, Nicola, Jenny and Heidi.

But the guilt he does understand.

'We should offer thanks for Ruth's safe return,' says Cathbad.

Ruth and Frank exchange glances. They are sitting in the tiny garden of the Cambridge house, made smaller by the trampoline that fills half the space. This was Frank's present to Kate on her last birthday. At the time Ruth had thought the gift too big, too much of a commitment to her daughter, but there's no doubt that Kate loves it. She is bouncing on it now, accompanied by Michael and Miranda. Ruth, Frank, Cathbad and Judy are drinking tea at the rickety wrought-iron table left behind by the previous owners. Is it possible to offer a libation in tea?

But Cathbad has other plans. 'It should really be wine,' he says. 'Wine is a powerful offering. The gods will be pleased.' He smiles beatifically at the gathering. Ruth has often noticed that the gods have similar tastes to Cathbad himself.

'We've got a bottle of white in the fridge,' says Frank. He goes into the house. Judy wanders over to the trampoline, where the children are practising forward rolls.

'How are you feeling, Ruth?' says Cathbad. 'It must have been a terrifying experience.'

'It was,' says Ruth, putting her hand up to touch the dressing on her forehead. 'But today it feels like a dream. Was I really attacked by a madman? Did I really run across the marshes in a storm? Did I really try to fight off a killer with a wooden spoon?'

'You fought him off with your strength and integrity,' says Cathbad.

'I don't think it works like that,' says Ruth. 'After all, the other women had strength and integrity too. I was just lucky. And, of course, it was really Nelson who saved me.'

'His strength is the strength of ten because his heart is pure,' says Cathbad. Ruth turns away so that Cathbad won't see her blushing. What happened after Bob Carr had been taken away could hardly be described as pure. Has Ruth fallen back into the quicksand again after trying so hard to escape? Why doesn't she feel worse about it?

Cathbad is giving her one of his uncomfortably under-standing looks. To change the subject, Ruth says, 'It was the strangest thing, when I was running across the Saltmarsh I saw this light, a weird light that kept moving. I followed it and it led me to safety. I thought all those marsh lights were meant to be evil. I heard a bird too. An owl, I think.'

'Swamp gas,' says Frank, arriving with the bottle and four glasses. 'Phosphorescence. Dead matter is trapped in the mud and releases methane which mixes with phosphines to create blue light.'

Cathbad disregards this, as Ruth knew he would. 'A glowing owl,' he said. 'They're often seen over the marshes. Some say it's the moon reflecting on their feathers, others that they glow because they eat phosphorescent plants. But an owl is a powerful symbol.'

'I thought owls were bad luck,' says Ruth, accepting a glass of wine.

'They're good luck for you,' says Cathbad, 'because of your connection to Hecate.'

Ruth remembers telling Kate that her dæmon would be an owl. She remembers the way the light had seemed friendly, lighting the path to home. She realises that everyone is looking at her.

'To Ruth.' Cathbad raises his glass.

'To Ruth.' Frank smiles at her.

'To Ruth.' Judy winks.

'Thank you,' says Ruth. The little garden is full of sunlight and the laughter of children. Ruth drinks her wine and thinks about the Saltmarsh.

CHAPTER 35

The good weather lasts all through June. Bob Carr is charged with five murders and for a while the press have a field day. 'How did Norfolk Police miss the killer?' 'Ten mistakes made by the bungling cops'. One paper describes Nelson as Norfolk born and bred, which upsets him almost more than anything. But at least Ivor March doesn't go free: he is charged with the murder of Sofia Novak and is still incarcerated at HMP Wayland. Chantal Simmonds, née Kiri Novak, has been charged with conspiring to pervert the course of justice but she doesn't seem to care too much. Sofia has been buried in the churchyard at Salthouse and Chantal visits every day. She is also having her garden landscaped by a handsome Serbian called Marko.

Ruth is grateful that her name has been kept out of the papers. She finishes the term in peace, marking papers late at night while Larry makes his rounds of the court, keys jangling at his waist. Frank continues to talk about summer holidays and, in the evenings, they look at brochures: Corfu, Santorini, the Amalfi Coast, Croatia. Ruth dreams about blue seas and crumbling castles, olive groves, white houses surrounded by cypress trees.

On Friday 22 June, the day after the longest day, Ruth and Frank go for a meal at their favourite Cambridge restaurant, overlooking the river. Kate is staying the night with Nelson and Michelle, a cause of great excitement, and tomorrow Laura is taking her to London, to see the Tower and Madame Tussauds. Rebecca is meeting them there and Kate has been counting the days, ticking them off on her Redwings horse lover's calendar. It makes Ruth feel slightly anxious to see time treated in this cavalier manner. She thinks of Nelson's story about the prisoners rejoicing on New Year's Eve. She has reached the age when she wants the days to last for ever but, even on the summer solstice, the earth seems to be turning at an alarming rate. She will be fifty next month.

It's a lovely evening though. They sit on the terrace having drinks and the swans glide by, luminous and mysterious. They talk about Kate and work and the famous holiday. When they are called to their table, the food is delicious. They drink a bottle of wine and are easy and comfortable together. It is only when they are walking back, across Sheep's Green, that Frank says, 'Ruth?'

Ruth stops. They joked earlier that Cambridge was like Oxford Circus, crowded with tourists and students who don't want to go home, but now, suddenly, they are on their own. It's ten o'clock but still not dark, the sky streaked with vapour trails.

'I would go down on my knee,' says Frank, 'but they aren't so good at the moment . . .'

'Frank . . .'

'Will you marry me, Ruth?'

Dear God, he has the ring there, in a blue velvet case that looks as if it has come from an antiques shop. He is smiling at her. Frank, good-looking, kind, intelligent and responsible. Frank who loves her, and Kate too. Frank, who has offered her the chance of escape.

And, perceptive as ever, Frank saves her from trying to find the words.

'You're going back, aren't you?' he says. 'You're going back to Norfolk.'

'I'm sorry,' says Ruth.

ACKNOWLEDGEMENTS

Many people have helped with *The Lantern Men* but I must stress that I have followed their advice only as far as it suits the plot and any subsequent mistakes are mine alone. The first thank you must go to Chris Rushby of Jarrold's in Norwich for giving me a book called *This Hollow Land* by Peter Tolhurst. In this treasury of Norfolk folklore I first found the legend of the lantern men. The story grew from there.

Thanks also to John Sutton who, in the course of many long drives, educated me about bicycles and cycle racing. There is no cycling club called Lynn Wheels, though, and, as far as I know, no race along the north Norfolk coastal path. Thanks to Linzi Harvey at the Natural History Museum for being brilliant on bones as usual, and to police consultant Graham Bartlett for his advice and support. Thanks also to Mary Williams, Associate Dean (Students) for the Faculty of Humanities and Social Science at the University of Portsmouth, for telling me what lecturers get up to in May and June.

Thanks to Ailsa Britain for taking part in a charity auction to become a character in this book. All proceeds go to CLIC Sargent, the charity supporting teenage cancer sufferers, so a huge thank you to Ailsa and everyone else who took part. Thanks also to my friend John Robertson who made a donation to Shelter in return for featuring in these pages. I hardly need say that the real Ailsa and John bear no resemblance to their fictional counterparts.

Grey Walls is imaginary but most of the places in the book are real. I'd especially like to thank the podcast Weird Norfolk for all the wonderful stories about this wonderful county. Do listen to their podcasts or follow them on Instagram. The Cley marshes are real, as is the amazing visitor centre. Thanks to David Fieldhouse and the team for making me so welcome there.

Heartfelt thanks to my publishers Quercus Books and the fantastic Team Elly: Therese Keating, Hannah Robinson, Ella Patel, Laura McKerrell, David Murphy and so many others. I'm so grateful for everything you have done for me and Ruth. Special thanks to my wonderful editor, Jane Wood, who has edited all the Ruth books and knows her as well as I do. Thanks, as always, to the one and only Agent Carter, Rebecca Carter, and all at Janklow and Nesbit. Thanks to Kirby Kim at Janklow US and to Naomi Gibbs and all at HMH. Thanks to all the publishers around the world who publish these books with such dedication and care. Thanks to my crime writer friends for their support and to anyone who has bought or borrowed my books. I appreciate you more than I can say.

The final thanks must go to my sister, Sheila de Rosa, printmaker extraordinaire, who provided invaluable information on the printing process. Sheila, this book is for you.

Love and thanks, as ever, to my husband, Andrew, and to our children, Alex and Juliet. And thanks to Gus who, like Flint, cannot resist a keyboard.

EG 2020

Read on for a first look at

The Night Hawk

Coming in hardback, ebook
and audio February 2021

PROLOGUE

All along the coast on this very eastern edge of England, the tide is coming in. It rolls over dark sand at Holme, it crashes against the multicoloured cliffs at Hunstanton, it batters windows at Happisburgh, reminding home-owners that this land is just on loan. And, on this spit of land jutting out into the North Sea, it approaches from all sides, turning streams into lagoons and lagoons into unfathomable lakes.

The Night Hawks are aware of the encroaching waters. This is dangerous territory, after all. But they are hunters and their blood is up. Iron Age coins have been discovered in the sand near Blakeney Point and there are rumours that they are part of something big, perhaps even a hoard. The hawks spread out across the beach, their metal detectors glowing and humming. The sea rolls in, white crests on black water.

A young man with a torch like a third eye on his head calls, 'There's something here!' The other hawks converge on him, their machines picking up the message, the call of metal below the surface of the earth.

'Could be more coins.'

'Could be armour.'

'A metal torque. Arm rings.'

They start to dig. Someone sets up an arc light. It's not until there's a shout of 'Tide!' that they realise the waters are almost upon them. Then there's another cry, coming from Troy, a young hawk stationed at the mouth of one of the estuaries winding back inland. His comrades splash over to him, taking care to keep their machines above water.

'There's something . . .' says Troy. 'I almost fell over it.' He's very young, still a teenager, and his voice wavers and breaks.

Al, an older detectorist, reaches out in the dark to touch his shoulder. 'What is it, lad?'

But another of the hawks is pointing his torch at the ground by Troy's feet. And they all see it, clothes swirling in the incoming tide, a movement that gives the appearance of life. But then, caught in a clump of sea grass, a dead body, arm outstretched as if asking for their help.

CHAPTER 1

Ruth parks in her usual spot under the lime tree and takes the well-trodden route through the Natural Sciences department to the archaeology corridor. This route is so familiar to her that she almost stops at her old office, the place where she first met DCI Nelson twelve years ago. But, with only a slight hesitation, she continues on her way and heads to the last door, on which there is a new plaque: Dr Ruth Galloway, Head of Archaeology.

This corner office, which boasts two windows and has room for a sofa as well as a desk, chairs and round table for meetings, was once occupied by Phil Trent, Ruth's old boss. But now Phil has taken early retirement and Ruth has the top job. Not that head of department at the University of North Norfolk is the toppest of top jobs (in fact Ruth's previous post as a senior lecturer at a Cambridge college was probably more prestigious), but on days like this, when she can see the ornamental lake glittering from her windows and the new freshers drifting across the campus, it does feel pretty special. I am in charge, thinks Ruth, putting her laptop on the desk and clicking onto the university intranet. It's a good feeling but she mustn't get too power hungry and start making her cat a senator or forcing the staff to call her Supreme Leader. It's still a medium job in a medium university. But at least she has her own coffee machine.

She's just about to have her first espresso of the morning when there's a perfunctory knock on the door. Before Ruth can say 'go away', the space in front of her is full of David Brown, the new archaeology lecturer. Her replacement, in fact.

'I've been thinking about our induction for new students,' says David, without even a *Good morning, Supreme Leader*. 'It seems crazy that we don't have them digging as soon as possible. We give them all that crap about research methods but don't let them get down and dirty until the second semester.'

Ruth sighs. In principle she agrees. Digging, 'getting down

and dirty', is one of the joys of archaeology. She would like her students to experience the thrill of discovery as soon as possible. But there are practical implications. Although Norfolk is one of the most archaeologically rich landscapes in the world, there are only ever a few digs running at one time and these could be ruined by overeager first years trampling all over the trenches. And the students themselves will be disappointed if, after a day in the bitter easterly winds, they only unearth a nail or a jubilee coin from 1977. Plus she despises the word semester. They're called terms in England, she tells David silently.

'We've thought about this before,' she says. 'Before you came and disrupted everything' is the subtext. 'But there's not really a suitable dig at the moment. Caister St Edmund needs Roman specialists and Sedgeford is only in the summer.'

'Then we should start our own dig.'

'We haven't got the funding,' says Ruth. She remembers how Phil used to irritate her with his constant talk of grants and funding, yet here she is playing the same tune. But the harsh reality is they don't have the money or the person-power to start a new excavation, not unless another Bronze Age henge magically materialises on a Norfolk beach.

'Our induction programme is out of date,' says David. 'There's not enough on isotope analysis or DNA testing.'

Ruth, who updated the programme herself, glares at him but is distracted by her phone ringing. 'Nelson' says the screen.

'Excuse me,' she says, ' I must take this call.'

David doesn't take the hint and leave but stands in front of her, blocking out the light.

'Ruth,' says Nelson. He, too, never bothers with niceties like 'hallo'. 'I'm at Cley. A body's been washed up at Blakeney Point. I think you'd better come and see it.'

Ruth doesn't know quite how David Brown manages to come along too. It certainly isn't because she invited him. All she knows, as she climbs into her lime-spattered Renault, is that David is next to her, folding his long legs into the passenger seat and adjusting it without her permission. She can't really tell him to get out. Teaching hasn't started yet. The only official business of the day is the 'Meet and Greet' with the freshers at five. She supposes that David has all the time in the world to inspect dead bodies.

'This might take a while,' she says, as she backs out of her space. 'I'm a special advisor to the North Norfolk police. They probably want me to look at the position of the body, provide some forensic analysis.'

All David says is, 'Mind the hedge,' as Ruth takes the corner too tightly. She grinds her teeth.

Ruth doesn't know quite why David annoys her so much. They have the same academic speciality, the prehistoric era, which doesn't help, but this is partly why Ruth employed David, to teach the courses that used to be her province. They even attended the same university, University College London, although David is five years older than Ruth so they didn't overlap. David then went to live and work in Sweden which is why he finds himself, aged fifty-five, applying for a job at UNN. But he was a good candidate and Ruth is lucky to have him on the team. It's just, why does he have to act as if he's all too aware of this?

It's a short drive to Cley and David is silent for most of it. Ruth is damned if she's going to make conversation, but she longs to point out the beauty of the landscape, the yellow grass and blue water, the flint cottages, the fishing boats in the harbour. But David hardly looks up from his phone. More fool him, thinks Ruth.

Nelson is waiting for them at the entrance to the car park. Ruth remembers, early on in their acquaintance, meeting Nelson at Blakeney car park on their way to interview Cathbad in his caravan. Now Cathbad owns a charming cottage in nearby Wells, where he lives with his partner and three children. Everything changes, thinks Ruth, as she parks the car and gets out her wellingtons. She is wearing her best boots in honour of the Meet and Greet and she's not going to risk them getting wet. David watches her sardonically. He is wearing a trainer/shoe hybrid that will probably fare very badly in the mud and sand.

'What took you so long?' says Nelson, as soon as Ruth comes within speaking distance.

Some things never change.

'This is a colleague of mine, David Brown,' says Ruth, ignoring Nelson's comment. 'David, this is DCI Nelson.' She doesn't give Nelson's first name because no one in Norfolk, apart from his wife, calls Nelson Harry.

Nelson nods at David and turns back to Ruth. 'The body's a little way along the beach. We'd better hurry because the tide's coming in.'

The walk from Cley to Blakeney is, by all accounts, an energetic four-mile trek. Ruth has never tried it herself. She has taken Kate on the boat trip to Blakeney Point, though, to see the seals who loll on the sand bank like drunks who have been thrown out of a pub. She hopes that today's walk isn't going to be too arduous. It's a beautiful autumn day but she doesn't want to spend hours trudging along the shingle in her wellingtons. Nelson strides ahead and Ruth has to scurry to keep up with him. She's not going to trail behind the two men. Luckily David dawdles along, taking pictures on his phone.

They walk along the beach, scrubby shingle on one side and the sea on the other. Occasionally Ruth sees sea poppies and clumps of samphire. A yacht goes past, its sails very white against the blue. In the distance is a curious house like an upturned boat. Just as Ruth's legs start aching, Nelson turns inland. There are patches of still water here and, as they pass, the birds rise up in clouds. Eventually they reach a promontory where yellow police tape is fluttering gaily in the wind. Two figures in white coveralls are standing at the water's edge.

'Should we be suited up?' says Ruth.

'No,' says Nelson, 'we don't need to get that close.'

Ruth looks at him quizzically but says nothing. They climb the shingle bank so that they're looking down at the inlet. Here the water comes to a point and starts to trickle inland. On the higher ground a tent has been erected but, through the open flaps, Ruth can see the shape of a body.

'Male,' says Nelson. 'Young. Looks to be about twenty.

We'll get his DNA, of course, but that'll only help if it matches someone on our records. My guess is that he's an illegal immigrant . . . a refugee,' he amends, looking at Ruth.

'Why do you think he's a migrant?' says David. 'Because he "looks foreign"?' He puts contemptuous quotes round the words.

'No,' says Nelson, scowling at him but keeping his voice even. 'We get a lot of migrant boats coming this way. They're heading for Southwold because there's no coast-guard there.'

Ruth looks across at the tent. She can see the head quite clearly, dark hair lifting in the breeze. A young man's body. Has he really travelled hundreds of miles just to end up here, washed up on an unknown shore? She says what has been in her mind ever since she got Nelson's call. 'If you know who he is and why he's here, why do you need me?'

'Because his body was found by some archaeologists,' says Nelson. 'Metal detectorists. They call themselves the Night Hawks. And I think they've found something else too.'

CHAPTER 2

'Night hawks aren't archaeologists,' says Ruth.

'Why do you say that?' says Nelson. 'They looked pretty professional to me. Lots of equipment.' They have moved along the beach to a point where the earth is lying in huge mounds, as if a giant child has been building sandcastles.

'They're not archaeologists,' says Ruth. 'They're amateurs who charge around looking for treasure. They've no idea how to excavate or how to read the context. They just dive in and dig up whatever looks shiny.'

'Wow,' says David. 'Elitism is alive and well and living in Norfolk.'

'What do you mean by that?' says Ruth.

'Archaeology isn't just the preserve of people with degrees,' says David. 'Detectorists are valid members of the community and these finds belong to the people.'

'Licensed metal detectorists are fine,' says Ruth, 'but Nelson called these people night hawks.' She can hear her voice rising and takes a deep breath. She doesn't want Nelson to hear her arguing with a colleague. Well, strictly speaking, an employee.

'It's what they called themselves,' says Nelson. 'Much as I hate to interrupt this academic discussion, as I was saying, the body was found by some metal detectorists who were looking for that.' He points at the mounds.

'What is it?' says Ruth.

'It seems like a lot of metal,' says Nelson. 'I thought you might like to have a look.'

Ruth feels her heart beating faster. This part of the coast is famous for buried treasure. There was the so-called jeweller's hoard at Snettisham, as if the contents of a Romano-British jewellery shop were lying underground just waiting to be discovered. Then there was the Sedgeford torc and the Iceni silver coins at Scole. Old coins, Nelson said, but he wouldn't know an Iron Age hoard from the contents of the slot machines on the Golden Mile in his beloved Blackpool.

'These metal detectorists,' Nelson is saying. 'They were here last night with their machines and lights and what have you. They found this and got all excited then one of them, a young lad called Troy Evans, found the body. They called the police and two local PCs attended the scene. They called me first thing this morning.'

'We'll have to secure this site,' says Ruth. 'Stop anyone else trampling over it. Can you make it part of the crime scene, Nelson?'

She's half-joking but Nelson says, 'I suppose so, as it was found at the same time as the body. Funny place to bury something, isn't it?'

'Not really,' says Ruth. 'Two thousand years ago it would have been well above the tide line.'

'But why bury something on the beach?'

'They could've been a votive offering,' says Ruth. 'An offering to the sea gods.' She looks at Nelson and knows that they are both thinking the same thing: bodies buried in the sand near here, murdered to placate nameless, vengeful gods. They have reached the hole – it can hardly be called a trench – and Ruth can see the dull gleam of greenish metal.

'Or sometimes you find escape hoards,' David cuts in. 'Warlords on the run, perhaps escaping back to Scandinavia. They buried their treasure, hoping they would come back for it.' He squats down to look. Ruth is rather pleased to see that his shoes and trousers are wet and spattered with sand. He leans closer and, when he speaks, his voice is different. Thick with excitement.

'Ruth! I think this is Bronze Age.'

Ruth comes forward to look. A Bronze Age hoard would be a find indeed. Rarer and older. Leaning in – uncomfortably close to David – she can see what looks like a fragment of a spear, shaped a bit like the club in a suit of cards.

'Broken spears,' says David. 'This could be Beaker.' Ruth knows that the Bronze Age, and the Beaker People specifically, is David's speciality.

'We'll get carbon-14 dating done,' says Ruth, 'and maybe some scans too.'

'Looks like we've got our dig then,' says David, standing up. He grins at her. It's the first time that she has seen him smile. The effect is actually to make his face look even grimmer than before. She doesn't smile back. A man is dead, after all.

'Glad someone's happy,' says Nelson. 'It's an ill wind.' This, too, suddenly sounds rather sinister, especially as the wind has been getting stronger in the last few minutes. Sand is rising from the beach in clouds, getting into Ruth's hair and eyes. Ruth suspects that Nelson got this particular adage from his mother and it's never a good sign when he starts quoting Maureen.

When Ruth and her follower have trudged back to the car park, Nelson returns to the crime scene. The forensics team are having to work quickly because of the incoming tide. Last night, the Night Hawks moved the body to higher ground. Normally Nelson would be cursing them for interfering but, in this case, it was the only thing to do. The tide was rising fast and, by the time the police appeared, the body would have been lost to the water. It does mean that they can't gain any clues from the surrounding area, 'the context' Ruth would call it. And, to be on the safe side, they need to move the dead man before the tide comes in again, at midday.

After exchanging a few words with the forensics officers, Nelson heads back inland. There's nothing more for him to do here. He's not a fan of the North Norfolk coast, miles of sand and rocks and mangy-looking vegetation. It whiffs to high heaven too, a horrible rank briny smell, not like the aroma of vinegar and chips which hovers over proper seaside resorts. As he treads carefully over the wet seaweed, he sees a woman coming towards him, dressed in a yellow raincoat. DI Judy Johnson always has the right gear for the climatic conditions. Cathbad, her partner, says it's because she's in tune with the weather gods.

'Hi, boss,' says Judy, when she gets closer. 'I saw Ruth leaving. Who was that with her?'

'Some dickhead from the university. They're all excited because some old coins have been dug up further along the beach.'

'Is that why you called Ruth?'

'Yes,' says Nelson, not looking at her. 'And because it was some of her lot who found the body. Though Ruth says that metal detectorists aren't proper archaeologists.'

'Cathbad goes out with the Night Hawks sometimes,' says Judy. 'He says that they're genuine questing souls.'

That figures, thinks Nelson. He doubts that there's a single group of local eccentrics that Cathbad doesn't know about. And, if they go out at night and break a few laws along the way, that's right up his street. Questing souls indeed. He never knows quite what Judy, his best and most rational officer, makes of her partner's beliefs. She certainly manages to say this sort of thing with a straight face.

'We need to secure the archaeological site,' says Nelson. 'It might be significant, and we don't want the public coming and nicking the lot.'

'OK,' says Judy. 'Do we know anything about the deceased? Any identification on him?'

'No,' says Nelson. 'I think he must have come from a migrant boat. Have the coastguard reported anything?'

'No. I rang round all the stations this morning. Of course, they could have come ashore somewhere where there are no checks. Who attended the scene first?'

'PC Nathan Matthews and PC Mark Hammond. Local boys. Good coppers. I came across them in Cley last year.'

'I'll read their reports. Shall I get them to come in for the briefing later? Might be good to hear about it in their own words. Especially as we won't have forensics from the scene.'

'Good idea.'

'The tide's coming in,' says Judy as, on cue, a wave sneaks over the shingle and breaks just in front of them. 'We need to move the body. I've got a private ambulance standing by.'

'I'll leave you to it,' says Nelson. 'Briefing at three. See you later.'

'Super Jo was looking for you,' says Judy, over her shoulder. 'I told her you were out.'

'Good work,' says Nelson. His boss, Superintendent Jo Archer, is always trying to make him have meetings with her. Avoiding her is his main form of exercise.

CHAPTER 3

When Phil was in charge, the Meet and Greet was one of Ruth's least favourite events of the year. Now, when it's her job to welcome the new students, the ordeal is even worse. The freshers stand in a nervous huddle close to the drinks, the staff are meant to circulate but often seem even more ill at ease than the students.

The Archaeology Department at UNN is small. As well as Ruth and David it consists of Bob Bullmore, an anthropologist cruising towards retirement, Fiona Green, a newish recruit who still has a bit of idealism and energy, and Peter Llewelyn, who specialises in Cultural Heritage and rarely utters a word on social occasions. Also present are Ted Conroy from the Field Archaeology team, who is only here for the beer, and several graduate research assistants circling the perimeter of the room.

Ruth stops to exchange a word with Ted, whom she knows from various digs.

'Congratulations on the new job,' says Ted, who is sticking two mini pork pies together to make a more substantial whole.

'Thanks,' says Ruth. She got the job almost a year ago but had to work out her notice at Cambridge and Phil wasn't going to be cheated out of a valedictory final term. She'd hoped that she could put off the move until her ten-year-old daughter, Kate, was at secondary school but has ended up moving Kate back to her old primary school for one last year. Kate has coped well and is clearly delighted to be back in their old cottage but it's one more thing to feel guilty about.

'We need a few more digs,' says Ted. Ruth eyes him suspiciously. It's natural for Ted to want more field work, that's his department after all, but has he been talking to David? Has Ruth already lost an ally?

'A possible Bronze Age hoard has been found at Blakeney Point,' she says. 'Could be a really interesting excavation.'

'Good,' says Ted, rubbing his hands together. 'A bit of leprechaun gold.' Ted is often known as Irish Ted although he comes from Bolton and has no discernible Irish accent. Ruth thinks that he makes remarks like this just to add to the mystique.

David appears, holding a glass of white wine in one hand and a mini kebab in the other.

'Are you going to say a few words?' he asks Ruth.

'I'm just about to,' says Ruth. Why does everything David

says sound as if he's criticising her? There's something so supercilious about him. Maybe it's his glasses.

She taps her wine glass and clears her throat. She doesn't mind public speaking – she's a lecturer, after all, and has even appeared on television – but there is something daunting about addressing the new students as head of department. She is conscious of David standing just behind her, no doubt looking deeply contemptuous. Ted raises his glass in a half-ironic salute.

'Welcome to archaeology,' says Ruth. 'I hope you'll have an interesting and instructive three years with us. I'm Dr Ruth Galloway . . .'

Nelson too is addressing the troops. The body on the beach is not necessarily a case for the Serious Crimes Unit but any unexplained death has to be investigated. Nelson runs through the details: 'Deceased male, probably late teens or early twenties, found on Blakeney beach in the early hours of the morning. Death looks to be from drowning but we'll wait for the autopsy results to be sure. By the looks of the body, the deceased had only been in the water for a few hours. The deceased . . .' He misses his former DS, Dave Clough, who would have given the dead man a name, probably taken from one of the *Godfather* films. The rest of his team are watching him intently. Judy, inscrutable, notebook in hand. Tanya, ever eager, hand hovering to be the first to ask a question. Tony, the new DC trying to look mature with a newly grown beard and an expression of carefully cultivated nonchalance. Nathan and Mark, the PCs who first attended the 999 call, sit awkwardly to one side. Nathan, in particular, looks nervous at finding himself in the CID lair. He's sweating profusely and keeps wiping his forehead.

Mark Hammond takes the lead in reporting their part of the story. 'We got the call at one forty-five a.m.,' he says. 'We proceeded to Blakeney beach where we found four individuals beside the body of a deceased male. They stated that they had found the deceased while searching for buried treasure on the beach. They had moved the deceased to higher ground because the tide was coming in. We secured the site and took statements, then we allowed the witnesses to return home. Their names . . .' he consults his notebook, 'are Troy Evans, aged twenty-one, Alan White, aged fifty-eight, Neil Topham, aged fifty-six, and Paul Noakes, aged thirty-one.'

'Do we know anything about these men?' asks Nelson.

'Alan White runs the Night Hawks,' says Judy, 'a local group of metal detectorists. They are a proper registered group. Alan is very respectable. Cathbad knows him. He's an ex-history teacher.'

Nelson nods but doesn't say anything. The words 'Cathbad' and 'respectable' don't exactly go together. And he'd like to know why Alan White left teaching. Once again, he misses Clough, who was promoted and moved on and who would certainly have been rolling his eyes.

'Did you get a look at the dead man?' Nelson asks the two PCs.

'We checked that he was dead,' says Nathan. His voice is

hoarse and his hands are shaking slightly. Nelson wonders if he has the right temperament for a police officer. 'We also looked for any identifying documents but there was nothing in any of his pockets. He was wearing jeans and a check shirt. No shoes. They had probably come off in the water.'

'Anything that struck you as strange?' asks Nelson.

'He had a tattoo,' says Mark.

'Nothing so odd about that,' says Nelson. He has one himself. It says 'Seasiders', a reference to Blackpool FC, his beloved football club.

'This was a bit strange though,' says Mark. 'It was on his neck and it was a snake with sort of spikes on its back. Looked as if it was about to bite his ear off.'

Tony laughs and turns it into a cough. Tanya, who has a discreet dolphin tattoo on the inside of her wrist, says, 'Maybe it was some sort of gang insignia?'

'That's what I thought,' says Mark.

'An unusual tattoo might help with identification,' says Nelson. 'Thanks, boys. Looks like this poor lad was just unlucky. Maybe he took his own life or maybe he was in a ship that got into trouble. Anything from the coastguard, Judy?'

'A blank so far,' says Judy. 'No reports of any migrant boats last night but there are lots of places along the coast where ships could land unnoticed. Cathbad says that's why there used to be so much smuggling in the area.'

'There's still smuggling,' says Nelson, 'only now it's people, not barrels of rum. We're only about a hundred miles away from the Dutch ports. But let's not get fixed on the migrant idea. Our boy might just as well be local.

We'll know more when we have his DNA. In the meantime, we'll make some enquiries. I don't want anything in the media just yet.' Super Jo will want to give a press conference. She's addicted to appearing in front of the cameras. Nelson, though, wants to avoid the world and its life partner claiming the boy as their own.

'Oh, and there's a bunch of old metal on the beach,' he says. 'It might be valuable so I'm putting a guard on them until the archaeologists can have a look.'

No one says anything. They all avoid mentioning archaeology in front of the boss.

It's seven o'clock by the time Ruth gets into her car to go home. Kate is with her friend Tasha and won't be missing her mother, but Ruth doesn't want to impose too much on Tasha's parents. Tasha was Kate's best friend before the move to Cambridge and Ruth is delighted that the friendship seems intact. She supposes that social media has its uses. Kate doesn't have a mobile phone yet but she's used Ruth's iPhone and her own tablet to chat with Tasha and the contact seems to have preserved their closeness. And Kate is good at friends, a nebulous skill that somehow seems essential for a successful and happy life. Ruth has no idea who she gets it from. Ruth has a few, close friends but shies away from making new ones. Nelson, Kate's father, often says that he can't see the point of friends. Family is everything to Nelson but, as this definition seems to include his team at work, he's not quite the sad misanthrope that this would suggest.

Ruth is just about to start up her car when a face appears at her window. She actually jumps.

'Have you got a minute?' says David, when she lowers the window.

'Can it wait?' says Ruth. 'I need to collect my daughter.' She curses herself for giving the classic single-parent excuse but, then again, it's the truth.

'I didn't know you had a daughter,' says David. 'I do too.'

'How old is yours?' says Ruth, wondering when she can put the window up.

'Eleven,' says David.

'Mine too,' says Ruth. 'Well, she will be in November.' David says nothing but he has backed away slightly. Ruth seizes her chance. 'See you tomorrow,' she says, closing the window and starting the engine.

As she drives away, she sees David still standing in the car park, frowning after her.

WHO'S WHO
IN THE DR RUTH GALLOWAY MYSTERIES
MYSTERIES

Dr Ruth Galloway

Profession: forensic archaeologist

Likes: cats, Bruce Springsteen, bones, books

Dislikes: gyms, organized religion, shopping

Ruth Galloway was born in south London and educated at University College London and Southampton University, where she met her mentor Professor Erik Anderssen. In 1997, she participated in Professor Anderssen's dig on the north Norfolk coast which resulted in the excavation of a Bronze Age henge. Ruth subsequently moved to the area and became Head of Forensic Archaeology at the University of North Norfolk. She lives in an isolated cottage on the edge of the Saltmarsh. In 2007, she was approached by DCI Harry Nelson who wanted her help in identifying bones found buried on the marshes, and her life suddenly got a whole lot more complicated.

Surprising fact about Ruth: she is fascinated by the London Underground and once attended a fancy dress party as The Angel Islington.

Harry Nelson

Profession: Detective Chief Inspector

Likes: driving fast, solving crimes, his family

Dislikes: Norfolk, the countryside, management speak, his boss

Harry Nelson was born in Blackpool. He came to Norfolk in his thirties to lead the Serious Crimes Unit, bringing with him his wife, Michelle, and their daughters, Laura and Rebecca. Nelson has a loyal team and enjoys his work. He still hankers after the North, though, and has not come to love his adopted county. Nelson thinks of himself as an old-fashioned policeman and so often clashes with Super-intendent Archer, who is trying to drag the force into the twenty-first century. Nelson is impatient and quick-tempered but he is capable of being both imaginative and sensitive. He's also cleverer than he lets on.

Surprising fact about Nelson: he's a huge Frank Sinatra fan.

Michelle Nelson

Profession: hairdresser

Likes: her family, exercising, socializing with friends

Dislikes: dowdiness, confrontation, talking about murder

Michelle married Nelson when she was twenty-four and he was twenty-six. She was happy with her life in Blackpool – two children, part-time work, her mother nearby – but encouraged Nelson to move to Norfolk for the sake of promotion. Now that her daughters are older she works as a manager for a hair salon. Michelle is beautiful, stylish, hard-working and a dedicated wife and mother. When people see her and Nelson together, their first reaction is usually, 'What *does* she see in him?'

Surprising fact about Michelle: she once played hockey for Blackpool Girls.

Michael Malone (aka Cathbad)

Profession: laboratory assistant and druid

Likes: nature, mythology, walking, following his instincts

Dislikes: rules, injustice, conventions

Cathbad was born in Ireland and came to England to study first chemistry then archaeology. He also came under the influence of Erik Anderssen though they found themselves on opposite sides during the henge dig. Cathbad was brought up as a Catholic but he now thinks of himself as a druid and shaman.

Surprising fact about Cathbad: he can play the accordion.

Shona Maclean

Profession: lecturer in English Literature

Likes: books, wine, parties

Dislikes: being ignored

Shona is a lecturer at the University of North Norfolk and one of Ruth's closest friends. They met when they both participated in the henge dig in 1997. On the face of it, Shona seems an unlikely friend for Ruth – she's outgoing and stunningly beautiful for a start – but the two women share a sense of humour and an interest in books, films and travel. They also have a lot of history together.

Surprising fact about Shona: as a child she won several Irish dancing competitions.

David Clough

Profession: Detective Sergeant

Likes: food, football, beer, his job

Dislikes: political correctness, graduate police officers

David Clough ('Cloughie' to Nelson) was born in Norfolk and joined the force at eighteen. As a youngster he almost followed his elder brother into petty crime, but a chance meeting with a sympathetic policeman led him into a surprisingly successful police career. Clough is a tough, dedicated officer but not without imagination. He admires Nelson, his boss, but has a rather competitive relationship with Sergeant Judy Johnson.

Surprising fact about Clough: He can quote the 'you come to me on my daughter's wedding day' scene from *The Godfather* off by heart.

Judy Johnson

Profession: Detective Sergeant

Likes: horses, driving, her job

Dislikes: girls' nights out, sexism, being patronised

Judy Johnson was born in Norfolk to Irish Catholic parents. She was academic at school but opted to join the police force at eighteen rather than go to university. Judy can seem cautious and steady – she married her boyfriend from school, for example – but she is actually fiercely ambitious. She resents any hint of condescension or sexism which can lead to some fiery exchanges with Clough.

Surprising fact about Judy: she's a keen card player and once won an inter-force poker competition.

Phil Trent

Profession: professor of Archaeology

Likes: money, being on television, technology

Dislikes: new age archaeologists, anonymity, being out of the loop

Phil is Ruth's head of department at the University of North Norfolk. He's ambitious and outwardly charming, determined to put the university (and himself) on the map. He thinks of Ruth as plodding and old-fashioned so is slightly put out when she begins to make a name for herself as an advisor to the police. On one hand, it's good for the image of UNN; on the other, it should have been him.

Surprising fact about Phil: at his all boys school, he once played Juliet in *Romeo and Juliet*.